Shadow Lane Volume 9

The History of Hugo Sands and other Stories of Spanking and Love

by
Eve Howard

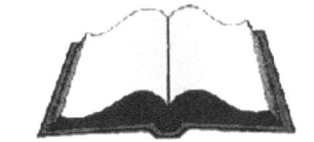

CCB Publishing
British Columbia, Canada

Shadow Lane Volume 9: The History of Hugo Sands
and other Stories of Spanking and Love

ISBN-13 978-1-926585-57-4
Second Edition

Library and Archives Canada Cataloguing in Publication
Howard, Eve, 1953-
Shadow lane : volume 9: the history of Hugo Sands and other stories of spanking and love /
written by Eve Howard – 2nd ed.
ISBN 978-1-926585-57-4
Also available in electronic format.
I. Title.
PS3608.O82S539 2009 813'.6 C2009-905737-9

Cover and interior artwork by Tarsis: www.briantarsis.com

Shadow Lane Volume 9 was first published by Blue Moon in 2004,

Publisher: CCB Publishing
British Columbia, Canada
www.ccbpublishing.com

Dedicated to every spanking enthusiast
who has made his or her dreams come true

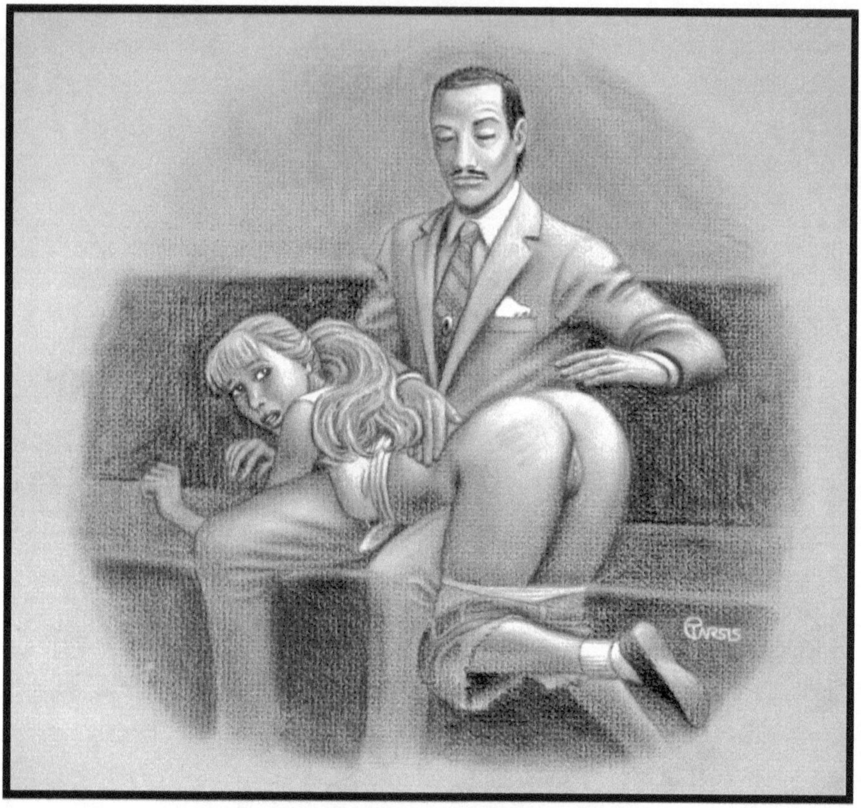

Hugo Sands spanks Susan Ross for disobedience

Shadow Lane

Volume 9

The History of Hugo Sands and other Stories of Spanking and Love

ꟹ

Contents

Chapter 1 – ***The Summer of Love*** 1
Chapter 2 – ***Never Trust A Hippie*** 15
Chapter 3 – ***Garda, Bettie and Brooke*** 60
Chapter 4 – ***Carter Takes Brooke*** 101
Chapter 5 – ***Scorpio Rising*** 142
Chapter 6 – ***The Business of Love*** 183
Chapter 7 – ***Modern Spanking Romance*** 222
Chapter 8 – ***At The Dutch*** 269
Chapter 9 – ***Love Isn't Born*** 300
Chapter 10 – ***Two Weeks*** 336
Chapter 11 – ***New Year's Eve*** 371
Chapter 12 – ***January*** 387
Chapter 13 – ***Marguerite and Michael Play House*** 402
About the Author 424
Reader Reviews about the Shadow Lane Series 425

There was a reason why all the girls wanted to play with Michael Flagg

Chapter One

The Summer of Love

In the Summer of 1967, Veronica and Virginia Grady were sharing a walk-up in an old brownstone on Charles Street, Beacon Hill, while Virginia completed her senior year at Boston University and Veronica earned excellent wages as a legal secretary in Back Bay.

One Saturday afternoon, Veronica returned to their apartment laden with packages from Bonwit Teller, where she habitually left most of her paycheck. On the way home she'd stopped at a salon and had her long, brown hair blown dry straight with bangs, and looking as smart as possible, ran upstairs and entered the flat, from which the aroma of baking and other sweet organic scents wafted and strange, wild, electric guitar music emanated.

All of this was normal. Virginia always found the best music, baked the best brownies and stockpiled the best weed in the commonwealth. But when Veronica entered the tiny, two bedroom flat an entirely incongruous image confronted her, in the person of Virginia, lying face down on their oriental divan, with a large icepack perched atop her skirted bottom.

"What's going on?" Veronica said, sitting down on a loveseat with her packages. "What's that record? Why the icepack? Did you fall down the stairs again? They're so dangerous! I can't wait to show you what I bought." And she proceeded to unpack her various bags, noticing the peace sign that Virginia had taken with her to the demonstration that morning propped up against the wall.

"It's Hendrix, on a cutout album from England. You'll never believe what happened to me," said Virginia with animation, tossing the icepack aside and sitting up. She was a lissome blonde in a pink midriff top, a print gauze skirt and sandals that laced to her knees. "On my way to the State House I passed a marine recruitment office, manned by this stereotypical jarhead who seemed bored, so I thought, here's a chance to have some fun."

"Fun with a marine? That doesn't sound like you."

"You know I have eclectic tastes," Virginia rejoined, then continued, "Well, I started out by just looking in the window, smiling at him and letting him ogle my bosom." Virginia paused to light a bong, draw on it and inhale deeply.

"Then what happened?" Veronica asked, taking the pipe from her.

"Then I went and got my sign and began to march back and forth in front of the window."

"Jesus, Virginia!" Veronica laughed.

"I know it was mad, but I couldn't resist. Well, naturally he came out and asked me what the hell I thought I was doing? But before I'd even drawn a breath to answer, this righteous defender of the military industrial complex starts telling me to move along or else. Or else what? I challenge, gratified by the shade of brick red he's starting to turn under his tan. God, he was pissed at me," Virginia laughed.

"So then what happened?" Veronica asked, finally expelling her long held breath. She pulled the white zip, micro-mini dress out of the Bonwit's bag and held it up to herself. "How do you like this?"

"I love it, but just listen to this. Guess what this joker says next?"

"Tell me."

"He threatens to spank me!"

"He what???"

"I knew that would get your attention."

"Why do you know that?" Veronica reddened.

"I've read all your Grove Press novels. Your Man With A Maid. Your Frank and I. Your Sadopaidea. I know what you're into."

"So you're saying that he spanked you? Right there in the street?"

"I really should have beat a retreat but I was having too much fun baiting him. We got into this argument about me not showing proper respect for the corps and after that it was mere seconds until he lost it."

"So he spanked you?"

"Wait a minute, let me change the record and I'll show you," said

Virginia, eagerly exchanging Are You Experienced for Surrealistic Pillow on the turntable. "You have to hear this one too."

"Oh, White Rabbit. I've heard that one. It's great. Show me what?"

"Look at this," said Virginia, pulling up her skirt and displaying her skimpily pantied bottom cheeks to her sister. "Can you see how pink I am? And this happened at least an hour ago."

Veronica saw that her sister's bottom blushed radiantly pink from hip to hip.

"He really spanked you in the street? Over his knee?"

"Oh it was horrible," Virginia laughed. "First of all, it hurt like fuck all, and then I absolutely hated myself for getting excited."

"Excited? You got excited? Where do you come off getting excited? I'm the one who's into it!" Veronica protested.

"It must have been a direct result of reading those books," Virginia admitted.

"So who broke it up?"

"No one. He spanked me until he got tired. And that took a while. We collected quite a crowd of horny guys spilling out of the bar across the street to watch. I probably would have cried if I wasn't so damned stoned, but I'd dropped half a tab of acid before I left the house and it started kicking in half way through the spanking. Weirdly, in my mind I eroticized the whole thing while it was happening and actually started humping his lap. I swear I felt his hand going between my legs for a second too. But then again, I may have imagined that."

"Jesus, is it still coming on?"

"You bet it is."

"Then what happened?"

"Then I made the mistake of looking into the face of the crowd and that was a lot more frightening than the Sergeant. That made me cry. Especially when they started sprouting tentacles, fins, claws, scales and jack in the box heads."

"You know you should never drop acid when you're going to be in an insecure environment. What's the matter with you?'

"Do you see how red I still am?" Virginia pulled her tiny panties up between her cheeks to fully display her pinkened bottom.

"Ginny, don't you know any better than to fuck with a marine?"

"I like fucking with marines. They always know how to use condoms," Virginia blithely replied, pulling several other mini dresses out of Veronica's shopping bag and holding them up to herself in the mirror.

"So, where did you say this recruitment center was?" Veronica asked idly.

"On Charles Street, just before you get to Beacon, across from the pub. Why, what are you going to do?" asked Virginia, following Veronica into the front bedroom.

"So how old was this spanking marine?"

"Hard to tell. Maybe thirty-five or even forty."

"Cute?" Veronica went behind a painted screen to exchange her jeans for the white dress.

"Would I get in grabbing distance of someone who wasn't?" Virginia retorted, opening the bedroom windows wider, as it seemed to be getting hotter and more humid as the afternoon waned.

"Are you going out tonight?"

"Yes," replied Virginia, "to see a foreign film in Cambridge. Want to come?"

"No thanks. Stay out late, okay?"

"Veronica, what ever you're thinking, you'd better reconsider," Virginia cautioned. "Spanking may be fun to fantasize about, but I found out that in reality, it hurts!"

"Mmmmm, you poor thing," Veronica ignored her sister while regarding her freshly frocked form in the full-length mirror. "Somehow it seems so cosmically wrong that you were the one to get spanked. Do you think this intuitive person has more than one spanking in him, or did you use it all up?"

"Are you kidding? He was getting off on it. I could feel!" Virginia asserted, leaning out the windowsill and gazing down on cobble-stoned Revere Street below. "In a big way too," Virginia added.

About an hour later in the Charles Street Pub, Sgt. Flagg wondered what it was about him that day that suddenly pretty young women were flirting with him on first sight. First there had been the blonde brat with her peace sign, insolently baiting him until he had no choice but to turn her over his knee, which event had been remarkably enhanced by being witnessed by ten rowdily enthusiastic onlookers pouring out of this bar. Now, here was a delectable brunette in the shortest skirt he'd ever seen, perched on a stool not five steps away and looking straight into his eyes in a way that could not be misinterpreted.

On the way over to talk to the girl in the white dress and high-heeled sandals, the sergeant was stopped to have his hand shaken vigorously by two different imbibers, in two different states of inebriation.

"What was that all about?" Veronica asked him as he slid onto the vacant stool beside her.

"Oh, they're just wise guys," said the weather-beaten marine, extending his rough hand to shake her small, well manicured one. "Doug Flagg," he said.

"Veronica Grady," she replied, allowing him to squeeze her hand briefly.

"What are you drinking?"

"Cosmopolitans," she replied.

"What the hell are those?"

"Martinis."

"May I join you?" he asked politely.

"Of course. I've been trying to catch your eye."

"Why's that?" he asked, hailing the bartender to ask for another tequila and beer chaser for himself and a second Cosmo for the girl.

"I can't resist a uniform."

After that the conversation flowed rapidly back and forth with all the ease of confident flirtation. Veronica's long legs were tanned and bare and her toenails painted dark red to match her fingernails and lips. Whenever she shook back her hair it fell into place perfectly. Her teeth were very white and she smiled a good deal. She seemed to get drunk fast and laughed at all his jokes accordingly. The looser she became, the less the wise Doug drank, leaving his last tequila on the bar before they emerged onto Charles Street in the heavy, humid dusk of evening.

"Are you hungry?" she asked. "Because I live very close by and I have an ice box full of food."

"Are you inviting me to dinner?" he asked, startled to make this sort of impression on such a fresh, pretty, well dressed and well spoken young lady.

"Pot luck," she explained with a grin, "but I think you'll be satisfied."

They walked the two blocks to Revere Street and then upstairs to the flat in the old brick building. Veronica sat Doug down at the small round table in the tiny kitchen and quickly laid out a spread of cold lamb sandwiches on crusty Italian bread, homemade potato salad and coleslaw, cranberry relish and a good red wine. Her guest was overwhelmed but immediately did justice to the simple repast thinking how much more pleasant this was than waiting for a table in a crowded restaurant on a busy Saturday night.

Even with two fans blowing directly on them, it was oppressively hot in the small apartment, especially after eating and drinking. Veronica encouraged him to loosen his collar and even take off his stiff white shirt. Stripped to his pants and sleeveless tee, the Viet Nam veteran was impressively lean and muscular and his hostess admired his ripped abs and tablet pecs accordingly.

They took their wine and crawled out the kitchen window onto the roof from which many assorted vistas and rooftops were visible including a sliver of the Charles in the dark. A nearby radio was blasting Take It As It Comes and Veronica made him get up and dance with her. They held hands and twisted to the music.

"This song makes me want to have sex," Veronica confided. Doug looked at her and marveled at how much girls had changed in the few years he'd been out of the country. For example, favors one had to practically stand on one's head and beg for in the early sixties were now apparently bestowed as a matter of course on the most casual acquaintance. And then of course the immense innovations of the mini skirt and noticeably absent brassiere had done even more to slide the pedestal out from under the modern American girl.

The next thing Veronica knew, she was being pulled back into the apartment, where she presently found herself sitting on his lap, with her arms wound around his neck and his tongue exploring her mouth.

Under her trim, firm bottom she could feel his excitement swell and she did not scruple to make matters worse by wriggling against and bouncing up and down on the truncheon like form through their clothes. Then she was being carried into her small bedroom, carefully undressed and thoroughly made love to in three or four positions until the leathery soldier finally allowed himself to expire in her embrace.

"You didn't come," he accused a few minutes later, as they put themselves back together and went out into the kitchen, their appetites stimulated by their exertions.

"It takes more than fortitude to make me come," she explained, setting the plate of brownies on the table beside a jug of milk.

"What does it take?" he asked, consuming the first brownie in a few bites and washing it down with milk.

"Maybe I'll tell you later," she said, pulling on a pair of short denim shorts and a dark red halter-top with a pair of denim espadrilles that laced to the ankle.

Sitting down to her milk, Veronica took her first bite of brownie as Doug demolished his second cake and reached for a third. Chewing thoughtfully she said, "Uh oh. I just realized something. Don't finish that," she said, an instant too late.

"Why not? I don't usually eat sweets, but these are great."

"You don't want to eat too much on a hot night," she said, sweeping the plate back into the refrigerator. "Listen, why don't we go out for a walk in the public gardens?"

"Sure!" he said agreeably and went to put on his clothes.

Walking through the small parlor en route to the bedroom he paused to look at some of the framed photos on the bookshelves.

"Ronnie, who is this girl with you?" Doug demanded, bringing one of the photos back into the kitchen with him. Veronica turned from the sink where she was quickly washing and drying their plates to regard the photo of herself and Virginia that he was brandishing before her.

"Oh, that's my sister, Virginia. Isn't she pretty?"

"You're not going to believe this, but I had a run in with her today at the recruitment office," he admitted.

"Really? What kind of run in?" Veronica affected amazement.

"Let's just get out of here before she gets home," he

recommended.

Once they were out on the street, where it was but a few degrees cooler than indoors, Veronica pressed her new escort for details.

"You're going to hate me when I tell you."

"Really? Why ever?"

"First of all, let me say that your sister is a little idiot. What does she do today but parade in front of my recruitment office with a goddamned peace sign!"

"No!"

"It's true. I guess she was on the way to that big anti-war rally outside the State House, but as soon as she saw me, she just had to make trouble. I warned her to beat it, more than once, but she just kept challenging my authority until finally..."

"Yes, finally what?"

"I told her if she didn't move away from the office I'd spank her."

"No!"

"But she kept standing there and arguing with me."

"And did you really do it? Spank her?"

"I did," Doug admitted.

"Gee, I wish I could have been there to see that!" said Veronica, pressing the traffic button for a green light on Beacon Street. They crossed over and headed towards the public garden.

"So the thought of me spanking your annoying little sister doesn't make you mad?" Doug asked, feeling suddenly wildly exhilarated. He'd never noticed that the sky above Boston proper could be so completely crammed with stars.

"Sure, mad with envy. I never meet any men who think of spanking me," she confided, leading the way into the gardens.

"Why? You don't think that's a bad thing?"

"No, I think it sounds exciting."

"Really? Do you?"

"Not that you were right to spank my sister. You'll be lucky if she doesn't sue you for battering a civilian."

"Your sister's a goddamned hippie."

"Hey, show a little respect. Thanks to hippie culture, you just got laid for free."

"God, you're a fresh girl."

"Go on, deny that you'd be headed for the combat zone right around now if you hadn't met me earlier?"

"You know, I was thinking that very thing earlier," he admitted, "how there used to be good girls and bad girls, but now there are only good girls who behave badly."

Veronica smiled.

"Come over here and sit with me," he said, leading her to a stone bench under a tree along a side path. "Should I show you what I did to your sister?" he asked, taking her smooth upper arm in his hand and pulling her easily across his lap.

"Right here? Right now?"

"It will only take a few minutes," he promised, patting her shapely bottom through her denim shorts and anchoring her waist to his lap with his free hand.

"Why don't we go back to my place?" she asked, leaning up.

"We can later," he pushed her back down and smacked her right cheek, then her left, somewhat sharply. "Now you need to be spanked."

Veronica squirmed on Doug's lap as the few dozen swats rained down on her upturned seat. "But, in public!" she cried, straining to get free.

"It was good enough for your sister. She courted the attention," he replied, ending the impromptu spanking with ten hard swats and setting her back on her feet.

"Oh!" she cried, flushed to the roots and humiliated to the depths when a young couple passed by smiling at them. "How could you do that in public?" she complained furiously, folding her arms and turning away from him.

"If you pout I'll do it again," he threatened. She began to walk away, her hands buried in her pockets. He caught up with her, picked her up and arranged her over one shoulder.

"Doug, put me down!"

"I'd rather carry you home," he replied cheerfully.

"If you want to be invited to sleep over you'll stop being horrid this instant!" she cried imperiously. Doug immediately put her down.

They walked along quietly for a few moments.

"You have a very hard hand," she said at last.

"You didn't like it, did you?"

"I didn't say that."

"I spanked your sister a lot harder than that!"

"Well, I'm not used to it."

"You could get used to it."

"What would be the incentive?"

"This time let me spank you just before we have sex. Then I bet you will come."

"I bet I will too," she agreed.

"Can we be sure your sister won't walk in?"

"Let's go back and see if she calls. She may decide to spend the night away."

The phone rang just a few minutes after they reentered the apartment. It was Virginia calling Veronica to let her sister know that she'd be spending the night with friends. Thus the gods continued to smile on their warrior.

"Obviously, it's no coincidence I picked you up," Veronica said, lighting her new lover's cigarette as they shared a brandy nightcap on the roof. "My sister came home this afternoon and told me about what happened in the street. Naturally, I was intrigued and when she told me you were kind of cute, I couldn't resist checking you out myself."

"Jesus, you must really be into it," Doug commented, noticing the stars were even closer now.

"I am. I always have been."

"Me too!" he agreed, astonished to be saying this out loud.

"So, how many women have you spanked?"

"Let's just say I've seized any opportunity presented."

"How about prostitutes? Have you spanked a lot of prostitutes?"

"No, of course not."

"Why not?"

"They wouldn't understand."

"Not even those cute Asian ones?"

"Maybe a couple of swats, but nothing to write home about."

"I'm surprised you didn't push that angle, into it as you seem. I mean, you just grabbed my sister, didn't you?"

"She was pushing my buttons. And she was warned."

"So when are you getting out?"

"This year, actually. How did you know?"

"You look old enough to be put out to pasture."

"You're really fresh, you know that? I'm not as old as I look."

"Really? How old are you?"

"Thirty eight."

"Wow, I thought you were at least forty two!"

"But you came looking for me anyway."

"That's right. I want a daddy to boss me around," she said, impulsively kissing him. "So what do you plan to do when you get out?"

"Well, I'm tired of talking orders. I'll probably start my own business."

"Really? What kind?"

"Maybe a little fixit shop."

"How exciting," she grinned.

"God, you're a brat. Well, what do you suggest?"

"How about a neighborhood photography studio? It's nice work, not too strenuous. And you could develop artistic photography as a side line."

Doug stared at her. "That's a good idea!"

"I thought you'd like that."

"Maybe I should hire you as my assistant. Then I could spank you every day."

"I have all the necessary skills."

"There's not much you don't have, including nerve," said Veronica's new admirer.

In a few minutes he took her back inside and stopped in the kitchen to pull out a straight-backed chair.

"You're a managing little female, aren't you?" He sat down and took her by the arm. "I'm not sure I like that!" He pulled her down across his lap in one motion. "Oh no, are these still on you?" he smacked the seat of her glove tight denim shorts a few times with disapproval. "Take them off. Take everything off. Right now!" He lifted her back off his lap and folded his arms to watch her undress for him. She unzipped and dropped her shorts slowly, then deliberately held his gaze while stepping out of them. Then she lazily pulled her stretch halter top up over her head revealing her small, firm, round, peach shaped bosom, rose nipples pointing insolently upward, skin like taut cream satin, with a torso tapering downward to an exquisite waist. Now she stood before him in a tiny pair of French cut blue panties and lacing cloth shoes.

"I'd like to photograph you for artistic photos," he said, pulling her back over his lap before she had a chance to remove her panties.

"Oh, that's been done. It's what gave me the idea for you," she revealed, turning to him.

"Are you telling me you've posed for nude photos?"

"Yes."

"You little slut!" he declared with mock indignation, liking her more every moment they were together. Then a strange and frightening thought came into his head. What if none of this was real and he was simply hallucinating off the brownies she had allowed him to eat?

He had only just identified the unusual euphoria he'd been experiencing for the past hour as drug induced. It suddenly all added up: the hippie sister, the classic medium of delivery, the subsequent sensations of wild elation counterbalanced by a tendency to over analyze every thought that occurred to him, the uninhibited sex and spontaneous confessions and most of all, his complete lack of concern about any of this. "You are a little slut, aren't you?" he demanded suspiciously.

"I'm a free spirit," she casually corrected him over one pretty bare shoulder, flipping back her long, smooth, shiny hair.

"Oh, I see, a child of nature," he amended, relieved that her responses still seemed to tally with her promise of being in the scene. He wasn't imagining that she was allowing him to pull her panties down, and yet he never recalled the color pink showing up so vividly on a bottom he had only briefly spanked. It looked electric pink. "I suppose you never get spanked," he ventured.

"Never! Who does?"

"I think it stays pink longer the first time," he told her, stroking her bare bottom with his big hand. "That's been my experience with the few girls I've spanked more than once."

"My sister was sure pink when I saw her and that was almost an hour after her encounter with you!"

"See, that's where this whole day somehow goes all Alice in Wonderland," he frankly admitted, pausing with his hands clasped on her waist. "Why did your sister pick me out to bait today? Why did you follow up? Things like this don't happen to me."

She wriggled against his sturdy thighs and murmured, "You were in the right place at the right time."

"So you've posed for photographers! That was very naughty. And dangerous," he told her, spanking her soundly for several minutes. "However, knowing that about you makes you coming to find me today more believable. You're a wild girl. Aren't you? You need someone to make you conform."

"You?" she looked back at him.

"I should punish you severely for playing that joke on me," he threatened, continuing to bring his palm down firmly on either cheek until each glowed magenta and radiated heat.

"What joke?"

"You know damn well what joke. Do you know how much it could jam me up to test positive for THC?"

"They'd bother testing a hoary old warhorse like you?"

"Keep it up and I'll make you get me a hair brush."

Veronica wriggled on his lap to entice him. He was rock hard again and she ground against it. The spanking began to hurt. She tried to breathe through it but finally she couldn't help but cry out.

"Oh please! I've had enough. I'm sorry for whatever I did!"

"All right. Spread your legs and jut your bottom up."

"Why?" she looked over her shoulder.

"You'll see," he told her, putting his palm between her smooth thighs and lightly spanking her public mound and vulva.

"Oh! How dare you spank me there!" she cried, delighted. Now he let one, then two long fingers slip up into her snug, creamy vagina.

"You're so wet. Maybe I'll show mercy and fuck you instead."

"Maybe fuck me without showing mercy?" she amended.

"Bent over the kitchen table? As though we were married?" he suggested.

"Is married life that exciting?"

"We'll see," he promised.

Chapter Two

The History of Hugo Sands Part One
Never Trust A Hippie

After graduating Harvard in the late 70's with a degree in art history, Hugo Sands found employment as a cataloguing assistant at the Boston Museum of Fine Arts.

At 23, the future esoteric publisher was already a man of the world, with several summers of European travel and a decade of sexual experience behind him. Longer if you counted that he had been playing "doctor" and "house" with little girls since kindergarten.

And now that he carried the additional éclat of a Harvard degree, his school ring was proving more potent than the signet of Castle Roissy in compelling young women to shed their outer garments and submit to his whims.

"It works with everyone but that one, the only one I want," Hugo complained to his companion, Van Milburn, of a tall, slim, young redhead sitting on a ledge by herself across the museum garden, with a book of Diane Arbus photos.

"Garda's not the type to be impressed by Ivy League degrees," Van informed Hugo on good authority, for the older man was a designer in the catalog department where Garda Hudson worked as a copy editor and knew her fairly well.

Van was 33, with refined features; short cropped, salt and pepper hair and a trimmed beard in the manner of a Greek coin. He and Hugo had become great friends due to their mutual interest in art history, but Van was just as happy to discuss the virtues of Garda, of whom he was also extremely fond.

"Do you know what makes her tick, Van?"

"I know that beneath that gauzy shift lurks a hardcore punk who spent the summer of '76 in London and owns a latex corset."

"That is so arousing to me!"

"I'll tell her."

"Would you? I'd love to get involved with a girl who isn't P.C.," sighed Hugo.

"Why don't you ask her out?"

"I have done. She keeps saying no."

"Maybe it's the ponytail," said Van, biting into a baguette sandwich.

"Garda dislikes long hair on men?" Hugo asked in surprise. His straight, sandy blond hair was the proper length for the era, complimentary to his features and had contributed to his general appeal for young women since high school.

"Never trust a hippie is one of her favorite expressions," Van helpfully revealed, amused to observe Hugo clutching his hair in a paranoid fashion.

"So, she's anti-love and peace?"

"She's a punk. Of course she's anti-love."

"Anti-drug?"

"No, actually. Now that you mention it, she was asking me where she could get some weed just today."

"Oh really? What did you say?"

"I said I'd find out."

"Are you going to?"

"I can't just now. My guy's out of town."

"Tell her I can help her. At once!"

Around three that afternoon, when Hugo was alone in one of the archive rooms checking catalog annotations against hand written item descriptions of 18th century cameos, Garda entered the cool, quiet area on her dainty espadrilles with the pretty ribbon ties around each slim ankle. She brought the smell of frangipani with her and her creamy skin appeared to advantage under the milky globe lights.

"Hi," she said uncomfortably and quickly, as one with business to conduct. "Van said I could see you about something."

"Yes. Absolutely."

"So, when?" Garda seemed perfectly desperate.

"Uh, whenever you like," Hugo replied agreeably, then drew a lovely cocoa and cream broach from the drawer and showed it to her. "Isn't this one pretty?"

"Beautiful," Garda appreciated the cameo in moderation, then returned to the more important subject with impatience. "You mean, tonight might be a possibility?"

"Definitely. You can count on it."

"Great! So, should I come to you?"

"Please!" Hugo couldn't help but laugh.

"What? Are you teasing me? Is this for real?"

"Of course I'm not teasing you. Look, here's my address," Hugo wrote it on a tiny pad in his neat, architectural hand. "It's right up the block from the Charles Street Steak House."

"You're kidding! I live on Beacon Hill too!"

"Where?"

"Myrtle Street. Two blocks up and one over from you."

"That is convenient. Would you prefer I come to you?"

"No, that's okay. What time?"

"Seven?" Hugo named the earliest time that would seem reasonable.

"That would be perfect. If I had to face another weekend in Boston straight I would have gone mad."

Hugo smiled as she exited, murmuring to himself, "Little drug slut." Then for luck he kissed the 18th century beauty on the broach before putting it back in its velvet slot. Like Casanova, he believed Venus to be his ruling planet and saw his life stretch before him as a series of romantic adventures with only the most interesting of women. This Garda Hudson counted. She was his first real challenge, who stood proof against all his usual charms and required extraordinary magicks to captivate.

Let the end justify the means, Hugo decided, stopping in at the barbershop on the way home.

Garda climbed the staircase to Hugo's second floor flat above the Italian grocery promptly at seven. He had seen her from his window and opened the door.

"My god, you cut your hair?" she exclaimed, as he ushered her into the small parlor whose dominant feature was an old, brick fireplace, with logs in readiness, should the perfectly mild October evening turn chilly. "How did you find this place? This building looks two hundred years old. And you have kittens!" Garda fell to her knees before the basket beside the hearth.

"I adopted them last week," Hugo said, handing her an exceedingly thick joint and lighting it for her.

"Kittens," she murmured, tentatively picking up the grey one, then the black one. "You have this whole place to yourself?" she asked, touring the tiny apartment with the joint in one hand and the grey cat in other.

"You don't live alone?" he asked.

"Yes, but I can barely afford it and I'm sure my place is cheaper than this one."

"I have a second job translating French for an art journal," he revealed.

"Why did you cut your hair?"

"Do you like it better now?"

"Is that why you cut it?"

"I'll bet you haven't eaten yet."

"Don't evade the question."

"I'll make some coffee," Hugo decided. Garda followed him into the tiny brick walled kitchen to watch him grind some beans with a hand grinder.

"Hugo, I don't want you to get the wrong idea about why I came over," she said firmly.

"Oh, I know why you came over," he rejoined.

"What I mean is, I know you're interested in me. But, haircut not withstanding, I must inform you that my affections are otherwise engaged."

"I see," Hugo murmured, unable to conceal his disappointment. "A long standing relationship?"

"Not a relationship as yet, but it might develop into one, in time."

"Oh!" Hugo brightened. "Anyone I know?"

"Yes, it is someone you know," Garda revealed, coloring.

Hugo mentally reviewed the rest of the museum staff with whom she might have come into contact and rapidly fallen in love, for she had only been in her position a few weeks herself when he had been hired. "Can't think of anyone who seems like a match off hand," he speculated, spooning coffee into his percolator. "Milk and sugar?"

"Uh huh."

Hugo cut some bread, cheese and fruit and served it with the coffee in the parlor. While she cuddled the kittens and nibbled at the food he studied her after work look, not sure if he liked or hated it. She'd changed from her delicately printed shift into a pair of black pegged jeans, shiny black ankle collared work shoes, a plain white cotton tee (beneath which her small, perky bosom appeared unfettered) and a green and blue plaid flannel shirt knotted around her slender waist. Her straight, shoulder length hair had been drawn back in a ponytail, her earrings were two dots of black onyx and her mouth was an exciting dark, red slash.

"I just can't think of anyone worthy of your notice," Hugo finally concluded.

"It's Van," she revealed.

"Van? Are you serious?"

"Why? He's a darling man!"

"Garda, you do know that Van's gay?"

"What?"

"You didn't know, did you?"

"Are you sure?"

"I'm positive."

"How can you be so sure of a thing like that? Did he tell you that?"

"No, not exactly. But it's true."

"Oh, I don't believe you. You're just saying that because you want me for yourself."

"If you don't believe me, ask him yourself."

Garda sat silently smoking, stroking the kittens and trying not to sob out loud. Finally she sprung up. "So, can I buy something now?"

"Here," Hugo handed her a small wrapped parcel.

"How much is it?"

"I don't know. Just take it."

"How much do I owe you?"

"Nothing. It's a present."

Garda unwrapped what looked to be at least a quarter ounce of something green, heavily resinous and very pretty. "I can't take this from you."

"Not even to assuage your disappointment?"

"First of all, I'm not convinced that you're right, so I'm not entirely disappointed as yet. Secondly, if I take all this weed I'll owe you."

"So owe me."

"Damn it, why won't you let me pay you for this?"

"Just take it as a present."

"You're not giving me all your weed, are you?"

"No."

"Why do I think you're lying?"

"Hey, Garda, on a different subject, was that you I saw in the audience of A Man With A Maid last week?"

Garda's color deepened, which more than cancelled out the work boots in restoring her delicate femininity. "You mean that movie in Back Bay?"

"Yes. I thought I saw you in the audience."

Garda reentered the kitchen, poured herself a second cup of coffee and looked in the refrigerator for milk. "Hugo, what's this?" She came back with a tiny glassine envelope containing a small square of paper on which was imprinted a pink dot.

"That's the stuff that dreams are made of," he replied.

"Acid?"

"You bet."

"Good?"

"I don't know. Someone said you could regress to childhood on it. Someone else said past lives. I'm sure it's speedy as hell."

"So, you just have the one hit, huh?"

"You can have it if you want."

"Seriously?"

"If I can be with you when you do it."

"Oh, right! You just want to be with me when at I'm at my most trusting and vulnerable so you can fuck me with the minimum of resistance, if any!"

"No, I want to be with you when you regress to childhood, so I can spank you."

"Look, I have to go now. I have to tie myself in knots over what you told me about Van," Garda protested.

"Can I walk you home?"

"I suppose that would be wise," she sighed.

Hugo and Garda climbed slowly up narrow, cobbled Myrtle Street, past a tiny playground, a small grocery, a laundromat and many close set thin, brick walk-ups.

"You never answered my question about whether you were at A Man With A Maid," Hugo asked, as she preceded him up the three, tall, narrow flights of stairs to her top floor flat. From this angle he could appreciate the girlish contours of her bottom and thighs as never before. The snug jeans molded to her lithe form delightfully.

Garda let him into her obsessively neat and tiny one bedroom apartment. Her own two Siamese cats came in off the roof through the bedroom window and rushed into the parlor to greet her. She showed him around in a minute, ending with the rooftop access, from which one could not only see a sliver of the Charles, but also the landmark flashing neon Citgo sign.

"You shouldn't leave your windows open like that. Someone will climb in and rob you at best and possibly do more," he scolded.

"Maybe you should -- spank me the next time I do it," she ventured to suggest. Hugo's heart jumped in his chest, for had she not just said, "...you should spank me..." which meant that she wanted a spanking and then added the tantalizing "...next time" which meant that she planned to see him again and perhaps often?

"You can count on it," he agreed at once, but smiled pleasantly with it, so as not to appear too anxious.

"People talk about spanking me, but no one ever does it," she suddenly complained, sitting at her industrial wooden spool with the red tablecloth thrown over it to roll a joint out of the bag he had given her.

"Really? Who talks about it?"

"The person I saw the movie with."

"I wish I'd been the one to escort you home after that flick!" Hugo said.

"So, what are you doing this weekend?" she asked him at length, for her cats were all over him and the bonding process begun.

"I'm at your disposal if you're feeling adventurous about the windowpane," Hugo said, rising to his reedy 6'2" stature and gently setting down both cats. They solemnly exchanged phone numbers.

"You do look handsome with your hair short," she said, walking him to the door.

Hugo, having made such tremendous strides, only ventured to press her hand upon parting. The purchase of the acid had been a last minute impulse item, very much in the nature of Casanova ordering vast quantities of oysters and champagne in order to reduce a beauty to a state of reckless, sensual abandon. He had studied the master well enough to know that the way to a woman's heart and soul was through all of her senses.

Hugo walked home in the chilly dusk on puffs of light and air. He had met an enchanting, abrasive girl who might truly be a fetishist, one whom he would not have to sneak the spanking by, but who might well regard it as the sacred aphrodisiac which he had always believed it to be. Congratulating himself for holding himself in check and not jumping her in either apartment, he stopped in at a pub and ordered a beer. Sitting at the bar, the friendly baseball game in progress above, the startling image of himself as clean cut in the mirror opposite and the fantasy of the weekend stretching before him, Hugo could not remember ever feeling more delight in being alive.

It was with additional titillation that Hugo pondered, a few moments later, his best opportunity of making a girl cry real tears from a spanking, without being a bully or cruel. On acid people cried, even when you weren't spanking them. Like alcohol, it freed the emotions, but without making the room spin around. This girl was either marginally or deeply perverse. She owned a latex corset. She would certainly let him spank her. And while she was getting her spanking, the psychotropic would translate the entire experience into epic proportions, and she would most likely cry. After that, she would be his, especially if he completed the softening up process with a home cooked dinner. Hugo put down his empty stein and set off for the market.

He predicted she'd phone him no later than ten the following morning; she called at exactly ten am. He invited her over for coffee; she was at his door by the time it was ready. Today she wore her hair down, with a white tee shirt, pegged blue jeans and black, stack-heeled ankle boots that by Hugo's lights made up for a multitude of sins.

"Those shoes are much more provocative than the ones you had on yesterday," Hugo observed, handing her coffee with the windowpane on the saucer to one side.

"Well, you did cut your hair, so I figured I should make some concessions," Garda smiled at him.

"Thank you."

"Why don't we cut this in half and both do it?" Garda suggested.

Hugo briefly considered the possible paranoia involved and shook his head, protesting, "One of us should be a grown up."

"And that would be you?"

"Yes," he replied cheerfully.

"What are you afraid of Hugo? The thought of not being in complete control on our first date?"

"Since you said first date, I'm prepared to throw caution the winds," Hugo candidly admitted, cutting the paper in half and popping one half in his mouth.

"You're doing the acid with me after all?" she cried.

"How could I not, you threw down the gauntlet, didn't you?"

He took her coffee cup away to refill it. When he came back they finished their coffee, each playing with one of the kittens. Then Garda burst into giggles.

"What?" asked Hugo, smiling. "Don't tell me you're feeling something already?"

"Look, don't get mad."

"Why? What do you mean?"

"I just kind of turned your experiment around."

"What experiment?"

"The one where you planned to use powerful hallucinogens to break me down sexually."

"Come on, Garda, give me a break."

"You didn't plan to do that?"

"No. Of course not."

"Anyway, I decided not to take the acid."

"Oh really?" Hugo felt his face growing warm.

"Yes. And I dissolved the other half of the paper in your coffee that you just drank. So you actually took the full hit."

"Damn you," Hugo said with admiration. "Are you serious?"

"Isn't it delicious?" Garda actually crowed with laughter.

"You are naughty!" Hugo accused, torn between amusement and annoyance. "Aren't you?" Suddenly Garda stopped giggling. "In fact," Hugo said, "you deserve to be spanked!" He took away her kitten, placed it on the table beside the other one, who had buried his face in the cow creamer and reached for her wrist.

"What are you doing?"

"Something. While I still can!" Hugo said, pulling her across his lap with determination. "You said no one ever followed through before. Well, someone is about to." He then brought his palm down on her slim, curvy backside a dozen times, spanking her on one cheek, then the other, evenly, like someone who had done this, not once, but many times before. "I'm sure you think you're very clever!" he accused, beginning the second dozen with renewed vigor. "But you're really very irritating!" Smack! Smack! Smack! His palm impacted against her taut, denim-clad bottom with a satisfying resonance. She gasped, panted and whimpered in response but did not dare to protest. "Of course I've longed to turn you over my knee, but I never dreamed you'd give me a reason to do so. I guess I should say thanks!" He finished with a final ringing dozen swats before letting her go. She staggered to her feet and started to stumble away but he pulled her back down to sit on his lap and taking her in his arms properly, kissed her wide, red mouth for the first time.

He was surprised to feel her cling to him so fiercely afterwards.

Then, when she sprung off his lap an instant later, and refused to let him see her face, her obvious embarrassment both touched and aroused him. He was certain he could have her right then, but his muse told him to let the day unfold.

A few minutes later, as Hugo consulted the telephone weather report to determine how they were to spend the day, Garda had emerged from her romantic stupor and was amusing herself flipping through his record collection.

"King Crimson, Traffic, Pink Floyd, Moody Blues --Hugo, don't you have anything that isn't completely extinct?" she complained, lighting a cigarette as she recoiled at Hugo's similarly Byzantine jazz-fusion collection.

"Shall we drive out to the country?" he asked her, determining that the day would be fair and fine.

"Oh, come on Hugo, do we have to behave like Druids just because you dropped acid? I want to go see that double feature at the Nu-Art this afternoon."

"You don't think we'll have time to drive out to the country first for a few hours?"

"Oh forget that. It's so clichéd. Since I've got you though, maybe you can do me a favor. There's something I've been wanting to do for a few weeks now, but I've needed an escort."

A few minutes later they had set off across the Common on the way to the Combat Zone, that seedy, red light district of downtown Boston, where adult bookstores, massage parlors and strip clubs nestled between discount sock stores, wig emporiums, dangerous Chinese restaurants and pawnshops out of the Twilight Zone.

Hugo couldn't understand why they were spending a glorious autumn day in one of the worst parts of the city so Garda could experience the depressing reality of late 70's pornography, but since she'd let him spank her and kiss her so prettily, he was ready to oblige her.

"You're not going to like it, you know," he said as they entered the shop twelve minutes later. He had been there before and went straight to the fetish section. Garda strode around the shop recklessly, then she came back to him at the rack of spanking magazines. Hugo showed her Crack and Sting. She drew back in repulsion. "These aren't great, but they're of some interest," he told her, handing two issues of the English magazine Janus to the clerk to ring up. What he really wanted to buy was an anal plug to insert in her bottom. "Want anything else while we're here? They have quite a nice selection of Doc Johnson vibrators."

Garda wandered over to the wall full of dildos and vibrators. Hugo wished he knew whether she was truly intrigued or just fascinated by the freakishness of the display. He stood beside her.

"What do you know about vibrators?"

"Plenty." Hugo told her, "My best friend in college was a lesbian."

"Meaning?"

"She forced me to read a book about female self pleasuring to prove to me how useless men are. I learned a lot."

"Enough to be useful?" Garda smiled at him.

"You'll see."

Garda colored and walked away. Hugo grabbed a few shrink-wrapped objects off the pegs on the wall and took them to the counter to be rung up with the magazines.

Now Garda wandered deep into the hardcore aisles, where only random males lurked, their eyes widening as she came into view. Hugo joined her and she whispered, "Is sex really that ugly?" directing his gaze to a magazine called Girls Who Eat Cum Vol. 6.

"Haven't you ever seen hardcore before?"

"No."

"Someday I'd like to put out my own magazine," Hugo said as they walked away from the shop. "But it would be nothing like these," he shook the bag containing the Janus magazines and the sex toys.

"What would it be like?"

"Oh, beautiful, tasteful and definitely something a woman would enjoy."

"Think you know what women enjoy?"

"Some women," he responded simply, for it was best to keep it simple when his brain had just clicked into Technicolor and Dolby sound. "But didn't I tell you this was no place to go on a beautiful day?"

"What's the matter? Can't you take it?" she goaded him.

"Sure I can. I'd just rather not," Hugo replied.

On the way to the movies they stopped back at Hugo's apartment to check on the kittens, drop off the toys and smoke a joint. Hugo noticed Garda watching him closely and he laughed at her.

"What?" she demanded.

"I'm still amazed you played that trick on me. Why are you so suspicious of me?"

"I'm not. It's just that every Ivy League guy I've ever met has been a total dick brain to me sexually. And Harvard men are the absolute worst."

"The worst in what respect?"

"It strikes me you may be the exception," she suddenly said, surprising him by placing a small kiss on his cheek.

"Of course I am!" Hugo assured her, returning her favor by kissing her hand.

"In fact, you're showing remarkable restraint," Garda complimented him, for she had noticed the effect she was having upon him.

"Maybe it will be more exciting for not rushing things," he suggested as they strolled through Back Bay a few minutes later. Determining they had almost an hour before the show, they stopped at a cafe for sandwiches and hot chocolate. Then they looked in the windows of antique shops discussing which objects they admired.

"I want to buy you something," he said.

"Hugo, where are you getting all this money?"

"All what money?"

"First you gave me all that expensive weed. Then you bought all those things at the sex shop. Then lunch. Now you're talking about presents."

"Hasn't anyone ever spoiled you before?"

"No," she said bluntly.

"Then I'll be remembered as the first who did."

Garda protested that there was no time to choose anything, but Hugo persisted and they quickly selected a gold tipped, white enamel, art deco cigarette holder for ten dollars.

And yet, five minutes later, Garda led Hugo remorselessly into the double feature of Todd Browning's Freaks and David Lynch's Eraserhead, not to emerge into the fresh air again until over three hours of desolation and degradation had marched before their eyes.

"Are you trying to kill me?" Hugo demanded, after they escaped into the late afternoon. "Or just drive me mad?"

Garda could not help laughing gleefully, "Didn't you enjoy that?"

"Sure, the parts where I was planning what I'm going to do you later."

Garda tried to put off going back to his apartment for as long as possible. She persuaded him to walk through the public garden and into the Mother Goose graveyard, so they could contemplate the old stone markers, with their irregular spelling and droll punctuation. The leaves were on the ground and the clear, crisp, blue day was waning as picturesquely as it had begun.

There being virtually no one else inspecting the tiny graves in the cemetery, Hugo boldly seized Garda by the arm, pulled her over to a charmingly positioned low, stone bench and sitting upon it, drew her down across his lap. "This is for drugging, mentally torturing me and attempting to deprive me of my reason," he told her, giving her a second spanking on her jeans, twice as hard and long as the first. In fact, only the entrance of several tourists with cameras into the graveyard finally stayed his hand. "That's just a prelude to what's coming when I get you home, young lady!" he promised her, putting her off his lap. She did nothing but blush furiously.

They continued their walk home and he received no reproaches for spanking her in public. He himself was amazed he'd been able to pull it off, considering that the entire time he was spanking her he felt as though they were hurtling through space together on a diamond bullet. Somehow the tourists peripherally entering the park had brought him back to reality and he had shown enough restraint to abort the spanking and transport his lady beyond the reach of prying eyes.

Although outwardly cool and collected, Hugo's brain was none the less overflowing with romantic sentiment for this sylph who had twice let him spank her without question, and indeed seemed to regard such treatment with awe rather than resentment.

"You know what would make me really happy, Hugo?" Garda asked as they climbed his stairs to his flat.

"What?"

"If we could go to see The Cramps and The Damned tonight. They're playing in Cambridge together."

"Okay, I'll make a deal with you," said Hugo, knowing she couldn't possibly do his brain a worse turn than she'd already done with the David Lynch movie, "I'll go with you to see The Cramps if I can see you in your latex corset before the show."

"All right," she agreed. "I'll go on to my place right now, feed my cats and put it on. You come by in a half hour, okay?"

"Okay, but don't forget this," he handed her the bag of toys and magazines they'd bought earlier that day. She grabbed it, kissed him quickly and ran off down the stairs.

"So far, so good," Hugo thought, trying not to pay attention as the kittens strobed before his eyes around their water dish, metamorphosizing into Tinkerbells. "Anyway, it's bound to start wearing off soon."

When he got to Garda's house she had uncorked a bottle of white wine. She was wearing the black latex corset, which had a row of thin, buckling straps up the front. Over the corset she had on blue jeans and a different pair of black boots, with higher but thicker heels. Obviously this was her club outfit from London. Her red hair was loose around her shoulders, a black, thin, studded leather collar ringed her slim white throat and her small, round, high bosom was displayed to maximum advantage by the skintight foundation.

"That suits you, Garda," Hugo complimented her casually, squeezing her waist as he lightly kissed her lips.

"The sun is going down. Want to watch it from the roof?" she asked. They took the bottle and some cigarettes. The two beige and brown cats joined them and began to jump to the neighboring roof top as the eighty year old buildings were extremely narrow and close together on that part of the hill. Garda put her Sex Pistols album on so Hugo could learn the error of his musical taste. It had the effect of making him want to fuck her immediately and hard. The Cramps album was even more sexually incendiary and before it was half over Hugo had dragged her back through the window, into her tiny bedroom, onto her tiny bed and began to pull her shoes and jeans off.

"Hugo, can I tell you something?" she asked, when he held her pretty foot in his hand.

"Tell me anything," he encouraged her, admiring her long, slim legs for the first time, then rolling her over on her tummy to behold the bare curves of her bottom revealed by the hip length corset. Besides this she wore only a g-string.

"How adorable you are," he rolled her back over. "But what did you want to tell me?"

Garda sat up against the windowsill and lit another cigarette. "This isn't easy for me to talk about," she explained. "But I'll start by saying that you're the first boy who's ever come close to doing something I like. I mean spontaneously."

"Really? I would have thought between Berkeley and London you'd have met your share of deviants."

"I won't say I haven't made a few converts," she smiled, then added fiercely, "but it's not the same!"

"I see your point. Of course I've always spanked my girl friends, but you're the first who ever seemed to want me to do it before I did it."

"I've always been this way."

"Me too."

"Do you know what I would really like?"

"Tell me."

"To be treated harshly," she replied candidly, going pink with embarrassment.

"That would no more than you deserve," Hugo said, altering his tone to suit her endearing request. "After what you put me through today, a lesson in basic civility is in order for you, young lady." In so saying, Hugo seized her by her bare forearm and positioning himself on the edge of the bed, drew her face down across his lap. "Although it's not just today you should be punished for," said Hugo, spanking her slim, exposed cheeks sharply as he scolded her. "You wouldn't have even gone out with me if I hadn't scored for you. Isn't that so?" Smack! smack! smack!

"Ow!" she cried, putting one graceful hand back to shield her pinkened bottom. "That really hurts!"

Hugo paused to rub her satiny cheeks in light, hypnotic circles, wondering whether this was her first real bare bottom spanking. "Mmmmm," she said, beginning to grind on his lap, then suddenly thinking better of it, modestly closing her thighs.

"I like them better open," Hugo told her, slapping her inner thighs sharply until she spread them again. He also pulled off the g-string and tossed it aside. "And I would have preferred you in actual panties. Please remember that."

Continuing to spank her firmly, Hugo looked across the tiny room and saw the bag from the sex shop on a small chest of drawers to the side of the bed. He reached out, grabbed it and dumped its contents on the bed beside him.

"So freak shows amuse you?" Hugo spanked her from pink to magenta over several minutes.

"No, not really," she finally cried, gasping for breath.

"You seem to prefer them to peak foliage."

"Just to push your buttons, since you're such an aesthete," she returned, in spite of her vulnerable position.

"Yes, well, now I get to push your buttons," he assured her, ending with a volley of six hard swats.

"Ow! What are you going to do now?" she craned her neck around to look at him and then at the bag from the sex shop he had grabbed.

"Embarrass you," he said, freeing a standard, 6" vibrator from its shrink-wrap and showing it to Garda. "By putting this in you while you're over my knee and spanking you until you come."

"No, that would be too humiliating!" she protested without attempting to escape.

"No, this will be the humiliating part," Hugo cheerfully explained, showing her the second toy he had grabbed, a 4" anal plug. "As you can see, it's designed for insertion in the rear."

"No!" Now she tired to wriggle off his lap, but he held her fast. "That's too much!"

"Just enough for the likes of you, my dear," Hugo replied, resuming spanking her.

"Did I not tell you to keep your legs spread?" he warned her, separating her thighs. "I want to see you." He pressed her pink cheeks open with his hands and spanked her in between them.

"Oh god!" she cried, squirming as he firmly tapped his palm against her two most private parts. "It's too much!"

"You protest, but you're wet, you naughty girl."

"Hugo?" she twisted the right way around on his lap and sat up, "I'll die if you do all that to me at once! Couldn't you just take me? Now?"

Hugo tightened his arms around her, kissed her, nibbled her ears, bit her shoulders and nuzzled her throat, all the while lightly squeezing her pert bosom through the corset. He felt her tension ebb away quickly as his hand closed upon her dewy Venus mound and a finger slipped into her glove tight vagina.

"I need to teach you about foreplay," he murmured against her ear.

"Hugo?" she suddenly looked at him. "Are you not potent?"

"Silly," he said, placing her hand against the rampant bar of iron in his jeans and causing it to theatrically throb as she touched it. "Don't worry, he's waiting for you. But tell me, when was the last time you indulged in anything like serious petting, junior high?"

"You're right, Hugo," she smiled ruefully. "You seem to know all my secrets." Garda stroked Hugo's erection through his jeans then tried to unzip them. "Don't you think it's very submissive for a girl to give a man head?" she asked. He captured her hands in his own and kissed them.

"Yes, very. But that's not what we're doing right now," he told her firmly, pulling his belt from the loops of his jeans. "Because I have a habit that I doubt I will ever give up." He placed her two pillows in the center of her single bed and summarily bent her over them thus elevating her bottom. Then he went in front of her and bound her wrists by looping and buckling the belt around them and then securing it to the shiny black wrought iron rail at the foot of her bed. "When I have to do with a girl I really like, it's a compulsion with me to get her off first."

Once Hugo had Garda face down on her little bed, over her little pillows, all the resistance left her and she surrendered herself to his whims.

The potent psychedelics still at work, Hugo was touched beyond expression at her complete and charming passivity. “She must really trust me,” he thought, but at least had the presence of mind not to sob aloud at the gift of her delicate pre-Raphaelite beauty spread out before him like a sacrifice. Coming to, he remembered that he was not there to stroke her bottom as though it were a kitten’s head. Her one request, that uncompromising demand, that he be harsh, reasserted its dominance in his brain.

Hugo scolded Garda for being arrogant and unapproachable at work while slapping her bare bottom vigorously. Then he forced her thighs apart and inserted the larger dildo into her vagina, while holding her down by the waist. Garda whimpered and squirmed but Hugo ignored this and let her feel her own, small, wooden hairbrush on her bottom while her pussy was filled. Garda yipped and wriggled. Hugo took the dildo out of her pussy and replaced it with the smaller one, but only long enough to lubricate it for her bottom, into which it then was inserted. Garda whimpered and squirmed even more violently. Knowing from experience that her climax was only moments away, Hugo untied her hands to have use of his belt, doubled it and began to first lightly, then harder, strike her across the exact center of her filled bottom with it.

“And another thing,” he told her, bringing the strap down harder, in order to leave light pink marks, “you should never be rude about another person’s record collection, to their face.”

Hugo held her down with his hand in the small of her back and strapped her bottom just a little harder than he had ever strapped any other girl friend before. He would have gone on a good deal longer as well, had she not succumbed, as predicted, to an intense orgasm. After which she was embarrassed enough to die during the delicate extraction of toys from her ultra tight and still pulsating orifices. For Garda it was too humiliating. The last twelve strokes of the strap had been effective enough, post-climax and three minutes later to cause her to cry several real tears. Of course, from such a poignant punishment, her eyes could only be expected to fill up once or twice. But those six or seven tears thrilled Hugo madly. He touched her face just to make sure he wasn't hallucinating and found they were adorably real. Hugo thanked his ruling planet Venus for helping him to make her come so fast. Now she wouldn't notice just how fast he was about to climax while fucking her for the first time, as he could never remember being quite so excited in his life.

Hugo cleared the bed, efficiently unbuckled her corset and had her naked and up on all fours in a minute.

"No head?" she asked, turning to see his impressive erection emerge from his jeans then become quickly sheathed in a condom.

"Some other time, darling," he gently pushed her head down, took her by the waist and proceeded to enter her tight, creamy vagina, still faintly throbbing from her own strapping induced climax. He nudged his large cock in slowly, gratified to feel her instantly clamping him tightly inside her. She was squeezing him so tightly he almost came at the moment of entry.

"Relax, Garda," he told her, "or I'll have to spank you some more." He smacked her once on each cheek. She loosened slightly, allowing him to penetrate her more deeply and finally, fully. "Good girl," he told her, pistoning his cock in and out, for she was wet as a young girl can be and the additional spanks set her afire afresh. She looked back at him, with a coquettish pout he would not have thought her capable of, as much as to say, there is my bottom, right in front of you, are you going to waste this opportunity to spank me? "Or should I say, bad girl?" Hugo spanked her rhythmically as he thrust his cock into her pussy. She virtually melted at this, coming a second time, as he achieved his first effusion in Garda's honor.

Then he was enormously hungry and they went back to his kitchen to cook. After which they saw The Damned and The Cramps and Hugo spanked and fucked her two more times that night.

After that, they were inseparable for the next ten months. They did everything that young cosmopolitans couples do, plus spanking; and never quarreled, unless Garda became unreasonably jealous. That was when the disagreeable side of the restrained beauty emerged to the full and Hugo felt compelled to beat her for it, which of course made her that much more his slave. But the idyllic relationship came to an abrupt though not unfriendly end when Garda was accepted to law school the following year and returned to California to complete her education. And that was pretty much the last he heard from her.

Then, one windy winter afternoon, twenty-two years later, Hugo Sands was standing behind the counter in his shop, about to make some phone calls, when he noticed a tall redhead enter through the front door and pause to look at him.

"My god, is that Garda?" he cried, coming from behind the counter to meet her, his heart contracting with excitement.

"You actually recognize me?" Garda cried, astonished. She was still slim to a fault, with pale lips, no jewelry, a smart suit and expensive shoes. "Hugo, your flaxen hair -- it's gone all sandy!" She allowed herself to be squeezed tightly and hugged him back hard. "But how handsome and urbane you've become!"

"How dare you not write me?" he asked, pulling away. "I should spank you for that right now. And hard!"

Garda put her hand to her throat. "Hugo, don't start with me the first second."

"What? You felt something just then, didn't you? Something here?" Hugo pressed his palm against her tummy.

"Hugo, how could you be just the same after all these years?" she laughed and let herself continue to be hugged.

"You found me by accident, didn't you?" he asked, releasing her and enjoying the delicate blush that suffused her cheeks. "God, you're still beautiful. But I don't like the pale lips. I remember that dark red lipstick you used to wear. So sexy."

"Yes, I found you by accident. I'm in town on business and I found your lovely little B&D journal in my room at the Inn. Naturally I devoured it and was agog to see you were the publisher, and right here in the village. Too good to be true!"

"See, I told you I'd make a magazine."

"I think I need to put an ad in it."

"Let me put up the sign and we'll have lunch."

"You own this place too?" she asked as he ushered her out.

"Yes, shortly after you departed I had a favorite aunt leave me some money and I used it to go into the antique business. The magazine is just a sideline. It barely pays for itself."

"You should charge more for it."

"Everyone's going on-line these days."

"I got off to some of the stories and illustrations last night in my room."

"Naughty girl!"

They strolled back to The Bone and Feather Inn and had lunch in the pub.

During the cocktail stage Garda confided that she had never married but had been in a series of failed relationships with highly competitive though not technically dominant men. She had tried attending local support groups in San Francisco and Los Angeles but never felt attracted to the people she met at their parties and was profoundly bored by their interminable meetings. Once or twice, out of curiosity and desperation, she had answered a male dominant ad in a local paper, but was consistently disappointed.

"Who are you in town to see?" Hugo asked.

"Randy Price. You know him? He's letting the studio I work for shoot at his estate and I've brought contracts for him to sign."

"Yes, I know him. He'll come on to you, but don't succumb. He's not our kind of people," Hugo counseled.

"Hugo, this isn't Ally McBeal. Mega millionaire clients do not come on to female lawyers old enough to remember life before pantyhose."

"You don't look your age," Hugo promised her, squeezing her leg under the table. Again she blushed. Then Hugo thought, "What am I doing?" and withdrew his hand.

"So what about now?" he asked, "in a relationship?"

"No," she said helpfully.

"Maybe you do need to place an ad."

"How about you, Hugo?"

"Well, I couldn't wait for you forever, so I finally did get into a relationship."

"Would she mind your squeezing my leg under the table? Is that why you suddenly withdrew your lovely hand?"

"Yes, I suddenly remembered Laura, who is conveniently out of town for a few days, but who deserves to be mentioned."

"Wife Laura?"

"Girlfriend. My illustrator too."

"For how long?"

"Well, I met her five years ago, but temporarily lost her to another. It took a few years to get her back, so I'd say we've been together about two years."

"Live together?"

"No. She lives up at the Cliff House. Her little sister landed the composer Anthony Newton for a lover off my introduction and he took to Laura as well."

"Convenient," she said.

"And rent free," he grinned.

"Oh dear," she frowned, sipping her cocktail.

"What?"

"I'm feeling that horrible jealous feeling again."

"Really?" Hugo couldn't help but be pleased that Garda still loved him. "You're so bad. You probably haven't had a good spanking in years."

"Hugo, stop, you're making me blush and I haven't done that in years either."

"Come visit me later. I have a great playroom."

"I have to have dinner with Randy, but I can drop by afterwards," she promised.

"With dark red lipstick and earrings on."

"Just as you like, Hugo," said Garda agreeably surprised that nothing had changed between them.

After lunch Hugo took Garda through the village on foot, stopping at a small, chic looking dress shop on Main Street. "A friend of mine owns this shop and my former-girl Friday works here," Hugo said, ushering Garda into the smart boutique. Inside they found one small and elegantly shapely brunette in her late 20's or possibly just 30, clad in a close fitting gray wool dress steaming the wrinkles out of some hanging suits while a second, taller and still more slender brunette, in another version of the grey wool dress, in her middle 20's, with her hair in a shiny black French roll, stood meticulously folding cashmere sweaters behind one of the counters. Both women looked up but only the smaller one smiled.

"Hi girls. Damaris, Pamela, this is Garda Hudson."

Garda said how do you do and shook hands with them while Hugo explained to her that Pamela, who had until recently been his own assistant at the shop, had just signed on with Damaris as a custom seamstress.

"She's got art and fashion degrees and was wasted behind my counter," he disclosed, smiling at Pamela, who returned the smile but faintly. "So for her own good, I let her go," he continued.

"My good too. I love my new assistant," said Damaris, delighted to be running her own business in Random Point with such a suitable partner. Indeed, the two women with their nipped waists, black hair and pale olive complexions might have been sisters.

"And I love my very first girlfriend in the scene," Hugo said, squeezing Garda's slender waist.

"Your first, Hugo?" Damaris seemed to appreciate the poignancy of this declaration much more than did Pamela and beamed with affection at the visiting redhead. "How unspeakably sweet! How long ago was that?"

"Please don't ask," Garda protested, responding charmingly to Damaris' warmth.

"Years and years before I met even Marguerite," Hugo confided, glowing in a way that made Pamela ill.

"Who is Marguerite?" asked Garda.

"She writes as Alma for my magazine."

"Do I get to meet her too?" Garda asked.

"Luckily for Hugo, she's in New York with Laura right now," said Damaris impertinently.

"Yes it is, but you oughtn't to have said so," Hugo agreed, thumbing through a rack of cocktail dresses.

"She would have been intolerably competitive with Garda," Damaris observed, "And it all would have ended in tears. She's a redhead too, you see and there's never been a second one in Random Point."

"Girls, won't you find me a perfect corset for this lady?"

"We just got some incredible ones in!" Damaris cried with excitement, going behind the counter to pull out a tissue packed box containing several black lace over beige nylon sewn full corselets, echoing the glory days of the Irving Klaw studios. "This small should fit Garda perfectly. Come with me, and we'll try it on," Damaris took Garda by the arm and led her to the lavishly appointed fitting rooms.

"You're buying me a corset, Hugo?" Garda asked over her shoulder with a bemused grin on her face.

He winked at her as she disappeared with Damaris. Pamela folded sweaters and sulked behind the counter.

"Well," she said, "I'm sure you hardly miss me."

"Sweetheart, of course I miss you," said Hugo gently, "but we couldn't go on working together. Things had gotten out of control. And by things I mean you."

"If I didn't love my new boss I'd hate you now," said Pamela. "As it is, I feel hurt and rejected! And now this, flaunting some blue-eyed redhead in front of me! Torturing me by forcing me to see her in a beautiful corset before imagining you together!"

"Pamela, I haven't seen Garda in 22 years. She was my first submissive. She's only in town for the weekend and she still likes me. Can you blame me for being happy?"

"Yes!"

"Pamela, you're not being reasonable. You belong to Sloan. What you are feeling for me is some sort of mild infatuation brought on by me spanking you."

"And fucking the daylights out of me!"

"Just that once."

"I haven't been able to forget it."

"That's why we couldn't go on working together."

"I thought when girls had sex with their bosses they got to keep their jobs," said Pamela recklessly.

"You're lucky we're not somewhere I could give that remark the reply it deserves," he said forcefully.

Damaris came out with a smile. "It's a perfect fit. How about a glorious new cocktail dress to go over it?"

"Do bring her something to try on, Damaris," said Hugo, unable to fully enjoy the experience because of Pamela's sulking. When Damaris disappeared with another dress over her arm Hugo lifted Pamela's chin, forcing her to look at him. "You're behaving like a very wayward girl," he told her.

She glared at him defiantly, her full red lips forming a Bardot-like pout.

"Give me your hand," he said sternly, picking up a small wooden ruler. When she saw that he was quite serious, she extended her trembling left hand towards her former employer. Hugo took it and turning her palm upwards smacked it sharply with the flat side of the ruler. She tried to pull her hand back but he held her wrist fast in his other hand and struck her two, three, four more times across her palm, hard enough to sting her and bring tears to her large, dark eyes.

"Wipe your eyes," he ordered, letting go of her hand. "Aren't you ashamed of yourself for acting like such a brat?"

Looking in the mirror behind the counter Pamela delicately dabbed her eyes with a white handkerchief. He came around the counter and hugged her briefly to him, his own heart beating fast at the enormity of having made her fall in love with him.

"Pamela, I'm not going to let you disturb your beautiful relationship with Sloan or mine with Laura, but that doesn't mean I plan to neglect you," he said, examining her hand, which was pink now. "Now go and run that under water," he told her. "And we'll continue this discussion at a later date."

Pamela was in tears and told herself severely in the bathroom mirror, "You have no pride." But when she looked at the palm of her hand she felt a terrible thrill of excitement.

Garda came out in a square necked, long sleeved, wasp waisted, straight skirted, flounced cocktail dress of which Hugo entirely approved. He handed Damaris his credit card.

"We thought we'd let you discover just how charming the corset looks later, yourself," said Damaris, and Hugo smiled, glad that Pamela had left the floor. That young lady's temper tantrum had almost cast a pall on the evening but the solution had been very much in hand and now a kind of order had been restored.

"I might as well give up even trying to do the honorable thing with regard to my buddy Sloan," Hugo confessed to Garda, while walking her back to the inn. "Basic chemistry is making that impossible."

"Sloan is?"

"Pamela's boyfriend. He runs the bookshop across the way from my store and he's a very good friend of mine. Anyway, he's got a pretty assistant who was driving our Pamela crazy with jealousy. So I decided to take her mind off that entire situation by being the boss from modern Gothic hell, kicking off the program with a spanking."

"And she promptly fell in love?"

"I would call it a crush that has developed over several weeks."

"I see the distinction," Garda laughed.

"Stop by my house on the way to Randy's and I'll get you stoned," Hugo promised, writing down the address on the back of his business card.

"Oh Hugo," she replied, fondly squeezing his arm, "nothing has changed, has it? I'll come now!"

Garda brought all the things she needed to Hugo's house in the woods and dressed for dinner in his playroom, in front of a gold scalloped cheval glass, while sharing a joint with Hugo as in the old days. He helped her hook the form sculpting new corset while sitting on the edge of a leather sofa, with Garda standing in front of him, enjoying their reflections in the mirror.

Garda said, "I think we look better together now than we did before, Hugo."

"Marvelous the way you kept your figure," he complimenting her, giving her a pat on the bottom before pulling her down on his lap to embrace her properly. "I'm glad you live in California. I could easily fall in love with you again," he told her. "Now put your stockings on and I'll hook the suspenders for you."

"You certainly know your way around foundations," Garda remarked with admiration.

"You were the first girl I ever met who owned anything even remotely fetishistic," he told her.

"Oh yes, my rubber corset. It always made me dizzy after twenty or so minutes."

"You never told me that."

"You wouldn't have let me wear it."

"That's true."

"You were so paternal with me," Garda smiled, seating herself on a leather pouf to pull on the seamed stockings gracefully.

"Goes with the territory," Hugo told her, entranced by the way she put on her ultra high, black velvet, tapering, stack heeled pump and extended her long leg to admire the effect.

"Is that why all the girls in town follow you all around?" she gently mocked him, slipping on the blue gown.

"Not all, but maybe one more than is necessary at the moment," Hugo replied, zipping her up then hooking the suspenders to the tops of the real silk stockings he had bought her as an additional present.

"I wish I didn't have to go to this dinner," she pouted, sitting down on his lap and impatiently wriggling her slim, muscular bottom while winding her arms around his neck. "Oh, it's so good to feel you just as you were, only more so!"

"Make it a short dinner and come right back to me," he ordered, patting her bottom through the velvet gown again.

She purred against his ear, "I love it when you tell me what to do."

A few minutes later, while putting her into her rental car Hugo allowed her to take a last hit. "You're so sweet," she murmured, checking her makeup in the mirror. She was back to dark red lipstick and her russet hair was twisted up and held in place by a velvet clip.

"Remember what I told you about Randy, Garda. If he makes a move on you, brush him off. He's developed the knack of pressuring women into giving him sex better than anyone I know, but there's nothing in his bag of tricks to interest the likes of you."

"Hugo," Garda laughed, "do you even know how old I am?"

"Are you saying that in L.A. no woman over a certain age gets the make put on her?'

"Yes, Hugo. That is what I'm saying." But Garda drove off gaily, merrily lit and looking forward with intense pleasure to the later portion of the evening.

Garda took the narrow coast road to Randy's estate, warmed by Hugo's compliments, but never expecting his predictions to come true. Randy Price was five to seven years her junior, frighteningly rich and according to Hugo, a ruthless operator. She expected to dine briefly, tour the shooting areas, get her contracts signed and leave without much ado.

Randy was tall, arresting and detached, but not unfriendly, as he showed Garda around and introduced her to their only other dining companion, his sister Marnie Price, a tall, raw boned blonde, very much in the New England mode, good looking, butch and crudely charming.

"I notice a remnant of an ex-punk past," said Garda, tapping her own earlobe, which like Randy's, bore the faint, ancient perforations of four piercings. "I'll bet you used to have a Mohawk, huh?"

Randy admitted he had and stories of bands and clubs were exchanged. Garda thought, "What was Hugo talking about? Randy's not so bad. And I love his sister!"

But less than three hours later, when she lightly rapped on Hugo's front door, he opened it to a badly shaken redhead.

"You warned me, but I didn't believe you," she confided a few minutes later as he took her into his prettiest sitting room and handed her a glass of burgundy. "I feel stupid!"

Hugo felt a terrible arrow of jealousy pierce his heart. "Garda, you didn't let Randy take advantage of you?"

"It all happened so quickly," she explained, gratefully accepting a cigarette. "One minute he was showing me his signed copy of the Necronomicon and the next thing I knew, he was jamming his dick down my throat!"

"Oh, Garda!" Hugo snapped with real annoyance. "Why in the world did you let him?"

"I felt pressured, as though if I refused he'd kill the shooting space deal."

"You let yourself be pressured into sex over something as trivial as that?"

"I'm not sure how it happened. I'm only sure it happened fast. He seemed to instinctively know all my vanilla buttons and pushed them in a row. The earlobe nibbling, the bosom squeezing, the digital penetration."

"Preceded, I imagine by liberal inhalations of cocaine?" Hugo accused, remembering that this was Randy's drug of choice, which also accounted for his general greed and irascibility.

"Gee, you know him well."

"Gee, I know you well," said Hugo cynically.

"Hugo, I feel wretched."

"It's the cocaine and cheap, meaningless sex. Smoke some weed, take the thrashing you deserve from me and you'll feel better."

"Hugo, this never happens to me," she explained, curling up on the hearthrug in front of the fire.

"Maybe if you wore blue velvet and corsets instead of austere business suits it would happen more often," he pointed out, sitting down beside her and removing her ultra high-heeled pumps one by one.

"Thank you!" she cried.

"I'll find you another pair to set off your corset," he said, disappearing upstairs and returning to her a few minutes later with a pretty pair of lower heeled black brocade pumps with high vamps. "You're the same size as Laura," he told her, slipping the 18th century style shoes on Garda's graceful feet. "Turn around, I'll unzip you," he told her. She let him help her out of the dress, which revealed her charmingly corseted, long, slim torso.

"You're just as delicious as ever," he told her, holding her waist between his hands. "But I'm highly incensed at your letting Randy Price see you, no less have you in this!" Hugo declared, pulling her across his knee and giving her eight or ten quick smacks on her fully pantied bottom, which appeared as taut and smooth as ever under the sheer briefs. "You've behaved shockingly, young lady, even for you!" he said, with a half dozen more spanks, before letting her up.

Garda, blushing furiously, took her wine across the room. He laughed at her embarrassment. "Has it been so long since you've been turned over somebody's knee?" he asked.

"About 22 years," she admitted, pretending to study his bookcase and presenting an elegant rear view.

"Is this true?"

"I kept trying out different masters. But as you know, they don't often specifically spank."

Hugo smiled, "I binged on slaves for a while myself."

"Really?"

"I kept meeting girls who'd grown up on The Story of O. I had three girl friends in a row who virtually wanted to be told when to go to the bathroom."

"What happened?"

"It warped my character. I started taking the scene too seriously and wound up alienating someone I really cared for."

"That would be the lady with the good taste in shoes?" Garda asked, extending her well-shod foot.

"Had you returned just a few years ago, you would have found me insufferable."

"I'm sure that even at your worst you were never as grisly as some of the creatures who've lured me into their dungeons. I've been suspended, hogtied, hot waxed, prodded, pinched, clamped, cinched, everything but wrung out and hung up to dry."

"No corporal punishment?"

"Oh, I've been able to obtain a few dreamy floggings from ripped leather men over the years, but I was never lucky enough to meet a straight one with the proper looks and brains to interest me."

"That's insane, Garda. California is probably the spanking capital of the world. I'll have you set up with a spanking boyfriend within weeks of your returning to L.A."

"You seem incredibly sure of your powers," Garda smiled.

"Trust me."

"It seems like I've been sublimating this need since the last time I saw you," she mused.

"I can't think why. You were always such a self starter."

"I've been remiss," Garda admitted.

"And should be punished."

"Hugo, this wine is lovely, but do you know what I'd really adore?"

"Tell me."

"One of those luscious Irish coffees you used to make us before we went skating at night."

"Come with me and I'll show you how it's done," Hugo said, leading her by the hand through the house to his rustic kitchen, with its wonderful hearth.

Garda watched Hugo grind the coffee beans, sitting on the wooden table and swinging her long, slim legs. "You always took such good care of me," she said fondly. "Remember that day we pretended that I was a baby and I crawled around the floor and talked baby talk all afternoon and you spanked me I don't know how many times?"

"That was fun," he agreed, measuring out a jigger of Bushmills.

"You used to literally spend hours spanking me. Remember?"

"Can you blame me?"

"And you're saying there are really others like you?"

"Can you honestly doubt it? You saw the magazine. Why don't you answer some ads while I begin researching my California resources? I promise you'll be playing regularly before you know it," he guaranteed her, pouring cream into a bowl and placing that under a blender.

"The truth is, I've become a boring corporate lawyer," Garda sighed.

"I still can't understand how you could have allowed Randy Price get the better of you!" Hugo exclaimed, remembering her lurid confession with annoyance. "He's not even your type."

"Hugo, you don't understand. Men just don't come on to me that often. I give off a spinster or dyke vibe. Or maybe it's that I don't flirt. Anyway, I seem to be seldom pursued these days. So I was flattered into submission."

"Oh, that's nonsense! What else did you do with him?" Hugo snapped, while whipping the cream.

Garda shrugged, "I just gave him head, let him finger bang me, trivial stuff."

"I can't believe you went down on your knees to Randy Price!"

Garda bit her knuckle.

"You're hopeless," Hugo declared, pouring coffee into a mug, adding the jigger of Bushmills and the whipping cream. Garda took the cup and a spoon to stir it. "Bring that with you and follow me," Hugo said, grabbing the whiskey bottle and a glass along with her smoking materials and leading her up three pairs of stairs to his attic playroom.

"Wow," Garda said, peering out of the porthole window and catching a glimpse of the half moon through the swaying boughs. Then she noticed the skylights, the sophisticated furnishings, all suitable for playing on and the looking glasses to reflect it all.

"All the dungeons in Random Point are traditionally located in the attics," he informed her.

"What are you going to do with me?" she asked, drinking her coffee fast.

"You mean to you, for making me angrier than I have ever been with you before! And after being back in my life just one afternoon!"

"But, you always said you're not the jealous type," she smiled.

"I'm not jealous, I'm just irritated as hell that you squandered the divine gift of your submission on Randy Price. After I warned you, Garda. That's what makes it so insulting."

"See, you shouldn't have warned me like that. You've heard of the Bluebeard Syndrome?"

Hugo ignored her flippancy and lifted the lid of a large toy chest to select implements. She came over to look in.

"Finish your drink and your smoke while I find the proper restraints," he advised her.

"Restraints? What for? I'll always stay in position for you, Hugo."

"Maybe I think you'll look good in restraints. Some black leather wristlets, linked by a couple of boat hooks, should be perfect for your wrists behind your back. And then, I can easily have you reach back and spread your bottom for my crop."

Garda pouted while she watched him gather toys. She smoked a joint while touring the room. Inevitably she kept coming back to the expensively upholstered table with the carved and varnished wooden legs in the middle of the room. Hugo demonstrated, at the touch of a button, that the elegant bondage bed could be tilted. Rather than sticky leather, it was covered in a smoky blue velveteen fabric, suitable for a lady to repose upon. Soft blue suede restraints were tucked into pockets at each corner and there were recessed o-rings around the perimeter at all the necessary points to make bondage possible in a variety of classic positions.

Hugo let her finish all her stimulants then summarily took her by the ear across to a long, high backed wooden bench, carved in the same style as the table, and with a padded seat covered in the same smoky blue plush fabric and turned her over his knee. "First, a good, hard spanking, to make you very sorry!" he promised, bringing his palm down on her trim backside, so glamorous through her sheer black on beige lace nylon briefs.

Hugo held her by her ear lobe while spanking her vigorously for ten or fifteen minutes. This worked the way it always had done. She squirmed, panted, whimpered and ground against his lap, lubricating copiously.

He lowered her panties and saw with satisfaction how pink she had already become. The texture of her skin was still smooth and fine.

"If I weren't so incensed at the way you've behaved, I would compliment you on your figure and skin more," he explained, running his hand across her slim hips, still girded by the charming corset he had bought her that afternoon. "However, it can be still pinker," he decided, commencing the spanking again. For her naughtiness, he wanted her bottom a solid color field of magenta against her snowy skin when he lay her face down on the table.

"Hurts you?" he asked, several minutes later. She was wriggling and panting but scarcely protesting. Distantly, she knew it must hurt, but she was floating in a heavenly sphere of submissive bliss. It had always been this way with Hugo. They'd play for hours, the next day she'd be as sore as if she'd athletically trained and not remember why.

Then it would come back to her, the spanking that had lasted an hour in the woods, or during the entire Oscars. The way he paced his smacks, and how he placed them, was quite an art, she had always felt. She felt it then and now, that Hugo spanked with symmetry.

"Now that you're entirely pink," he observed, transporting her to the table and placing her on it, face down, "we can continue in the place that seemed to intrigue you."

Hugo thrilled Garda by roughly spreading her ankles as wide as they would go and binding them with the soft suede straps.

"Remember how I told you I wanted your hands, Garda?"

She obediently put her wrists behind her and allowed him to enclose them in the soft leather cuffs and link them together loosely so that she could turn them either palm up or palm down. First Hugo turned her palms up and very sternly spanked each of them once. She whimpered more at this than all the hard spanking that had come before. "Are you going to obey me tonight, Garda?"

"Yes," she murmured sincerely.

"And please me?"

"Of course, if I can."

"Show me your bottom," he ordered. Garda slowly responded by turning her hands palm down on each cheek and faintly spreading them. "Is that the best you can do?" he asked, pushing her hands up so that her forearms folded against each other and rested on her lower back. Now he selected a small, oval shaped paddle of varnished red teak, about a half an inch thick, and began to apply it firmly to either cheek. She squirmed and yipped. Finally he stopped, unfolded her arms and placed her hands on her cheeks again. Without being told she pulled them apart.

"That's just the way I want you to stay, Garda, dear," he told her, selecting a short crop with a two inch square leather spanker at the end. "Because of all things you really need to have your bottomhole disciplined tonight."

She made some inarticulate noise of protest, but timidly kept herself spread as he began to methodically spank her anus.

"Oh god!" she cried, feeling bitterly ashamed and on the edge of an orgasm at once. "Please!"

Hugo took this to mean, please don't stop, which he didn't intend to. "This is only the beginning, darling," he promised, cropping her quickly. Then he laid down the crop. Again, he removed her hands from her cheeks and folded her arms up on her lower back above her pink cheeks. "Don't move," he told her, touching the button and causing the table to tilt up 30 degrees, to elevate her bottom and drop her head.

Then he went to a console where he'd left the whiskey, poured himself a shot, drank it, then decanted a cigar from a silver tube. But he didn't light the cigar. He screwed the lid on the tube and returned to Garda. Placing one hand on her wrists on the small of her back, he inserted the smooth, rounded end of the cigar tube into Garda's exceedingly creamy pussy.

"Oh! What are you doing?"

"You'll feel it in a minute," he warned her, withdrawing the fully lubricated cylinder from her pussy and inserting it firmly into her freshly pinkened bottomhole.

"No! Oh please!"

"I'm sorry," he said insincerely, twisting the tube deeper into her rectum until only a few inches of it protruded. "But nothing short of total humiliation will due tonight. Now don't move," he told her, reaching for a thin leather strap. Bound, with her thighs apart and her anus filled for her strapping, Garda was incoherent with embarrassed confusion.

"I'll be good," she promised wriggling with shame. Again and again the strap came down, scoring her dark pink bottom rose. He would only stop every twenty or so strokes to roughly, deeply fingerfuck her pussy. The third time he paused to do this she came.

But that was not the end. He removed the tube, unfastened her bonds and ordered her to set herself to rights. When she returned to him, still in a sort of daze he took her to a couch, turned her on her tummy, pulled her up by the hips, inserted his cock in her pussy and drove into her with the robustness that she so fondly remembered. She came again as he held her by the waist and pistoned into her relentlessly for ten or fifteen minutes, until expiring in a flood of personal pleasure himself.

The next morning, while Hugo's large black tomcat lay heavily against her, Garda was served her cappuccino in bed by her host. Meanwhile, Damaris and Pamela, again in two similarly styled, smart woolen dresses, their shiny black hair perfectly groomed, were enacting the rituals of opening the shop.

As Damaris set the steamer opposite a rack of sleek, short suits and Pamela started the coffee, the doorbell tinkled and Laura Random entered, the picture of a New England tomboy in cords and a tucked out plaid shirt layered over a solid one. She was in her early 30's, exceedingly pretty and youthful, with an extremely long, chestnut brown ponytail and dark eyes. Her voice was softly pleasant as she cheerfully greeted them, placing a small but heavy looking carton on one of the glass countertops.

She announced, "I have our second book!" Opening up the carton she pulled out a thick, elegantly covered graphic novel. "And Anthony didn't even have to finance this one. Susan and I were able to pay the printers ourselves out of what we made from the first one."

"Laura, it's spectacular," said Damaris, leafing through the thick, all color pages, from back to front.

"Damaris, you're not reading Hebrew, start from the beginning!" Laura cried, happily, for she and her sister had just published their second book and it would soon be in the stores, which brought an intense feeling of happiness to the artist-author.

"Yes, it's beautiful," echoed Pamela, her own pulse racing with that mixture of jealousy and excitement she always felt when she encountered Hugo Sands' lover.

"Can I leave some in the store with you?"

"Of course!" Damaris agreed.

"You keep half of everything you sell, okay?"

"Deal!"

Pamela gazed at Laura and Damaris with bafflement. How could Laura Random be so cordial to the woman who now lived with her ex-husband? Then she reminded herself that Laura now had Hugo Sands all to herself. Except for the redhead.

"Listen, Laura," said Damaris, suddenly remembering the redhead too. "Something came in yesterday that you have to have. Here, try this on!" She thrust a size 6 cocktail dress in cranberry silk into Laura's hand.

"That is pretty," Laura said, obediently walking into the fitting room.

The instant she disappeared, Damaris dialed the phone.

"Who are you calling?" Pamela demanded.

"I'm warning Hugo to get homegirl dressed."

"Why? Don't you think it would be more fun to let nature take its course?" Pamela suggested.

"P., have you forgotten he spent five hundred dollars here yesterday? And that we love him?" Damaris chided. The phone was answered and Damaris delivered her important news into Hugo's ear.

Hugo felt his heart jump as he gazed as Garda looking so handsome in Laura's grey cashmere dressing gown with her light red hair down on her shoulders. "How thoughtful of you to let me know that," he told Damaris, looking at his watch. It was already a quarter to ten. He could see he wasn't going to open the shop on time today and longed wistfully for the not so distant past when he had an assistant to rely upon.

"So, what do you want me to do?" Damaris asked.

"That's a good question," he mused, feeding Garda a small piece of buttered toast.

"I can keep her here at least an hour if you need time to think of a good answer," Damaris said helpfully.

Hugo laughed and said, "Just tell her the truth, that a dear friend of mine was in town yesterday doing business with Randy Price and I brought her to visit the shop before sending her over to him."

"I didn't know she was meeting Randy," said Damaris, distinctly repelled by the name.

"She met him alright," Hugo disclosed in a tone that spoke volumes.

"He can be so loathsome. Was he rude to your darling?"

"Let's just say you made her look a little too good."

"Oh my god, you don't mean he tried to take advantage of her?"

"Since when did Randy Price ever just try to do something?"

Damaris hung up and reported to Pamela, "Hugo said that Garda saw Randy last night."

"Randy Price?"

"I think he may have forced himself on her."

"No, Mr. Price doesn't rape. But he knows how to take better than any man I've ever met," said Pamela bitterly. Never had she given in to a man so quickly and for so little reason.

"Tell me about it! You have no idea what misery that man caused me at one time," Damaris replied, heading for the fitting room with a copper silk dress over her arm.

Laura had put on the cranberry dress and was admiring the effect in the three-way mirror when her friend joined her.

"So guess who was in yesterday?" Damaris begin.

"Who?"

"Hugo and a very old girlfriend."

"An old girlfriend?" Laura stared at Damaris in the mirror, her heart contracting painfully as she sat on an upholstered pouf, her legs gone to sand.

"A pre-1980's girlfriend. Just about the same age as Hugo, give or take a few years," Damaris said soothingly.

"A leggy redhead?"

Damaris nodded.

"Garda," Laura sagely concluded, for she had been Hugo's companion long enough for him to have told her about all his important lovers. "Still a beauty I suppose?"

"Very cool, smart and slim."

Laura took off the red dress and exchanged it for the copper one as Damaris told Laura of Garda's encounter with Randy Price. Like Damaris and Pamela, Laura had also been had by Randy Price, knew Randy for the extraordinary piece of work that he was and felt a pang for Garda, of whom Hugo had always spoken so fondly.

While getting back into her clothes Laura asked Damaris, "How come Pamela is here? Did Hugo lend you her for a few days?"

"He gave her to me permanently."

"You mean she's working here now?'

"Has been for a week."

"But, why?"

"She won't say."

"What about Hugo? What was his reason for sending her to you?"

"He claims her talents are better suited to my shop than his. And he's right. She's been to design school you know."

"There's got to be more to it than that," Laura guessed. Damaris lead her back out to the shop with the two dresses over her arm. "Did you want these?"

"Yes, please," said Laura, getting out her credit card.

"You're not to pay for anything, per Anthony," Damaris said, refusing the card. "He said I was to send all of your and Susan's bills to him."

"How sweet," Laura smiled. "I'm sure he's delighted to encourage your new enterprise."

While Damaris was zipping the dresses into a smart carrying bag Laura wandered over to Pamela, who was behind one of the counters folding bias cut silk slips from Paris with extreme care.

"Pamela, I was surprised to hear you've left Hugo," Laura said.

"Yes, me too," said Pamela, without raising her eyes.

"You don't mean he dismissed you?"

"I think I was beginning to get on his nerves," Pamela observed not completely untruthfully.

"This is very mysterious," said Laura to Damaris as her friend walked her out of the shop. Overhead lightning was striking. "Why do you suppose Hugo fired her?"

Damaris shrugged, though she had already formed a good idea.

"Do you think I should call Hugo before going over today?" Laura asked as thunder struck noisily above.

"Most definitely," Damaris counseled.

"So it's like that between them, is it?"

"She was his first scene girlfriend, Laura."

"I know. I suppose she was amiable?"

"Laura, she has an important job in California to return to forthwith," Damaris reassured her as the rain began to fall in the street.

Laura took the dresses and hugged Damaris. "Maybe I won't call him until tomorrow," Laura mused, getting into her car.

"Yes, I'd worry about this one more than that one," said Damaris, jerking her thumb towards the boutique where Pamela was still brooding and folding slips.

Hugo Sands was thinking along the same lines as he put Garda into her car and watched her drive out of the village in a windy, driving rain, later that afternoon. He walked aimlessly back from the inn to his shop, glancing at his watch and wondering if it was even worth it to open up that day. If Pamela were still in his employ, he wouldn't have given a thought to taking the entire day off. Why had he fired her anyway? Pausing with the key in the door of his shop he abruptly put it back in his pocket.

He looked at his watch. It was three. "No, it's too late. And no one will come out in this rain," he reflected, walking across the cobbled street to the bookshop.

Hope Lawrence was wiping down the wooden coffee bar and Sloan was ringing up sales behind the back counter. Hugo waved at him, Sloan waved back and Hope began to automatically prepare a double cappuccino. Hugo slid onto a stool and brooded at a copy of the Boston Globe as Hope produced her usual stream of cheerful chatter. Something was nagging at Hugo. And he wanted a cigarette. If Pamela were still working for him, he could get one from her.

Laura's return troubled him not at all. He'd already spoken with her over the phone, told her about Garda's visit and promised to cook her a welcome home dinner that night in his own kitchen. She'd asked him at once about why he'd dismissed Pamela and he'd replied at once and frankly that it was because Pamela seemed to have developed a crush on him. These were not words calculated to do anything but please and soothe a worried girlfriend and Hugo realized with a start that although he had ostensibly given up continuous access to Pamela out of respect for his friendship with Sloan, Laura provided an even stronger reason for exiling the willowy beauty from his immediate realm.

But who deserved the real blame for what had occurred? It wasn't Pamela. It was himself, for being a wise guy. He retraced the sequence of events as they had unfolded. First Pamela had returned to Random

Point after a year away. At which point she'd been shocked and violently jealous to find that Sloan's new assistant was the remarkably beautiful Hope Spencer Lawrence. Desperately, Pamela had asked Sloan to let her exchange work places with Hope, putting her in the bookshop and Hope in Hugo's antiques shop across the street. But Hugo had firmly objected, on the grounds that, charming as she was, Hope talked too much to bear as an assistant.

Also, he took exception to Pamela deciding who was to work for him and being so disloyal as to want to leave him and punished her for her temerity with a good spanking, thereafter behaving towards his employee in a fashion that could only be described as Gothic.

Hugo had been cold and harsh to Pamela for several weeks, over-working and stretching her to the limit in every possible way. The result was that she fell in love with him and when the feeling built to such a fever pitch that it could no longer be ignored by the sensitive girl, she declared herself to him, with some embarrassment and he was forced to do the confession the honor it deserved. He made love to her, in his usual style, which only inflamed her more. The situation rapidly becoming untenable, in a panic of conscience and common sense, Hugo decided that the only possible solution was to dismiss Pamela.

He told himself he was actually doing Pamela a favor. Damaris had promised to make her a partner if Pamela designed for the shop, and this after all, was what she had gone to school for. But after seeing her beautiful eyes filled with tears yesterday and knowing that it was his fault, he spent the entire afternoon feeling restless, guilty, angry and desperately aroused by the tall girl's passion for him.

He finished his coffee, borrowed an umbrella from Sloan and walked back across the village in the rain to Damaris' shop. Pamela was standing outside the shop under the bottle green awning in a beige wool dress, moodily smoking a cigarette. She gave a start at seeing him, followed by a trembling smile.

"Can you get away for an hour?" he asked without preamble.

"Yes," she replied, crushing her cigarette underfoot and running inside to get her raincoat and umbrella. A young woman who lived by the weather report, Pamela had on smart black thigh high boots that disappeared under her skirt and gave Hugo a romantic notion.

"Let's go for a walk," he said, leading her several blocks across the village and then along the brook that ran behind it. The rain had lessened to a fine mist and the gusts of wind had died down. "Do you know about the marble summer house?" he asked. Pamela shook her head. "Very few people do," he told her as they walked along the gravelly bank.

This open structure, nearly a hundred years old, overgrown with ivy and lined with marble benches stood in the woods about a half-mile out of town.

"What am I going to do with you?" he asked, drawing her to sit down beside him on the driest bench seat he could find. Taking her gloved hands in his, he kissed her full mouth lightly. Then he peeled off her gloves, examined the palms of her hands and kissed them. His act of tenderness washed through her like a balm, soothing away all the hurt and confusion of the last week.

"You're a willful girl who doesn't know what's good for her," Hugo scolded, slowly drawing her down across his lap. He curved one hand around her tiny waist and used the other to push up the skirt of her raincoat and wool dress. Pamela had on black panties of Calais lace through which her pearly flesh gleamed. These he promptly rolled down to her thighs, which caused her to gasp as the chill air touched her satiny skin. Then he began to spank her and the sound of his slaps rang through the woods for many minutes to follow. "Players ought to be able to separate spanking from sex," he reasoned during a pause, as he smoothed his palm across her bare pink cheeks and white thighs above the boot tops. "You never should have come on to me the way you did that day in the store room."

"I know," she assented meekly, and was duly rewarded with additional spanking, this time on her tender, creamy thighs. "Oh god! That really hurts!" she cried, wriggling on his lap. He caught her hand to her waist and held her fast, but proceeded to again spank her rhythmically, first on one cheek, then the other, until both were colored rose.

Presently he pulled her back up into a sitting position. "No, get those off," he told her sternly as he saw her attempting to pull her panties back up. "You heard me," he told her, briskly assisting in this operation, matter of factly folding them up, putting them in his jacket pocket and then pushing her back down on the bench, on her back. "Get your skirt up," he told her, yanking his zipper down and freeing a condom from its foil. Straddling her he captured her wrists and drew them together up over her head as she lay looking up at him in passive though breathless expectation.

"Keep your hands above your head," he told her. Her complete submissiveness to his will caused his cock to throb like an unruly fire hose in his hand as he nonetheless coolly rolled the rubber down over its lengthy shaft.

Before penetrating her, Hugo paused to undo the top two chunky buttons of her dress. Pulling it open he squeezed each small, firm round breast through the black lace under wire brassiere that supported it so elegantly. She gave a little whimper and he responded by spanking her breasts once each, which caused Pamela to gasp. He pinched her nipples lightly as she gazed at him with huge black eyes.

"Don't take your eyes from mine," he instructed her, guiding his cock between her creamy labia and penetrating her one inch at a time. This requirement making the act unbearably erotic, Pamela succumbed to the confluence of stimulations to which she was currently being subjected and whimpered her way through the first face-to-face orgasm she had ever experienced. As he felt her climax, squeezing his imprisoned cock madly, Hugo also orgasmed copiously before pulling out, rolling off and lying on his back beside her on the broad marble bench. It was natural at that moment, after making themselves more decent, to loll decadently on the cool, moist stone, gazing out at the rain drenched woods all around them.

"Cigarette?" she asked, lighting one. He took a puff then handed it back to her and relaced his fingers under his head.

"Hugo, thank you for not ignoring me today," Pamela said softly. "Between Garda's leaving and Laura's return you still managed to find this perfect hour for me. I will never doubt you again."

"I want you to get over me, not go into a decline over me. Is that understood, young lady?" Hugo leaned up on his elbow and looked down at her.

"Yes," she nearly sobbed, receiving a momentary flash back of him forcing her to gaze straight into his cool blue eyes while he took her. He pressed his hand against her flat tummy, just above her Venus mound through her clothes. "Oh!" she cried, as he reawakened her g-spot simply by resting his hand there.

"You're so responsive," he said, continuing to pat and rub her through her clothes. "I could make you come again just doing this."

"Will you?"

"No," he said, sitting up. "I'd rather leave you worked up so you'll have to go see Sloan."

"I wouldn't dare," she admitted, sitting up herself and checking her lips in a pocket mirror.

"No? Why not?" Hugo took her hand and they left the summer house.

"I don't believe we're seeing each other, as such, anymore."

"Oh Pamela, you told him didn't you?"

"I had to."

"Oh, you did not."

"I couldn't deceive him."

"Well? What did he say?"

"He said he understood perfectly, reminding me he'd done pretty much the same thing with his boss, Mrs. Branwell, last year."

"Then, he wasn't upset?"

"No, simply detached. He said in view of my confused emotional state we ought to take some time off from seeing each other."

"If he said that last week, perhaps enough time has elapsed," Hugo suggested encouragingly as they began the misty walk back to the village.

"Hugo, may I have my panties back?"

Chapter Three

Garda, Bettie and Brooke

Garda returned to L.A. distracted by the pleasures she had experienced so recently in Random Point but pessimistic about ever finding the like in her city.

On arriving home at her cottage in Laurel Canyon, she was delighted to find that Hugo Sands had already emailed her about a possible playmate, a creative businessman, of the proper age, personable and possessed of sterling references. But Garda perceived a possibly snag when she accessed Augie Rose's photo online, remembering that she had already met this gentleman, across a bargaining table several months before.

The incident occurred while Garda was helping a friend in private practice with her case overload, unbeknownst to her own employers. Garda's client, a small bookstore owner, was suing Augie Rose for recovering and retitling the same erotic paperbacks that had been sold to the book dealer several years before.

Augie Rose claimed he had bought the books without covers from a printer after a publisher defaulted on a large order and had no idea that the books had ever been printed before. A shrewd and amiable arbiter, Rose annoyed Garda by striking a deal with the bookstore owner whereby he would pay the damages in paperbacks rather than actual money. Garda's fee was barely enough to purchase one pair of shoes on sale at Barneys.

There was a second complication involving the ubiquitous Augie Rose, for the studio had just arranged for her, in her capacity as contract lawyer, to visit his house in Nichol's Canyon and secure it for a location shoot. She received this dispatch from Jeffrey Jardine, the new head of her division, a singularly charmless young dynamo, to whom she privately referred as: The Barking Crewcut, but whom she had no wish to irritate with potential conflicts of interest.

She was now scheduled to go up to Rose's house, negotiate an acceptable fee and hope that through all this he wouldn't recognize her from the previous mediation.

But Augie Rose was not one to forget a sleek, striking redhead, even if met over the bargaining table during a dull, legal dispute. In fact, Garda was fully appreciated by Augie Rose at the time, though she had treated him with the haughty contempt she felt deserved by any bandit. (Garda didn't believe a word of Augie's innocence in the matter of the recovered titles.)

Garda drove her convertible up Nichol's Canyon that brilliantly sunny, hot morning, in a new fitted suit of French grey jersey that clung elegantly to her slender form and complimented her straight, shoulder length russet hair to Technicolor perfection. Augie Rose had seemed an agreeable if unctuous fellow. No doubt the oiliness was necessary to lubricate the cogs of his business, she mused, turning up his long, winding driveway to the ivy covered, pocket mansion where he lived.

It was obvious to Garda that if she did go out with Augie Rose, she could expect only the most refined wining and dining. While ringing the bell she tried to compose herself, for her heart had begun to beat fast. Something pink and luscious in bloom around the doorway was perfuming the air exquisitely. A Latina cleaning woman opened the door and showed Garda the way to the patio garden, where Augie Rose was enjoying his morning coffee and papers.

"Hi, remember me?" Garda asked, extending her hand to shake his. Augie looked at her.

"Oh, hello. Of course, you were Manny's mediator."

"You have a good memory, Mr. Rose. I'm Garda Hudson."

"You get around. Have a seat. Would you like some coffee?"

"No thanks," Garda said, sitting opposite him in the charmingly landscaped garden overlooking the canyon. "It's lovely up here, and so secluded. Perfect for a quick, little shoot."

"So what's the going rate for a shoot?" he asked innocently.

"Depending on how many rooms we use, between five and fifteen thousand a day."

"I can make the whole house available to you," said Augie helpfully.

"May I take a quick tour?"

"Please, come with me," Augie said, leading her back into the house while idly wondering if she'd notice that most of the rooms weren't big enough to shoot in.

"Mr. Rose, I have a favor to ask," Garda began as he was conducting her though the kitchen and pantry.

"Yes, Miss. Hudson?"

"Well, I took that mediation case to help a friend. The studio doesn't like us to do that sort of thing though. I could get in trouble if it became a matter of record. May I count on your discretion?"

"Absolutely. As long as you believe me when I tell you I had no idea that Manny had ever bought those titles previously. I had a definite feeling throughout our proceeding that you considered me a species of literary pond scum."

Garda colored. "I'm very sorry," she murmured. "I'd never even heard of a case like that before and I didn't know what to think."

"I don't want you to think that I'm some sort of chiseler."

"Honestly, I don't."

"But, you did. Admit it."

"Don't tease me, Mr. Rose. I have apologized."

"Teasing you could be fun. You blush."

"Mr. Rose, you have no idea," Garda said, as he led her through the lower rooms.

"No idea about what?"

"For one thing, what a small world it is."

"You're being very enigmatic," said Augie.

Garda looked at him. He was tall and wiry, with dark hair, penetrating eyes, a straight nose and wide, handsome mouth. His sand colored gabardine suit and white shirt were tailored and like all of his things, showed discriminating taste. His house smelled of sandalwood and spa minerals, with hot tubs both inside and out. Suddenly Garda felt a stab of excitement pierce her tummy, as though perhaps she too belonged in this little corner of palm fronded paradise.

"Someone told me I should get in touch with you."

"Someone?"

"Someone unrelated to the studio or the bookstore."

"I'm terribly intrigued. Let's go upstairs and you can see the bedroom suites."

"Someone in The Scene!" she said dramatically, turning toward him as they mounted the winding staircase.

"The Scene?" Augie seemed mystified.

"You're registered with Matchmakers in Random Point, aren't you?"

"Matchmakers! Yes, I am. Don't tell me you work for them too?"

"No. But they told me to look you up."

"You don't say!" They emerged onto the second floor landing and he began to lead her down the hall to view the rooms. Now Augie took a new look at Garda, from the rear.

"I never met a man here in L.A. who could give me what I wanted in a scene," Garda bluntly admitted while touring the suite with the wet bar, pink and brown marble hearth and panoramic view of the city stretching away in the distance far below.

"Tell me what you want. I'll give it to you!" Augie agreed cheerfully, quite willing to accept this unexpected boon without question.

"I will. But not now."

"Know what? There's a party at a friend of mine's house Friday night. Why don't you let me take you?"

"What kind of party?"

"The fun kind."

"Well, what should I wear?" Garda asked practically as Augie Rose put her into her car a few minutes later.

"Let your mood be your guide."

Garda was charmed enough to nearly forget why she'd come.

"Oh, Mr. Rose, what about the contracts?" She pulled them out of the portfolio on the front seat of her BMW convertible and handed them to him.

"Where do I sign?" he asked, putting his hand out for a pen.

"Why don't you look them over and call me if you have any questions," Garda said, handing him her card.

"I'll do that," he smiled.

When they met at The Ivy for dinner on Friday night it was not as strangers. Several lengthy phone calls had stimulated both their imaginations and appetites for each other. Garda was so attention deprived in this area that just talking to Augie in detail about what she might expect from him, was enough to simulate hours of foreplay.

Thus she found herself in a state of intense excitement as she consulted the exquisite menu and Augie Rose informed her that they would shortly attend a party in Beverly Glen at the home of his attorney, Crossjay Patterne, whose lover, Lucy Burke, enjoyed collecting, assorting and mating ornaments of the L.A. scene.

"Will people be playing?" Garda asked, after cocktails were served.

"I wouldn't be a bit surprised!"

Ninety minutes later, Augie was ushering her into the impressive home of a more successful attorney than Garda. Their host, Crossjay Patterne, a tall, blond, buff, country club dom, was holding court at the downstairs bar while his girlfriend, Lucy Burke, a blonde in white leather, mixed martinis enthusiastically.

The high ceilinged downstairs suites were milling with denizens of the Hollywood subculture, ranging from professionals to sophisticates, tattooed and profusely pierced streets waifs in a few pieces of good leather to female CEOs in satin evening suits. The mix was not incompatible and due to the profuse amounts of high-grade liquor and catered food, everyone seemed enormously content with their evening's destination.

Augie walked Garda around the house, upstairs, then down again into the back gardens and pool area, running into people he knew here and there, but mostly just holding her hand tucked in his and smiling quietly at his prize while always keeping an eye out for the perfect corner.

The pool was lit by Japanese lanterns and looked glamorous in the star spangled moonlight. Augie had taken Garda to sit beside him in a big, wooden swing and was on the point of kissing her for the first time when the moment's dreamlike quality was firmly shattered by the completely unexpected salutation, "Garda Hudson, what are you doing here?" bellowed disagreeably from above.

"Jeffrey!" Garda jumped away from Augie and to her feet. "I could ask you the same thing! Jeffrey Jardine, Augie Rose," said Garda. The men casually shook hands.

"Did you bring her?" Jeffrey demanded of Augie Rose.

"I did!" Augie replied, smiling at Garda.

"So, were you aware of what kind of party this was going to be, Garda?" Jeffrey demanded, in the hoarse, husky voice that grated so on her nerves.

"Why? What kind of party is it, Jeffrey?" Garda replied carelessly, still somewhat intoxicated from the wine at The Ivy and sipping a fresh champagne.

"Excuse me, Garda," said Augie tactfully. "I have to go say hello to someone." He slipped away and left Garda confronting her boss with some hostility.

"Who's that man you're with? Where did you meet him? How do you know he isn't one of these freaks?'

"What do you mean, freaks? Or rather, aren't you one of them, I mean, us, too?"

"I'll tell you one thing, I don't have a padlock through my penis!" Jeffrey revealed indignantly, as though he'd just confronted a half dozen men who did. In reality there was only one, securely bound to a whipping post in the attic and annoying no one. Which was more than Garda could say for Jeffrey.

"Jeffrey, what are you doing here?" Garda asked, suddenly convinced he'd arrived at the party either by mistake or as a gatecrasher.

"The hostess is my ex-girlfriend," Jeffrey growled, glaring in the general direction of the ground floor rotunda where Miss Lucy Burke was dancing with a cat suited lesbian, herself in a sweetheart cut dress with long sleeves that hugged her slender curves like the skin on hot milk.

"That firebrand Lucy Burke is your ex-girlfriend?" Garda nearly reeled. "And why pray did she dump wonderful you?"

"For not being rich enough to keep her like this," Jeffrey rancorously admitted.

"Does that mean that you are truly in The Scene?" Garda asked. Jeffrey's chin came up and he looked at her.

"That depends on what you mean by that statement."

"Well if you're going to be coy about it, forget I ever asked," said Garda, tossing back the rest of her champagne and grabbing another glass off a passing tray.

"What about you? That's what I want to know!"

"I'm sure you do."

"Who is this Augie Rose? The name rings a bell."

"Oh hell," thought Garda. "I'm not supposed to fraternize with property lessors either!"

"Well, it's been all too real. I'll see you at the office," Garda said, attempting to walk away. He caught her by the arm and pulled her back down into the swing to sit beside him.

"Wait a minute. Let's finish our conversation."

"I have to go find my friend."

"He'll amuse himself. I just remembered who he is too! He's the owner of the house you got the contracts signed on this week. Right? The one you let over bill us by ten grand a day?"

"What is that supposed to mean?" Garda cried, her heart jumping.

"That property was assessed as a five thousand dollar day rental site by the production manager's assistant. You let Mr. Rose sign off the contract with the fifteen thousand dollar per day figure. Didn't you, Garda?"

"Well, that's what the property looked like being worth to me," she replied, though faint of heart.

"I'm not surprised, since you seem to be dating him!" Jeffrey snapped. "I have a good mind to report you for this."

"So report me!" Garda snapped, feeling her face redden and her heart begin to pound.

"If I did you'd be fined, you know. And reprimanded."

"So report me," she repeated, though a bit less enthusiastically now. "Fined how much?"

"Obviously, the extra $30,000."

"Great! Thanks a lot," she replied, getting up to flee her persecutor. He pulled her back down.

"Not so fast, young lady."

"Why not?"

"Why don't you try to persuade me to be nice?"

"And how might I do that?"

"Why don't you offer to take the reprimand from me personally. It would go a long way to wiping out the debt. In my mind, anyway."

"What in the world are you suggesting, Jeffrey?"

"Take the reprimand from me."

"Okay, what would that entail?"

"Allow me to spank you. Right now. Right here!" Jeffrey enclosed both of Garda's hands in his own large ones. She looked up at him.

"What?" she stammered.

"Let me spank you and I'll forget about the over billing. You'll save thirty thousand dollars. Just like that."

"But why do you want to?" she wondered, not believing her ears. Was it possible the Barking Crewcut had been looking at her? Thinking about her?

"Why do I want to spank you? I only think about it every time I see you totter down the hall in those tight skirts and high heels. You often run. It's very cute. Only I'd like to see you in even higher heels. Heels so high you'd be perfectly helpless without me to carry you around in them. Are you ready?"

"I can't take this in," Garda protested, springing up and away from Jeffrey. "You have to give me a few minutes to - to rethink you!"

"Why? What do you mean by that?" Jeffrey barked, flipping open a black cigarette case and extracting a cigarette. He let her light it for him, holding her shaky wrist while she did, then pulled her down again beside him and after taking a drag handed her the cigarette.

"I haven't been accustomed to thinking of you in these terms," she unsteadily admitted.

"Oh? And how have you been accustomed to thinking of me?"

"I'm sorry Jeffrey, but to me you've always been just The Barking Crewcut," Garda admitted, quite deliberately.

"Well, to me you've always just been The Arrogant Slut, but meeting you here, somehow I feel it all fits," said Jeffrey, taking the cigarette out of her hand, putting it out and then swiftly and ably, pulling her over his lap. "You weigh nothing," Jeffrey said, arranging her on his football player's thighs. "Just relax, Garda. This will be over before you know it," he assured her, gently but firmly capturing one of her slender wrists again and pinning it back to her waist.

Garda was bereft of speech and powerless to move, awed by the deftness of Jeffrey's attack, how solid his lap felt and how securely he held her to it. It was beyond belief that the hateful Jeffrey Jardine, who was always so trying under the office lights, should be suddenly so enchanting in moonlight.

The spanking was as promised: brief and to the point. Or maybe Garda only perceived it that way. For in reality, it was fully sixty swats of Jeffrey's big, hard hand.

"You should wear satin at all times," Jeffrey told her, rubbing the sting away after each volley of spanks. "With your curves, it's irresistible."

"Jeffrey," she turned her head, "this is a very different side of you than I've seen."

Jeffrey continued spanking her firmly, alternating smacks on her slim, oval globes, now so glowingly encased in ivory satin for a little while longer. As she received the smacks with little pants of surprise but otherwise complete docility, he wasn't quite sure whether Garda was in shock from the summary treatment or off in a female submissive dream world. So presently he let her up.

"Since you're here with someone else, I won't make a pest of myself for the rest of the night," he promised, taking her hand and lightly kissing the back of her ivory satin glove. "But next time I have you over my knee, young lady, you won't get off so easily!"

"But, I still don't understand," she murmured, setting her clothes to rights. Jeffrey knelt to straighten the elaborate gold tasseled fringes on the folds of her form fitting, late-Victorian flavored evening gown and when Augie Rose rejoined them, he assumed that Garda had merely put the impertinent lawyer in his place, at her feet.

"Augie, can we go?" Garda asked, linking arms with her date and mincing away on her high heeled, brocade evening shoes, conscious of Jeffrey's eyes focused on her swaying, corseted form. The entire outfit was assembled in one shopping spree on Melrose. Even as she was spending the twelve hundred dollars on the dress, shoes and corset that afternoon, she had thought, this will be an investment in my wardrobe. Now she had learned that that some investments pay off immediately.

All the way home Garda was distracted. She liked Augie Rose. But she also liked what the Barking Crewcut had done to her and how he had done it. But by her calculations, Jeffrey was seven to ten years her junior! (Perhaps he'd realize that in the light of day.) Augie was the proper age for her. But now she felt she'd already been unfaithful to Augie, by letting Jeffrey spank her.

"Did you play with anyone?" she asked casually as Augie Rose pulled into her driveway. "Oh, and do come in!" Garda was never loath to entertain friends in her small but tastefully managed quarters. She had cats, trees, wine glasses from Florence, comfy poufs, in short, everything a sensualist needs to enjoy a modern, modest and slightly artistic lifestyle.

"Would you open that bottle of wine on the table, Augie? I want to change my dress."

Garda kept the beautiful, ivory corset on and over it threw a matching dressing gown, which, when it feel open, created the perfect frame to display the exquisite, hip length, waist cinch corset.

"Augie?" Garda called from the bedroom. Augie joined her with two glasses of white wine. "Please, do loosen my stays before I expire!" she cried, dropping the robe from her shoulders to show him how tightly she had laced herself.

Augie untied the central laces at Garda's waist, then paused, confounded by the intricate crisscrossing network of laces that ran from the middle of her back to below her waist. "You know, I don't have much experience with foundations," Augie admitted. "Isn't there a way to get it off fast?"

"Well, of course, it could be unhooked in front, but then it would be off entirely."

"Don't you think that would be a good idea? You could still wrap up in that dressing gown, couldn't you, dear?"

"All right. It's a good idea. I'll take it off," she conceded. "You wait out there. I have to undo all the garters and take off the stockings that are attached. I'll be out in a minute."

Finally taking off the corset felt like its own sort of orgasm. The stockings also went away and her slim, pretty feet went into ivory satin slippers with high vamps. "Oh, he's smart," thought Garda of her guest and went out to him feeling deliriously relaxed.

They lay on the hearth rug together in front of the fire, she with her back to him, but pressed against him, he with his arm around her, her waist under his hand, talking for several hours, then kissing and finally petting, which suddenly led to spanking. She was easily pulled across his lap and so accessible in the satin robe, with only her scrap of panties between his hand and her smooth, white bottom.

"I knew you'd have a beautiful bottom," Augie said, caressing her baby smooth skin. She had finally ceased to feel the imprint of Jeffrey's hand upon it but was grateful for the firelight in case her so seldom spanked bottom should still bear the traces of pink from her associate's hard, calloused, weight lifter's palm. "I couldn't believe it when you said you were in The Scene the other day at my house. It's been my dream to date someone like you." But these fond words didn't stop him from spanking her hard!

Garda and Augie played on Friday night, met again on Saturday, at a Hollywood B&D club, in order to be able to esoterically gambol in a dungeon, then spent all of Saturday night and most of Sunday together as well, continuing to play and make love. Since Garda hadn't had a regular spanking boyfriend in over twenty years, she couldn't seem to get enough.

They played all over his stylish little estate, established a safe word, which was never used and spent a portion of Saturday afternoon visiting Dream Dresser, where Augie bought her several outfits in leather and PVC.

By the time she ascended to the Noho offices of her firm on Monday morning, she had all but forgotten about Jeffrey Jardine, and what had happened between them at the party.

He was giving one of his Monday morning pep talks and looking particularly Clark Kentish in a crisp shirt and slim tie, when she walked in. Garda remembered the party and promptly exited the meeting without paying the slightest attention to the injunctions her supervisor was forcing on her hapless associates. When they next ran into each other, some hours later, at The Eagle Coffee Shop, he appeared to take umbrage at her earlier act of insubordination.

"So guess what, Jeffrey," she lightly murmured while dropping into the next booth, "I cleared up that awkward misunderstanding with Mr. Rose about the rental of the house. He's agreed to a reduced fee of 5K per day."

Jeffrey reddened, imagining her to be purposely insulting him. He had extorted her temporary submission to him at the party on the basis of her costing the company an extra 30k. Now that she had erased the debt, the spanking he had given her seemed all the more gratuitous and he felt rebuffed by her exuberance.

"I see!" said Jeffrey darkly, which gave Garda that certain feeling. "You obviously went home with him that night!"

"I beg your pardon?"

"When can I see you?" he demanded. "I want to spank you for a long time, uninterrupted."

Garda felt Cupid's dart pierce her heart. "I might be free tonight. Call me." She wrote her home number on the back of her business card and gave it to Jeffrey.

"What about your address?"

"Let me come to you." Garda was far too fastidious to wish two different men to appear in her bed in the same week.

Jeffrey lived in a small, plain beach house in Zuma, smelling of fresh pine and sand. She arrived on the later side that evening, with cheese, bread and wine and was charmed to dine on the lanai overlooking the ocean. It would be pleasant to fall asleep to the sound of the waves in the big, muscular arms of the aggressive business school freak who ran her department so stupidly. His nearly empty boy's house rather held the scent of him and she enjoyed breathing it in from the start.

"I don't want you to do anything until we finish the wine," said Garda to Jeffrey as the sun went down.

"That will take for ever," Jeffrey protested. Garda laughed at his eagerness.

"We'll go up in the little attic," he tempted her. "I've built a few pieces of custom furniture that you'll find interesting."

"I hate surprises."

"Even a spanking bench, a horse and a sturdy armless chair?"

"So you really did spank me the other night at the party in Beverly Glen!"

"Did you doubt it?"

"Well, I was drinking."

"You know damn well I spanked you. I enjoyed it too. I've been thinking about nothing else since."

"I'm surprised by that. A strapping young go-getter like yourself must be inundated with submissives," Garda buttered.

Jeffrey snorted with derision, "I'm still reeling at the fact that you work in my office. You don't know how hard it was for me to keep my hands off you today."

"Is that so?"

"You have a beautiful waist."

They went up to the charming attic. Jeffrey was particularly proud of a carved, solid oak spanking bench, padded down the center with black leather and designed to elevate the bottom while spreading the knees. There were grips in front and on the sides and rather smart retractable straps affixed at various points for holding the culprit or starry eyed submissive in place at the waist and knees. Around the attic were freestanding mirrors to reflect whatever activity took place therein from several interesting angles. Garda was suitably impressed.

"Why don't I have a room like this?" she wondered, bitterly reproaching herself for being so ignorant about what was happening in her own back yard. "So, what do you plan to do now?" Garda asked, quickly gulping the remainder of the wine.

"You did let me spank you the other night."

"Yes, I let you extort me into compliance."

"Was that the sheer force of my will, or do you really enjoy this sort of thing?"

"Both, I guess."

"So, if I now proceed to spank you again, you are likely to again enjoy it?"

"In all probability," she smiled.

"Is there anything you'd like to ask me?"

"The sight of all this superb equipment answers most of my questions," Garda sighed, "although I'm still not sure this is proper."

"You mean because we're associates?"

"No, because I don't think I really like you," Garda let slip out, due to having drunk most of a bottle of wine. "That is, I didn't like you at all until the other night. Now I seem to like you to a certain degree, but maybe that's because I'm starved for playmates."

"So, you really don't like me, huh?"

"Then there's also the age difference," she declared. "You're quite young, aren't you?"

"You're seven years older than me. Big deal."

"You know exactly how old I am?" she sputtered.

"I looked up your records."

"Damn you."

"Did your bottom stay red from your spanking? It must be very fair with your coloring."

"Go to hell."

"Did you go home with Augie Rose that night?"

"I took him home with me!" said Garda deliberately, lighting a cigarette and blowing blue smoke up to the skylight.

He took the cigarette away from her and crushed it in an ashtray then took her by the earlobe and led her to the big wooden chair.

"No!" she resisted him, pulling back.

"Come over here, you little slut," he told her sharply, thrusting her down across his lap. "I don't like that arrogant way you just bragged about taking Augie Rose home!" Jeffrey's hand came down hard on the back of her khaki Capri's. "But I like this little J. Crew outfit you have on," he said, flipping up the tail of the thin white cotton shirt that had been clinging so provocatively to her pert, upstanding, erect-nippled bosom. Then he dusted off her slim, oval bottom through the thin trousers with his big palm. She wriggled and twisted on his lap so he clamped his other hand to her waist. "You should not have taken Augie Rose home. Not after I had spanked you for the very first time. It was promiscuous and very wrong!" he scolded, slapping her cheeks alternately in a manner both robust and stinging.

"I thought it was great. Getting foreplay from one man then going to another for the conclusion!" she taunted him.

"Is that so? I can see I have my work cut out for me here," he told her, spanking her harder but more lingeringly, making her wait breathlessly for each resounding smack.

"What work?"

"Taming you."

"Never!"

"Well see about that!" Smack! It was then that Jeffrey discovered the trousers had an elastic waist and could be easily tugged down.

"Hey! Wait! Don't!"

"Stop fussing, young lady," he told her firmly, lowering her khakis to reveal her thin white cotton panties. Under them her gym-pampered bottom was that of a woman half her age, smooth and firm, with just a tinge of pink against the white where his hand had struck. Again he began to spank her, slowly and effectively, pausing a few beats between each swat so that each could be appreciated separately. Soon he had her half whimpering, half panting in expectation of his now more rapidly descending palm. Presently he pulled her panties down to her thighs and started all over again.

The sting of his large hand soon caused her to yip. Then she cried, "Oh Jeffrey, can't we take a break?" She twisted to bewitch him with her sapphire gaze. "A shoe shopping break?" she added meaningfully. In a second she'd slid off his lap and was whipping her Capri's back up. "You fascinated me when you mentioned fetish pumps," she admitted, reminding him that Dream Dresser was open until midnight.

"All right, but they have to be at least seven to eight inches high," he agreed, grabbing his car keys and ushering her out into the night.

After the shoe event it was all over for Augie Rose with Garda but for the Dear Augie letter. It wasn't that Garda didn't like Augie very much. It was just that she seemed suddenly to like Jeffrey Jardine much more. Augie was charming, deferential and sincere. Jeffrey was bossy, cynical and sexually aggressive. There was no question that Jeffrey would conquer.

Naturally, Augie reacted with customary grace and good humor but the affectionate rejection left him feeling deflated for a couple of days.

Garda, ridden with guilt at having played with the emotions of a deserving gentleman, appealed to Hugo to supply Augie Rose with a proper replacement. By the end of the day, Garda had received the following email from Hugo:

Hi Red,

I'm sure Mr. Rose is inconsolable. So near and yet so far to spanking heaven. There could never be a replacement for you. However, I do have a niece out there, attending UCLA, who might prove of great interest to your new friend. She's not a blood relation, by the way and I only met her for the first time last summer, when she deliberately came looking for me after she found out I publish The New Rod.

Her name is Bettie Brandon. She's of age and has been a complete spanking fetishist since toddlerhood. She's a lit. major, pretty and mature for her age.

She has a boyfriend in the scene, a young shark from the Harvard Business School, now working for a real estate broker uncle of his in Westwood, but Bettie doesn't care for realtors. I understand your Mr. Rose is a paperback book publisher. That would be more in Bettie's line. Maybe he can even give her some freelance or start publishing her stories. Little Bettie Brandon is bored with her lover and has begged me repeatedly to put her onto an interesting older man in the scene. Mr. Rose cannot lose with this proposition. I'll have Bettie email him tomorrow.

I highly approve of your thoughtfulness.
But what a bad girl you were to disappear from my life for so long!
Missing you,
H.

Garda ran over to Augie Rose's offices during lunch to apprise him of the incoming email from Hugo Sand's 18-year-old half niece.

"Can they even write when they're that little?" he asked.

"Her ad specified older men."

"I've seen those ads but they never made any sense to me," said Augie, escorting Garda out to lunch at Le Chardonnay.

"Dearest, you don't understand. Younger girls adore older men. If you need to ask why you've probably forgotten how awkward you were at nineteen."

"I've never thought much of men in their forties who run after teenaged girls," Augie confided to Garda as they shared a bottle of wine, "I'd feel like an idiot dating one."

"Hugo suggested you might give her some editorial work. College girls are always strapped for money, you know."

Augie smiled at the innuendo, tremendously touched that Garda had taken such a personal interest in his happiness on such short acquaintance. He kissed Garda's hand and murmured, "I feel so connected." And yet he also felt a twinge of unease at the entire proposition.

Bettie Brandon's email was waiting for Augie upon his return from lunch. It simply introduced herself and stated that Hugo Sands had indicated that Augie Rose might possibly have some freelance editorial work for her.

He sent her a reply at once, telling her to come and see him the following day.

The next afternoon at around two p.m., Augie Rose was looking out his 10th floor window when he saw Bettie Brandon get off the bus on Little Santa Monica Blvd. and begin walking up Roxbury Dr. towards his building. A slight girl with shiny black hair that hung in a waist length ponytail of tight, rippling curls, she was dressed in pegged blue jeans, a checked shirt and hiking boots.

In a few minutes Augie's secretary was buzzing to inform him of Bettie's arrival. Augie had her sent in directly and rose from his desk to firmly shake her hand. She was a small, olive complected beauty, delicately formed, with large, dark eyes and a wide, full mouth. After thanking him for the interview, she disposed of her backpack on the floor and timidly waited for him to speak first.

"My friend Garda tells me you could use a little freelance," Augie began, in a detached but not unfriendly manner.

"I'm not quite sure what that means," Bettie replied.

"Freelance means assignments you complete outside of the office. I just lost my in-house editor and have quite a few small jobs I could give you. I notice you got off the bus. Don't you have a car?"

Bettie shook her head, saying, "It's not a long bus ride from Westwood."

"See those paperbacks?" Augie indicated a small stack of books with plain pastel covers and provocative titles. "I'm about to recover them and I need back cover synopses. There are eight titles there. I'll give you $50 per synopsis."

"Wow," Bettie took the books and looked at them.

"You don't have to read them. Just skim them. Give me between a hundred and a hundred and twenty words each. Think you can do that?"

"Yes."

"By when?"

"When do you need them by?"

"Think you can do them over the weekend?"

"Yes."

"Okay. Email them to me," Augie said by way of dismissal.

Bettie Brandon left with the books in her pack, noting that Augie Rose had barely looked at her and feeling that the handsome publisher was completely uninterested in her scene affiliations.

Bettie neglected her schoolwork all weekend to complete the assignment and was still working on it Monday morning. The sex novels were awkward and her summarizations of them lackluster. She hadn't enjoyed the assignment and wondered how such inept writers were ever able to have their manuscripts published. She also disrespected Mr. Rose for buying and recovering such brain drool. By noon she'd received an email from Augie Rose asking her whether the assignment was finished. Bettie emailed it straight back to him, realizing it would be better to keep to her deadline than try to rework her paragraphs any longer. Then she went off to her afternoon classes and her early evening stint in the library, where she already had one part time job shelving books.

Bettie wasn't enjoying her freshman year. She had no affinity for her roommate, a cheerleader named Randi. She hated her dorm room, with its cinderblock walls and metal desks. She missed the lush trees and refreshing rains of New England. Her instructors either confused or failed to engage her.

She had also become disenchanted with her suitor, Gilbert Rush, a driven young realtor. He however, was becoming less of a problem since beginning an affair with one of his silicon enhanced, thin, blonde associate sharks. Bettie was untroubled by the development and felt quite ready to cut Gilbert loose, for since coming to L.A. her lover's topics of conversation had narrowed to stock options, real estate envy and designer consumerism, none of which interested the college freshman.

Bettie Brandon hated L.A. The sky was ugly and the landscape virtually devoid of trees. The air held no scent. Bright, glaring concrete and soul killing post-Bauhaus architecture set the scene for general despair. Scrawny palm trees, useless mini-malls and appalling plastic signage dominated every vista. Public transportation was a cold, unfriendly thing. Libraries were few and far between. All restaurants and offices were kept icy cold, apparently by law. And the local newspapers were unreadable.

Westwood was only marginally pretty, massively inconvenient and almost completely without charm. Without a car or bike, distances even to and from the bus stop from within the village, where Gilbert's condo was located, exhausted and deflated Bettie. Getting anywhere in the city other than Beverly Hills on the buses seemed to take half the day, and the end goals inevitably disappointed. Hollywood Blvd. made

Bettie want to cry. The beaches were crowded, chilly and bleak. Parks were one square block of grass with no hills to climb, no trees to shelter behind. Downtown was but a dozen skyscrapers, divided from skid row by two blocks of food stalls, jewelry marts and pawnshops. The Civic Center stood desolately apart from restaurants and other city life. Indeed, there was no city life except in West Hollywood and Hollywood, venues which Bettie was just beginning to discover as she searched for cutting edge music and fetish clubs.

And then there was the onset of winter to contend with. Day after day low clouds hovered above and chill breezes blew in off the ocean, reaching all the way to the campus. Again and again she questioned her choice to come out, the only positive side of which was the considerable distance now extant between herself and her mother.

Then came the introduction to Mr. Rose. She had felt a fierce attraction for him the moment he shook her hand, partially because she knew he was a dominant and partially because he was an attractive, confident older man.

While her high school girlfriends hung portraits of Brad Pitt and Keanu Reeves in their lockers, she had worshiped black and white glossies of Cary Grant and Robert Taylor, ordered from Movietime News. For it was while watching old movies that Bettie had first become attracted to suave, assertive men. As a small child she had noticed that these early 20th century heroes were somehow more charming then the men she saw around her at the turn of the millennium, when she was coming of age. She liked the way the men of the silver screen were always threatening to spank their ladies or were throwing them over one shoulder or tucking them under an arm to carry them off somewhere in order to smother their mouths with kisses.

Bettie had come to associate men in their late thirties and early forties with such romantic images. Augie Rose, for example, had short hair and wore crisp suits, just like Melvin Douglas or Franchot Tone. He had the proper look, was undoubtedly in The Scene, and in fact was in every way, Bettie's notion of a real leading man.

But Bettie sensed that Augie Rose was not interested. His body language confirmed it. Which made her wonder why he had given her the work at all. She had already been affected by Gilbert's cynicism and didn't expect something for nothing in Los Angeles. Bettie sent Hugo an email asking his opinion after reporting the results of their first encounter.

Hugo wrote back:

Dear Bettie,

He probably took one look at you and thought you were fifteen. Next time you see him, dress like a lady.

Hugo

Bettie didn't own many grown up outfits. She did have several pair of outrageously high pumps that Gilbert had bought her and which she had only worn with lingerie (in that deliciously sleazy adult motel with the mirror on the ceiling) for him. And she had a stretch jersey dress or two.

When Bettie arrived at Augie's offices the following Tuesday to pick up her check she was dressed in a long sleeved cream wool sheath dress and a pair of black pumps with four inch heels and elegantly high vamps. Over the dress she had thrown a black cashmere princess cut topcoat that had been Hugo's going away present to her at the end of the summer. She had knotted her long, thick hair into a full chignon at the back of her head and colored both her lips and nails dark red. The effect was to add several years to her appearance and she looked like a different young woman entering Augie's office the second time.

"Bettie?" Augie asked, rising from behind his desk. She tottered in and unsteadily sat down. They looked at each other for a moment, neither knowing what to say and both coloring as they tried to decide.

"Don't you look different today?" he finally remarked, raising his eyebrow at her as though the change did not entirely please him. In reality his heart was thumping at the thought of how easily he might possess the sophisticated little dreamboat who was so obviously offering herself to him for a second appraisal.

"Do you not like me this way?" she asked tremblingly.

"Well, I'll admit you were a bit casual during our first interview," he replied, writing her out a check and tearing it out of a large book.

"Thank you, Bettie." She took the check and put it in her purse.

"Thank you," she said. "I hope my work was satisfactory."

"Oh, fine. Call me next week. Maybe I'll have something else for you."

"Okay," she replied, realizing with a heavy blush, that she was being dismissed.

By the time she had tottered to the bus stop, Bettie was sobbing. She was a beautiful, 18 year old submissive, a chic fashion angel in pure wools and fetish pumps. She had essentially wrapped herself up as a present for a 40-year-old man in the scene and he had simply dismissed her. Bettie was crushed. What had she done wrong? Why was he indifferent? She felt too ashamed at the lack of impression she had made on Augie Rose to confide in Hugo as yet.

Somehow she lived through the week, forcing herself to think about her schoolwork rather than Augie Rose. At least he had given her the invitation to call him. She did this mid morning on Monday, unaware that this is the busiest time for all businesspersons. She stammered out that she was calling to see if he had any more work. He seemed harried and said he'd call her later in the week.

More torment. Bettie had found Augie Rose's website, which displayed several excellent portraits of the pulp fiction publisher. Therefore she was able to look upon the countenance of Augie Rose while she wondered and waited. Finally on Thursday afternoon he emailed her that if she cared to stop by on Friday afternoon he would have work for her.

Bettie was wildly excited at having a fresh opportunity to interest Augie Rose, but less than eager accept another tedious editorial assignment, the excellent money not withstanding. She had lost much valuable study time the previous weekend and dreaded another such laborious task.

This time Bettie arrived at Augie Rose's offices dressed in a charmingly conservative little coed outfit composed of a skirt and matching cardigan over a fitted blouse, with well behaved two and a half inch pumps, rather reminiscent of the forties. She wore her hair loose and it rippled down her back. Augie was irresistibly attracted to its glossy luxuriance and in spite of his determination not to flirt with her, blurted out, "God, you've got beautiful hair."

Bettie felt some pleasure at these words but they really meant nothing to her. What she wanted to hear was a threat or a promise of something which she knew interested Augie Rose as much as it did her.

"Anyway, I thought I'd talk to you about doing some writing for me. I'm putting out some erotic magazines. One will be vanilla, the other fetish. I have a lot of space to fill and I need someone to write the letters sections. I'll need about six thousand words per magazine. I'll pay you three hundred dollars for each letters section. Do you think you could handle that?"

"You mean edit letters or make them up?"

"After the magazines are out for a while you'll get real letters from readers," explained Augie, "but initially you'll write them."

"Where are they supposed to have come from then?"

"The vaults of Augie Rose," said Augie with a smile.

"So I just make up jack-off letters?"

"Exactly. A vanilla set and a fetish set."

"When do you need them by?"

"How about the first set next week and the second one the week after?"

"That sounds like a lot of writing."

"You mustn't be a perfectionist about it," Augie advised. "This stuff is ephemeral. Just write it off the top of your head. "

"Okay."

"Here's a list of topics to cover," said Augie, handing her a piece of paper. Bettie looked at side marked: Erotic Fantasies. Under this heading Augie had penciled in: head, three ways, adultery, virginity, wedding night, bachelorette party, jumbo endowments, etc. The other side was marked: Exotic Fantasies and included: spanking, bondage, flagellation, cross dressing, exhibitionism, water sports, corsetry, shoes and boots, feet, bosom worship, bottom worship, goddess worship, leather, latex, S&M, B&D, transvestism, etc.

"Mr. Rose, can I just do the fetish letters?" asked Bettie with a sigh. It suddenly seemed to her that Augie would never pay attention to her as a woman, so she decided that she'd better get the most out of their business together.

"Oh? You just want the fetish magazine? Why is that?"

"The other one seems beyond boring. And I don't have that much free time."

"Okay. Take the fetish letters only."

"And I think I'll need the whole two weeks to complete them," she meekly observed.

"You really need that long to write six thousand words?" Augie shook his head.

"My school work," Bettie pleaded, shrugging her slim shoulders.

"H'm. Well, all right," Augie said pleasantly, by way of dismissing her again.

Bettie could have cried. But this time she didn't. Instead she went back to her dorm room and logically plotted to capture Augie Rose's attentions through her writing. She had always done well writing letters. A letter had brought her to the interest of Hugo Sands, which had started her on the road to becoming a player. Now she was determined to write the best letters anyone had ever written on the subjects he had given her.

While Bettie knew very little about most of the topics on Augie Rose's list, she had an invaluable research tool at hand, in the person of her new friend, Brooke Neuman. They had met at a campus B&D support meeting and were even in the same class. Brooke was a native of Hollywood and like Bettie shared a lifelong fixation on spanking. Brooke was in the film school at UCLA. She also had an interesting part time job, working at The Keep, a friendly little player's club on Las Palmas.

Through working at The Keep as a submissive-switch, Brooke had come into contact with every variety of (civilized) kinkiness and was happy to recount specific sessions for Bettie's letters column. Brooke had so many experiences, in fact, and so nice a turn of phrase in describing them, that Bettie decided to split her assignment with Brooke and let her write half the letters, all the truly esoteric ones, for half her fee. This enabled Bettie to fulfill her assignment faithfully, creatively and with integrity without infringing too brutally on her required study time. Becoming wrapped up in her first West Coast romance it was easy to forget that she was out here to get a degree.

Even so, what with spell checking and reorganizing the materials several times, Bettie was three or four days later in delivering her assignment than promised. She emailed the entire document to Augie Rose on a Thursday evening and awoke the next morning to a summons to Beverly Hills.

His email had been terse but it set her heart racing: "Good job. Come by at three and I'll have a check for you."

By noon it had begun to rain, with lightning and thunder. It became dark and cold, nature conspiring against a smart outfit. Instead Bettie went in jeans tucked into boots and a thick woolen sweater (with a matching beret) over a soft flannel shirt. At the hat and sweater set, Augie Rose almost went to pieces, but held himself together until she had been seated in his office with a cup of coffee before her.

"Well, young lady, you're quite a good writer," Augie told her, lighting a cigarette and offering her one, which she accepted. Smoking was a new habit in which she occasionally indulged, especially in nervous making situations.

"Half of the letters were written by my friend Brooke. She works at a B&D club and I thought her perspective would add verisimilitude. I marked each of my own letters with an asterisk."

"You didn't have to tell me that," he said, smiling faintly.

"I have no reason to conceal it. Besides, I wanted you to know which ones I wrote myself."

"I'll give you creative work on a regular basis if you'd like it," Augie promised. "Providing you can learn to write a little faster."

"That would be wonderful," Bettie admitted.

"I like to develop new talent," said Augie, writing out and handing her two checks for $150 each. "I split it for you and left the pay to blank for your friend so you don't have to put her check through your account. If we do this regularly, I'll need her to come in and fill out an employment form for tax purposes, just as you did."

"Thank you very much. Shall I bring her with me next time?"

"Please do."

Bettie felt desolate as she realized that she was being dismissed yet again. Even after reading her stories! It was simply unbearable. She tried to rein in her emotions. Perhaps he was doing and saying nothing simply because he didn't realize just how much she wanted him to do and say something. She opened her lips to speak, but closed them again and dropped her eyes, not daring to express her thoughts to a man who was essentially nothing more to her at this point than a disinterested employer.

"Bettie? Is something the matter?" he asked.

Bettie heaved a sigh and murmured, "Are you really going to make me say it?"

"Say what, dear?"

Bettie's eyes widened and met his at the first endearment that had ever passed between them.

"Say why I keep coming back here," she replied, meeting his eyes with an adorable pout, finally tired of pretending.

"I'm sorry?" he said, as though he didn't understand. "I thought you kept coming back here because I've been giving you work."

"That's part of it. But not the important part," Bettie explained.

"Tell me about the important part."

"I would have thought you'd have figured it out by now!" Bettie accused. "Being as you've read my letters. And knowing that I was virtually sent to you by Hugo Sands via Garda Hudson!" Bettie had worked herself up. She no longer cared that she might be humiliating herself. She had to make her position clear to this dense man.

"Bettie, you're just so impossibly young," Augie protested. "It doesn't seem proper for me to think about you in that way."

"So why dangle me along by giving me work?" Bettie demanded, seeing a swift, unsatisfying end to her day's work looming in the next half minute and feeling close to tears of frustration.

"I always need editors," Augie replied honestly. "You need to use your spell checker more, but you're sharp. I'm ready to be your publisher. Doesn't that make you happy?"

"Well, yes. Thank you," she replied, forcing herself to focus on the positive aspects of the situation, as he advised, and calming down somewhat.

"Have you had lunch yet?" he asked kindly. Bettie shook her head, suddenly feeling butterflies in her stomach.

"No? Then let's go celebrate the commencement of your literary career," he said, leading her out of his office. Augie had seen a tear start in her eye and realized that to pretend that there was nothing going on would benefit no one any longer. For some reason, she wanted him, and now, having read her marvelously erotic stories, he wanted her too.

They went to a Beverly Hills brasserie and she was served the wine of his choice without question. The fare was of an elegance she'd never tasted before and she feasted with intense pleasure while basking in her new patron's gaze. Then, over dessert he said, "Bettie, why were you four days late?"

Bettie stammered out several excuses to which Augie did not appear to be listening. "You know, you ought to be spanked for missing your deadline like that," he interrupted her to remark, studying her casually, leaning his chin on his hand. Bettie's color rose. "I notice you don't argue with that," Augie observed, their dark eyes meeting.

"No," she replied, "I don't argue."

"I wouldn't think of spanking you directly after lunch, however; I'll give you cab fare and directions to my house and later this evening you can come over. And I'll take care of you."

And that was how Bettie and Augie's first date came to be arranged. He told her to arrive promptly at six thirty, dressed in the same boots, but with a skirt on.

It was raining, but the air had become warmer. It felt like the height of sophistication to climb into a taxi and be driven up the windy, lush canyon to Augie Rose's house as the sky became silvery grey, then black streaked with silver clouds. Under her black watch plaid skirt her legs were bare from her boot tops to her panties. A soft, cream wool polo shirt under a thick navy cardigan rendered her cuddly. There was nothing wispy about her after all, she was simply slim with good leg muscles from hiking and running and as Augie Rose would soon discover, fantastically firm, well rounded buttocks and thighs. The soft leather boots came up above her knees so that just a few inches of silken thigh was exposed to the chill air in the taxi.

Around her Bettie had wrapped the black cashmere coat, for good luck as well as warmth. Her small bottom, encased in the sheerest white cotton French briefs, was only a pleated wool skirt and topcoat away from his hand as he took her from the cab.

Suddenly Bettie was seeing a different California. Augie's house was quite wonderful. It even smelled delicious. He lived among splendid trees and thick foliage with twinkling views of the city below.

The moment he took her hand she realized that he had resigned himself to her. He now allowed himself to look at her with something like warmth, though not smiles. "I'm glad you weren't late," he told her. "That would have made me cross."

He never relinquished her hand, but took her straight upstairs to his bedroom, a large, round room, the walls papered forest green and gold, with a cream and gold gilt domed ceiling. One of the most charming features of the room was a long, wide green velvet recamier. Two matching armless chairs were of similar interest to Bettie.

"Shall we get the unpleasantness over with at once?" Augie asked, moving one of the large velvet chairs away from the other, sitting down on it and saying, "Come over here, young lady."

Bettie approached Augie, was caught by the wrist and pulled across his lap as though she were no more substantial than a dinner napkin. She flashed him one minx like smile over her shoulder, then made her face completely sober and wide eyed before dropping her head back down. Meanwhile, as he smoothed her little skirt down over her pert backside Augie was experiencing an epiphany re: the adorable girl, now draped so submissively over his lap. To wit: maybe Bettie was a gift from the gods, not to be questioned. Perhaps fate had introduced them at this particular juncture in time because they could be useful to each other. Augie thought, "There had to be a girl for me sooner or later. Even if it only lasts a year or two, neither of us are doing anything else. Besides, I didn't plan this. She's a gift."

Scolding her about missing her deadline, Augie spanked her on the seat of her skirt, just hard enough to get her attention. She wriggled and shifted on his lap, thrusting her small bottom up for more smacks. This naughty and flirtatious behavior was acknowledged by more and harder spanking, which caused her to grind into his lap in a most sophisticated style. Augie spanked her on her skirt until heat radiated from the entire area, one hand wrapped around her tiny waist all the while. She caught her breath and whimpered now and then but gave no indication of distress or wanting him to stop. After spanking her vigorously over her skirt for at least five minutes, he raised it to her waist to glimpse her endearingly pink bottom glowing through her sheer white panties. Her thighs were milky in contrast to the portions of her slim bottom cheeks left uncovered by the high cut French briefs, now stained so rosy from his hand.

"You write like an experienced submissive and take a spanking like a seasoned player; I guess I have to assume that you're not the baby I thought you were," Augie remarked, smartening her up again with his palm, through the thin panties which so snugly wrapped her shapely backside.

"I don't mind being treated like one though," she told him. So Augie pulled her pristine panties down to expose her freshly pinkened bottom.

"You're as smooth as one," he told her, caressing her tender skin. "This may be the prettiest sight I've ever beheld."

"I was wondering when I'd get a compliment out of you," Bettie murmured.

"Don't be fresh when I have you in this position," he warned, resuming the spanking, this time with her panties pulled down to mid thigh. In a very few minutes, Bettie's excitement became palpable. Augie was pleased but still hesitant to go any further. Even though she parted her legs invitingly and seemed to arch towards his hand every other moment, as much as to say, penetrate me, now! Soon her parted legs, dewy sex and dainty bottom began to mesmerize him blatantly.

"You're a very naughty girl," he told her, holding her apart and spanking her labia lightly, then spreading her bottom and spanking her bottomhole, though not so lightly. Bettie moaned and whimpered, grinding against him frantically, as though he'd just found her on switch. Deliberately spanking her sex a little harder, he observed the dynamic effect this treatment had upon her. Bettie whimpered and squirmed on his lap, eager for more discipline but nearly sobbing when she got it.

Finally Bettie noticed the pulsing rod beneath her. She turned to look at him and innocently said, "Mr. Rose, I think you have a hard-on."

"Of course I have a hard-on. Look at what I'm doing to you?" he replied impatiently, pausing to rub her rosy cheeks in circles with the palm of his hand.

"I have condoms," she informed him.

"Do you now?" Augie stopped spanking her and rubbing her and pulled her up off his lap. "Don't you think that would be a little sudden, young lady?"

"Why? You're not getting any younger, Mr. Rose," she replied with a grin.

"All that spanking and you're still this fresh?" Augie shook his head in amazement but punished her by taking her by the ear and turning her back over his knee for several dozen hard swats, each of which made her yip and kick.

Then of course he had to soothe her by caressing her bottom again, which lead to spreading it, spanking her pussy again, then her bottomhole, then when the glistening promise of her almost untouched pussy was simply too creamy to resist, penetrating her with his fingers, deeply and dominantly, for a very long time.

"Didn't I say I'd take care of you?" he asked, masturbating her deftly over his knee until she gave up a delightfully girlish orgasm. If she wasn't in love before, she was when he let her up.

"But now I want to take care of you," she declared a few minutes later, bouncing on his lap, which still cradled the engine of his desire in a fully rampant state.

"No, that's absurd," he told her sternly, seizing her around the waist and putting her off his lap before going to wash his hands. She followed him into the marble bathroom with the matching sweetheart sinks.

"Why is it? You got me off. Now I wish to reciprocate."

"I won't hear any more of that, young lady," Augie warned her.

"It's not like I haven't had lovers," she pointed out. "I've had five!"

"Have you now?" Augie was amused and relieved by her candor. But when she boldly laid her hand upon his pulsing organ through is trousers he deliberately slapped it hard.

"Ow!" She held her hand to her cheek like a bad little girl. Which made Augie melt and take her in his arms. Which led to him kissing her deeply. Which led to Bettie Brandon not leaving the house until the next morning.

Brooke Neuman was taking a nap in Bettie's dorm room, face down and ravishing on Bettie's little bed, in pegged blue jeans, black ankle boots and a black cashmere cowl neck sweater. Her dark hair streamed down her back, thick, straight and long. Her face was turned to one side, pillowed on her arm, young, lovely and peaceful. Then Gilbert Rush walked in, jolting the girl out of her dream state, causing her to sit up with a start and stare at him.

"Oh, hi Gilbert," Brooke said.

"You know me?"

"Bettie showed me your photograph."

"Where is the little termagant anyway? She's been harder to get an appointment with than a grown up lately."

"I'm expecting her momentarily. We're going shopping," Brooke reported, frankly though carelessly appraising Gilbert through her sophisticated, 19 year old, UCLA freshman's eyes. "You are good looking," Brooke declared, granting him a quarter of a smile.

"You make it seem as though I haven't a single other valuable quality," Gilbert bristled at the superior tone Brooke had adopted but was instantly attracted by her tall, elegant form and charming face. Brooke shrugged and gave him the second quarter of the smile. "What's Bettie been telling you about me?"

"Only the truth, I expect," said Brooke. "That you're a soulless, grasping businessman whose been running around lately with dyed blonde silicon jobs."

"That was a passing obsession. It's over and done with now," said Gilbert cheerfully.

"Interesting. Well, I'm sure that someone as attractive and

upwardly mobile as yourself will have no problem acquiring a new one."

"I don't want a new one. I just want Bettie. But she's been almost impossible to track down these past few weeks. What's going on?"

"Well, she does have a part time job you know."

"Shelving library books."

"No, freelance editorial work. It's been keeping the both of us busy. Of course, I'm not the writer she is. I'm in the film school."

"Oh, are you the one who videos everything?"

"Yes. You should let me video you. I could document a day in the life of a young realtor."

"No thanks," replied Gilbert emphatically.

"Why not? It would be ever so useful to me."

"Why should I want to be useful to you?"

"Gallantry?"

"Strange things are passing for that these days," he returned.

"The more I look at you the more I see what a marvelous subject you'd be. I don't only film journalistically, you know. I could create a scenario for you instead."

"What sort of scenario?"

"I'd have to think about that."

"And what would I get out of this venture?" Gilbert smiled.

"The chance to work with an important filmmaker to be."

"You're pretty confident for a freshman."

"I've always been that way. I think it has to do with being tall," Brooke replied, still look at him with the eyes of a hungry casting director.

"What's the freelance connection all about?" Gilbert changed the subject abruptly.

"Erotic magazines. We've been writing copy for a publisher called Augie Rose in Beverly Hills. He pays us well and the work is easy. Augie Rose said I could video him for my businessman in L.A. documentary."

"What's this you say? Bettie's writing stroke books?"

"Don't sound shocked. We got the introduction through her uncle Hugo," Brooke revealed pointedly.

"What? You mean to say this publisher is also a player?"

"As I understand it," said Brooke.

"As you understand it from whom?" Gilbert was beginning to feel sick with apprehension that an older, more successful male had annexed Bettie for his own plaything.

"Who do you think?"

At that moment, there was a knock on the door. Gilbert opened it to confront a delivery boy bearing an enormous bouquet of Birds of Paradise surrounding a heart of crimson roses. Gilbert dismissed the boy and tore open the card.

"What do you think you're doing?" Brooke cried.

"I see I'm too late," said Gilbert, the color draining from his face as he slipped the card back in the envelope. "How old is this Augie Rose, anyway?"

"Oh, forty, I suppose. Hey, you're not really upset, are you?" Brooke asked with some perplexity.

But Gilbert had no chance to reply because Bettie walked in at that moment, gave a start at the occupants of her room, then smiled at the large bouquet. Gilbert noticed her carelessly toss the keys to a Volvo on the dresser before burying her face in the roses.

"What's everyone doing here?" she asked, tucking the card into her pocket without reading it.

"You're driving a Volvo?" Gilbert demanded, picking up the keys as his world went spinning around. Was he really losing his dream girl to a relic in his 40's??? Why hadn't he thought of helping Bettie get a car?

"It's fifteen years old and I'm only borrowing it," Bettie explained.

"I'll meet you downstairs, okay?" Brooke said, tactfully disappearing.

"So I'm out, am I?" Gilbert said caustically as soon as they were alone. Bettie blushed, her heart pounding.

"I never promised I'd be yours forever," she replied. "I told I was looking for a different kind of man right from the start."

"So all those nights you spent in my arms meant nothing to you? You don't care for me anymore?"

"I'm very sorry. You're a good lover, but we don't want the same things out of life. Mr. Rose is more my type."

"You're going out with man old enough to be your father?"

"I'm sorry, Gilbert," Bettie said, her eyes filled with sympathetic tears.

Stabbed in the heart, Gilbert stumbled out the door, choked by emotion. Bettie joined Brooke downstairs, still dashing tears from here eyes.

"What's the matter? Did he yell at you?" Brooke demanded.

"No. He just seemed devastated."

"He'll get over it. Maybe I'll help him."

"Really? You want Gilbert?"

Brooke got into the car beside Bettie, musing, "Only if you really don't want him anymore."

"I'll give you his number."

"Okay, I'll bug him some more about letting me film him and see if he asks me out."

Bettie pulled out the card from Augie Rose and read its contents aloud to Brooke, "Dearest Bettie, What a night that was and what a girl you are. I am slain. Augie Rose."

"So they can still get it up at that age?" Brooke asked as they headed into West Hollywood via Beverly Hills.

"Get it up? He had me both ways!"

"Wow. I've barely ever been sodomized. I keep hoping I'll meet a man who's interested but the closest I've come are men at the club wanting to put toys in me."

"Do you let them?"

"We're not supposed to let the customers take those sorts of liberties, but I have a few regulars I grant special privileges to."

"Look what Augie gave me when I was going out this morning," said Bettie, pulling out two new hundred-dollar bills.

"Wow," exclaimed Brooke. "He even gave you allowance. I'm so impressed."

"Let's go to Melrose. I want one of those PVC slip dresses and a pair of four inch heels!"

Over the next week, Brooke did not call Gilbert, but she thought about him at least once a day. Consequently, on Friday night, he showed up at The Keep to book a session with her. She was somewhat disappointed when all he did during the session was turn her over his knee and spank her (rather hard!) for the entire half hour, not even pulling down her panties until minute twenty-two. He neither scolded nor flirted, so she did not know what to think. But when she did catch a glimpse of his expression in the opposite mirror, it was one of grim determination. Brooke could only conclude that he was using her as a surrogate for Bettie, just to have someone to punish for Bettie's betrayal. The entire situation felt so B&D Gothic to Brooke that she began to dream of Gilbert every night.

Meanwhile, Bettie found it nearly impossible to concentrate on her studies. She longed to see Augie Rose again, but didn't quite know how to make this happen. She had called and left a message about bringing back the car, which he had breezily replied to in a quick email, telling her to keep it for a while. Bettie didn't realize that Augie was as hesitant to rush her as she was to dog him.

But finally, thirty-six hours later, her passion overcame her better judgment and she typed a reply to his last that demanded attention: "I'm starving."

Thirty minutes later they were meeting at a favorite bistro of Augie's at the bottom of Nichols Canyon. She was wearing the new black PVC slip dress and the matching fetish pumps, under a leather jacket that Brooke had lent her.

"That's a great outfit," Augie told her as they consulted the menu, "for a B&D call girl." Bettie instantly looked stricken. Then she saw by his eyes he was teasing.

"I used the allowance you gave me to buy it and the heels. Do you like them?" Bettie extended one slender ankle to display one of her spectator pumps.

"You're a good shopper," he commended her, "but you're attracting a lot of attention, young lady."

Bettie melted and murmured, "I just want you to notice me."

"I think everyone is noticing you. That dress clings to your bottom like ink."

"I apologize for dressing inappropriately," she offered.

"You're lucky you don't get your first public spanking for that."

"A public spanking?" Bettie was intrigued beyond words.

"I saw a tree with a circular bench facing the front entrance."

"Brooke told me her ex-boyfriend spanked her outside of Yamashiro once," Bettie confided.

"I didn't realize it was becoming such a trend!"

"I'll cut you a break," Augie told her, as they left the restaurant an hour later.

"What do you mean?" she asked as he took her by the hand and strolled towards the tree.

"I'll spank you on the side facing away from the entrance," he replied, taking her there, sliding onto the bench and pulling her lithe form over his lap. The PVC skirt was so shiny and taut it seemed to reflect the moonlight on the crest of each small, jutting, oval bottom cheek. The skirt only came down to Bettie's upper thighs and her black fishnet tights looked adorably naughty outlining her shapely legs. The fetish pumps were perfection on her tiny size five feet.

"No my dear, this is not an outfit to wear in public, unless you are working," he declared, spanking her pert backside firmly and resounding at least thirty swats. Bettie had no idea whether anyone was leaving or entering the restaurant at that moment or how much they could see, but the unmistakable sound of crisp smacks connecting with a patent leather girded rear was unmistakable to her sensitive ears. When pulled her by her hand back to the valet station, he seemed perfectly indifferent as to whether anyone had heard or seen what he'd just done. Nor could Bettie raise her eyes. Her face felt warm, as did her bottom under the skintight skirt.

Augie Rose may have been just a little too civilized for Garda, but he was just edgy enough to electrify the much younger Bettie, who soon became his spoiled darling. Possessed of the natural authority that comes from achieving an early and steady success in the business world, Augie didn't have to try to impress Bettie; just being who he was and doing what he did accomplished that. Even weeks after they began their affair, she still felt pleasantly intimidated by him.

For Augie's part, it was all too easy to become accustomed to the company of a charming and compliant young lady whose pure and unrestrained love seemed to envelope him from their first night together. The way she clung to him each night, the way she fussed over his morning coffee, the glow on her face when she waved to him from a table in a cafe where they were to meet, all were clear indications of her affection. It was but a step from complaining about her roommate to having a suite set aside for her own use in Augie's house. He never asked Bettie to spend up to five nights a week there, but this is what transpired naturally. With the old Volvo to take her back and forth to school this scarcely inconvenienced her at all. Since he was gone during the day, the house made the perfect secluded study palace, with her choice of computers and refreshments.

A late autumn heat wave permitted Bettie to swim in Augie's pool every day of the first week of November. Suddenly she began to see the virtue of a California winter. Brooke was also of course encouraged to visit Bettie at Augie's house and the girls made it their haven in the afternoons whenever they could meet there.

Neither Bettie nor Brooke could quite understand what was going on in Gilbert's mind when he came to see Brooke once more at The Keep. Again, he only took her over his knee and spanked her, eschewing conversation. Glimpsing his face in the mirror, Brooke saw that Gilbert was still angry and bitter about losing his girl.

But the second time he came to see her was slightly different. She was amazed when he gave her a hundred dollar tip after the simple, though stinging spanking. "Really?" she sputtered incredulously.

"I sold my first house today," Gilbert admitted, smiling faintly.

"Congratulations! Where was it? Who bought it? And for how much?"

"Brentwood, a movie star and five million dollars," he modestly reported.

"A female movie star?"

"Yes," he nodded wryly.

"A female movie star over the age of thirty five?" said Brooke shrewdly.

"How did you know?"

"That creeping blush. It's a sure indication that you exerted more than just your powers of persuasion in making that sale."

"What are you implying?"

"You did her, didn't you?" Brooke accused her tall, dark, handsome client naughtily.

"You know what? Let's extend the session. I don't think I've spanked you enough!"

"Sure, but you fucked her. I can tell you did!" cried Brooke with glee. "Bet that restored the old ego, eh, Gilbert?"

"I have no idea what you mean," he said, throwing the bolt on the door again and removing his jacket once more.

"Wait a minute, how much over thirty-five was she? I do hope you're not starting to feel cheap."

"Come over here, wise guy," he threatened, picking up a wooden paddle and pointing to his favorite chair in the wood paneled dungeon room.

"Can't I hear the details first? Was she a face-lift queen? How many times were you required to get it up before she signed off on the house? And most importantly, was she kinky?"

Gilbert didn't answer, but instead stalked her, grabbed her by her wrist and dragged her across his knee. "You're not only irritating, you're rude," Gilbert accused, whacking her vigorously with the paddle through her copper latex apron dress. He was mad for her tall, slender body but hadn't gone beyond punishing her yet. Not even a stray caress had he spared the cheerful young cynic. Her bottom-arching body language he had been pleased to ignore. She had laughed at him and he would not give her the satisfaction of openly lusting after her. If she wanted to go anywhere else with him besides over his knee, she would have to tell him so. Meanwhile, it was nice to have her to spank. Especially now that he'd have his first commission to defray the expenses of an ongoing session relationship.

Brooke felt that it was a significant day for Gilbert. He had sold his first house and seemed to have no one to celebrate with. So after the second half hour was over, and Brooke was released, very sore, she mildly remarked that she got off at ten that evening.

Gilbert was back at ten, but was told by Hildegarde that Brooke had unexpectedly gone into a two-hour session that would not conclude until midnight. Gilbert had to be in the office at seven thirty the next morning but went to a nearby sports bar to kill two hours until midnight anyway. When he got back to The Keep he was told that the client had extended the session with Brooke for yet another half hour. This time Gilbert waited.

When Brooke stumbled downstairs after her two and a half hour bondage, whipping and hot wax session, she was nearly asleep on her feet. In fact, she didn't even have the energy to put her heels back on and carried them in her hand as she padded downstairs. Gilbert saw the perfect opportunity to scoop the sleepy girl up in his arms before she even saw him at the foot of the stairs. He carried her out to his convertible and dumped her in the front seat. "Some ten o'clock scholar you are," he accused.

"I'm so sorry," she protested, laying her head on his shoulder as he pointed his car towards Westwood Village.

"You're going the wrong way, I live up Laurel Canyon."

"Alone?"

"No, with my dad."

"Then come to my place instead," he said, continuing on his original route.

"Starting next semester Bettie and I are getting a place together."

"Don't tell me, let me guess. In Hollywood?"

"West Hollywood."

"God forbid you're ever more than three blocks away from the Pleasure Chest," Gilbert said.

Gilbert took Brooke to his stark white enamel and brushed metal condo in Westwood with the track lighting and flat TV and on site spa. Brooke could easily see why Bettie preferred Augie's warm, textural canyon aerie, but for a youthful bachelor the cool, postmodernist lines of Gilbert's domicile seemed exactly right.

"I know it's boring and ugly. I'm moving soon," he told her as soon as he closed the door behind them.

"It's sexy as hell, Gilbert. In fact, I'd be delighted to spend the night with you here."

"Really? Even after I spanked you so hard?"

"Oh, I enjoyed that. I almost cried."

"Why?" he asked, opening a bottle of white wine. Brooke sat on a barstool and watched him pour two glasses.

"I felt excited by your anger at Bettie, and me."

"I'm not all that angry anymore," he smiled.

"I know."

"Do you think you could like me?"

"How could I not like you? You're smart, hot, even a little bit older, if not wiser. Plus, I've already cleared the annexation with Bettie, which eases her conscience considerably."

"Now there's a remark to make a man feel dominant!" he bristled.

"I'm sorry."

"I think I'll start all over again on you with my strap."

"Goody! I need something to wipe away the two and a half hours of bondage boredom I just endured."

"And after your strapping?" Gilbert said, after kissing her long and hard for the first time.

"Then you decide."

"*Dear Hugo,*" Garda emailed her first lover in the scene, "*All's well that ends well. I met your darling Bettie today at the home of Augie Rose. A film crew from my studio was shooting at his house for the day and I popped over to give Mr. Rose the rental check.*

Miss Bettie was sunning by the pool, a la Lolita, but she snapped to when she heard my name. The adorable girl jumped up to greet me and affectionately hugged me for some moments, whispering her thanks for the introduction.

Augie had been supervising some of the crew who were moving around his possessions and seemed a little embarrassed by Bettie's bikini.

She took me aside to tell me of Mr. Rose's many kindnesses to her, including an automobile and the keys to his house, since she doesn't like her roommate and U.C.L.A. is five minutes away.

She also asked me to tell you that Gilbert Rush is now courting her friend Brooke, who appreciates the lad a bit more than she did.

As for Augie, he is plainly enchanted and seems to be doing all he can to gild your niece's existence.

My new boyfriend came along to keep an eye on me. Jeffrey Jardine is a piece of work. He's my superior at work, though somewhat my junior. (Compared with what Augie is up to, seven years hardly seems worth mentioning.) He has nothing to recommend him but athletic looks, a strong right arm and an attractive portfolio, but I'm drawn to him. Let's just say he's good enough for me.

Please come visit me one of these days.

Your adoring,
Garda."

Chapter Four

Carter Takes Brooke

After Aurora Milne left Los Angeles to continue her studies in England, Carter Webster was once again without a lover in the scene. Not eager to immediately acquire another girl friend, especially since he and Aurora planned to visit each other often, the screen writer decided to satisfy his most immediate urges by visiting The Keep, Aurora's former work place, run by the charming Mistress Hildegarde and staffed with the nicest mannered submissives in the city.

It was at this discreet little two-story house on Las Palmas Street in Hollywood that Carter first met Brooke Neuman, whom he engaged for a session the moment he glimpsed her tall, elegant carriage and refreshingly youthful face. She appeared to be under twenty, but exuded sophistication and confidence in her leather slip dress and thigh high boots, her dark hair smooth, her mouth wide and sexy. She was so striking, that Carter immediately quizzed her as to whether she had a portfolio, for he made it a rule to avoid actresses whenever possible. Brooke informed him that she planned to occupy a position behind the camera, not in front of it, and was currently studying at the U.C.L.A. film school to that end.

Carter recoiled, as it never seemed to go well between him and ambitious women eager to penetrate his world. He had never asked anyone for favors and resented those who did, conveniently forgetting that his own degree from Yale had often served as his consummate connection.

It bored Carter to date industry types. All they talked about was their projects and he had plenty of his own with which to concern himself. In fact, Carter was already bored and decided to call the session before even playing. He paid Brooke anyway and strolled out of the house with a scowl.

Brooke, who had never felt affronted by a client before, even when they had beaten her black and blue, handed the allowance to Hildy with a shrug. "Wha'd I do?" she murmured, checking her reflection in the dressing room mirror to make sure nothing was amiss. But the mini dress was the epitome of sleekness, the boots graced her long legs to perfection and not a hair was out of place on her naturally beautiful head.

"Exactly what did you say to him?" asked Hildegarde.

"Nothing! He asked me if I was an aspiring actress and I told him that I was a film student."

"There's your answer, Brooke dear," murmured Hildy regretfully. "He's much too important a Hollywood figure to casually consort with up and coming young film makers. He's either afraid of you outing him later, or hitting him up for a job or introduction now."

"You mean that snotty piece of work is someone?" Brooke gasped, for she had never come close to playing with a real celebrity so far and longed to do so, in the hopes that their magic dust would rub off on her budding genius.

"Didn't I tell you that was Carter Webster you just let slip through your fingers? I'm sorry, that was remiss of me." Hildegarde had the grace to blush.

"Carter Webster, the intellectual's Tarrentino? That was him?" Brooke's heart leapt painfully in her pert bosom. "I'll bet he can be a real bastard in a dungeon!" she added, recalling the rough treatment that women received in his scripts.

"No, he's a darling. But don't worry, he'll be back," Hildy promised. "He found his last girlfriend here."

Brooke's best friend at college was a freshman named Bettie, an attractive brunette who was also in the scene and currently seeing an older male dominant, a pulp magazine publisher named Augie Rose, who spanked her delightfully well.

Bettie had thrown over her summer romance, Gilbert Rush, in favor of the older man. Brooke, observing Gilbert's heartbreak at losing Bettie and feeling sorry for the handsome, young MBA, was allowing him to date her and dom her instead. But as one can sense a summer storm, Brooke felt as likely to break off the connection as maintain it. Gilbert was very nice, but he was no Mr. Lawrence.

Brooke told Bettie how she had scared Carter Webster away from the club, who then related the story to Augie Rose, who stunned Bettie by revealing that he and Carter Webster had been friends for some time. The story of how Carter met Aurora in Random Point (and then followed her back to The Keep), enchanted Bettie, who had just spent the summer in that tiny Cape Cod village, wherein she herself had first discovered the scene.

Augie told Bettie that if Brooke wanted another opportunity to charm Carter Webster he was prepared to invite him over for dinner. Bettie begged him to proceed with this plan, thinking Brooke would be pleased enough to justify surprising her with the celebrated author. At eighteen, Bettie was not yet acquainted with the concept of circumspection.

The dinner party took place on Augie's canyon patio, with glowing outdoor heat lamps to warm the guests. The moon was full, the fountain which sprang around a nymph Diana rushed, night birds sang and a thousand stars shone down. Dinner was delivered by Augie's favorite restaurant but served by Bettie in a smart red apron over her blue jeans and blue chambray shirt, dressed down so as not to distract Carter from appreciating every aspect of Brooke's willowy charms.

Brooke was late and they began without her. Augie had been casual about the unseen guest. Bettie had said nothing beyond hello to Carter, vastly intimidated by his importance. At first the writer seemed edgy at Bettie's presence, as though he couldn't understand what she was doing there. But when she went into the kitchen to get the first course, Augie explained how the college girl was one of his freelance copywriters but also the niece of Hugo Sands, who published the New Rod out of Random Point, MA.

"And she's into it," Augie added with a grin.

This put Carter a little at ease, taking the focus off himself and placing it on the petite coed serving them. Knowing Bettie was an adorable, compliant young submissive, rather than a typical L.A. nerve case caused the much sought-after bachelor to finally begin to untense.

Carter began to interrogate Bettie as to her experiences, what she'd done in Random Point and other amusing topics. He had met Aurora in Random Point and still found that young lady enchanting. To Carter, who was coveted by so many, a girl who wanted nothing more from him than spanking and dominant sex embodied the quintessence of feminine charm.

The exquisitely shy Aurora had stayed as well out of the way of his other friends and associates as any man of the world might wish. Aurora had no desire to parade with him in public and cringed at the thought of an interview. She was for firesides and wooded glens, not paparazzi. Which had led him to suppose that a B&D girl could make the perfect mistress. His friend and fellow Eli, Anthony Newton, had proven it could be done for the last five years with his own youthful companion Susan Ross. Yet another Hugo Sands referral, Susan had been a constant presence in Newton's private life without intruding into his professional one to the slightest degree. This wasn't something Newton worked at, Susan simply had no interest in appearing in the pages of People magazine. She was much more content to draw Newton into her own private world of the scene.

Carter preferred a passive, undemanding playmate, who would leave him alone when he needed to work, which was most of the time. Aurora had been as timid around him the year after they met as on the first day, a lovely trait that he continued to relish.

But Carter was about to realize that there are all types of submissives.

Brooke arrived in a clatter of platform boots and flung herself into a chair, still in her work clothes of a leather mini jumper and short, fitted, matching leather zipped jacket. Her hair was in a long ponytail and she smelled of both perfume and leather. She was tall, slim and magnetic, with legs that mesmerized. She greeted Augie gaily as she sat down but started with surprise at Carter.

Carter recoiled. He did not remember the circumstances under which they had first been introduced but vaguely perceived her as someone who wanted something from him. Damn, how did she find him here? Why was she a welcome guest? When Augie went into the house to tell Bettie of Brooke's arrival, Carter followed.

"What's she doing here?" Carter demanded.

"What do you mean? She's Bettie's best friend. She's over all the time. I thought you might like to meet her under better light than at the club."

"What club? What are you talking about?"

"Brooke told Bettie you walked out of a session with her."

"Oh my god, is that the same girl I almost played with at The Keep? The film student? Damn it, Augie, why didn't you tell me she was going to be here?"

"She's really a very nice girl. I don't know what you have against her."

"Oh, hell!" Carter snapped, returning to the patio to make his peace with Brooke, who had poured herself a glass of merlot and was nibbling on some crusty rosemary bread.

"I'm sorry," he said at once, "I didn't quite remember where I'd met you." The smile he produced to accompany the insincere apology was only tepid.

"That's not surprising," Brooke replied agreeably and with a complete lack of concern.

When Augie and Bettie sat down with them Bettie began to quiz Brooke about her day at the club and Brooke did not hesitate to unselfconsciously regale them with the details of the four sessions she'd enjoyed during the afternoon and evening there. Brooke was the top girl at the Keep that season being so young, statuesque and spankable. She was also an excellent switch and half of her sessions were dominant ones. She described her various playmates colorfully while appearing to completely ignore Carter, knowing her subject matter to be of sufficient interest so as not to feel inhibited by his presence. Carter watched her face rather than listened to her words and could see that for all her affected coolness she was still angry with him for having rejected her the other day.

"I don't see how you can do it," said Bettie, twirling pasta around a fork. "I could never let myself be touched by a man I wasn't attracted to."

"You'd be surprised," Brooke told her with a wry smile.

"How so?" Carter asked.

"A good player doesn't have to be pretty," Brooke asserted. "He just has to be good." Then added with a grin, "And of course, smell good."

"And then what?" Carter persisted.

"Then it's all about sensations instead of emotions and that works okay for me."

Suddenly stuck by her intelligence and maturity, Carter felt rather sick at the way he had walked out on her at the club. Just as he began to wonder whether he himself felt threatened by her glowing youth and keen penetration Brooke announced that she had to go rent a video to watch for a class the following day.

"What video?" asked Carter casually.

"Trouble in Paradise," she replied.

"Lubitsch, 1932?" Carter asked. Brooke nodded. "You're not going to find a store that would have that movie open at this hour," he told her.

"Damn it!" Brooke swore.

"I have it on tape," Carter told her. "Stop by my place on the way home and I'll give it to you."

Brooke agreed and they soon left together, she following his sleek sports car in her limping Dodge Dart. In twelve minutes they arrived at his house in Malibu Canyon. Brooke killed her motor but made no move to get out of the car. When he came around to open her door she blandly smiled up at him and said, "I'll wait here."

"It'll take me few minutes to find the tape, why don't you come in?"

"I don't think I'd better," she replied.

"Why not?"

"I have an early class."

"Come in for a few minutes anyway."

Brooke paused, looked at him, then shook her head, "No."

"Damn it, then what was the point of stopping by Augie's tonight?" he snapped.

"I didn't know you were going to be there," she protested.

"Right, honey," said Carter, becoming annoyed by what he

perceived to be her coyness.

"I didn't!" Brooke returned.

"Then how did Augie know about us meeting the other day?"

"I may have told Bettie I met you and she may have told Augie about it, but I certainly didn't authorize them to arrange for us to meet!" Brooke cried, furious at being accused of such a blatant act of man chasing. She threw her car in gear as if to leave right then.

"Wait a minute, don't you want the tape?"

"I'll get it tomorrow!" she replied.

"What time is your class?"

"Ten!"

"Eddie Brandt's doesn't open until one tomorrow and that's the only place you'll find your movie," said Carter with some authority. "Come on in and help me find the tape, why don't you? It's the least I can do to make up for walking out the other day."

"You don't owe me anything, Mr. Webster. You paid for the session."

"Come on," he coaxed her, reaching in through the window to pop the door button, opening the door and extending his hand to help her out. She looked at him, took his hand, got out of the car and allowed him to lead her into his splendid residence, which was even more impressive than that of Augie Rose.

Carter led Brooke directly to his research library, which featured wall-to-wall bookcases filled with videotapes, CDs, DVDs, monitors and sound systems. The films were alphabetically arranged by title and neatly labeled as to year and cast. Rolling ladders went up to the ceiling allowing access to the entire collection, which ranged from silent cinema to the current era worldwide. Brooke was lost in the wonder of the collection for some time, going up and down the ladders and across the hardwood floors on them as she searched for and found titles she'd only heard about for years but had never seen. To Brooke, the fleet of German sport cars, the modest mansion, the Oscar nominations for best screenplays of the previous two years, made some slight impression. The fact that Carter owned copies of Prix de Beaute and Gosta Berling delighted her.

After finding her Trouble in Paradise Carter tried to tempt her into watching it with him. "I've got killer weed," he murmured, instinctively crooning the siren song no Hollywood bad girl can ever resist.

Brooke weighed the alternatives while still gazing longingly at the various classic films on the walls. If she returned home now to the small cottage she still shared with her father, a marginally successful stand up comic who supplemented his income emceeing at a strip club, she would still have three or four hours of privacy in which to watch her film and then quietly retire, thus getting a good night's sleep and preserving both her brain and her looks for the following early morning. Whereas if she tarried in the luxe canyon retreat of her first real celebrity, she would no doubt be fed that $2,000 an ounce weed that had become so legendary in fin de millennium cinema and which she had yet to sample, and she would also no doubt be seduced by this very important man and then tossed out with the empty Perrier bottles the following morning. She remembered how Carter hadn't scrupled to walk out of the session with her with no explanation whatever. That insult still stung Brooke.

"You think I'm a climber, don't you?" she asked coolly, taking the video she needed out of his hand and attempting to effect a swift exit.

"Why do you say that? Haven't I been nice so far?"

"Is that some sort of minor miracle?"

"I'm sorry, that came out wrong. I apologize. And for leaving you the way I did the other day. Please forgive me."

"I do. After all, you're lending me the video," said Brooke with a degree of calm, which Carter decided should be immediately shaken out of her.

"Brooke, I want you to stay. I want to get to know you better."

"I'm sorry but I don't trust you."

"Don't trust me how? Surely you don't think I'll try to take advantage of you."

"No, but you can be very insulting and I don't like exposing myself to that kind of crudeness."

"I certainly never meant to insult you," Carter protested, shocked at Brooke's perception of him. He had always thought himself exceedingly civil!

"You're so important that you automatically assume everyone you meet wants a piece of you. You even think I arranged for dinner tonight. Well, I didn't. Do you think I wanted to see you again after the way you acted? Hildy explained that you thought I wanted to use you as some sort of industry connection. I didn't even know who you were until she told me. Then I was actually kind of glad you'd walked out."

"Oh? And why was that?" Carter bristled.

"Because I've seen your movies."

"And?"

"And you're obviously an extreme sadomasochist!"

"Nonsense!" Carter protested. "I'm actually an astonishingly wholesome over the knee spanker!"

"Huh! That's moderately intriguing, but I have to go!" she said, starting for the door. He caught her arm and guided her back to a large, tufted, brass riveted sofa, making her sit down beside him and retaining her hands while he spoke to her. "No, you don't," he insisted. "You have to stay and let me redeem myself."

"You don't have to redeem yourself with me."

"I do. I've misjudged you. As in the many dozens of depression era movies wherein spunky shop girls, sassy show girls or madcap heiresses were misjudged by their insolent, but well meaning leading men and in revenge spent the next sixty two minutes confounding and fleeing the poor saps. But I have no intention of pursuing you for over three reels before taking you in my arms," said Carter, adding, "Or turning you over my knee."

Brooke stared up at him, allowing a smile to emerge at last. "I wish you'd let your characters talk like that rather than the way they do. This indeed is an unexpected side of you. But still I must go."

Brooke got up but he pulled her back down. "I've said I was sorry, haven't I?"

"You still think I'm playing you," said Brooke. "You don't believe I didn't know you were going to be there tonight. You assume I so desperately wanted another chance to snag my celebrity that I set this entire evening up in aid of it."

"What does it matter? Now that I know you better, I find I

genuinely like you."

"That's handsome of you."

"Brooke, don't be so sensitive. You have no idea how many drippy girls I meet day to day. A man in my position has to guard his privacy. And speaking of privacy, you shouldn't have told your friend Bettie about meeting me at the Keep."

"Why not?"

"If you really have to ask then it's time I held a discussion with Mistress Hildy on the subject of discretion among her employees!" Carter said sternly.

"What do you mean?"

"You're not supposed to bandy names about the way you have mine!"

Brooke replied, "I only told Bettie."

"And she told Augie Rose."

"But he turned out to be your friend."

"Coincidentally, and thankfully, for my sake. Remember, he's recently gone into the erotic magazine business. Through Bettie, you gave him extraordinarily inflammatory information about my private sex life. He might well have written it up in his next gossip column! Do you begin to see how terribly indiscreet you've been?"

'Well, anyway, I haven't told anyone else," Brooke declared, completely resistant to his attempted infliction of guilt.

"How do I know that?"

Brooke shrugged, "You'll have to take my word for it."

"I think you need a good spanking for violating my privacy like that."

"Maybe some other time," said Brooke, again attempting to leave him.

"What's wrong with now?"

"I told you, I have to get up early. And I've already played four times today."

"I wasn't talking about playing, though of course I'm willing to provide you with allowance for the privilege of disciplining you." In so saying, Carter pulled eight or ten hundreds out of his wallet and placed them in her hand.

"No, thank you," she said firmly, handing them politely back and withdrawing from him with a finality that he knew could not be breeched that evening. "I'll be going now."

Carter resentfully walked her to her car and put her in it. "I don't understand," he snapped. "What's wrong with me?"

"Nothing. Good night, Mr. Webster. Shall I mail you back the tape?"

"When do you work next?" he demanded.

"Friday night."

"Maybe I'll be by then," he grumbled and walked back into the house sparing her but one irritable backward glance before disappearing inside it. Her heart still pounding, Brooke threw her car in gear and puttered back down the hill with a bemused smile on her face.

Brooke didn't honestly expect Carter Webster to drag himself back to the Keep on Friday but he was waiting for her when she arrived a half hour late for her shift. Carter seemed in a vile mood as she led him upstairs to the blue painted room known as Bishop.

Brooke could tell that she was in for it when he didn't make small talk or smile, but rather busied himself choosing implements and restraints from the wall outside their dungeon. He appeared grimly determined to fulfill the role of strict disciplinarian, if not master, that afternoon and she only inflamed him with such candid observations as, "I can't believe you didn't have something better to do on a Friday night."

"While we're in this dungeon, you'll speak when you're spoken to. Understand?" said Carter, closing the door, throwing all the gear he had gathered onto a leather bondage bed and taking off his jacket. "Why were you late?" he asked, buckling a soft, leather cuff around each of her slender wrists and linking them together with a boat hook. Then turning her to face the whipping post and taking both wrists in one hand he fixed the cuffs to a "d" ring on the post about a foot above her head. Brooke was clad that day in a zippered black PVC miniskirt and matching vest, black fishnet stockings and a black lace lingerie combination underneath. Her perkily proportioned bosom, tiny waist and long, shapely legs all contributed to the impression of elegance and grace. She wore no makeup save for dark red lipstick and no jewelry except for pearl stud earrings and an Olympia's pearl pendant suspended on a black velvet ribbon around her neck. Her hair was loose and hung to mid shoulder in a straight, silken black curtain.

"I'm always late," Brooke admitted, turning to look at him over one shoulder.

"Didn't I tell you I'd be here today?"

"Sure, but I didn't think you would be. And certainly not first thing."

"Always late, are you?" Carter slapped her on the bottom several times hard. "What's this you have on?" He found the zipper going up the back of her skirt and jerked it down in one swift motion. The thin patent leather garment fell to the floor at her feet revealing a pair of sheer black French cut briefs over a black lace garter belt. Her slim bottom was oval cheeked and gleamed palest cream through the sheer mesh panties. His two initial smacks had left a clearly discernable pink handprint on either cheek, but Carter wasn't sorry.

Reaching around in front of her while pressing his front to her back, he unzipped her glove tight vest and it too fell to the ground. He circled Brooke, taking in every aspect of her semi nude form and finding her very lovely. She followed him with her dark eyes, pouting at him with her wide mouth, flicking her smooth hair away from her face whenever she turned her head. Carter thought, "The camera would love her." Meanwhile, Brooke, the filmmaker in embryo, was thinking the same thing about her handsome, 30 something persecutor. His jet black hair and whitest skin, athletic frame and tailored, monochromatic shirt and trousers, combined with the way he held a riding crop, added up to a masculine appeal that was suddenly overwhelming to the romantically inclined submissive.

"Being always late is nothing to brag about!" Carter flicked the spanker end of the crop against her cheeks. Then he greatly embarrassed her by summarily yanking the panties down to her upper thighs and touching up her now bare buttocks with the very hard palm of his hand. Brooke caught her breath but didn't cry out. He wasn't being very nice and so she didn't intend to give him the satisfaction of reacting. How lacking in finesse, thought Brooke, not to give her a warm up over her panties.

"Are you always this cold to your clients or do I rate special treatment?" he asked, confusing the issue by sliding his left palm in between the post and herself and pressing his fingers firmly against her lower abdomen, atop the region under which her "g" spot slumbered, while continuing to spank her with his other hand, striking her repeatedly in the exact middle portion of each cheek, neither too low or too high to please her.

"Stick your bottom out and spread your legs," he ordered at length. When she complied he dropped his left palm down to completely enclose her sable triangle. Surprised, she pulled away, but Carter spanked her back against his hand. "Don't tell me you're shy about being touched," he accused cynically. She glared at him and gave her head a toss but didn't reply. He squeezed her silken muff and insinuated one long finger into the tiny slit. They looked at each other because she was wet. She wanted to tell him not to be too flattered, that she was perpetually wet, but had decided to speak the minimum amount of words necessary. "Well? Are you averse to being penetrated or not?" he demanded, smacking her several times more.

"No," she replied, though not in any manner that could be considered encouraging.

"I didn't think so," he said, deliberately inserting his finger deep inside her. She tried not to throb but couldn't help doing so. The next thing she knew he was unhooking the cuffs from the post and leading her by her wrists over to the bondage bed, which he briskly bent her over. Then he caused her to first step out of her panties, then separate her legs as far as she could on the floor, thus revealing all her pink, creamy charms to him.

Now Carter selected a broad black leather paddle and began to strap her upturned, spread bottom with a stinging report. But he soon became dissatisfied with the position and desiring her still more accessible to his eyes, hands and implements, made her mount the leather padded table and kneel with her chest down and her knees spread wide. This position revealed even more than the previous ones and Carter began to pay special attention to her bottomhole, smartening it up with the spanker on the end of his crop. This imparted to Brooke a highly interesting sensation that had little to do with pain and she couldn't help but react with a gasp and a pant as he began to stimulate this key erogenous zone.

"I can't see you properly," he told her, somewhat cruelly. "Lie down flat on you stomach, put your hands back and spread yourself open for me."

Brooke sat back on her heels and looked at him. He gazed coolly back. "Today," he advised, giving her a smack on the thigh. Brooke got into position with a glowing face, unable to process this degree of humiliation in any way other than to blush.

Circling the table Carter took in every aspect of his submissive, including the comically pained expression with which she awaited the renewal of the spanking. Her eyes were squeezed shut to block out the shame, which he found charming.

"Open your eyes," he ordered. She did so to look daggers at him. "I can see you're not used to being embarrassed," he remarked, walking around her again, this time to run one hand up her leg from her trim ankle to her soft knee back to her satiny thigh and flank. Her black patent leather spectator pumps had ravishing 5-inch heels and Carter could not help but caress each one upon her slender feet as well. "I expect you're more accustomed to being worshipped than humiliated," he observed, repositioning her hands on her bottom cheeks to afford the maximum exposure to his fascinated gaze. "But that's just not the kind of day you're having," Carter told her, positioning himself behind her and beginning all over again with the crop against her anus. Repeatedly he brought the square leather spanker down on her tiny rear portal, just hard enough to make her flinch and squirm but not so hard that she was tempted to remove the target area. "I don't know why I knew you were anal, I just knew," he murmured, infuriating her.

Finally he tossed the crop aside, moved her hands and standing to one side of her, spread her open himself with one hand while alternating spanking her pussy and bottomhole with the other until she gave up a shuddering climax, which didn't take more than a minute.

A mere fifteen minutes had passed since he'd entered the dungeon. While Brooke composed herself, sitting up on the bondage bed, Carter coolly put his jacket back on. He handed her her panties and she slipped them back on, unable to meet his eyes, her flush not yet receded.

"I want to see you outside," he told her, handing her his card. "Do you understand me, Brooke?"

"No!" she sputtered, still in shock from having been made to give up so much of herself to him so soon. "You're horrid and I hate you!"

Carter smiled and handed her her skirt and vest. She put them on while resentfully glaring at him. "Why?"

"You're just as fast and crude as the characters you write about!"

"You're upset that I got you off?"

"It was the way you did it! Anyway, I'm not supposed to get off. No one is. It's just supposed to be a play session."

"I feel like I played," he admitted, stuffing some bills in her hand. "Look, if it's the allowance issue, we'll come to a regular arrangement. I hope you trust me not to take advantage of you."

Brooke uncurled the bills and counted the same eight hundred he was going to give her the other night.

"Thank you," she said, "you're very generous."

"What's the matter?" he lifted her chin.

"You want me to be your B&D prostitute," she accused him.

"Have I asked you to do anything for me?" he cried indignantly. "Do I seem like a bad person to you? I met my last girlfriend here and I assure you, young lady, she was none the worse for it. You'd better get down off your high horse. You're leggy and look good in leather, but you're still just a college brat. You should be honored that someone like myself is taking an interest in you!"

Carter had worked himself up to such a degree that the only logical follow through was to grab a hairbrush, turn her over his knee and spank her hard!

"You've got the worst attitude of anyone I ever met here!" he continued to excoriate her, whacking her smartly through her shiny, skintight black mini skirt. Brooke stubbornly took her spanking without making a whimper, for the first sixty seconds. Then she couldn't help kicking and squirming as the hairbrush came relentlessly down on either cheek. He had to renew his grasp on her waist just to hold her on his lap. Finally she began to gasp and sob, unable to control herself any longer, completely reduced to the state of a punished child.

"You don't want to be my friend? Have a key to my house? Be courted by me? Fine, I'll come here and thrash you instead!" he told her, laying on a final dozen swats that reduced her to copious tears across his lap.

Carter let Brooke up and saw her wet face. "An orgasm and real tears all in twenty minutes," he thought, impressed, "she's the most responsive girl I've ever played with." But aloud he said, "I didn't mean to make you cry."

Brooke couldn't meet his eyes and was horrified by the prospect of being taken in his arms and consoled after all he had done to her. "May I go now?" she murmured.

"You won't even let me hug you?" he asked with renewed exasperation. But Brooke looked so miserable at the prospect, her lower lip beginning to tremble again, that he scowled, "Just go!" And she fled the dungeon at once, leaving him feeling like the worst heel since Sir Stephen.

Carter wondered, driving home, why he had been so brutally cynical with Brooke, why he had felt the need to shame her so deeply. Was it to attract or repel her? He remembered that he was the one who had initially insulted Brooke by walking out on their first session. But he had tried to make up for his unfair behavior by inviting her home, giving her the tape and trying to bribe her to play with him, kindly, civilly. True, he had given her to understand that he still mistrusted her, still regarded her as a climber who might be using him as in industry in. But he had also assured her that it hardly mattered anymore, since he had decided that he liked her very much. But still she was obstinate, making him come to see her at the club and so forth. That was what had driven him to humiliate her into coming for him. And what a turn on that had been. The girl was divine. Why had he abused her so? But he hadn't. He had offered her what every woman wanted, a corner of his life. And she had reacted like the spoiled brat that she was. It was no use. The more he revolved the paradoxical afternoon, the more he felt convinced that the girl was still more greatly at fault than himself.

Meanwhile Brooke went through the rest of the day in a trance, for now she was deeply in love. And yet her success in arousing Carter's passion seemed to hinge on resisting him. She didn't know how long she could maintain an air of indifference around such an exciting male. It wasn't that she didn't still hate him for doing what he'd done. But she gave him credit for originality. If he was auditioning for the position of boyfriend, proving he could get her off was not a bad reading. She took it back about his being crude. No, he was merely blunt but very focused. Certainly he'd read her correctly. She didn't really care for kissy face anyway, so why was she whining to herself about his lack of chivalry?

Brooke decided that the only honorable thing to do would be to break off with Gilbert. Clearly Carter had developed a passion for her that seeing all she had to give had not satiated. She was young but highly intuitive. She knew when she aroused that certain something in a male that made him want to nurture and keep her. There was suddenly no question in her mind that Carter could quickly be made to fall in love with her. Perhaps it was already so. Hadn't he spoken about keys to his place? Brooke realized that she had reached a milestone in her life, her first real, post-high school love affair was about to commence. And it was going to be with a man who was possibly not even nice.

"You're back already?" Brooke cried, throwing open the door of The Keep that Wednesday afternoon to Carter Webster, who was dazzlingly groomed in a grey cashmere suit and bore dozens of hybrid pink roses for her.

"I had a feeling if I caught you right after school you'd be dressed like a regular girl for a change," Carter said, handing her the flowers and taking advantage of her arms being full to kiss her on the cheek. Brooke had come directly from campus and was adorably clad in a short, grey pleated skirt, a black wool polo shirt, bobby sox and black oxfords with stacked heels. In this outfit her slim white legs went on forever and had the same mesmerizing effect upon Carter as on the previous occasion of their meeting here.

He followed her into the kitchen where she put the flowers into several milky green cut glass vases then helped her carry them back into the sitting rooms. Both were uncomfortable and at a loss for words, though she recovered her sang-froid first and opening a black book bag, pulled out a sheaf of paper, which she thrust into his hands.

"What's this?" he asked.

"My Lubitsch paper. Note the grade, Mr. Webster. I was the only one in class who was able to track down Trouble in Paradise, thanks to you," she announced gaily. He glanced down at the paper and saw a big red "A" at the top.

"May I read it?" he asked.

"No," she took it back and put it away. "I just wanted to show off."

"But I want to read it."

"No. It would only make you realize how smart I am and then you'd pester me to go out with you again. I'd refuse again and you would, uh, lose your temper."

"That's going to happen either way," Carter snapped, displeased by her flippancy.

"Oh really?" she tried to look defiant but was suddenly overcome by embarrassment as she remembered how effectively he'd subdued her the last time they were alone in a dungeon.

"Why do you think I came back so soon?" he asked.

"To make me cry again?" she asked with a sinking heart.

"Suppose we get a dungeon."

"The schoolroom okay?" Brooke asked.

"Perfect," he replied without smiling.

She brought her book bag with her and led him upstairs to the attic that had been decorated in the style of an Edwardian home schoolroom. The painted wooden rocking horse was oversized and large enough for a big girl to straddle. Brooke disliked the schoolroom because it contained many humiliating devices, such as a stool to one side of the blackboard with a dunce cap on it. Many a client had caused her to sit on it, after a spanking, with her skirt up and the dunce cap on.

After taking the allowance and going downstairs to have Rusty start their session, Brooke hastily returned to her impatient client, who had already transferred the Lubitsch paper from Brooke's book bag to his inner jacket pocket.

"I'm back," she said, pressing her back to the door and dropping her gaze as a blush of vulnerability suffused her cheeks.

Carter melted at her trepidation but affected indifference as he sat her down at one of the two school desks and then assumed a position of authority behind the podium lectern.

"To continue with our discussion of books into film," said Carter, taking up the pointer, "who can name an American film of the 30's which contains a schoolroom corporal punishment scene?"

"Tom Sawyer!" Brooke cried eagerly.

"Miss Neuman, don't talk out of turn. Raise your hand politely first," Carter chided. "Tom Sawyer is correct. And I see here a birch of the same variety as was used on little Tom's breeched backside here in this stand." He pulled out a birch of golden brown twigs, smoothed and lightly glazed for a handsome appearance. "You're familiar with the scene, Miss Neuman?"

"Yes, Mr. Webster."

"Well, are you going to get up here or do you want me to come and drag you back by your ear, like in the movie?" he demanded.

Brooke sprung up and came to him. He took her under his arm, flipped up her skirt and mercilessly pulled her black cotton high cut French briefs down to her milky mid thighs. He heard her catch her breath with indignation as her slim, oval cheeked, white bottom was summarily exposed.

"Tom Sawyer didn't get it on the bare!" she protested.

"Never mind that. Just hold still," he told her, then delivered a series of hard, fast swats with the whippy birch rod, using the rhythm identical to the one used by the schoolmaster in Tom Sawyer.

Carter was pleased with the bouquet of pink lines, which now blossomed across Brooke's fair skin. "Becky always should have been the one to get the whipping," he declared.

Brooke was gasping (with excitement) from the stinging but not unpleasant birching. How clever of him to use the birch quickly and rather lightly at first!

"The problem with movie spankings is that they're always over far too soon," said Carter, subjecting her to another volley of birch strokes, this time switching the position of his arm from over her back to under her tummy. As slim as she was, this gave his supporting hand access to her delicious young charms, growing ever moister as he birched her bare bottom.

They both remembered the ease with which his fingers had slipped up into her the last time they had played. Now Carter couldn't resist giving free play to his hand below while still continuing to birch her from above. She was forced to grind against his hand and inevitably, a finger slipped in, and out, and in again. After two or three minutes of this, Brooke became embarrassingly wet, which caused her to whimper, at least once, in shame.

Carter led her over to her school desk and bent her over it, throwing aside the birch and spanking her upturned bottom with his hand until she was carnation pink from buttocks to upper thighs. He pulled her panties down to her knees, careless of the way they hobbled her, to have full command of her thighs.

Brooke thought him excessively cruel to spank her thighs. She was on the point of asking him not to spank them when she realized that this might make him double up on spanking them. Others had been so perverse. Besides, she had resolved never to ask him for mercy. She had much rather burst into tears, because at least that inflicted guilt.

Then something shocked her! Carter had stopped spanking her. He was standing behind her and unzipping his trousers! "What? What are you doing?" she cried.

"Relax, I'm not going to fuck you," he assured her. "Just let me look at you," he said, stunning her by hauling his huge erection out of his pants and casually looming with it over her bottom.

"I can't believe you're doing this!" she cried. Not that it didn't happen now and then, but it rather took Carter down to the level of a dungeon masturbator. She was familiar with this stamp of B&D Romeo, who sought his thrills in the semi dark, stroking himself off, with the girl's face turned away. Normally she would not have made a murmur. But with Carter it somehow seemed wrong. Why was he treating her so coarsely? It was true that he'd gotten her off last time. She supposed it was his turn. But she expected him to exhibit greater self-control and felt disappointed.

"Don't blame me," he said, reading her mind. "This is all your fault. Forcing me to see you here like this. I wanted to treat you like a lady. But you insist on being treated like a B&D slut."

"I don't want to be treated like anything by you!" she turned to cry, still amazed at the sight of his handsome cock, fully erect, almost nodding at her from his hand. "God, you get hard fast!"

"Are you kidding? I've been hard since the florist shop," he said, gently pushing her head back down, caressing her punished bottom and simply pointing his engorged organ at her. He pulled off her panties and fully spread her legs, opening her petal pink labia with his fingers and slipping one in deep. She was so wet and clinging that he almost gave it up at that moment.

Then something made him pause, abruptly sheath his weapon and collect himself. He'd suddenly caught sight of his own reflection in a round nautical mirror opposite them, standing over Brooke with her pleated skirt up and his dick in his hand. Of all the times he had entered the club, his zipper had never come down. But this girl seemed to bring out the pervert in him like no other.

To calm his tattered nerves he dragged Brooke, by the earlobe, over to the sturdiest wooden chair he could see, turned her over his knee and began to give her the sort of spanking she deserved, which used up the remainder of the hour. He didn't trust himself to bend her over anything else. It was safer like this, with Brooke prone across his lap, her little school skirt flipped up and her bottom growing pinker by the minute. He spanked her until her skin radiated heat.

She meekly submitted, allowing herself to go limp across his lap. It meant something to Brooke that he had stopped just short of jacking off all over her bare, spanked, upturned bottom. Clearly he'd resisted the temptation as a mark of respect. "How big and beautiful he is," Brooke thought with anticipation, so glad that she had broken off with Gilbert.

The knock on the door that came to let them know the hour was up surprised them both. Brooke turned to look at him.

"Tell them we'll extend," said Carter, helping her off his lap and handing her another hundred and twenty dollars. Brooke ran downstairs and gave the money to Rusty, stopping in the dressing room to check her hair and lipstick.

Hildegarde was leaning against the counter with a needle and thread, shortening the straps on a peach satin slip for Cherry, who perched on a stool in a peach lace combination, beige hose and stiletto pumps, leafing through Cosmo. "I knew the boy was in love," Hildegarde commented, when Brooke told her Carter had extended. "It only remains to be seen when he'll take you from me," the pretty young mistress added with a sigh.

"Ask him if he wants another girl in the session," Cherry suggested with that particular brightness that Brooke found so irritating. Cherry, a pretty, petite flirt tended to compete heavily for clients with Brooke and through sheer tenacity managed to snag some away from the willowy coed.

"The contrast would be charming between the two of you," said Hildy, looking from her cupcake to her thoroughbred.

"I'll be sure to run it by him," Brooke promised, exiting the room with a shudder. She had once done a double with Cherry and the small submissive's manipulative obsequiousness had aroused Brooke's most vitriolic contempt.

When Brooke arrived back in the dungeon she was surprised to find Carter busily wiping down the saddle on the hobbyhorse with alcohol. As soon as she closed the door he gave the horse a pat and said, "Sit here."

Brooke was about to mount the horse when he stopped her. "Take your panties off first," he said, selecting a short, thin rattan cane from the wall. Brooke pouted as she pulled her panties off and folded them. Then she walked slowly to the horse.

"You're going to embarrass me again, aren't you?" she demanded.

Carter smiled insolently at her, decanting a fine cigar from a silver tube and snipping the end off. "Do you mind if I smoke?" he asked. She shook her head. The tube went back in his jacket pocket, he lit the cigar and she straddled the horse.

Carter arranged her so that she was leaning forward, with her head against the horse's mane and her bottom thrust up nicely. Now he flipped up her skirt to reveal her bare bottom, still faintly pink and perfectly split by the position he had placed her in. "Now lift up so I can see your pussy," he instructed. When she obeyed him he slipped his hand under her and momentarily cradled her damp sex in his palm. Her dark public curls felt silky against his fingers, several of which he slipped inside her. After she was thoroughly creamy he stepped away from her and began lightly caning her bottom. Pressing one hand down on the small of her back, Carter forced her Venus mound flat against the saddle as he continued tapping the thin rattan rod against her spread cheeks. When she arched her bottom up he brought the cane down harder. Now it made a little whoosh as it went through the air toward her tautly stretched skin. It connected with a snap, quickly, several dozen times in a row, the impact growing imperceptibly with each volley. Now she was straining up and grinding down as he paused and struck, paused and struck.

The rhythm of the strokes accelerated as the caning intensified in severity. Fast and whippy came the swats, leaving a sting behind. It was starting to hurt now, but Brooke felt inflamed and saved her voice for whimpers rather than protests. Then all at once, he stopped caning her.

"Don't move," he told her, scandalizing her by inserting the silver cigar tube into her vagina gently but deeply.

"You can't do that!" she cried helplessly, trying not to wriggle her painfully throbbing clitoris against the saddle.

"Wait, it gets worse," he said, taking one more puff on his cigar before putting it out. Then, extracting the thin, aluminum cylinder from her pussy, he divided her bottom cheeks and began to insert it between them. "This is a classic disciplinary device."

"Oh god, don't!" she cried, twisting to evade the intrusion.

"Hold still," he said, slapping her smartly and spreading her tiny bottomhole for the slick silver tube. "You're so creamy this should slip right in," he declared, delighted by the one last outraged glance she cast him before dropping her head.

"I've always wanted to have a girl like this," Carter admitted, once the tube was fully inserted and Brooke was both spread and filled. He now took up a standard black leather dungeon paddle and began to paddle her soundly. The visual, of Brooke prone and straddling the wooden pony, with her pleated skirt pushed up, long, bare legs, punctuated by the oxfords and white anklets, bent at the knees and hugging either side of the horse, and her exquisite pink bottom filled was one to store up and treasure for all time. Again and again he brought the paddle down across both cheeks, until two spots of bright magenta stood out upon either side of her bottom.

Now he tossed the paddle away and came to stand beside her and spank her by hand, pausing only to finger her pussy deeply. She was soaking wet and her eyes were squeezed shut, just moments away from a climax. Now he held her fast with one hand while spanking her hard with the other. "Come on, little girl," he said, "give it up for me." And Brooke couldn't help but obey him. She ground against the saddle and came. Then she collapsed in shame.

Carter was quick to unstrap her but let her collect herself, de-tube and get off the horse in her own time and style. This was quickly managed and Brooke disappeared for a few minutes into a nearby bathroom. When she returned he was gone, leaving another extraordinarily large tip behind.

Brooke felt somewhat uneasy at Carter having left so abruptly. She wanted to believe he had done so to minimize her embarrassment at having succumbed to yet another humiliating orgasm at his hands. But she couldn't help but think that perhaps after this last excess, he had finally had enough of the Brooke ride, was bored and eager to get onto the next diversion. At any rate, she now had enough money to put down first and last month's rent on that apartment that she and Bettie had been talking about getting on the back streets of West Hollywood.

For days the erotic image of Brooke on the horse haunted Carter. He'd remember what she'd let him do to her and feel a keen thrill of possession. She was so real that it was hard to fault her, even for being a film student. Certainly he had mixed feelings about her being a professional, but not though any distrust of her integrity. He had interviewed enough girls at The Keep to know which were there for the money and which for the thrill. Brooke fell into the later category. In fact, she didn't know the first thing about working a wealthy client. What liberties he took with her were freely allowed and not bartered for additional allowance, which was the mark of a true enthusiast. There were girls who worked for Hildegarde who would have charged him by the mark if given the chance. It would never have occurred to Brooke to negotiate the cost of inserting an object into her, for example. But it disturbed him that Brooke was available to all who asked for her. As with Aurora, Carter was more concerned for her welfare and safety in this questionable environment rather than jealous of her favors or possessive of her purity.

Carter expected that it would be even more difficult to make Brooke give up the silly job at the Keep than it had been with Aurora, which in itself had taken some figuring out. Meanwhile, he hadn't even gotten her to consent to a date, though he'd already given her two climaxes. But after reading her beautiful paper on Lubitsch he was more determined than ever to make her his. The glimpse it gave him into her mind and sensibilities convinced him that she had every right to voraciously pursue a career in film production and that it actually behooved him to help her towards realizing that goal, if only to assure himself of a chapter instead of a footnote in her future life story. He messengered the paperback to Brooke at The Keep with a note saying, "*I would have given you an A plus. Do you realize I don't even have your phone number? My card is enclosed. If you know what's good for you, you'll call and give me leave to take you out on a civilized date. Soon, young lady. If I don't hear from you by next Wednesday, I'm showing up for our next session with a medical bag. And if you think I embarrassed you before, you have no idea.*

Sincerely,
Carter."

Carter Webster couldn't understand why Brooke wouldn't see him outside the Club. Or why, no matter how many orgasms he gave her in session, or how much extra allowance he pressed into her hand, he couldn't seem to erase the initial bad impression he'd made upon the U.C.L.A. coed, part time B&D girl and future film maker, by walking out on their first session, for no good reason.

Because the wildly successful screenwriter was hunted daily by ambitious young Hollywood women, and because Brooke herself had ambitions to some day become a film maker, he'd initially suspected Brooke of having designs on him as a powerful networking device. However, Brooke was not behaving like any female go-getter he had ever met.

Apart from being available for sessions with him, she seemed to barely notice he was alive, behaving as though she could take or leave him, in spite of the patina of power and prestige which clung to him like fairy dust wherever he went.

Every time he showed up at The Keep, a battle of wills ensued. She seemed determined to show her distain for her handsome and influential client, while he was equally committed to possessing her, in various humiliating ways, with meticulous indifference. It didn't take much penetration to see that they were falling in love.

As hard as he tried, Carter found it physically impossible to stay away from the Club for more than three days at a time. So he was actually glad when business called him out of town between their second and third session, leaving Brooke to wait a whole week before seeing him again.

While away he hadn't called her. She hadn't called him either, which irritated him tremendously, for he could sense that the willowy brunette was no longer indifferent to him. Based on this instinct, he had threatened that if she persisted in refusing to see him outside, and made him come back to the club yet again, he would arrive the next time with a medical bag, to humiliate her ten times worse than he had already done, which was saying a good deal.

Brooke wasn't exactly sure of what he meant by that stern promise. Possibly that he would invade her with some sort of clinical apparatus like a dilator or even an enema! This supposition was based upon the direction that their last two sessions had followed. Uncannily, he had guessed just how anally oriented Brooke was during their very first encounter, which had ended with him making her come by simply cropping her bottomhole. At the end of their second session, he had given her a climax by inserting a silver cigar tube into her bottom and paddling her hard.

Brooke was frankly intrigued about the medical bag. After two sessions with the deft young dominant, the top-earning girl at the club was becoming addicted to his methods. Other men had given her enjoyable sessions, but never to the point of orgasm. Besides, Carter was good looking, a Yale man and a brilliant writer. Through his generosity and continued interest he had pretty much cancelled out the churlishness of walking out on their first session, but a certain cynicism still tinged their budding relationship going both ways.

Neither could quite bring themselves to admit aloud that they were glad to see each other or that they had missed each other upon his next appearance at the club, timing his visit so as to be Brooke's first session of the day.

Brooke's eyes went to the black bag, which looked heavy, as she ushered him in. "What's in there?" she asked casually, leading him straight upstairs.

"Wouldn't you like to know?" he asked, following her to the second floor landing.

"All the dungeons are open. Which one would you prefer?" she asked, opening the four doors off the hall.

"The examining room, of course," he replied, selecting some paddles and other implements from the pegs on the wall.

Brooke led him into that newly decorated room, which was painted apple green with pale rose accents. The examining table was covered in pink leather while the cabinets that lined the room were of white painted wood with green trim. Some of the glass doored cabinets contained real medical equipment, while others housed objects that would have been more appropriate to an inquisitor's closet. Before she had a chance to close the door he handed her the money to start the session and she ran down stairs to give it to Rusty.

By the time she had returned Carter had taken several popular Pleasure Chest items out of his bag and disposed of them handily. Brooke blushed to notice a translucent bottle green hot water bag now suspended from the IV stand with a large nozzle attached. Also sitting insouciantly on one of the white, rollaway cabinets, was a pink toned rabbit pearl vibrator and beside it a small glass jar of cinnamon lube.

"So, why didn't you call me?" he asked, still arranging his equipment. "Did you lose my number?"

"No," she hesitated before adding, "but I'm not really a phone person. Do you have an email address?"

Carter looked her as much to say, "I should slap you silly," but only replied, "That you could have gotten from Augie Rose any time."

"Oh. Right," she agreed with a hint of impudence in her dark eyes.

"Too bad you didn't think of that," he said, throwing the bolt on the door. "You could have saved yourself a lot of humiliation."

Brooke didn't admit that the current scenario pleased her more than dinner at The Ivy and sixth row center seats at the ballet would have done, but Carter was perceptive enough to read the pliancy in her body. She seemed neither tense nor afraid. Her embarrassment had flushed her cheeks pink, but her eyes were sparking with excitement as they followed his every move and expression.

"Mr. Webster, why are you doing this to me?"

"Why are you still calling me Mr. Webster?"

"I was just being respectful."

"Really? That's not like you."

"Sorry," she murmured.

"That's okay. I can see you're trying. You actually wore a color today. And my favorite one too."

She was clad in a 50's style pink gingham playsuit of snug, cuffed shorts and a halter top with matching pink ankle strap sandals and dark red toe nails.

He took her by the hand, found a seat on a green straight-backed chair and pulled her rather gently down across his lap.

"It's better we talk like this," he told her, smoothing down her cotton shorts with his hand and giving her a friendly warm up with his bare hand. Brooke noted that this was the first time he'd begun in so affectionate a manner and wondered whether it had to do with her wearing pink instead of black. She recalled that he himself generally wore only black or grey. Perhaps he'd been so assertive with her their first few sessions because he subconsciously felt she was competing with him for dominance!

He brought her back to the present, reflecting, "You know, outside in the world, with all its distractions, I might behave more gallantly." Smack, smack! His hand now left a sting behind. "But you insist all our encounters must take place in a dungeon." Smack, smack, smack! "So what choice do I have but to discipline you severely every time I see you?"

"That's okay. I deserve it," she murmured softly and agreeably.

Brooke would never admit to hoping that a disinterested someone would some day walk into the club, desiring to punish and purge a submissive. This was the first time it had happened on her shift and she was positively eager to comply.

Brooke traced her interest in enema discipline to discovering a collection of magazines in the back of her father's closet at age eleven. They were mostly from the 70's and frighteningly tacky, yet fascinating glossy black and white scenarios of men with bad hairdos giving women with worse ones enemas. The photos were weird on a Diane Arbus level but intensely intriguing to Brooke. Over the next several years, every now and then she would feel drawn to the closet and when she was certain that she was alone, she'd review the magazines. Later that night, alone in bed, she'd remember the photos, fantasize and masturbate, enjoying the first orgasms of her life just thinking about girls being punished with enemas.

Later, at age fourteen, she discovered her first Victorian novels, read about sodomy and various other forms of anal eroticism and began to understand that an interest in such subjects was simply an expression of her own individual sexuality rather than an aberration. By fifteen she had a boyfriend ready to initiate her into every esoteric form of sex she cared to submit to and by sixteen she had had her bottom taken in several ways. But the one place they hadn't gone together was the "E" place. That she wished to reserve for a total or near stranger, one whom she might never have to meet again, in case the experiment went terribly wrong.

As Carter continued to spank her, Brooke became painfully aroused. Enema videos were almost impossible to find, but she'd managed to finally rent The Wet One, a scatological saga of fetishistic obsession, wherein Jamie Gillis kidnaps girls to give them enemas. Violent and sleazy enough to give a normal person nightmares, the vintage pornography, supposedly based on a true story, both repelled and enraptured Brooke, who found the opening scene, of a candy striper face down on the examining table, ready to be probed and filled by the stern medical staff, to be deeply thrilling. Now it was about to happen to her.

She wondered, as her bottom grew warm under Carter's smacks, whether she ought to protest the treatment, for form's sake. No, she thought, this was his idea. She was simply submitting to it. Unconsciously she wriggled on his lap, freshets of bliss coursing through her in contemplation of the awesome punishment she was about to receive.

Carter was in love with her little waist and long legs. He noted her shorts buttoned in the back; undoing and tugging them down, he exposed her pale pink, figured silk panties.

"Pink panties instead of black? I'm touched," he remarked, spanking her.

"You feel hard enough to touch others," Brooke replied, grinding her flat tummy against his robust erection.

"Never mind that!" he said, slapping her smartly. "I want you to behave."

"All right."

"And this time you do not have permission to come," he warned.

"That's not really in my control," she replied, turning to look at him.

"No?" He picked up a round leather paddle and gave her a dozen resounding smacks. "Well, what say we give it the old college try anyway? Just so I can maintain the illusion of punishing you."

He pulled her shorts down and off, tossing them aside. Then he pulled the snug pink panties down to her upper thighs and instilled fresh roses in her cheeks with the spanking paddle.

"Forgive me, but I need to spank your bottom deep, rose-red in preparation for your enema. You'll see that it makes all the difference," he assured her. Brooke looked up and noticed opposing mirrors angled above and below the examining table and wondered if he could possibly intend to make her watch the entire proceeding as well as submit to it.

Several minutes passed as he continued to bring the paddle down repeatedly on her bare cheeks.

Then he tossed the paddle aside and spreading her cheeks with one hand, spanked her bottomhole with the other for several minutes more. Brooke whimpered at the hard smacks but didn't try to wriggle away. Her clit had begun to throb and her pussy to ache with desire. Craving penetration, she thrust her bottom up for the smacks as they fell. Carter only stopped when he noticed how slick her pussy had become. Thrusting a finger into her vagina he probed that velvet glove firmly. "I hate to think you let just anyone do this to you," he couldn't help but remarking.

"I don't," she murmured reassuringly.

"Good!" He disengaged his hand and pulled her panties entirely off, helping her off his lap. "Well, you're ready," he declared, leading her over to the examining table, lifting her to sit on it, then bidding her to kneel on all fours for him. He then disappeared with the hot water bottle.

Carter returned shortly, hung the filled bag on the IV stand, removed his jacket and rolled up his sleeves. Slipping one hand between her legs from behind he squeezed her muff softly. Her wetness embarrassed her.

"Anyone ever give you an enema before, Brooke?"

"No."

"Well, if you don't want to disgrace yourself just remember to keep your bottom tilted upward while you're on the table."

"Okay, but isn't that too much water?"

"It's a standard two quart bag."

"That seems like a lot for me."

"It's what you're getting though," he told her, adjusting her head so she could look into the mirror on the floor in front of the table, which reflected the mirror above the other end of it, which showed her rosy bottom in contrast to her ivory thighs. While she watched he went behind her, spread her bottom and parted her labia. Then he poised the rounded head of the rabbit pearl vibrator at the entrance to her vagina and gently inserted it a few inches into her. "Feel that, naughty girl?" he demanded, smacking her bottom a few times.

"God, yes!" she panted, praying he wouldn't turn it on just then. She had heard about the legendary vibrating, undulating rabbit pearl for years but had never tried one. They cost about $75! But she knew she could never have one in her, vibrating and undulating, without succumbing to a climax in seconds flat. This was not fair!

"Oh, please, no!" she begged. Gesturing for him to remove it.

"What's wrong? Is it too thick?"

"Yes! Too thick!" she cried. Carter withdrew the vibrator all at once and laid it to one side. She was teetering dangerously on the edge of an orgasm even from that much. Now he made things even worse by stroking her muff and kneading her abdomen. "This flat, little tummy is about to become very full," he warned.

Now he unscrewed the top of the cinnamon lube. Again she protested. "Oh god, not that!"

"Why not?"

"It will feel all hot!"

"Yes, that's kind of the point."

"It might make me come," she speculated.

"If you do, you'll be severely punished," he warned, smacking her sternly. But heeding her words, he applied only a microscopic dab of the scented lubricant to her tiny, pink anus with the tip of his finger. The 6" nozzle of the hose he lubricated generously with Brooke's own copious juices, which he got by inserting it deeply into her pussy. She moaned and wriggled, getting smacked again. "Don't move so much," he warned. "You're to be completely passive. Understand?"

"Yes."

"Now hold perfectly still," he told her, removing the nozzle from her pussy and slowly inserting it into her anus. Making sure it was lodged to the hilt he checked her position, including the proper arch of her back and rear end, gave her stomach one more pat and pointed her face toward the mirror so she could observe what was happening. Pinching her earlobe to make her open her eyes and actually look, he told her, "Watch."

"I can't! It's too embarrassing!"

"You're a film maker. You watch," he ordered.

"Now I remember why I hate you!" she cried, squeezing her eyes shut rebelliously.

"You want me to put you back over my knee and use a hairbrush on you this time? Huh?" Carter smacked her hard on either cheek, determined not to let the color fade.

"No," she murmured.

"Then do what I tell you."

Brooke opened her eyes and beheld her own bottom, with one of Carter's hands on each cheek, adjusting the white hose depending from the centermost portion of it. "I can't!" she cried, "I just can't watch this! Please, I beg you, mercy!"

"All right, don't look if you don't want to," he replied with irritation. "But you're missing something worth seeing!"

"I'm sorry," she murmured.

"Forget it. You're sensitive. I forgot," he patted her bottom.

"And young. Very young!" she reminded him.

"Really? How old are you?"

"Going on nineteen."

"See, that makes me mad," he warned her, smacking her soundly five or six times on each cheek.

"What?"

"You're much too young to be even playing in a place like this, no less working here. I can't tell you how much it distresses me, feeling about you as I do."

"I've been here since my 18th birthday," she declared.

"That's just shocking," he reflected, folding his arms and appraising the picture Brooke made. "But we can discuss that later. Perhaps tonight you'll visit me at home for the first time. I'll be there from ten p.m. on. I left my card with the address and phone number in the bag. And you can keep all the equipment I'm leaving here too. Did you hear me Brooke?"

"Oh, sure. Phone in the bag," she replied, with her eyes still shut, not knowing how much longer she could continue to ignore the persistent aching in her clit, due the positioning and nozzle. Not to mention how warm her bottom still glowed from the long spanking. He was torturing her by delaying and she was enjoying it immensely.

"Well," he said with a sigh, "I won't postpone this any longer." Now Brooke heard him release the clasp on the hose to allow the warm water to flow into her through the nozzle so deeply embedded in her bottom. She felt it right away, not painfully but excitingly. But it was all so embarrassing. Especially when he slipped his hand under her tummy to cup and gently squeeze it as the water filled her.

Presently it became somewhat uncomfortable. She squirmed in such a way that Carter stopped the flow. "Are you all right, Brooke?"

"Yes."

"Does it hurt?"

"No, not exactly, but maybe that's enough for now."

"We'll just wait a minute," he decided, picking up a small, oval hairbrush and smacking her cheeks.

"Oh!" she cried. "Oh god!" she squirmed.

"Intense?" he asked, pausing with the brush against her bottom.

"Yes!"

"Ready to take the rest of the enema?"

"But that's a lot!"

"It's the recommended amount."

"I'll have an accident."

"You wouldn't dare," he said, resuming the hairbrush spanking. "Anyway, you should have perfect control. Just concentrate. You know what muscles to contract."

"Oh, please????"

"All right, we'll compromise. No more water."

"Thank you!"

"But you go back over my knee."

"Oh, no!"

"Come on, off the table," Carter said, scooping her off the table and taking her back to the chair. Before resuming the seat he grabbed the hairbrush again and something wrapped in cellophane out of the medical bag. Then he sat down and pulled her down across his lap carefully. "Arch your bottom and hold still," he ordered, positioning her to his satisfaction, placing the brush close at hand and unwrapping the cellophane package.

"What's that?" she asked, craning her neck to see.

"Retention plug," he replied, holding the five-inch rubber pacifier in front of her face. "To preclude any accidents while I'm spanking you."

"Oh god!" she cried, deeply mortified.

"Feeling uncomfortable yet?"

"A little."

"Does this help?" he asked, slipping his arm under her waist to support her upper torso and take most of the pressure off her stomach.

"Yes. Thank you."

"It's not that I don't trust you to maintain perfect control," he explained, spreading her cheeks and positioning the tip of the rectal plug between them, "but you'll get a better spanking this way." Brooke sobbed with humiliation when he pushed it all the way into her bottom, the confluence of sensations very nearly bringing her off. "Still with me, honey?" he asked, tapping her lightly with the brush.

"Yes," she replied, gasping at the ticklish thrill she was getting from the butt plug.

"Oh, wait," he said, unbuttoning the back of her halter-top and slipping it off. Deliberately reaching down, he tweaked each perky nipple and firmly squeezed each perfectly proportioned breast. Brooke groaned with deeply submissive excitement. "Are you my girl?" he asked.

"Yes," she sighed.

Carter almost did the same, in relief. "So, this is for playing so goddamned hard to get," he told her, before bringing the brush down, vigorously, and continuously on her bare, plugged bottom for several minutes. The spanking built in intensity rapidly, going from taps to smacks to thwacks as he held her firmly in place. He spanked her on alternate cheeks and then directly on the plug, driving her punishment home in the most intimate way, at least every third swat.

"Come for me," he told her, as he felt her tense to do just that. Once again, she climaxed under his hand. Carter was gratified and bent to kiss her shoulders and neck. "You did well. I can't believe that was the first time you ever did that," he said, gently helping her to her feet.

"It was!" she said, grateful he was releasing her without making her looking at him, for her face was still rosy with embarrassment. "May I go now?"

"Sure," he smiled as she ducked into the adjoining bathroom.

When Brooke emerged, some time later, Carter was gone and Mistress Hildegarde was setting the room to rights.

"Well, young lady," purred the voluptuous club owner, "you seem to have made quite an impression on Mr. Webster. And I can see why." Hildy gazed at Brooke's nude charms with unselfconscious appreciation.

"He did it again," said Brooke, slipping her under things and playsuit back on. "He made me come. Embarrassingly. Anally."

"I rather inferred that," said Hildy, patting dry the cleaned equipment and folding it up to go back in the medical bag.

"He said I could keep all the equipment in the bag," said Brooke gleefully. "I've always wanted a rabbit pearl."

"Honey?" Hildy peered into the bag. "Did you know that Mr. Webster left you a video camera?"

"What?" Brooke sprang over to Hildegarde, who was taking an expensive DV cam out of the black leather bag. "Oh, he must not have realized it was in there. Well, I was going by his house tonight anyway. I'll take it back then."

"Going by his house, are you? Bad girl!"

"I'm sorry, mistress, but he won't give up and we've used up every extreme thing I'm willing to do in a dungeon. After this, it has to be actual sex between us and that wouldn't be appropriate within these hallowed walls."

"You're quite sensible, my darling," murmured Hildegarde, kissing her favorite fondly. "But I'm going to miss you."

"I'm not leaving."

"You will be, dearest."

Brooke left work at nine p.m. and rushed home to shower and change. She despaired at the sight of her wardrobe, which contained mostly black and grey. Then she remembered the stack of Christmas sweaters from her mother still neatly wrapped in tissue in her cedar chest and merrily dug into it.

"Mother! You're good for something after all!" she sang as she found a complete selection of pastel polo sweaters in cashmere or merino wool, matching shell and shrugs sets in shades from blue to gold, cardigans in berry red and creamy beige and all manner of knit pullovers in a range of neutral hues. Smoking a joint and trying the sweaters on, Brooke felt so elated that she called her mother in NY and left a message on her answering machine thanking her for the sweaters and admitting that she had finally found the kind of boyfriend would admire them.

After a long, perfumed bath, Brooke slipped into an extravagant, hip length, Felina corset she had bought with part of the tip money Carter had given her the previous week. It was made of sheer pink tulle, ruched and edged with cream and rose lace. With her pretty bosom, slim waist and long torso, Brooke's lithe form was ideally suited to model corsetry. The eight garter straps were of rose satin, garnished with insouciant rosettes.

She matched the exquisite foundation garment with a pair of real silk stockings, squared at the heel and seamed, along with 5" high heeled black maryjanes. Brooke anticipated that Carter would be profoundly moved upon discovering the perfect fetish outfit beneath the fawn brown pleated skirt and rose sweater set that she was about to put on. Brooke arrived at Carter's Malibu Canyon home by ten seventeen. She parked in the driveway, as before, grabbed the medical bag, which was heavy, and teetered up to the front door.

The door opened just as Brooke was about to knock. Carter was alone and had been listening for her car.

"You came," he said.

"I should be all out of blushes, but somehow I feel my face getting warm again," she admitted, unable to meet his eyes. He pulled her in, shut the door and took her in his arms. They stood clasping each other for several minutes, his arms tightly wrapped around her for the first time.

"Wait! Don't leave the bag outside. The camera's in it!" she cried, reluctantly pulling away.

"The camera? You brought back the camera?" Carter sounded annoyed as he opened the door again and brought the bag inside. "That was a present for you. Now that you're here, you can have the light kit and tripod that goes with it too."

"You're giving me a camera? Why?"

"You need a new one, don't you? That's what Bettie told Augie when I asked him to ask her what you needed."

"You can't be this sweet. It doesn't go with my image of you."

"It's no big deal. I bought it on a whim. Never even used it. Knock yourself out."

"Thank you."

"Is everything else still in the bag?" he asked dangerously.

"More or less," she replied.

"Let's go straight upstairs then. I'm sure you're exhausted after your busy day."

"As a matter of fact, I am a feeling a little over tired," she agreed, adoring the idea of being fussed over by Carter.

"You just get comfortable," he said, leaving her in his bedroom suite, "and I'll get you a little snack."

"Really? I am hungry!" she declared, gratefully dropping down on an invitingly upholstered chaise.

Carter returned a few minutes later with a dish of pasta and sautéed chicken. He carried a bottle of chilled white wine and two glasses. Setting the dish before her on a wooden tray and pouring a glass of wine, he watched as she took a bite.

"Mmm, that's wonderful. Where did you get it?"

"I made it myself," he announced proudly. "I often cook."

"I wish I knew how to cook," she said, having no choice but to take tiny, delicate bites, as tightly corseted as she was.

"You can help next time," he told her, taking the camera out of the bag and setting it aside. "I'll be back," he said, disappeared into another part of the house while she continued to nibble at the pasta.

He reappeared pushing a wheeled cart containing a tripod and some lights. "You who video everything should want documentation of our first official date," Carter told her, working with impressive speed and dexterity to set up the equipment.

"If you're going to do that, let me reveal what I have on," said Brooke, carrying the plate out of the picture frame and then unself-consciously stripping off her outer garments to display herself in the beribboned, gauze-on-brocade, hip length Victorian corset with the sheer sewn in bra that allowed her cherry nipples to peek through so naughtily.

"Rolling on three," said Carter, "Carter and Brooke, Act 5, Scene 2. Action."

Brooke looked solemnly into the lens.

"I said action, dear. Show us the corset, do," Carter teased, still adjusting his camera. Brooke obeyed, smiling quietly as she pivoted and displayed her body from various angles, including bent over with her bottom towards the lens and face forwards with her cleavage towards it. She showed off her fetish shoes and shook out her long hair, still not saying a word. Already thinking like a film editor, she knew it would save trouble not to have anything extraneous on the tape that was to be archived as the first one shot with her new camera.

"What have you been up to since I saw you last?" Carter asked, as she disposed herself once more on the recamier.

"I did three more sessions," she replied.

"They must not have been corporal punishment ones, you're bottom's lily white."

"Not everyone spanks as hard as you," she smiled.

"Tell me, what brought you to the place where I found you?"

"Adventure and romance," she replied with poise.

"You're something, all right," he chuckled. "But tell me more about yourself. What gives an eighteen year old the nerve to go work in a club?"

"I was born and raised in Hollywood. Fetish has surrounded me from the start. I've always been attracted to dominant men and never questioned this. The club seems the perfect way to put myself through college. I can make more there than at any other job and learn about the scene at the same time."

"Yes, well I'm sure you're neglecting your classes through keeping such late hours!" he observed. Brooke looked momentarily unhappy. "Right, young lady?"

"I'm falling way behind in French," she admitted.

"I'll get you a tutor," he replied cheerfully.

"Are you my daddy now?" she asked, not displeased.

"You'd better believe I am."

"But I'm afraid that we're about to have our first quarrel," she said wistfully.

"Oh? Why is that?"

"Because you'll video me, but you won't let me video you," she replied.

"Who says I won't? And we are not going to quarrel, ever," he declared, deliberately raising the height of the camera, leaving it set in position and walking into the frame. "I'll give you a film of me spanking some of the insolence out of you!" And with that succinct statement, he sat down beside her, pulled her straight across his lap and gave her a brisk, proper, fifteen second movie style spanking, over the sheer gauzy pink panties that covered her bottom so daintily. Then, with equivalent dexterity, Carter rolled her over and swept her into a classically cinematic embrace, smothering her lips with a long, hard kiss while crushing her to his chest.

He let her go and turned off the camera.

"That's enough for posterity," he told her.

"You did a spanking movie with me!" she cried with excitement. "Can we watch it? Please???"

"We'll rewind it and watch it," he said, rolling back the tape. Then with their heads pressed together above the viewfinder, they reviewed the quick, pretty spanking and romantic finial. "God, don't we look gorgeous together???? I want to keep that tape," she cried possessively.

"Of course, it's your camera."

"I'll make you a copy of it though," she assured him.

"Kind of you."

"Can we watch it again?"

"No. I want you. Now."

Brooke blushed, feeling like a child. "It's not like you couldn't have had me, until now," she pointed out.

"Are you still being difficult?" he snapped, grabbing her by her earlobe and dragging her over to a sofa arm of the proper height to bend her over. "As if I would take you in a dungeon!" He pushed her down, giving her a half dozen smacks for good measure. "Arch your bottom," he told her, pulling her filmy panties down and off. "And spread your legs." More smacks hastened her compliance. Pressing one hand in the small of her back he freshened the color in her slim, oval cheeks to dark pink through brisk spanking. In a minute or two he tested for results, insinuating a long middle finger into her tight and flatteringly creamy girlhood. "That's my girl," he said, whipping out a condom and a rampant organ for it to contain.

"Now you're gonna get it," he told her, positioning his smoothly sheathed mushroom knob between her velvet labia and fastening his hands to her tiny, cinched waist before plunging slowly but completely inside her. "This is the way I like to do it," he told her, expertly pistoning into her sleek, smooth, clinging inner depths. "How about you?"

"Yes!" she gasped, amazed and thrilled at the ripples of excitement, which radiated through her as Carter mastered her in the most traditional way with his oversized penis. Mini buds of ticklish pleasure pulsed and burst within her as her lover rammed his cock home hard and fast, only her extreme lubricity making any of this possible.

"You're such a bad girl," he told her, making her sob and come, with inner spasms so intense as to bring him off as well. "I mean, you're such a good girl," he amended, as he disengaged, turned her around and took her in his arms.

"I suppose I could be nicer to you," Carter mused a little later, after they had put out the lights and climbed into bed together. The skylight above them was crammed with white stars and birds were trilling in the trees that lined the canyon.

"God, don't do that!" she murmured, pressed up against him in the circle of his arms.

Chapter Five

The History of Hugo Sands Part Two
(Perhaps the most important part!)
Scorpio Rising

Hugo Sands was about to turn thirty on the sparkling October day when he rolled into Random Point, Mass, in a glossy new green Jaguar, to open his second antiques shop.

The old stone house he'd bought in the woods off Shadow Lane was little more than a handsome hull whose interior had been falling to pieces for thirty years. Hugo planned to camp in the old fashioned kitchen, with its enormous hearth and arched doorway into an overgrown garden, while conducting the renovations of the sturdy, ten-room cottage. He deposited his two cats there before going into town.

Shadow Lane, which bisected the woods and ran into the village, was also the cobbled street upon which the antiques shop stood, across from a pretty duck pond. Like the house, the shop needed a great deal of work prior to habitation, but this was mostly of the dusting, polishing and cataloging variety and Hugo planned to accomplish this in easy stages over the next few weeks, intending that it should be ready to welcome clientele by the start of the holiday season.

That afternoon he traversed the village, buying provisions, introducing himself to the local shop keepers and stopping at the hundred and fifty year old Ball and Feather Inn for lunch. His final destination was the head shop, located on Rumple Street, upon which also sat a food co-op, a Thrift store and fire station. Rumple Street, unlike Shadow Lane, would probably never become gentrified. It was home to aging hippies, unappreciated artisans, impoverished students and other lower middle class townies of various stamps.

The smoke and incense shop, called The Pearl, commanded a large and busy storefront, crowded with the artifacts of Eastern religions, occult talismans and brass water pipes. Inside, a confluence of exotic scents, rich fabrics, carved pagan images and tinkling chimes vied for the visitor's attention.

When Hugo strode in, impeccable in his first Armani suit, worn casually, with an open collared shirt and Italian shoes, the clerk, a slim young woman, in raw silk, gauze and gold, with light brown hair down to her waist, looked up sharply from the velvet box of toe rings she'd been displaying to a customer and gazed at Hugo for a moment as if mesmerized.

Hugo strolled around the shop, examining the pyramids of candles, the bins of incense, the numerous books and icons representing the arts of divination, spell casting and other mystic topics as the girl shopkeeper's monologue to her customer on the art of becoming more centered permeated the air. Chirpy, helpful, overflowing with arcane lore and equally useless New Age philosophy, this not unattractive young lady represented a type of female that Hugo found perfectly repellent. She had just begun a dissertation on "The Goddess" when Hugo cleared his throat. He didn't have an hour to waste in the shop while his hostess held fourth.

In a moment, the girl was before him, making a small, and Hugo thought, ironical bow while greeting him as "Master!"

"Why master?" Hugo replied with a start.

"Aren't you the Wiccan priest from Boston who was coming down to give a talk at the shop tonight?" the girl returned, gazing so deeply into his pale blue eyes with her tawny hazel ones that he received the sensation she was attempting to read his mind.

"Certainly not!" he rejoined roundly.

"Oh, I do beg your pardon. May I be of some assistance then?"

Now he took a second look at the girl, who was clear skinned and graceful, with a firm, round bosom thrusting against the royal blue midriff vest edged with gold braid, a flat stomach, bare, with a sapphire in her navel, and a long, filmy skirt of dark, sheer blue fabric spangled with gold stars, from beneath which tiny blue and gold embroidered slippers peeped.

She was rather a small girl, extremely slender, save for the curves of her bosom and bottom, which Hugo had yet to take note of. Her eyes were very large and fine, her nose straight and aquiline and her mouth wide and full. Hugo did not think her more than tolerably pretty, but she did begin to improve in his eyes, now that she had ceased to lecture her customer and merely stood waiting for his words.

"Yes, I need a few things. Perhaps you could get them for me," he said, handing her a short list.

"Certainly, sir," she replied agreeably looking at the piece of paper and handing it back to him. Hugo followed her while she went about the shop collecting the candles, incense, incense burners and rolling papers he had requested. At length she glanced at him and casually asked, "But you did come out from Boston, didn't you?"

"Yes, I did."

"And it wasn't to visit a shop?" she asked.

"Actually, I came to take possession of the antiques shop on Shadow Lane."

"Oh! Wonderful! By the way, my name is Cassandra Campi."

"Hugo Sands," he replied, still not terribly interested in the girl.

"You know, Hugo, I'm getting a very strong sensation as I look at you that you are most definitely some sort of master," Cassandra declared, in bafflement. "Are you not a virtuoso of some type?"

"A psychic, are you?" he smiled indulgently. "I do have a masters degree in Art History," he added, hoping to end the inane exchange as soon as possible while noticing that Cassandra had somehow chosen his exact favorite brand and scent of incense, his preferred brand of rolling papers and even the size and color of candles he'd wanted but hadn't specified.

"The aura you're projecting contains much more power than even an art degree from Harvard could endow."

Hugo wasn't surprised she'd guessed his school, as his signet ring was recognizable, but he couldn't understand what she was getting at with her strangely flattering remarks.

"Do you normally see auras around your customers?"

"Oh, by no means! Only special people have them."

"Uh huh."

"May I ask what your birthday is?"

When Hugo told her the girl smiled. "What?" he demanded.

"Oh, I just figured it out."

"Figured what out?"

"You're a Scorpio. That's the sex sign, you know. Your power is the power that you have over women. An extraordinary one, I think."

Hugo finally had to smile back. "Young lady, are you flirting with me?"

"Not that I'm aware of," she replied thoughtfully, "but of course I would be honored to know you better."

Hugo was nonplussed by her deference and began to feel somewhat uncomfortable about the entire encounter. "Well, I'm sure we'll be seeing each other frequently. My shop is only three square blocks away from yours," he said.

"That will be fifty dollars even," she said, ringing up the sale. "I thought you'd want the best we had," she said, indicating the fine brass incense burners.

Hugo handed her the cash.

"Thank you," she said. "Oh, may I ask you one more thing?"

"Sure."

"Where were you born?"

"In Boston."

"You don't happen to know the hour of your birth, do you?"

"Why do you ask?" Hugo grew irritated.

"I'd like to cast your horoscope," she replied.

"You do and I'll spank you," he warned, grabbing his package and strolling out the door.

"You'll do that anyway," Cassandra said, under her breath as she watched his tall figure disappear down the street from her doorway a moment later.

Hugo didn't see the girl again for twelve days or even give her a thought in that time. But on the thirteenth morning, while he was arranging the first display of his own in the front windows of his shop, he suddenly remembered his fellow shopkeeper with a grin. It was certainly true that she wasn't his type. But she was a female, young and not unappealing in her way. Most importantly, she seemed available and Hugo was getting a little lonely for companionship.

One hour after he had visualized Cassandra, she came walking into the shop, carrying a small, purple tissue wrapped package and a fragrant bunch of violets.

"Good morning," she called, then saw him in the window. He stepped out to greet her.

"Hi."

"Some welcome to Random Point presents," she said, placing the flowers and package on the closest counter top and looking around the still highly disorganized shop.

"Thank you," he replied. "Would you like coffee?"

"Oh yes!" she agreed and he took her into the back of the shop, where he had already set up his office. A new electric typewriter sat atop his desk and sheaves of manuscript were stacked beside it.

"Oh, are you writing a novel, Mr. Sands?"

"Call me Hugo. No, I'm putting together a little literary magazine that I'm going to publish myself."

"I'm sure that will be very interesting," she said enthusiastically.

"What did you bring me?" Hugo asked, pouring her some strong, fresh ground coffee then picking up the purple package.

"Mushrooms," she replied with a twinkle in her eyes.

"Mushrooms?" he looked at her with a new appreciation.

"Sure. It's just about the perfect time to take them, considering we're in the midst of peak foliage."

"Have you tried them?"

"Oh yes! You'll just adore what they do."

"Awfully nice of you, Cassandra."

"Did you think I'd forgotten about you?" she smiled.

"As a matter of fact, yes."

"Oh no. I've been thinking of you constantly since the day we met. It was just that Mercury was in retrograde for the last twelve days and I felt it would be dangerous to pursue anything while that situation was in effect."

Hugo looked at her and sighed. "Cassandra, you don't really subscribe to that hokum, do you? Think carefully before you reply."

"You don't approve?"

"Let's just change the subject," he said, suddenly remembering her kindness in bringing him the mushrooms and his longing for a girl in his bed.

"I'm eager to hear your opinions though," she insisted. "I had a reading last year during which I was informed that a tall, fair man would impart to me a quantity of highly useful knowledge. I believe that man is you."

"Is that so?" Hugo leaned back against his desk, lit a cigarette and regarded her over folded arms.

"May I be completely frank with you, Hugo?"

"Please!"

"I think you could help me with something that's been bothering me for years."

"Really?"

"Remember I told you that Scorpio is known as the sex sign?"

"How could I forget that?" he smiled.

"Well, I wasn't wrong, was I? I mean in assuming that you know your way around sex better than most men your age."

"Well, no, you aren't wrong about that," he admitted with a complete lack of self-consciousness. "Though I'm sure that has more to do with all the Grove Press novels I read as a kid than my astrological sign."

"Then I'd like to make a confession."

"Sure."

"I'm twenty three years old. I've had many love affairs. I know how to orgasm five different ways. But I've never experienced what I've heard described as 'incredible sex' and I'm wondering if it really exists."

"The five different ways, what are they?" Hugo asked, out of academic interest.

"Masturbation, intercourse, oral sex, anal sex and sex with inanimate objects," she recited matter of factly.

"Ever try sex with B&D?"

"No! What is that?"

"I'll send you some books on the subject," he promised.

"Only books?" she seemed disappointed.

"To see if you might be interested."

"Why not just plunge in?"

"That wouldn't be very subtle, would it?"

"I don't know."

"The first rule of exciting sex is anticipation."

"It is?"

"Absolutely."

"I've been anticipating this discussion for almost two weeks, doesn't that count?"

"Yes, but the fact that it took two weeks for you to come by because Mercury was in retrograde counts against you, I'm afraid. Time flies by too quickly to waste it."

"I'll remember that. But we might have clashed severely while Mercury was in retrograde. Because your personality is so strong. I couldn't risk that at the outset of our relationship."

"That was very silly of you," he scolded.

"I'll go now and await the books," she said with resignation, receiving a strong sensation that with or without the excuse of B&D, she would shortly be beaten by Hugo Sands.

"What am I getting myself into?" Hugo asked himself that afternoon as he packaged up a batch of erotic novels for Cassandra in his library in progress at home. "She's has remarkable intuitive powers but look what she's doing with them!" Yet he couldn't help but be touched by her confiding manner, charmed by her acquiescence and inflamed by her air of submissiveness around him.

And then Hugo knew with inescapable certainty that he had just put a name to what she was. She was his new submissive, although she didn't even know what that meant. It was a strange way to come by a new submissive, simply meeting a girl with a sexuality like a blank page ready to be filled in by himself. He just wished he could feel more attracted to Cassandra, the woman.

A change of look would help, he thought. He was used to the smart, late 80's style of Boston businesswomen, in their tailored menswear suits with mini skirts and stiletto heels, sleek, upswept hair and long, silken legs. Hippie chicks wore clothes like wilted cabbage leaves, though at least Cassandra managed the richest silks and velvets in her costumes. He had also noticed today as she walked out of his shop, that her bottom jutted splendidly for one so pert in size. But magenta and aquamarine together, even in raw silk well cut, made Hugo shudder deeply.

Several days later Cassandra mailed Hugo a hand-made invitation to dinner at her house, Cobweb Cottage, situated on a pretty little cove a few miles down the coast road. She greeted him at the door, dressed in a short, black velvet sheath with a sweetheart neckline and matching high vamped, high-heeled pumps. Her mouth was a wide, dark red slash, just the way he liked a mouth to be, full lipped and almost pouty. She wore no other make up but had pulled her long hair back in a black velvet clip and wore little pearls in her ears and around her throat. Three small tabbies of various shades emerged from behind her to approach and sniff at Hugo, who stooped to admire and pet them.

"Don't you look sophisticated?" said Hugo, presenting her with flowers and wine. "Turn around and let me look at you," he said, easily spinning her around. The back of the dress had a provocative flounce that hit the backs of her knees and he noticed she was wearing real stockings with seams up the back and Chanel #5 rather than patchouli. "Are you the same girl I met the other day in my shop?"

Cassandra squeezed his hand, modestly beamed at the compliment and apologized, "I'm afraid I'm a vegetarian. I hope you like bread and cheese."

"I love bread and cheese," told her agreeably. "So did you get a chance to look at he books I sent you?" he decided to get over the awkward part immediately.

"Oh, yes!"

"Well? What did you think?"

"I thought that most of the men weren't very nice," she observed, handing him a corkscrew in the small kitchen of the cottage. She'd laid out a repast of French bread, imported cheese, autumn fruits and nuts on the rustic table. Her wine goblets were painted with bunches of grapes and peaches. Hugo opened the red that he'd brought. "Especially those ones set at Roissy and Ironwood."

"You're right. There aren't many decent male role models in the scene," Hugo agreed. "That's why I'm starting my own publication. Just to prove that it's possible to conduct a viable scene without necessarily ceasing to be a gentleman."

"Your publication is to be an erotic one?"

"Yes, but it will to be the kind women will like as well as men. That's my plan."

"I preferred Frank and I of all the novels," said Cassandra. "It seemed more good natured than the rest."

"I agree."

They sat and drank wine with their simple meal. Then she passed him a pipe and they smoked.

"I'm sorry I'm not your type," she said sincerely, startling him out of his reverie.

"Why do you say that?" he sputtered, getting a little fed up with her uncanny penetration.

"I drew up your birth chart as best I could without your exact hour of birth, and even with such sketchy data it revealed that you and I will never suit."

"Cassandra, what did I tell you about that?" Hugo demanded.

"What?" she looked up startled, for he had gotten up.

"Didn't I tell you not to do that? Didn't I warn you I'd spank you?" he dragged her off the chair by the hand, took her seat on it and pulled her back down across his lap.

Without pausing for further discussion, Hugo brought his hand down firmly on either velvet cheek, at least a dozen times. He heard her catch her breath, but that was all the sound she made as he positioned her more securely on his lap, pushed her snug, flounced skirt up over her hips and revealed a classic black lace garter belt and sheer panty combination. Cassandra's thighs were creamy white between her cheeks and stocking tops, but when Hugo pulled aside her panty legs he saw how pink his palm had already made her.

Spanking her pinker through her sheer black panties, he pulled them down at length and continued smacking her firm, small cheeks until the color turned from blush to the same magenta she had worn when she'd visited his store.

Cassandra took her spanking with more than academic interest. Unlike the harsh Victorian novels, which Hugo had chosen to give her, his hand did not sting like a hot iron, nor did her flesh burn like fire. She did feel sensations the likes of which she hadn't felt before, but not of pain precisely. Overwhelming pulsations of pleasure accompanied each sharp smack he visited on her bottom. He held her fast to his lap about her small waist, reinforcing his control over her body and will.

Cassandra very nearly went limp, giving herself up to the sensations that now swept her away on wave after wave of gripping excitement. It was a whole new thrill, being seized by a man and treated like this. She suddenly realized that she never had been taken by a man before, she had merely had sex with boys.

"Is this the type foreplay that works best for incredible sex?" she finally lifted her head to ask.

"Yes, honey. That's exactly what it is," Hugo said, inspecting her to find that she was as ready as a girl would ever be to have a man. He carried her into the sitting room, where an upholstered hassock had been conveniently placed in front of the fireplace. Hugo put her down and bade her kneel across the stool.

He lifted her skirt to her waist a second time, pulled off her panties entirely and spread her knees as wide apart as they would go on the thick hearthrug. Kneeling behind her, he spread her thighs and caressed her deeply, making her wetter and more desirous with his fingers. Then he unzipped and unsheathed the noble engine of his manhood that Cassandra had been wondering about all day and was soon to feel filling her to the depths and perhaps a bit more.

"Are you going to be a good girl and take it all without a fuss?" he asked her, positioning himself gently but firmly between her labia from behind and placing one hand under her public mound to spread her and ease his cock in.

"That depends on how big you are," she replied, turning to see that he was big enough to give a small girl pause. "Wow."

"Pay attention," he told her, patting her Venus mound with the palm of his hand. She caught her breath again and lubricated copiously. "Now," he told her, starting the patient process of penetrating her fully, for she was very narrow but also very slick. In a moment or two he was half way in. "Relax," he told her, patting her more firmly from below and inserting a little more in. She shuddered against his hand and began to climax violently before he was even fully inside her velvet sheath. "Good," he said, "you relaxed!"

Hugo let her recover her senses before taking her as she had never been taken before. While it was seldom his habit to sodomize a woman on the first date, the lubricity provided by the twenty three year old girl's orgasm was copious enough to make the attempt viable.

"Spread your bottom for me," Hugo ordered.

"But why?" she trembled, looking back.

"Because you know why," he told her, dividing her cheeks with one hand and lightly spanking her anus. "You had no business coming so fast. You need to learn better control. I'm going to take your bottom as a penalty."

"Oh!" she sobbed, partially with fear and partially with excitement. "That will hurt too much!"

"No it won't," he assured her, continuing to spank her bottomhole until she squirmed under his hand. "Now hold perfectly still," he told her, inserting his cock into her pussy again to lubricate it. "If you come again before I start fucking you, I will punish you severely."

"Okay," she murmured, responding with abandon to the pistoning of his slick rod inside her. But suddenly he withdrew and placed it between her bottom cheeks, pulling them apart with his hands and forcing his knob into her tiny bottomhole.

"Be brave, darling," he advised her before beginning the plunge deep into her bottom.

"Oh!" she cried. "Oh God!" But it was more from the shame of the invasion than any type of pain. For she was wet and excited and holistic as she was, had purged herself completely before this all-important date. Expert at the art of sodomy, Hugo knew just how far and hard to nudge. He also knew the secret place to hold her, right above her Venus mound, firmly, in the palm of his hand, to give her a second climax in a matter of moments.

Again Cassandra was overwhelmed by the experience of being handled so effectively. Her faith in Venus affirmed, she fell into a dreamless sleep that night in Hugo's arms.

When Hugo awoke the next morning, Cassandra had already left the cottage. This made him glad because he didn't know whether he even felt like being with her that day, or ever. Of course, the girl was nothing if not agreeable, but perhaps she was a bit too agreeable. The way she had propositioned him for example. She really had thrown him off balance by being the first to raise the subject of sex. He would have liked to feel desire specifically for Cassandra, rather than for just a woman in general when he made love to her for the first time. It wasn't that he didn't adore easy girls. In fact, he rather disliked the other kind. But he at least liked to be the one to ask first.

"Why kid myself?" he mused as he drove back into town, "I can't possibly enter into a relationship with a New Age airhead." Then he guiltily stopped at the florist shop and had two dozen pink roses sent to Cassandra at The Pearl. He had no idea of what to write on the card to placate without encouraging her, so he merely signed his name with three xxx's after it. That done, he decided to try to forget the whole thing ever happened.

While Hugo Sands was a good deal less psychic than Cassandra Campi, he had a pretty good notion of how the girl felt about him. Therefore, he fully expected to be chased by her continuously thereafter. Much to his surprise, she neither called nor visited for the next three days. Finally realizing that Cassandra might be either politely, patiently or intuitively waiting for him to call her, Hugo told himself that not to do so would be the worst example of incivility and picked up the phone.

This time he invited her to luncheon at his house, for he had gotten the kitchen in good working order and his furniture and wine had arrived from Boston that week. She accepted joyfully and asked if she should bring him anything special. He advised her to bring walking shoes and a jacket, as he wanted to eat the mushrooms with her and spend much of the day in the woods. Not that either of them needed anything to either loosen their inhibitions, see beauty more clearly or sharpen their perceptions of themselves and each other, but there is a uniquely intimate comradery in sharing a consciousness altering experience that Hugo had learned to appreciate on a level with foreign travel and haute cuisine.

"I knew you had cats," she told him, entering by the garden door with a grey one under one arm and black one under the other.

"Of course you did. You know everything," said Hugo dryly, while pouring out tea for them. "Sit down," he ordered. Cassandra accomplished this with both cats still gathered in her arms like a bouquet. They were sniffing her wool cardigan, which bore the essence of her own feline family.

"Thank you for calling," she said simply, placing both cats back on the floor and shrugging out of her short suede jacket. "I had no idea whether you would want to see me again."

"I wasn't sure myself," Hugo admitted.

"I understand," she murmured, not meeting his eyes. "I made a poor first impression on you, which I compounded by proposing we have sex as an academic experiment. I've been quite unacceptably forward and put you in an awkward position as well. I only wish there had been some other way to attract your attention," she concluded with a sigh.

Her humble yet brilliantly acute analysis of their relationship to date left Hugo speechless for some moments. Finally he only remarked mildly, "Don't worry, honey, by the time I'm through with you, you'll have learned how to attract a man's attention without saying a word."

"Yes, Hugo, I do see you in the role of educator. And I vow to do my utmost not to irritate you."

"Just stop reading my mind, damn it!" he said, dropping the mushrooms into the herbal tea he'd poured them.

"Aren't we going to chew them up and swallow them?" she asked.

"The tea will leech the psilocybin out and then we can it drink it. Otherwise, don't you think it will be too strong?"

"Not for me," she replied.

One hour later, having both drank the tea and chewed the mushrooms, Hugo and Cassandra were walking through the woods, which let out at the beach behind William Random's house in the cul de sac at the end of Shadow Lane.

"I suppose you'll need models to pose for the photos in the magazine," she startled him by saying, as they trampled through great heaps of red and gold leaves.

Hugo had indeed been musing on just that problem. But he didn't recall telling Cassandra that his journal was to be anything other than literary. The books, which he had given her to read, were of text only. So what made her think about photos?

"Yes," he answered at length, "I certainly will. But how in the world did you know that was just on my mind this morning?"

"Hugo, don't be cross. It was simple logic. My sister has done extensive modeling for bondage magazines, so I know all about photo spreads."

"You have that kind of sister?"

"Yes. Carola's working her way through law school in Boston by doing bondage outcall," Cassandra replied without embarrassment. "She's got a great look too, kind of like that 50's pinup girl, Bettie Page. I'm sure she'd be happy to pose for photos or drawings for some allowance."

Hugo just looked at her. Then he said, "That would be extraordinarily helpful."

"Are we stopping at William Random's?"

"Why? Do you know him?"

"Of course."

"He is doing the renovations on my house, but he's more of an acquaintance than a friend," Hugo explained, "I don't know that he'd welcome a drop in visit."

"I think he'd look marvelous posing for some of your photos," said Cassandra.

"He does seem highly photogenic. But what makes you think he'd be up for it?"

"I've always had a feeling about him. I think he may be the type. Let's go ask him!"

"If you think so, it's probably worth a try," Hugo agreed and fifteen minutes later they were seated around the fire in William Random's den as their host displayed his own private album of erotic photography.

Still in his middle twenties, William was a working architect, whose family construction business had passed entirely into his capable hands in recent years. He spent half his time running the company and the other half working on interesting remodeling and small building jobs around the Cape. He was the one who had told Hugo about the fine, half ruined stone house in the woods when they had met by chance at an estate auction in Boston the previous spring.

William was interested in restoring the house for someone who would appreciate and preserve it and saw his man in Hugo. Thus their friendship was commencing on little other basis than their mutual interest in the applied arts.

"William, you would look good in photos," said Cassandra without preamble. "Would you consider posing with myself or my sister Carola for Hugo's elegant new spanking magazine?"

"Spanking magazine?" William smiled. "I would love to do that!"

"Are you sure you know what Cassandra means?" Hugo asked. "I mean, have you ever done it?"

"Spanked a girl? Yes, I have!" William replied confidingly.

"Is this true?" Hugo demanded.

"Hell, yes!" William laughed, for this was the first time in his life he'd ever discussing his favorite subject in mixed company. "But where do you find one when you want one?" he added.

"Apparently there's been one here in Random Point all along," William nodded towards Cassandra.

"Tell me about this sister," William said, "is she the one I'll be spanking in the photo spread?"

"Well, if you're perfectly willing, why not spank the both of us in different scenes and thus create two photo sets? Then you could in turn photograph Hugo spanking us. Also, we could be spanked together, or spank each other!"

Hugo looked at Cassandra in astonishment, for he had been thinking of exactly those combinations. William said, "Sounds fine!"

Several minutes later, as they walked through the woods to the beach, Hugo felt the mushrooms begin to take effect. The burnished leaves shimmered glossily in the light breeze from the sea and the sky above was a rich, cornflower blue. When they reached the rocky shore the waves were lapping gently and the water was slate grey. Gulls wheeled above while sand pipers hopped and pecked below. They sat on a rock and looked out at the sea for quite some time. At length he pulled her into his arms and kissed her full on the mouth.

Reentering the woods a half hour later, Hugo realized that Cassandra hadn't uttered a word since leaving William's house. He would never have imagined her to be the type of girl who could keep quiet for a minute, no less an hour and was suitably impressed. Now as they walked, he took her by the hand, a small hand in a chestnut brown suede glove that matched her jacket. He liked her in the pegged blue jeans and little walking boots, the cream wool polo shirt and sweater and the small Basque beret angled atop her finely shaped head.

"I like you like this," he told her.

"Do you?"

"You ought to give up dressing like a hippie."

"What about my hair? Should I cut it short?" she asked.

"You do and I'll wear out my belt on you," he threatened, stroking her hair.

"At least you like something about me," she grinned.

"You mustn't make self deprecating remarks, Cassandra. You're perceptive enough to know that you're an extremely desirable young woman."

Cassandra saw it made him cross to have to tell her this and colored. Then Hugo eyed a likely switch. Giving her one steely look, he fished a Swiss army knife out of his pocket and began to trim the nubs from the long, thin branch he had taken from the forest floor.

"Come over here, young lady," he said, taking her rather sternly by the earlobe, leading her to a sheared off tree stump and bending her over it.

"But why?" she asked, turning to look at him. He swished the switch through the air and made it whistle. Then he tested it against his hand.

"What did you ask William just before we left the house, Cassandra?" he asked, slapping the switch against his Donegal tweed trousered leg.

"Oh. That!" she murmured, pillowing her head on her folded arms and turning it in his direction, to catch his profile and see when he might raise his arm in order to prepare herself for something that had never happened to her before: punishment.

"Well?"

"I asked William his birthday, hour of birth and where he was born," she sighed.

"What did I tell you about casting horoscopes?"

"You just said not to do yours."

"Well, I'm amending that now to everyone else's as well."

"But I can't stop drawing up birth charts, it's part of my livelihood," she protested, rearing up. He pushed her back down in the small of her back.

"I'm highly distressed to hear that, Cassandra. I consider such occupations adventures in charlatanism."

"I'm sorry," she murmured, resigning herself to an extremely severe lecture. For even without configuring his hour of birth into Hugo's chart, she had been presented with a pretty clear picture of his character, not the least facet of which was a harshly critical bent.

"If indeed there are individuals chuckleheaded enough to pay for such services then you have even less reason to pester people with working brains about their signs and ruling planets."

"But most people enjoy having their charts done or getting a reading."

"Well, most people are idiots. You, on the other hand, should know better. You appear to have an excellent mind in every respect. In many ways, you're one of the most rational women I've ever met. Yet in this one area, complete illogic rules. But I intend to try to cure you of that."

Hugo took careful aim and brought the switch down lengthwise across the center most portion of the seat of her snug jeans with a smart report. He had meant it to be little more than a warm up tap but he was not yet expert with a switch and the sharpness of the rod across her tender bottom, even clothed in jeans and panties, caused hot tears to spring instantly to her eyes. She gave a little sob, bit her knuckle and turned her face away.

It was very humiliating to be told that one needed to be broken of one's favorite hobby, though the thing did no one harm and many people good. But Cassandra reminded herself that Hugo had been sent to her as a teacher and resolved to at least try to understand the present lesson without rejecting it out of hand. Meanwhile, the switch came down two more times, once slightly above and the other slightly below the original stroke. Since she hadn't made much of a murmur after the first, Hugo delivered the next two a little harder. Now she couldn't help but cry out pitifully in response. After the fourth stroke she broke down completely and sobbed, causing Hugo to throw the switch aside in alarm and take her in his arms.

Cassandra sobbed against his chest for several minutes, quite overcome by the intensity of the pain just four strokes of a twig had imparted. Enfolding her in his arms he kissed her face again and again, apologizing with his eyes if not in words. Finally feeling this first glimmer of honest affection from Hugo, Cassandra managed a rueful smile and giving her bottom a rub, murmured, "That really hurt!"

"Come on, I'll give you a ride home," he told her, lifting her to stand on the stump, then allowing her to sit on his shoulders. She was light, easily balanced and had no fear of falling. Thus she felt as though she were walking through the trees when her psychotropic reverie began to blossom. Not wishing to spoil the extremely beautiful moment with idle conversation, Cassandra waited until they were back at Hugo's house and sitting down to luncheon to introduce a topic which might possibly result in a fresh quarrel.

"You know, being an empath is a thing quite apart from the arts of divination," she began bravely, for she felt she had to set him straight on this one point.

"What are you saying now?" Hugo had opened a crisp Pinot Grigio and was pouring out two glasses.

"I'm saying that my being empathic has nothing to do with

horoscopes or any other forms of arcane superstition. It's simply a quality of consciousness slightly more sensitive or intuitive, if you will, than the average. Many people possess it to a greater or lesser degree. In fact, I'm sure you do yourself!"

"Your point being?" Hugo removed a homemade pasta casserole from the warming oven in the stone wall and set it on the table.

"My point being that I'm not consciously attempting to read anyone's mind. I just sense things that other people miss."

"I'm glad to hear you put it that way. But your excellent powers of observation notwithstanding, you were indeed trying to read my mind the day we met. I felt it too strongly to believe otherwise. And I also think that you succeeded."

"Why? What do you mean?"

"Uncanny the way you knew the exact type of incense, candles and rolling papers I wanted. I'm still puzzling over that one."

Cassandra laughed. "Don't, Hugo, dear. I just brought you all my own personal favorites. They happened to be the same as yours."

"Okay. Good. That makes perfect sense," he replied approvingly, though it made no sense whatever, since they shared the same taste in almost nothing else.

"And if I stared at you the day we met it's only because you're the handsomest man who ever found his way through my door."

Hugo smiled and ruffled her hair.

"You know, this is a marvelous house," Cassandra said a few moments later. "There's magic here."

Hugo sighed. "Can't it just be a wonderful house without any magic attached?"

"It could, but isn't. Cobweb Cottage has it too."

"Is that so?"

"You'll see, if you stick around town long enough. As far as this house goes, the power emanates from the cellar."

"I hope its wine friendly then," Hugo replied.

"May I look?"

"Sure, we can go down if you like. I had the cleaning crew work on that area first," said Hugo, switching on the cellar light and leading her down the steps through a door in the kitchen floor.

Hugo had already loaded his new wooden racks with vintages he'd collected over the past few years. There was also a large, oaken table with turned legs and a few matching chairs, all dating from the late Victorian era, when the house was built. Brass sconces with saffron frosted bulbs cast a muted light about the large, cool room.

"Yes, the energy is very strong down here," she said, walking about and poking into crannies in search of something, though she knew not what. "Perhaps you'll find a diary in the house some day," she mused, "to explain the origins of the force."

"You'll be the first to know if I do," he pledged.

"I wish you'd let me do a reading for you," she said. "It would answer a lot of questions."

"When hell freezes over," he remarked shortly, snapping at the rows of wine with a dust cloth.

"Most people consider it fun," she protested.

"Cassandra, do you want another spanking?"

She didn't reply but continued idly poking into corners.

"You're a funny kid," he told her.

"Am I?"

"Don't you mind what happened in the woods?"

"Didn't Poor Richard say: love well, whip well?"

"And that goes down okay with you?"

"Naturally. I subscribe to all of Poor Richard's advice."

"Come here," he said, pulling her towards him and unzipping her jeans. "I want to see if I marked you." He bent her over the table and pulled the jeans and then her beige cotton lace panties down to mid-thigh. Four faint pink lines scored her bottom crosswise, exactly where the rod had fallen. He caressed them with his fingertips while she almost unconsciously began to wriggle her hips. It was the most ancient gesture of seduction known to mankind and it did not fail to arouse the stud primeval in Hugo. The next moment his zipper was down and his blood engorged cock thrust inside her. The image of the switching in the woods still vivid in his memory, Hugo held Cassandra fast by the waist and took her hard.

After making love to her two times, spanking her once and

switching her to tears, Hugo felt it logical to assume that Cassandra now belonged to him. This was never stated in so many words, or even any words on either side, but he felt it to be true all the same.

Spending most of the following week in Boston, seeing to his business affairs, Hugo didn't trouble to call Cassandra. He was as sure of her as he had ever been of any girl and took it for granted that she would sense his good intentions, as she seemed to sense everything else, without being told directly of them. Therefore, it was with a disagreeable pang of surprise that Hugo beheld William Random lingering (for what appeared to be hours), at Cassandra's booth at the Woodbridge Pumpkin Faire the following Saturday.

Hugo had gotten back to town the previous night and planned to get in touch with Cassandra sometime that weekend. That morning he decided to visit the arts and crafts festival, unaware that The Pearl would be represented by a table. Around that table William Random hovered, drinking endless bottles of water and talking almost nonstop to Cassandra, who constantly looked up, smiled and appeared to agree with everything William said. As Hugo gazed across the Woodbridge Green at their amiable tête-à-tête, he felt a surge of emotion as yet unidentifiable, but highly unpleasant, course through his entire body from his head to his feet.

In order to observe the dynamic between Cassandra and William Random, Hugo traversed the fair some hundred minutes before finally approaching the table of The Pearl. At last he did so, coming over just a few minutes after William finally departed.

"Hugo!" cried Cassandra with delight.

"Cassandra."

She was startled by the sternness of his greeting and fell quite silent before it.

"Well? How are you doing?" he nodded towards the cash box.

"Oh, very well indeed!" she smiled, letting him peek at the salad of fives and tens she'd already amassed.

"I'm surprised you had time to make any sales!" he observed tartly, in spite of his resolve only a moment before to show no outward signs of jealousy. Meanwhile, Cassandra dimpled and blushed, instantly taking his meaning.

"Oh, you saw William keeping me company, did you?"

"I could hardly help it, could I?"

"My sister is the one he's interested in. I've been clueing him in as to what she likes so he can make a big impression on her when they meet."

"Oh!" Hugo's blood pressure dropped significantly. But Cassandra went on blushing as she felt his eyes upon her face. It thrilled and embarrassed her to realize that just for a moment, Hugo had been jealous.

"You're being very severe with me," she murmured softly.

"I would be if I thought you were flirting with William all day."

"I may have flirted, just a little."

"Then I may have to turn you over my knee."

Cassandra bowed her head in submission though her cherry lips curved into a smile.

That night at Cobweb Cottage Hugo was determined to give Cassandra a new erotic experience, that of feeling completely controlled while the object of all attention and desire. Lacing her tightly into her own brocade corset, a remnant of the last Renaissance fair, he caused her to kneel on her own little bed, lower her bosom to the counterpane and at the same time spread her legs apart as far as they would go. Next he used two equal pieces of soft nylon rope to gently but securely bind her wrists to her ankles, further dividing her thighs, labia and the slim, oval cheeks of her bottom.

Once she was completely spread, Hugo spent a great deal of time methodically disciplining every exposed portion of her intimate anatomy. Deploying a miniature leather flogger on her soft curled pubic mound, parted pussy and small bottomhole, he soon had her tingling with excitement. Then he paused to spank her cheeks dark pink. Several pillows placed under her abdomen kept her backside properly elevated without unduly straining her back. He noted how prettily she squirmed when he also spanked her sex and anus. She was very wet.

Leaving her spread and still lightly bound, Hugo went away to get insertion toys. After she was filled and spanked and made to come three times, she was only then made love to. During which she came once more. Her feeling about Hugo being a master was thus proven to her. But she still felt she had to know more. She had to know the hour and minute of his birth in order to properly execute his birth chart, and then, she had to do a reading.

The brief flare up of jealousy was enough to convince Hugo that he had somehow fallen in love with Cassandra. That his love was returned tenfold was a given. Which was the only boring part. Certainly he expected to conquer any woman he set his cap at, but not without some effort, some figuring out, some delicious delay.

It seemed he had possessed Cassandra from the moment their eyes met. She herself had called him master before he'd even said good day. Her attitude was flattering, but he didn't crave flattery. He preferred to use that tool of manipulation himself, but only when necessary. And yet, she had a brain. If she was abjectly submissive, at least she did it without fawning. She seemed sincere, honest, ingenuous and in her own native way, charming. So why did he feel the need to be so cruelly sarcastic? Why was he cool towards her rather than warm? Was theirs was to be a strictly dominant-submissive relationship, with him always feeling superior to her?

"You're lucky I'm so nice," he told her, later in the week as they strolled through Bartlett's exclusive department store in Woodbridge. Hugo was determined to make Cassandra a present of several smart outfits and she let herself be led by the hand through the various boutiques in a glow of contentment.

As they walked through the leather shop Hugo paused at the bin filled with riding crops. A slender, shapely clerk emerged from behind the counter in a clinging jersey dress and helpfully informed Hugo that they carried Hermes crops as well.

"An every day crop seems more useful at this point," Hugo smiled, laying the chosen object on the counter and passing her his credit card. "Cassandra, try on one of those riding pants and jacket outfits," he ordered, leaning against the counter to watch the passing parade of fashionable young matrons as he waited.

In fifteen minutes he ran up a fifteen hundred dollar bill on

Cassandra's behalf. She emerged in boots, pants, jacket and tailored shirt, all retro cut and suggestive of English country houses in the early portion of the 20th century. With her long brown hair down to her waist and her pert figure clad to perfection, Cassandra would have charmed the pen of John Willie. Her tiny waist and full, beautiful bosom, her slim, shapely legs were everything they ought to be, all in perfect, petite womanly proportion.

"I am lucky that you're nice," she murmured as they rode the noiseless escalator upstairs to lingerie, "but what did you mean by that remark?"

"Your submissiveness may get you into trouble some day."

"Oh?"

"Men may try to bully you."

"Which is something you would never do," she grinned.

"Come on, we need to find the perfect underpinnings for the equestrian outfit," he changed the subject.

"How you're spoiling me!" Cassandra observed as they left the lingerie department with her Lejaby combinations and Loire silk satin slips some minutes later.

"I've always liked playing dress up dolls with my girlfriends," said Hugo, causing a pang of pleasure to pierce Cassandra's heart. Girlfriend? Her blush betrayed her emotions and Hugo then realized what he had said. "Yes, Girlfriend," he told her, patting her warm cheek.

But the sweet, warm freshets of nonjudgmental love were not to flow from Hugo to Cassandra uninterrupted.

One slow Tuesday morning, Cassandra left her shop in the hands of her assistants and volunteered to help Hugo set his house to rights. This meant working around William Random's crews, who were still fine-tuning various parts of the infrastructure to Scandinavian standards of excellence.

Hugo wasn't quite sure he wanted Cassandra poking about his things, but when she made the offer he hadn't seen her for a week and had begun to long for her soft presence. Cassandra was nothing if not reluctant to pick up the phone and call, and in fact only did so to return a call of his. With impeccable timing, she never made herself available until he had somehow begun to miss her.

Finally he decided that she could do no harm among his books and set her to the task of alphabetizing the volumes by author and loading them onto the shelves that lined that room he would used as a study. William had left a sturdy wooden ladder on wheels, nicely varnished, for access to the uppermost shelves and Cassandra looked cute seated on it. Hugo went off to the village to bring back sandwiches and cake.

But he returned a few moments later, having forgotten his car keys. As he did so he surprised Cassandra removing an extremely yellowed piece of paper from a leather box of his marked "documents" which she had unearthed from a packing crate on the floor.

"Why are you going through my papers?" he demanded icily. She jumped at his voice, paled at his anger and hid the piece of paper behind her back.

"I just wanted to see what a Harvard diploma looks like," she replied quickly.

"What's that behind your back?"

"Nothing."

"Cassandra!" He advanced and she stepped back. "Give it here," he demanded.

"No, not until I've looked at it!" she replied with some spirit and then utterly infuriated him by slipping out the French door that led to the side garden. He chased her out but she was already running into the woods.

"You'll be sorry when I get my hands on you!" he promised, chasing her through drifts of leaves and carpets of pine needles. Cassandra was no match for Hugo's long legs, but she managed to get far enough ahead to thoroughly examine the purloined document before he ran her down a few minutes from the house.

Catching her by the arm he spun her around, wrested the crumpled, waxy piece of paper from her hand and found it to be his birth certificate. "What in the world did you want with this?" he asked.

"It lists your hour and minute of birth," she explained guiltily.

"Don't tell me you're still working on my birth chart!"

Cassandra hung her head.

"You see why I have to spank you?" he demanded, grabbing her and turning her under his arm. Smack, smack, smack! His palm rebounded and resounded against the seat of her snug pants. "You still don't get it, do you?" Smack, smack, smack! His hand came down many times causing her to wriggle and try to break free. "Don't you understand that annoys me?" She tried to dance away but still he held her fast. "Or maybe you're doing it on purpose, just to make me mad!"

"No, no! Never!" she maintained, trying to turn to him and make him look at her face. "I just needed accurate information."

"Accurate information in order to divinate! Do you know how idiotic that sounds? This is exactly why I've been reluctant to commit to a relationship with you," he explained, pulling her up to look at him.

"I'm sorry," she murmured, looking at her shoes.

"Do you like being thought of as a New Age ninny?"

"No," she replied, a healthy shade of resentment creeping into her voice as she rubbed her bottom vigorously. "But what makes you think you're right?"

"Logic, reason and 20th C. science."

"There are natural phenomena which defy explanation, even by your holy trinity," she retorted, lifting her head to look at him.

"That's the bunk," he replied, "and if you had half a peach pit for a brain you'd know that as well as I do!"

"Well see about that!" she returned stubbornly, marching back towards the house.

"What do you mean by that?" he pursued and turned her around to face him again.

"I mean that some day, many years from now, you'll see that I was right and you were wrong!"

"If you're that delusional, I feel sorry for you," he said coldly.

"I understand," she replied, suddenly more unhappy than rebellious. "You certainly can't love someone you feel sorry for, can you?" She began walking again, hot tears forming in her eyes. She gave him one backward glance, declaring, "Don't worry, I won't bother you again!" Then she broke into a run for his house where all she wanted to do was grab her jacket and depart in shame.

She knew she shouldn't have spoken as she had, for it meant losing the most interesting lover she had ever known, but Cassandra was true to herself and it was damaging her soul to have to pretend that she didn't have a gift, simply because the man she loved chose to disregard it.

Being meek and mild did not come naturally to Cassandra. She had achieved the attitude only through a tremendous force of will. From the outset she had strongly sensed Hugo's aversion to forward and aggressive woman and had fought monumental battles with herself to suppress her characteristic tendency to take control of every situation, inform every person and leave behind her a lasting impression of her own unique power and influence. Her initial assessment of the strength of Hugo's character had not diminished, but her belief in her own peculiar talents was about to reassert itself.

She stopped running, straightened her shoulders and slowed her pace to an indignant stride. She looked back again, but slowly this time, tossing her long hair and catching his flinty gaze with her feline one. She too was a Scorpio and she had the riding habit on. Better he be right behind her, to watch her walk out of his life with a defiant swish of the most beautiful hips in Random Point.

She re-entered the library by the garden door, picked up her things and prepared to exit the room. But Hugo was right behind her and caught her by the hand.

"Wait a minute, where do you think you're going, young lady?" he pulled her around to face him and was surprised by the look of insolence she tossed back.

"I'm leaving now," she announced. "But before I do I'd like to inform you that you are an extremely arrogant, narrow minded and earthbound individual. So much so that you failed to appreciate me. And I am hot stuff!"

This short lecture leaving Hugo completely amazed, Cassandra stepped to the door. "Oh, and by the way, if you want Carola and me to model for you, you'll have to pay a price. You'll have to let me do a reading for you. This is not negotiable."

Hugo let her go, torn between anger and laughter. "It's not over yet," he said to himself, "she looked too good in that riding outfit."

The minute Cassandra stopped trying to please Hugo, she became exponentially more interesting to him. The next morning he sent her flowers with a short note of apology for the uncalled for remarks insulting her intelligence. She was touched by his honest acknowledgement of a fault but hardened her heart and refrained from calling him.

The next time Hugo stopped into The Pearl, which was the following day, he was stunned to see Cassandra walking around the shop in a leather cat suit and lacing 4" heeled thigh boots. Her fingernails and lipstick had been painted dark red and her hair had been blown silky straight. For an instant Hugo thought this was finally Carola come to visit, but no, on second glance, the hair was brown, not black and the girl really was little Cassandra. Only not looking quite as little as before in her power fetish gear.

"I'm moving in a whole line of B&D paraphernalia," she explained, indicating a newly installed pegboard hung with a selection of classic black leather paddles and floggers. "Don't you think it's a splendid idea? There's a shop in Provincetown that stocks the stuff, so why shouldn't I? Perhaps you could help me pick out other things."

"Sure," he agreed, still reeling at the transformation he was witnessing. "But why?"

"Oh, because it's fun, sexy and a little on the dark side," she replied.

"That's a glorious outfit," he said without reserve.

"Thank you. You were right. It was time I changed my image."

"Don't change too much, huh?" he smiled.

"I won't."

"Did you get my flowers?"

"Yes. Thank you."

"I'm so sorry I hurt your feelings."

"It's okay," she replied as though the incident were trivial.

"I do appreciate you, Cassandra. I appreciate the way you told me off without using one swear word."

"That was the old Cassandra. The new Cassandra swears like a sailor."

Hugo smiled, took her by the hand and unerringly led her back to her own stockroom. Just inside the door he pulled her into his arms and crushed her mouth under his, with one hand to her bosom and the other on her skintight leather clad bottom. Her waist was also extremely fascinating, seeming tinier than ever before.

"Do you have a corset on?"

"A glove-tight one," she replied, placing his hands on her waist. "Carola says I'll either get used to the sensation or faint a lot."

He kissed her as he'd never kissed her before, not only on her lips, but also on her ears and exposed throat. Inwardly rejoicing, she gathered all of her resolve and gently moved away. "Not during work, Hugo," she chided mildly and quickly tottered back to the floor in her stiletto-heeled boots.

"She's beating me at my own game," Hugo brooded, leaving the shop in a state of arousal. "Suddenly she's free wheeling and independent, dabbling in B&D, wearing leather head to toe. And damn it, other men are going to notice. Right away!"

Hugo wasn't wrong about this, especially considering the spectacular things the cinching was doing to Cassandra's already exquisite figure.

Old boyfriends began emerging from the ether. Young craftsmen and clerks on Rumple Street came in for rolling papers once a day rather than once a week. And William Random, in what seemed to Hugo a supreme act of pandering, built a wooden pyramid in the herb garden behind The Pearl for Cassandra's readings.

The pyramid was completed on the very afternoon Carola arrived from Boston. Cassandra had asked Hugo to pick her sister up at the train station and bring her to the shop, so that he might judge for himself the desirability of having the leggy and elegant brunette pose for his magazine.

Carola was quite different from her sister. To begin with, she was taller and possessed a more willowy figure. Her hair was inky black and naturally straight. Her eyes were also dark and her skin very white. She was dressed in a grey pinstriped pencil skirt, white blouse and five inch heeled spectator pumps. Over her shoulders she had casually thrown a coat to match the skirt. A tiny, charming black hat and gloves completed her ensemble and she carried two round, hatbox shaped, black leather traveling cases. She seemed detached but not unfriendly as Hugo handed her into his car.

"So you're the soon to be famous Hugo Sands?" Carola remarked as they set off.

"Soon to be famous?" he smiled.

"According to Cassandra you're about to become a very big fish in that very small pond known as American B&D."

"Funny her making such a prediction when I only just introduced her to B&D two weeks ago."

"She's not called Cassandra for nothing, you know. But seriously, Mr. Sands, I have a definite bone to pick with you about my sister."

"Oh?"

"My sister's not as stupid as you think."

"I never thought she was stupid."

"Oh sure you did. You've been attempting to chip away at her confidence in her own abilities for weeks now."

Hugo threw her a look and saw she was sharply serious. With a shrug he replied, "I see you're just as silly as your sister."

"And I see you're just as arrogant as Cassandra warned me you would be!" returned Carola with spirit.

"I'm glad I don't disappoint you!"

"I'm glad you don't disappoint my sister. There should be at least one logical reason for her enduring such disrespect!"

"Has Cassandra been complaining of my treatment of her?"

"Not your treatment, only your attitude. She says you don't value her and I see now that's perfectly true."

"Carola, let's not quarrel," he threw her a conciliatory smile and even lit her cigarette.

"Don't worry, I'll still pose for you," she returned, artlessly displaying the family trait of casual mind reading. "I need the allowance."

The photo shoot was arranged for the following afternoon at William's house. The young architect took lighting seriously and it was over an hour before the first set up was ready. Hugo saw that at this rate, two set ups would be the utmost that could be accomplished in one afternoon. It was decided that William would photograph him spanking Carola first, then Hugo would photograph William spanking Cassandra. It was going to be the reverse configuration, until Hugo drove Carola from the station. After their conversation in the car Hugo had no intention of postponing spanking Carola.

"Have you ever been spanked before?" Hugo asked Carola as he checked his hair and tie in a mirror before taking the designated seat on a straight-backed chair in the center of William's solidly furnished, lodge like downstairs sitting room. Hugo wore a casual brown tweed suit and Carola was dressed in a short wool skirt, turtleneck and boots, with her hair in a ponytail. Cassandra checked every detail of the outfit and her sister's makeup before stepping out of the frame.

"Yes, every now and then, by a girl in a bondage shoot," Carola replied, peeking into the hand mirror Cassandra held for her. "And once in a while, by a client."

"Think you can take a real spanking?" Hugo asked her.

"If it's too hard, I'll say mercy," she replied matter of factly.

That afternoon passed rather like a dream for Hugo, who was fully sensible of its importance to his life. Like most enthusiasts, he had been obsessed with spanking and related forms of domination since early childhood. With his high sex drive, good looks and determination, he had seduced dozens of girls and women into going submissive to him in one way or another, spanking girl friends as early as kindergarten. But it was never enough. The spanking fantasies continued, longing to be even more fully realized and perfected. His artistic soul yearned to create that which he had never partaken of, sublime male dominant spanking erotica.

Like most enthusiasts, he had searched hungrily for beautiful spanking erotica, but the magazines he found in adult bookstores had made his Ivy League blood run cold. He really didn't know which was worse, the pictures or the text.

His vision was to present a town and country version of the fetish, with a philosophy of spanking that was strictly adult but esoterically decadent. And this was the first afternoon during which he was to realize his dream. As the film was shot, the magazine layouts unfolded before his eyes and he was infinitely pleased.

"Shoots are quite fatiguing," Carola told Hugo as William caused them to pause for yet another lighting readjustment. "You'd get tired of this very quickly if you did it as often as I do."

"Why do you do it?" Hugo asked.

"I love having my picture in magazines," she replied honestly. "And I have a lot of friends who model with me; it's a bit of a kinky sorority. Anyway, it suits my personality." He began to warm to her.

"Don't worry, I won't spank you hard," he promised. "Just look as though I am for the camera."

"That's all right, I have a panty girdle on over my pantyhose. Spank me as hard as you think necessary to get a reaction."

"You have a panty girdle on???"

"Long line," she replied smugly while William snapped away. "Why don't you look at it before you decide it's not sexy?"

So Hugo pushed her skirt up to her waist and revealed a figured black lace over beige lycra foundation garment, worn over shiny, seamed pantyhose. Her small, firm, oval cheeked bottom received an ample warm up through the substantial foundation garment that kept in the heat. When Carola began to wriggle and kick up her beautiful, long legs, William caught it all. But then he had to pause to reload.

"Are you all right?" Hugo asked.

"Of course!" she laughed.

"That wasn't too hard?"

"Oh, no!" Carola laughed. William and Hugo looked at each other. The sisters were two of a kind in this respect anyway.

When William was ready the spanking continued, with Hugo now lowering the girdle and pantyhose and revealing her pearly pink bottom for the first time. It was a lovely, fitness-firmed backside, velvety and blushing like a peach under his hand. "How beautiful you are," he commented.

"But wasn't I fresh in the car?" she asked, looking back at him. William caught the glance at that moment and the photo became the cover of Hugo's first magazine.

"You were downright terrifying in the car," he agreed, bringing his hand down hard on her bare bottom. Now she was a perfect little minx. Hugo mistrusted Carola but was quickly becoming intrigued. He spanked her for a long time as William circled them with his camera. Then he had to pause to reload.

Hugo didn't want to stop spanking her, but did, for form's sake, and because Cassandra was watching. Then, as though emerging from the dream, he remembered that they were also to photograph William and Cassandra that afternoon. It was now time to conclude Carola's spanking and the final roll of film was devoted to poses of Carola with her skirt up, standing against the mantelpiece, in Hugo's arms, etc., to the conclusion of the photo story.

Instead of breaking for lunch they ate sandwiches which Cassandra had brought while Hugo plied them all with good wine. Carola began to flirt with William Random.

They agreed that one more set up was all that could reasonably be managed that afternoon and that they should carry over the photo shoots into the following day. Carola whispered something to Cassandra, who relayed the question to Hugo, who murmured, "Yes, dear, you will receive two full day's pay." Carola relaxed.

Then William invited her to spend the night at his house, since it was so big and roomy, with so many empty rooms, and Cobweb Cottage so small, with only one bedroom.

"I'd hoped a room at the inn would be in the budget," said Carola idly. Hugo looked at William with a shrug.

"Of course it is," Hugo acquiesced, certain she had photographed quite beautifully and not caring about much else. Except perhaps his dislike for that dreamy look Cassandra seemed to be casting William.

Their scene was to take place in an old, abandoned barn on William's property. She was wearing the riding habit Hugo had bought her and William was in breeches, boots and a white shirt with the sleeves rolled up. They looked extremely good together and this gave Hugo a pain in his stomach, especially whenever Cassandra tossed her long brown hair, which was often.

Hugo instructed Carola to pack a basket with bread, cheese, more wine and some fruit and they proceeded to the barn. The light was fading fast and Hugo was not the perfectionist that William was, but he managed to capture some excellent action shots outside the barn and some moodily lit set ups within before they had to wrap their session up.

Somehow Hugo never got around to snapping any bare bottom shots of Cassandra over William's lap or bent under his arm. When Cassandra suggested there was more than enough time to get a few of these, knowing that Hugo would kick himself later for not having taken them, she was yanked outside the barn by Hugo, given a shake and promised all the bare bottom spanking she could stand, but from him and no other that day!

Cassandra was so touched she almost cried and threw her arms around his neck in a violent hug. Hugo smiled in spite of himself and squeezed the breath out of her in return.

Carola proved an invaluable assistant and they were putting away William's equipment by six p.m. Hugo was pleased.

"Well, Hugo? When may I expect you for the reading?" asked Cassandra.

"How about tonight?" he asked, resigned, because he was more than satisfied with Carola as a model and potential model magnet. Cassandra had also photographed well.

The reading was immensely uneventful from Hugo's perspective. Cassandra looked shrewdly at him each time he turned over a colorful card but told him nothing of her findings or conclusions. This left Hugo plenty of time to examine the excellent workmanship that had gone into the freshly erected, cedar lined pyramid in which they sat. Only a man intensely determined to impress a woman would have gone to this much trouble, Hugo brooded.

"You know what you are?" Hugo confronted Cassandra that evening at Cobweb Cottage, after they had deposited Carola at the inn, with William staying on to buy her dinner and tuck her in. "You're a chameleon! You determine exactly what it is you think a man wants and then you attempt to facsimilate it! You're not submissive, you're a traditional managing woman, masquerading as a mild cosmic lamb."

"Hugo, what on earth are you talking about?" said Cassandra, kneeling by the hearth to kindle a fire. Several striped tabbies came over to nuzzle her. Sitting on her heels, her bottom looked magnificent in the leather pants she had on.

"I saw you kittening up to William today. What I want to know is why?"

"I was doing no such thing," she insisted.

"Oh yes you were! You figured out that he's susceptible to that sort of thing."

"Well, most people are," she laughed. "So I'm a flirt. Why is that a surprise? You yourself accused me of flirting with you the first time we met."

"Are you saying that you're interested in William?"

"Why draw that conclusion?"

"So you're saying you just like the attention?"

"I'm not saying anything. I'm just interested in men," she shrugged, pouring him a shot of whiskey without being asked. He looked at her, tossed it back then put the shot glass down with a shudder. He walked away from her, turned back and looked at her again. She refilled the shot glass and handed it to him. Again he drained it, but this time didn't shudder.

"What the hell are you up to, Cassandra?" he demanded.

"Not one single thing," she serenely replied, strolling out of the room in her tight leather pants with the laces up the back, worn with a sheer, fitted, black nylon shirt, through which a charming black bustier could be glimpsed. She had her hair twisted up and her boots had 4" heels. Carola's influence was obvious. Between the heels and the hair, Cassandra had gained both stature and dignity. Hugo suddenly felt that this was the real Cassandra, a woman who was born to dominate rather than submit to men. He followed her into the bedroom.

"I hope William manages to charm your dear sister," said Hugo, lighting the fire in the small hearth. "I don't fancy competing with him for you." He stretched out on his back on the hearthrug. She sat down beside him.

"I noticed!" she laughed.

"What do you mean?"

"You barely let him touch me this afternoon!"

"Why should I let him touch you?" Hugo pulled her down into his arms and kissed her. "You're my discovery and I plan to keep you for a while."

"I don't know if that will be possible," she mused, sitting up and looking at him.

"Why not?"

"You're bad for my ego."

"You need a dose of reality."

"That's just the kind of remark I would find unbearable on a regular basis," she declared, starting to get up. He sat up and pulled her back down.

"Don't get temperamental with me, young lady," he told her, pulling her across his lap. He smacked her through the tight leather pants. "Remember the prophecy. I was sent to instruct you. You should listen to me instead of arguing."

"All right, I'll listen!" she cried, shocked by the sting of his hand but overwhelmed with excitement at being summarily seized. The leather pants trapped the heat generated by the spanking and caused her to squirm across his lap. The fire so close by added to the tangible warmth.

"Hold still!" he ordered, loosening the laces at the back of her pants and opening them. Now there was only a scrap of black silk panty between Hugo's hand and Cassandra's pink skin and this he briskly tugged down. The tight pants he'd pulled down to the tops of her thighs, which they hobbled together. Now he brought his palm down hard and fast, dozens of times successively on alternate cheeks, staining her smooth flesh magenta in due course. Hugo held her fast by the waist, barely allowing her to wriggle.

"Now I don't want to hear any more nonsense about us not being possible," he warned, after a final quick volley of stern smacks. "Do you understand me?"

"But you're so intolerant of my interests," she protested. "And I will not have my personality crushed!"

"And to think I was worried about your being too submissive!" Hugo laughed, pushing her off his lap. "I'm promising nothing!"

"Then neither am I!" she replied, yanking her pants back up.

"Fine, just don't let me catch you flirting with William Random again."

"All right, I won't let you catch me!"

"Here," said Hugo, placing a key in her hand. "I had this made for you. I want you to stop waiting until I miss you before you come to see me."

For the next two years, Hugo and Cassandra loved and helped each other. Carola brought him many models and Cassandra proved a capable copy editor. Hugo began to advertise and his New Rod Quarterly flourished. He soon created a personals department, which led, quite unexpectedly, to an entirely new social life for himself and his friend William Random. Suddenly Cassandra faced a whole world of competition in the form of eager and frustrated female spanking enthusiasts who were discovering the scene for the first time through Hugo's publication and in some instances, moving heaven and earth to meet its editor and experience his techniques first hand.

Cassandra was willing to be steeped in the scene and often accompanied Hugo to B&D support group meetings and parties in Boston and New York. He, in turn, allowed her to sometimes use his handsome home for readings. Which was how he acquired the entirely undeserved reputation of being an occultist, which was still hovering uncomfortably around him at the time that Marguerite Alexander came into his life.

Carola and William Random saw each other frequently, though theirs was more an arrangement than a relationship, in the sense that she slept with him in return for presents and allowance. Carola was an enormously practical young woman and believed in Du Barry's advice, to never give anything away.

The parade of young and older women who began finding their way to Hugo's door were entirely different in psychological makeup than Cassandra, who was always self possessed and in control of her emotions. These true submissives, spanking enthusiasts from childhood, were easily understood and satisfied by Hugo. But this often led to big problems for him. For example, almost every girl he spanked those first few years fell in love with him while he fell in love with none of them. And the disentangling maneuvers which followed were always painful and sometimes messy.

In contrast to the numerous cloying submissives that attempted to attach themselves to him, Cassandra's quiet independence seemed infinitely preferable. And though her tendency to develop warm friendships with other men gave him momentary pangs of jealousy, he rather admired her for this trait.

The wearing of boots and leather, the attending of B&D functions, began to bring Cassandra a following of submissives herself. A pattern of dominating men began at parties, when slave after slave would beg her to discipline him. Finally Cassandra gave in and picked up a crop. It was never the same for her after that night.

Instead of doing readings in her spare time, she began doing sessions with submissive men. At first she merely repeated the same activities she had experienced with Hugo, spanking, paddling, flogging and caning her adoring clients to a state of ecstasy. If the clients were very attractive, she sometimes shared with them other forms of stimulation she herself had been initiated into by Hugo Sands.

Carola tutored Cassandra in less domestic methods of mastering males, such as cross dressing and humiliating them, forcing them to worship boots and bottom, riding them like hobby horses, and finally, the complex and demanding art of submitting them to rope bondage.

Thus fitted with a deep grasp of corporal punishment and freshly schooled in the more esoteric fetishes, Cassandra was ready to place her first leather-clad ad in a national contact magazine. She simultaneously announced her intention to move to San Francisco and start her career as a mistress in one of the fine, new salons that had just opened its doors in that city.

Hugo didn't know whether to feel good or bad about having turned a submissive into a dominant but he did know that he missed her dreadfully for several months after her departure from Random Point. And yet, how like her, he thought with a smile, to leave him still a little hungry for her rather than sated!

Hugo kept in close contact with Cassandra for a couple of years, while she was in San Francisco. Her sister had joined a legal firm connected with the motion picture industry in Los Angeles. But when Cassandra took up residence in Hamburg, Germany, they finally lost touch.

Hugo hadn't heard of Cassandra for many years, though he thought of her fondly and frequently, when Laura found Hugo's horoscope on the top shelf of the bedroom which she occupied several nights a week in Hugo's house. Along with the chart was a map and a short page of verse, stiffly transcribed in an old fashioned calligraphic hand, entitled: Forecast for HS. Laura spread the map out on Hugo's study desk and they examined it together.

"It's Random Point and environs," said Laura. "But what's all this about?" She referred to a pentacle drawn in a circle of red. The five points of the star were deeply familiar to them both, marking: William Random's house, where Laura had lived as William's wife during the first year of her acquaintance with Hugo, Hugo's house in the woods, Marguerite's bookshop in the village, Anthony Newton's house on the cliff, where Newton, (Hugo's wealthiest collector-client) and Laura's sister Susan, (whom Hugo had introduced to Newton when she was just eighteen), often resided; and Cobweb Cottage, currently inhabited by spanking enthusiasts Hope and David Lawrence, who would both have willingly attested to the magic still at large in their aerie on the cove.

"Oh, I know what this is," said Hugo, picking up the complex astral chart, "Cassandra drew it up for me, expressly against my will, about a million years ago."

"But what does it all mean?"

"Who the hell knows?"

"So, how many years ago did she work on this?" Laura picked up the hand drawn map again.

"It would have to be about seventeen years."

"Really? I didn't think the book store went back that far."

"It didn't. It was an art supply store before Marguerite bought it."

"Who was living in the Cliff house then?"

"I have no idea. It was vacant for years before Anthony bought it."

"Hugo, this map places your future circle of friends in and around

Random Point."

"You're right!" Hugo agreed gloomily.

"Let's look at the poem," said Laura, unrolling the parchment and reading aloud:

"Seven Sisters' gift to you,
Two Siblings and one Friend;
Patronage to one is due,
Then on Her depend.
Hair of Russet, hair of Gold
Hair of Sable Brown;
Three to have, One to hold,
Jewels in your crown.
Fairest sister will you cede
To Supreme Maestro
Wife of comrade must be freed
'Ere true Love you will know.
Means for lovers to unite,
Gift that you are giving;
Subtlety replacing might,
Leads to gracious living."

Laura and Hugo looked at each other.

"Hugo, she's talking about Marguerite, Susan, William, Anthony and me. People she never met when she wrote this."

"She knew William," he replied uncomfortably.

"Big deal. What about the other references, things she couldn't possibly have known? The sister schools reference, and the comrade's wife freed allusion. That is obviously me. And this bit about subtlety replacing might. That clearly refers to your becoming less of a grouchy dom and more of a human being these past few years."

"Oh, it's all so typical of Cassandra," he said, tossing the poem on the table and the birth chart in the trashcan. "She always did have to get the last word in!"

"Wait, there are a few more lines here, and they seem to be written in gold ink," Laura noticed, taking up the prophesy once again reading aloud,

> "*Lover, though I leave you now*
> *You will still be with me*
> *Later I may tell you how*
> *We two have become three*
> *Never doubt your influence*
> *Which has changed my life*
> *Never doubt that for two years*
> *I was your first wife*."

"I wonder what she meant by that last stanza," Laura mused, somewhat disconcerted by the hidden emotions and obscure implications embedded in the verse she'd just read.

"Oh, it's just more of her nonsense," Hugo asserted, suddenly vaguely uncomfortable himself. "Silly New Age Nonsense. I should have spanked her harder when I had her to hand."

Later that day Laura retrieved the birth chart and putting it together with the verses and the map, returned the package to the top shelf of her closet.

Chapter Six

The History of Hugo Sands Part Three
The Business of Love

After Cassandra departed Random Point to reestablish herself in San Francisco, Hugo Sands was left without a lover for some time, for Cassandra was not the type of woman who was easily replaced. Then, on the first wet, windy Monday morning of that late 20th century year, an interesting young woman entered his antiques shop.

The doorbell tinkled as Hugo gazed out his front window at the duck pond on the other side of cobbled Shadow Lane. The scent of cinnamon hazelnut coffee, counter pointed by the ticking of numerous clocks and the glow of a crackling hearth instantly enfolded the first visitor of the day in comforting New England warmth as her casually natty, flannel suited host came forward to greet her.

"Good morning," said Hugo pleasantly. "Would you like some coffee?"

She was in her middle twenties, of medium height, slim, with honey blonde hair pulled back in a tortoise shell barrette, with eyeglasses to match. She was dressed in a beige trench coat and black boots; but wore no gloves or hat, and her face and hands were red with cold.

"Thank you!" she replied gratefully, unbuttoning one button on her coat and looking around.

"Milk and sugar?" he asked, going back towards his office.

"Please," the girl said, mesmerized by the Federalist portraiture hung about the upper walls. When he brought the coffee out to her in a fine china cup and saucer she handed him her card.

"Mercedes Vonderai," he read aloud, "what a pretty name." He looked at the card again. "Oh, you're with the Chamber of Commerce in P. Town, are you?"

"I've come to invite you to join us." she began her memorized speech; "The annual fee isn't large and a membership includes many benefits, not the least of which is a Storefront of the Month guarantee within your first eighteen months as a member."

"Storefront of the month, huh?" Hugo grinned. His displays were always exquisite and he had enough vanity to be pleased by the promise of formal recognition, even if funded by a membership.

"Yes, Mr. Sands, according to the county records, you've been doing business in Random Point for two years. Isn't it about time your fine shop was represented by the Chamber of Commerce?"

"Yes," he agreed. "I'd be happy to join."

"Oh, wonderful!" Mercedes gulped her coffee, immediately warmed through. Then she loosened her coat completely. The pinkness faded from her hands sooner than her face. She was fair complected to match her light hair with hazel eyes large behind her glasses. Without earrings, jewelry, makeup or a manicure, she was a remarkably pretty young woman, with regular features, velvet skin, chiseled lips, a graceful throat and small hands.

When she took her coat off and threw it on the counter he was able to fully appreciate her long torso, girded to perfection in a black wool cowl neck sweater and salt and pepper tweed straight skirt. She was fashionably lean, with a well formed bosom, incurving waist and firmly rounded bottom. With her elegant figure beguiling to a fault, her glasses suggesting intellect, her good boots indicating taste, her absence of frills betokening gravity and her lack of hat and gloves implying vulnerability, Hugo felt a sudden desire to know her.

As he walked Mercedes around the cavernous shop he deftly interviewed her, quickly discovering that she was single, twenty-six, a native of Baltimore and in possession of a degree from Sarah Lawrence, where she had majored in history.

She held the title of "Vendor Liaison" from the Provincetown Chamber of Commerce, where she had worked for the past year as a door-to-door solicitor of advertisers among the shopkeepers of Cape

Cod. Guessing that her job was exhausting, unfulfilling and poorly paid, Hugo unconsciously adopted a soft and soothing attitude towards his guest, who seemed anything but eager to forge out into the wet, whipping wind again.

"My special collections room," said Hugo, opening the door to his cedar scented repository of first edition books and curiosa. The phone rang and he went to answer it, leaving Mercedes to walk in and inspect several rare, illustrated editions of 18th century literature and even more numerous examples of 19th and 20th century erotica.

"May I look more closely at one of the books under glass?" she asked hesitantly, emerging to find her host.

"Certainly, I'll open the case," he said, preceding her back with his keys in his hand. "Which book did you want to examine?" he asked, removing a fresh pair of thin, white cotton gloves from a side drawer and handing them to her. "Better put these on, to keep the pages fresh."

"This one here, Frank and I," said Mercedes, putting on the gloves.

"Frank and I, eh?" he raised his eyebrows. "Do you just like the illustration or have you read it before?"

"I've read it. But I had no idea it had ever been illustrated," she revealed, taking the book from his hands and sitting down at the library desk.

"I'll leave you to it, then," said Hugo, walking out reluctantly. When she didn't emerge after fifteen minutes Hugo returned to her.

"If you're interested in that subject matter, I have other books with similar content," he revealed casually. She looked up from Frank and I wide-eyed.

"Do you really?"

"Are you interested?"

"Yes, academically, I am," she replied, somewhat equivocally.

"Oh? Are you doing historical research on the flagellation arts?"

"I guess you could say I've been researching the subject all my life," she sighed.

"If that's the case, you might be interested in my magazine," he said and went back into the shop to retrieve several issues of his self-published, New Rod Quarterly. Though the covers of his magazines were designed to appear Edwardian, with vintage illustrations and decorative borders of lotus and acanthus leaves, they had all been printed in Random Point within the last two years.

Hugo gave Mercedes the magazines and locked up the illustrated Frank and I in the glass case again. The girl leafed through each issue quickly, from back to front, then closed and hugged them to her heart. "Thank you!" she said. The next thing he knew she was putting her coat on.

"Would you like a check for the membership today?" he asked.

"That would be optimal, but I didn't have the heart to ask on a day like today. I'm sure business is slow."

"Nonsense. I had an extremely good Christmas," he told her, getting out his checkbook. She told him the rate for a year and he filled in the amount.

"I'll be back with your window placard next week," she promised. "Perhaps between now and then you could write up a little press release about you and the shop and I'll put it into the directory this Spring."

Hugo agreed and saw her to the door. That afternoon he visited Bartlett's Department store in Woodbridge, impulsively selected a pair of black suede gloves and a cloche to match and had them sent to Mercedes Vonderai at the Provincetown Chamber of Commerce with his compliments.

All week he wondered about the girl and her interest in books like Frank and I. His questions were answered the following Monday morning, when Mercedes Vonderai returned, in the same coat and boots, but with the addition of the hat and gloves which he had sent her, bearing the window placard proudly proclaiming Hugo Sands' Antiques a member of the Chamber of Commerce.

"Why did you send me presents?" she smiled with the embarrassed delight of a girl who doesn't get fussed over often.

"You looked so cold last week," he replied.

"I had a hat and gloves," she explained. "I just forgot them."

"That hat is very becoming on you though."

"Bartlett's is very expensive!"

"Honestly," he replied, "they were having a clearance sale."

"I probably shouldn't accept presents from a strange man," she confessed, "but they go so well with my coat and boots that I couldn't resist."

"Did you get a chance to look at my magazines?"

"Of course! I read them cover-to-cover several times each. In fact, I was hoping I'd be able to buy the back issues from you today."

"Don't be silly, I'll just give them to you," said Hugo, immensely encouraged, going back to his office and finding the five or six back issues she needed to make up a complete set of everything he had published so far.

"Thank you!" she said, tucking them into her leather envelope portfolio at once.

"I'm going to be in P. Town tomorrow on business. Might you be free for lunch?" Hugo asked.

"I'll be free."

"That's fine. About one?"

"Sure."

"Maybe you'll tell me what you think about my magazine in detail then," he suggested. She smiled faintly but looked uncomfortable. Just then the set director of a theatre company walked in and demanded to see any object remotely like a 19th Century Swedish stove. Mercedes used the distraction to politely slip out the front door with a wave and a nod.

Hugo looked longingly after her. So much had been left yet unsaid!

The next day was dry, very cold and windy. Hugo picked Mercedes up and drove her to a favorite inn off the coast road where he had called ahead to expect them. They were placed at a table by the fire in a small jewel toned dining room. Menus were brought quickly and orders placed. Wine was decanted and served.

"Thanks for getting everything going so fast," she said. "I really shouldn't be late back to work."

"That's a hell of a job you've got. Is there any future in it?"

"I doubt it," she replied with a wan smile.

"What did you expect to do with your degree?"

"Eventually write and teach. But I need to learn more first."

"Are you working towards a second degree?"

"Yes, I take evening classes at a pretty good local college. I've got one more year to go before I get my Masters."

"So you're working and studying full time?"

"That's about it."

"What do you do to unwind?"

"What's that?"

"How about letting me take you out sometime?"

"Of course."

"So, you liked my magazines?"

"...Yes," Mercedes replied, a hint of color coming into her cheeks.

"Good," he said. She parted her lips to say something more, then thought better of it and sipped her wine instead. Hugo was nonplussed by her taciturnity, for he'd never encountered the like in a spanking aficionado before.

Baffled and unsure as to how to proceed, Hugo changed the subject to her proposed master's thesis and sat back and listened to her expound, for the next half hour, on what she called "the business of love" in 18th century society. He had majored in Art History at Harvard and was perfectly happy listening to her analytical theories on Boswell and Casanova.

When Hugo delivered her back at the Chamber of Commerce building he told her he would call her in a few days. She smiled, nodded and ran inside, leaving him with the sensation that even if she wasn't in the scene, she was still worth pursuing for her brains, good looks and restfully reserved demeanor.

For the next several days Hugo pondered the puzzle that was Mercedes. Was it bashfulness, fear or disinterest that prevented her from discussing the materials he'd given her with him? He had grown so accustomed to being approached by wildly enthusiastic, spanking-starved women who seemed to discover life itself when they found his magazine, that he had to try hard to remember what a challenge it had once been getting ordinary girls to play.

From kindergarten on, Hugo had spanked his female playmates. Prior to puberty, he'd invent games to make them compliant, like doctor, teacher and house.

From junior high school on, he would spank as a form of flirting, instinctively fastening on the most playful of his female classmates to tease and make up to, thus he was never rebuffed when he found some excuse to turn them over his knee.

He attended a coed prep school, where by tenth grade, all the kids were reading paperback erotica, had seen various R-rated movies and fully understood the concept of foreplay. So again, spanking was blended into his seduction technique as smoothly as a band of chocolate ribbon into a butterscotch pudding.

In college finding tractable playmates was more challenging, as this was the era of Ms instead of Miss, of women instead of girls and of an aggressive backlash against the time honored American institution of benignly patriarchal, but integrally insidious male chauvinism. In college Hugo exerted care in seeking out the most uninhibited, if not classically "kinky" young women he could find at Harvard, Radcliffe and the other sister schools where he roved.

Following his own keen intuition as to which girls were naturally compliant and which unapproachable for anything beyond ordinary sex, he had never experienced the unpleasant adventure of being told off by an irate, self-actualized woman of the modern era as to why it was being a caveman to ever employ corporal punishment as an aphrodisiac. But that didn't mean it would never happen, and Mercedes was just austere enough to suggest that this would be her response.

Two days later, the next enormous rain front moved in over the Cape, bringing with it slightly warmer air. Hugo took Mercedes to dine at The Golden Owl Inn at Woodbridge and afterwards to see Rumble Fish.

This proved an excellent choice, as the moody sexiness of the production appeared to heat Mercedes' blood. When he asked if she wanted to see his house, she assented.

Taking the historical scholar over his old stone house took upwards of an hour, as he responded to questions about every interesting piece of furniture or painting they passed.

At last they migrated to the tiled kitchen, dominated by a large, stone hearth, in which he built a fire, while his several cats emerged from the pantry to greet her.

Pouring her a glass of wine and serving her a slice of pink and green marzipan cake, Hugo made a place for her across the wooden table and then sat down opposite.

"Wine and cake is very Henry James," she observed, reminding him once again that she was a woman of parts far beyond the perfect bosom, concave waist and insouciant hips in the clinging grey wool sweater dress. "May I take off my boots?" she asked, this time referring to shiny black rubber knee boots.

"Let me," he said, kneeling before her to pull each one off. Her small feet in white wool sox felt very wet. "Shall I take these off and put them by the fire to dry?" he asked.

"Yes, but do so quickly. I'm very ticklish!" she insisted, rosy-faced from the warmth of the fire and slightly reckless with wine induced courage.

"What pretty feet," he said, holding each one firmly as he took off her sox, so as not to tickle her. "They look so small."

"They're a size six," she said, pleased at the compliment.

"You're not very tall are you?" he asked. "You fooled me with the other boots."

"I'm five four," she said, awarding herself an extra, imaginary half-inch. "How tall are you?"

"Six-foot two," he said, now beginning to firmly massage the bottom of one foot between both hands.

"Oooh, that feels good," she sighed. "Normally I can't stand having anyone touch my feet."

"You just need a firm touch."

"That was such a good movie," she remarked once again. Hugo translated this to mean: "I am now aroused," and leaned up to kiss her on the mouth once, deeply, but not hard. When he pulled away her bosom heaved. She put her arms around his neck and drew herself towards him, opening her lips to his.

A few minutes later he was bending her over the table, pulling up her skirt, pulling down her panties, penetrating her with his fingers, manipulating her to a fine state of lubricity, deftly rolling on a condom, driving into her deeply from behind, holding her by the hips and filling her snug, pink, dewy glove with his rampant engine.

"Too deep, too deep!" she cried suddenly as Hugo's tightly sheathed knob hit the back wall of her very shallow channel. He immediately pulled out half way and began to slowly rotate then pull back and plunge forward, back and forward, never going in as deeply as the first time that had made her cry out in pain.

"You're such a little girl," he said fondly, lightly patting her bare bottom on each cheek. She looked back at him over her shoulder with either a shudder or a thrill. Hugo stopped himself from spanking her just then, and instead drew both her hands back behind her and pinned them to her waist by the wrists, held together under one of his hands.

When he felt by her grinding and panting and whimpering that she was possibly close to a climax, Hugo released her wrists and leaning over her, slipped one hand into the top of her dress and under her bra, captured one erect nipple between his thumb and forefinger and pinched it firmly. He pressed his other palm against her lower abdomen and drummed his long fingers against the specific region that had only recently been identified by a sexual researcher as the potent female "g" spot, just above her soft fleeced pubic mound.

Mercedes said, "Oh god!" and clutched at the table under her, squeezing him with every delicate inner muscle as she experienced her first orgasm at his hands.

Hugo allowed himself the same release, proud of having made her come so quickly and enthusiastically without resorting to anything more esoteric than a trapped pair of wrists, a lightly pinched nipple, a manipulated lower tummy and a virile penis.

Helping Mercedes up he turned her around, took her in his arms and kissed her. She clung to him affectionately, shudders still pulsating through her.

"No one ever took me like that before," she confided a few minutes later, as he plied her with additional wine and Parisian bonbons to restore her energy.

"You mean from behind?" he asked, gratified by her implicit

praise of his technique but still not certain she had fully understood what had just happened between them.

"I mean so... forcefully." (She understood!)

"You didn't seem to mind it," he suggested.

"...I didn't, while it was happening," she replied hesitantly, "but the moment afterward I felt uncomfortable, almost guilty about having an orgasm that way."

"Why?" he sputtered in surprise.

"It's hard to explain."

"Try!"

"Letting a man treat me like that goes against everything I believe in."

"What exactly is it you believe in?"

"That the sexes are equal, that neither should attempt to dominate the other, either physically, emotionally or financially."

"Mercedes, nothing we did violated any of those precepts. I obeyed my impulse to take you and you obeyed your impulse to yield to me. There was never any conflict, never any force. You know that."

"I know, but the way that you did it, pinning my wrists, pinching my nipples...it was more an act of conquest than of love."

"I'm sorry you see it that way, Mercedes. But obviously, you've yet to realize that hot sex and political correctness are pretty much mutually exclusive for people like us."

"What do you mean, people like us?"

"People who read spanking magazines from cover to cover."

"It's getting late, I should go," she said, beginning to don her sox.

"Really, Mercedes, I'm surprised at you, a highly educated woman expressing such backward sentiments about her own sexuality. Do you even know who you are?"

"Apparently you think I'm a pervert!" she returned unhappily, pulling on her boots.

"That's your word, not mine. But I do think you're being needlessly neurotic about a subject that should give you nothing but joy."

"Why should it give me joy to think that I can't get off unless I can play a completely passive role in any sex act?"

Hugo digested this statement while watching her struggle to pull the tight rubber boots on. Finally he replied, "What's wrong with that? Simply choose partners who enjoy playing the aggressive role, like myself and you'll guarantee yourself satisfaction."

"At the cost of my principles?" she shot back, roused to indignation.

"Certainly not," he disagreed. "Isn't self-actualization one of the cornerstones of modern feminism?"

"Yes," she replied, still frowning with emotional indecision as she slipped her extremely plain black bikinis back on.

"Don't you see, Mercedes, to repress your most basic sexual desires just because they happen to be a little esoteric is foolish, ungrateful and self destructive."

"Why?" she stopped violently combing her straight, collar length hair and shook it back so that it fell about the curves of her head like silk. Then she replaced the glasses that had come off during her sojourn across the tabletop.

"Foolish because you're trying to fight your own nature and Nature with a big "N" besides; Ungrateful because you're attempting to extinguish the single most bountiful aspect of your entire libido, your own innate and brilliantly responsive submissiveness; and self destructive because in leaving these desires unexpressed, you're causing yourself to experience year after year of acute sexual frustration."

"What did you mean by Nature with a big N? That whole theory of a racial unconscious? We fear and crave what our cave ancestors feared and craved?"

"I'm sure you're familiar with the notion of animal spirits. In our case, they go back about a million years."

Mercedes shuddered and continued setting her clothes to rights. Hugo gazed at her over folded arms shaking his head.

She looked at him and murmured, "I'm sorry, I know I'm repressed. You're probably right about everything."

"Of course I'm right about everything!" he agreed enthusiastically.

"But I just can't see it your way," she insisted.

"You're not really going out in the cold now? Please stay the night."

"No. I... I think becoming any more intimate with you would be dangerous for me," she said bluntly.

"It's true that the more nonsense you talk, the more I want to spank you!"

Mercedes blushed and put on her coat.

"Do you want me to call you?" he asked, walking her to the door.

"You'd better not."

"All right, you call me when you're ready to play like a grown up," he said, opening the door for her. Impulsively she turned, threw her arms around his neck and kissed him full on the mouth.

"It's not that I don't like you," she cried in a rush, "I like you very much!" Then she ran down the gravel walk to her car.

"Silly girl," Hugo said to himself as she drove off into the cold, wet night.

That weekend he ignored her injunction and invited her to accompany him to an estate auction in Boston. She allowed him to call for her at her untidy loft in a Provincetown Victorian on Saturday morning. Her front room with a bay window view of the main street was set up as a research study and Hugo found her library interesting.

"I love that you're a scholar," he told her, determined to avoid any incendiary topics until he'd plied her with dinner and drinks later on. "Oh, pack a small valise," he added. "I thought we'd stay overnight at an inn."

"You're taking me to Boston for the weekend?" she asked, coloring with pleasure. His heart contracted momentarily at the notion that Mercedes might have lived twenty-six years without ever being properly courted or spoiled by a man.

He explained, "I want to show you my other shop, take you to tea at the Copley Plaza, proceed to the sale and a few book stores, pause for a leisurely dinner, then catch a band at one of the clubs later on. I don't think we'll want to drive back after all that. Do you?"

"No," she replied, pleased by all these promised civilities.

"Good. You need to relax. And don't worry, I booked us two rooms, in case you're still afraid of me, yourself or Simone de

Bouvoir. Now pack!" he encouraged her with a single sharp pat on the back of her jeans, then continued to peruse her bookshelves with admiration.

"Damn it, it's the end of the week and nothing's clean!" she muttered on her knees before her bedroom bureau, attempting to ignore the sensation that the casual smack on her bottom was creating in the pit of her stomach.

Hugo overheard and called, "I'll take you shopping in Boston."

"Rooms at inns, shopping, costly gourmet dining, are you rich, Hugo?" she asked, coming out of the bedroom with a hastily stuffed overnight satchel.

"By your standards? Yes!" he replied. "And I don't mind going shopping with women. Besides, I have very good taste."

"Frighteningly so." she agreed, "If I didn't know better I'd think you were gay."

"I am fussy," Hugo agreed, without taking offense. "But that's part of my charm."

"You're a perfectionist, aren't you?" Mercedes asked as they strolled along Newberry Street several hours later in the cold, bright early afternoon sunshine. "I could sense your disapproval at my sloppy housekeeping."

"You're busy and impoverished. Some day you'll be able to afford a maid," said Hugo, leading her into Bonwit Tellers.

They went straight up to lingerie where Hugo unerringly selected a French lace combination, a quilted dressing gown in copper satin and matching slippers.

"Try on the camisole and tap pants," he told Mercedes, pointing her towards the fitting room.

"I can't let you buy these things for me," she protested.

"You need them," he insisted, inwardly deploring the trend towards wearing plain, unadorned lingerie, which Mercedes already embraced.

Twelve minutes later they walked out of the intimate apparel department, Hugo with a large, shiny, ribbon tied box under his arm and Mercedes with a smaller one under hers. They stopped in sports clothes on the second floor on the way down and Hugo picked out an

Irish sweater and a pair of heavy woolen trousers to replace the thin jeans she had on.

"There's a new cold front moving in tonight and I don't want you freezing if we stay out late," he explained as they exited the store, now each laden with packages.

"Do you get pleasure dressing women up like dolls?'

"Yes," he replied, ushering her into Maison Robert a few minutes later, where he'd reserved a table for lunch.

"I don't really feel comfortable with all of this," she told him after he ordered wine for them.

"I can see you're not used to being pampered. Don't worry, I'll turn you into a sensualist yet," he promised.

"Do you really think I'm worth the investment in time and energy?"

"What a thing to say," he shook his head in disapproval.

"I mean considering our difference of opinion on certain subjects."

"Oh, that."

"Nothing's really changed for me since the last time I saw you," she said, sipping her wine as soon as the waiter filled her glass.

"You mean you're still in puritanical denial about your most basic physical needs?" he sighed.

"I mean I still see inherent dangers in the practice of sado-masochistic foreplay."

"And I still can't comprehend your utter lack of curiosity about a subject which fascinates you!"

"I don't want to open Pandora's box."

"There's such a thing as being too timid."

Mercedes drank her wine without answering.

"It's ironic," he commented at length, "my last girlfriend was the most naturally dominant woman I've ever met, yet she willingly played the submissive all the while we were together, and here you are, obviously a life long enthusiast, frustrated to tears and you don't have the nerve to take the first step on the road to exploration, even with my perfectly trustworthy self here to guide you!"

"Why did your last girl friend play the submissive?"

"Because she was curious about every nuance of sexual power and saw me as someone who could teach her more about it."

"And did you?"

"I'll say. She learned enough to become a mistress and followed her destiny to San Francisco."

"Did you expect something like that to happen?"

"Not the mistress part, but I never expected to hold onto Cassandra for long. She was very independent."

"Are you still getting over her leaving?"

"I had been missing her terribly until the day you walked into the shop."

Mercedes hid her nose in the wine glass.

"When you let me make love to you the other night with so little preamble, and proved so receptive, I thought we had perfect chemistry. But your prejudices are discouraging."

"I'm sorry," she found herself unable to meet his eyes.

"It breaks my heart to think you're too ideologically rigid to allow yourself to enjoy the type of sex you crave."

"Let me think about this," she petitioned. "This is all so sudden for me. I never met anyone like you before, so sure of themselves about something like this. I don't know whether you're talking sense or spouting sophistry to undermine my political beliefs."

Hugo simply shook his head and sighed, convinced he hadn't made the slightest progress but resolving once again to let the subject drop. The rest of the afternoon was taken up with the estate auction on Boylston Street.

After dining and stopping briefly at their hotel to change clothes, Hugo took her to a club in Cambridge where X was performing. It was the first time Mercedes had ever been exposed to hardcore punk and as Hugo expected, the experience aroused her. They stopped for a few nightcaps at a favorite bar of Hugo's in Back Bay on the way back to the inn, which was situated just off the Boston Common. By this time the temperature had dropped to the single digits and Mercedes was extremely grateful for the thick woolen leggings Hugo had thoughtfully supplied her with earlier that day.

The drinks had begun to make her sentimental, and she was

disposed to allow him to tuck her in. But upon reaching their inn, Hugo merely saw her to her door and then retired to his own room.

Mercedes put on the satin gown, quilted robe and matching slippers he had bought her earlier that day and waited in bed for his knock on the door. Meanwhile, Hugo went downstairs to the parlor, poured himself two complimentary brandies from the snifter on the sideboard, smoked a cigarette and watched the fire in the hearth ebb to cinders. Then he simply went to bed.

Mercedes didn't understand why Hugo never came to her that night and in the morning she awoke with a large question mark over her head. Why had he bothered to pay for her to stay overnight with him in town if he didn't plan to take advantage of her proximity? Why buy her expensive clothes, if not to divest her of them in the jewel box of a room where he had deposited her? None of this made any sense to Mercedes as she had her morning bath, then dressed once more in the wool pants and sweater he had given her.

It had grown warmer overnight and the morning sky was white with snow as they met in the dining room to help themselves to breakfast off the sideboard.

"Too bad you weren't able to buy anything at the auction," said Mercedes.

"Oh, didn't I tell you?"

"What?"

"That young man who kept outbidding me on everything turned out to be Anthony Newton. He came over and introduced himself to me while you were in the powder room."

"The Broadway composer?"

"Yes."

"No wonder he was able to bid like that."

"He cheerfully admitted he'd been following my lead. He actually knew who I was. He gave me his card and told me to call him whenever I came across an interesting piano and he'd buy it."

"Sounds like you made a good connection," she observed.

"I couldn't be happier," Hugo agreed and indeed would never forget that Mercedes had been his lucky charm the day he first met Newton, who would become his most important client as well as perhaps his closest male friend.

Mercedes felt her shoulders untense as the onus of the weekend's success was lifted from them by Hugo's superb networking coup. She saw herself relax in the mirror opposite their table and smiled at how it had all turned out. But then she remembered her frustration and indecision of the night before, how she had longed to be taken again by this cool headed, confident male, in spite of every trepidation.

"Is something wrong?" Hugo suddenly asked.

"No, why?"

"You were wrinkling your brow."

"I was just wondering whether it was really worth it to you to bring me along this weekend."

"Of course it was worth it," he replied with an enigmatic smile.

"Really?"

"Why not? I find you an extremely pleasant person and you don't talk too much."

"Is that really enough to merit the Casanova treatment you've been giving me?"

"The what?"

"The lavish meals, deluxe accommodations, perfect wardrobe pieces, in short the big investment in a seduction that's already been accomplished and obviously left you lukewarm at best."

"I'd like to express greater warmth towards you," he said.

"Then why didn't you come to my room last night?"

"Why didn't you come to mine?"

"I didn't think you were interested."

"Were you interested?"

"Yes," she replied, looking into his eyes.

"Then why didn't you let me know?"

"I suppose I felt it wasn't my place," she demurred.

"How hopelessly old fashioned of you."

"That's true, it isn't in the slightest bit liberated to wait to be asked."

He covered her hand with his and said, "Next time don't wait. Ask me."

"I don't know if I can."

"Mercedes, a sophisticated woman articulates and gets what she wants," he told her firmly.

"I accept that in theory, in practice I've never been forward with men."

"I think you'll find that most men appreciate encouragement."

"I thought just coming along with you was encouragement."

"Coming along with me did indicate a certain degree of availability but I thought I made it clear that I don't feel we should pursue any further intimacy until we agree that D&S is to be an integral part of our relationship."

"But what exactly does that mean?"

"D&S? Why, dominance and submission, of course, particularly as expressed through corporal punishment."

"Corporal punishment?" her hand fluttered unconsciously to her bosom in the manner of a silent film siren.

"Yes, as in Frank and I, the book that riveted you so completely the first day we met, and my New Rod magazines, which you claim to have devoured whole. I'm talking about spanking, Mercedes, or did you not realize?"

Mercedes blushed at the lecture and excused herself from the table to run upstairs and pack. It was the second time the word spanking, pronounced, had made her wish to flee his presence.

A few minutes later she opened her door to his knock. Hugo walked in and closed the door behind him.

"Some say the surest way of dispelling a fear is to confront it," he told her, dragging the room's one armless chair into its center.

This time both slim, white hands flew to her throat in disquietude and she cried, "What are you going to do?" Then, as he pulled her down across his lap, she added, "Hugo, stop! You can't do this to me! I haven't agreed! Please don't. I'll die! I'll just die!"

"I highly doubt that," he replied, "but it is nice to finally see you come to life!" Hugo noticed that in spite of her protests, she didn't even try to struggle as he positioned her with absolute precision, locking his arm around her small waist and pinning her wrist to her side.

Upturned and encased in the nubby woolen trousers, her bottom although small, was ideally formed.

"Mercedes, what am I going to do with you?" he asked rhetorically, smoothing her tweed-upholstered seat with his palm until he felt her begin to untense slightly. "So intelligent, so cultivated, such an impressive vocabulary, yet I've known fourteen year old girls better able to express their emotional needs."

Mercedes gave a little sob at this humiliating charge but murmured, "It's true, I'm pathetic. Why else would I be submitting to this indignity without question!" she reproached herself bitterly.

"Because you've already asked all the questions. Now it's time to get the answers," he instructed, still stroking her through the thick woolen cloth of the snug fitting trousers.

"Go limp so I can feel your full weight pressing against me," he ordered, drawing her in even closer to his own center. The moment she obeyed him his manhood sprang to vigorous life. Feeling it throb beneath her, she gave a little wriggle on his lap. "Notice the effect of your compliance?"

"Yes," she replied, turning to show him a calm but curious profile.

"It's simply nature taking its course, my dear. You blurted out in a moment of clarity that deep down you long to surrender. That's all I'll ever ask of you."

"I doubt that can be true," she protested, leaning up on his knee to look at him.

"Why? Whatever do you mean?" he said, brushing her fine, ash blonde hair behind one ear and giving her pink earlobe a pinch. This tiny gesture caused her to shudder, blush and subside on his lap again, hiding her face. He noted this and again reached down to capture her velvety earlobe between his thumb and forefinger. "Why won't your surrender be enough for me? Do you know something I don't know about me?"

"I've read the books," she softly replied. "I know about the services required of submissive women!"

Hugo let go of her earlobe and lightly caressed her cheek and throat. "Is that what you've been worrying about, having to service me?" he laughed. "Silly. I couldn't care less about head. This excites me a million times more!" he insisted, patting her bottom lightly.

Finally he began to spank her, not severely, but hard enough for her to feel a sting even through the thick pants. He spanked her evenly and meticulously, first smacking one cheek and then the other, then lengthwise across the middle, again and again. After a few dozen swats he paused and said, "You see how you aren't even close to dying from this?"

"Yes," she replied, breathlessly.

"You can grind against me as hard as you like," he told her. "I have very strong thighs from skating."

The spanking continued, Hugo's hand descending metronomically on all the spankable portions of her dainty backside for sheer minutes on end. Then again he stopped and holding her tightly against his lap, one arm across her waist and the other across the backs of her thighs he began another conversation.

"There's something you can say to me, in case it starts to hurt too much," he informed her.

"What should I say?" she stopped herself from grinding against his hockey hewn thighs long enough to reply, though it was difficult returning to the earth after floating aloft in a pink gauzy ether of sensation.

"When you've had enough, say: I'll be good."

"Okay."

"Have you had enough yet?"

"I don't think so," she said softly.

"But you're feeling it, I hope?"

"Oh, yes!" she replied, reaching back to rub her bottom in demonstration.

He caught her wrist, locked it to her waist again and continued spanking her, slower and harder. Unconsciously she ground deeper against his lap each time his large palm descended, now aware of a sexy and pervasive heat radiating between the surface of her skin and the fabric of her clothes. "You're so responsive," he observed, pausing to stroke away the sting. "I'll bet I could get you to come like this."

Right, left and middle, his hand kept coming down, vigorously warming her entire bottom from her lower hips to her upper thighs and everything in between through the comforting protection of her tweed pants. As the rhythm of her breathing increased, so did the intensity of the spanks raining down on her backside, which at last caused Mercedes to kick up her legs and wriggle to and fro to dodge his hand.

"Hold still," he told her, firmly pulling her back into place and anchoring her to his lap with his arm thrown heavily across her waist. "I hope you realize that I'm doing this for your own good," he advised her, concluding the session with two dozen solid smacks, evenly distributed across both cheeks and resoundingly delivered, with enough empty space in between each swat to allow her to feel its penetrating impact and react with a pant and a kick.

On smack five she reflexively threw her hand back to shield her belabored bottom. He caught it, slapped it on the back and pinned it to her waist. She shuddered inwardly and subsided on his lap. Hugo had no way of knowing how profoundly aroused she'd become, for she scarcely breathed through the last of the paddling, no less indicated that she had actually climaxed.

When he let her go she slipped down off his lap and onto her knees by his side. As her palpitations faded, she clung to him, her arms tightly wrapped around his wiry torso, too embarrassed to raise her eyes to his or accept the tender kisses he was ready to bestow upon her face.

Finally she looked up at him. "I can't believe that happened. Just like in the Heinlein book."

"I Will Fear No Evil?" he asked, ever ready to accurately identify a reference, no matter how obscure. "You mean you had 'a female orgasm' " he quoted the scene gleefully, "just from getting spanked over your clothes?"

"Not one. They kept coming, from the moment I put my hand back and you caught it," she marveled, still feeling the echoes of the exquisite sensations resonating from her sex to her heart center and back, not once but many times. "I wish I could understand why."

"You got a good spanking. That's why," he said, lifting her to her feet and enfolding her in his arms.

Mercedes was unusually quiet on the drive back out to Random

Point, as she mentally relived the spanking over and over again. Like a magical incantation, whenever she came to the moment when Hugo slapped her hand, the memory of this gesture would cause a mini aftershock to reverberate through her entire inner core. She hadn't felt so inflamed since the first time she caught Across the Wide Missouri on The Late Show then spent the rest of the night dreaming of a spanking from Gable.

"Coming from a spanking the way you did, over your clothes and with no other form of stimulation - that sort of thing only happens to hardcore spanking enthusiasts," Hugo informed her cheerfully as he let her off at her house, which was already frosted with several inches of snow. "So welcome to the Scene," he said, grabbing her gloved hand and kissing it before she got out of his sports car.

Too overcome by strong feeling to reply coherently, she murmured her thanks for the weekend and presents and fled quickly into the gaily-painted triple-decker without a backward glance. Attributing her lack of articulation to her usual shyness, Hugo triumphantly returned to his house and cats, without a doubt in his mind that Mercedes was now his.

Therefore it was with extreme amazement that he received the following typed letter two days later at the shop.

"Dear Hugo," it began, "I am writing to explain that I am still confused and somewhat troubled by this affair that we seem to have begun.

I don't know if you planned to call me again, but if you did, perhaps you should not, at least until I have a chance to consult one or more qualified therapists about the possible ramifications of pursuing a romance based on fetishism and psychosexual perversity.

Please do not think that I am ungrateful for the magnanimous attentions with which you have showered me, the genial hospitality to which I have been treated every moment in your company and the delicate restraint with which you have conducted the more intimate portions of our brief relationship.

May I add that your physical charm, personal magnetism and

intellectual refinement have so completely enchanted me that I have scarcely thought of anything but you (and spanking), and you spanking me, from the day I walked into your shop.

You're a gentleman and scholar who has shown remarkable patience in the face of my tortured indecision. This is why I petition your further forbearance, while I attempt to sort out my future plan of action with regard to my own erotic evolution.

This week when I go into Boston to baby-sit some of my accounts, I'll also be arranging for counseling with the experts to whom I've referred. I hope I have your support in this endeavor.

Yours truly,
M."

Folding up the note with mounting anger, Hugo strode back into his office, threw himself into his chair, rolled a piece of thick, letterhead stationary into his machine and began typing rapidly. Feeling his pulse accelerate with his frustration, he dashed off the following reply to her humbly helpless missive:

"Mercedes,

You irritate me more than I can say.

How dare you question Nature's gift - the perfect zipless orgasm - flawlessly delivered, with the total cost to you of one slightly pinkened backside!

Haven't I explained how all of this works?

Hasn't my magazine proven to you that you're not the only one?

Who could possibly be more qualified to analyze your obsession with spanking than an experienced lifelong enthusiast who has played with dozens of women in The Scene?

What therapist has letter files crammed with effusive testimonials from scores of women whose sex lives went from hell to paradise in the few short weeks that followed them discovering my magazine, answering its ads and finally meeting the men who could and would give them precisely the kind of thrills they'd been dreaming of their entire lives?

Was I anything but patient and gentle with you? Did I even pull your pants down for your very first scene?

In retrospect I'm astonished by my own misplaced sensibility. I should have worn out my strap on you for your willful insularity.

You claim to be an intellectual, hold a degree from one of our best colleges, whose major field of interest is the Enlightenment, no less, yet you're less tolerant of alternative sexualities than the average reader of The National Enquirer. At least tabloid fans confront and attempt to understand anomalies. You merely seek to conform to a sterile standard of reactionary feminism that's already fifteen years out of date!

And don't get me started on that subject. You aren't even fit to call yourself a feminist, with your persistent repression of the most essential part of your sexuality.

Now you're going off to actually pay good money to an asinine assortment of casebook and textbook bred mental health technicians who will only validate your own fears and repressions, urge you to strive to be normal and force you to conform to some standardized version of lovemaking as alien to your true psychological makeup as is possible!

You'll do anything to avoid satiating your own most pressing desires and why? Do you have that many friends who would judge ill of you if they knew you simply enjoy being turned over a man's knee? And even if you did, would their opinion matter more than your own sexual gratification, if not salvation?

Anyone who can write a thesis as complex as the one you described to me, ought to be able to master a subject as elementary as her own sexual response without recourse to so-called experts, most of whom have never gotten within a mile of a real fetishist, no less ignited one into flames!

Yours in disappointment bordering on despair,
Hugo Sands."

After ripping the note out of the typewriter and reading it over two or three times, Hugo crumpled it up, tossed it in the trash and started again, much more calmly.

"Dear Mercedes," he now wrote, "Do not call me unless you're ready to submit to the thrashing you deserve for embarking on this idiotic course of action.

Sincerely,
Hugo Sands"

This too he crumpled up and tossed in the trash. Then he took out her letter again and reread the portions referring to his good looks and charm, noting her appreciation of his generosity and marking her tacit admission of an infatuation for him. But it was no use, the instant his eyes fell upon the words "qualified therapist" he became choked with resentment. Her naiveté with regard to what made a person "qualified" in this field was inexplicable to Hugo, when he considered the acute mental clarity and psychological penetration she seemed to bring to every other subject.

Perhaps she really wasn't for him after all. He'd never met a girl less intuitive about sex or less willing to trust him with her secrets. This frustrated and made him sad. Critical and highly judgmental by nature, Hugo was now ready to label Mercedes an emotional misfit and entirely give up the chase.

Always certain of the wholesomeness of his own desires, it was almost impossible for him to comprehend a like minded enthusiast not being similarly confident and self assured. As a successful and experienced player, erudite publisher and intelligent matchmaker, Hugo considered himself one of the Prime Movers in the Scene and therefore pretty much the final word on what was morally ethical, psychologically beneficial and stylistically correct about the phenomenon of modern, recreational D&S. That Mercedes wasn't ready to acknowledge this seemed to Hugo nothing so much as the injurious expression of a willfully stupid and neurotic disposition.

The more he dwelt on the subject, the more irritable he became and thus resolved to put a period to their brief and unfulfilling relationship that very hour. He decided not to answer her letter and (after rereading the portions relating to her growing affection for him several more times), with one final grunt of severe disapproval, slipped her note into his desk.

Two days later, while lunching with an associate on the second floor of a fashionable restaurant in Copley Square Hugo happened to look out the window and spotted Mercedes going into the Boston library with her leather envelope portfolio under her arm. It was an extremely cold day but clear and the three-day-old snowfall had become encrusted with a coating of glassy and dangerous ice. He saw Mercedes slip on the stairs but steady herself instead of falling and then hurry inside. Concluding his meal rather more quickly than he had planned, Hugo departed from his friend and went across the street to the library.

He found his girl in the Special Collections department, seated alone at one of the polished wooden tables and carefully taking notes from one of several old tomes.

He slid into the seat beside her as she looked up from her books with a start.

"Hugo! What are you doing in town? Gee, I'm glad to see you!" she exclaimed, going pink with pleasure and surprise as gales of butterflies took flight inside her.

"I was having lunch across the street and I saw you come in."

"Oh, Hugo, I'm very glad to see you!" she reiterated, going so far as to throw her arms around his neck and press her cheek briefly to his. After this type of greeting it was difficult to remain cool and remote but he managed. "In fact, can we talk?"

"It seems to me we've done nothing but talk," he protested mildly.

"Please, Hugo?" she asked, with endearingly meek persistence.

"Will it be worth my while?" he exchanged severity for wolfishness.

"I don't know. That's for you to decide," she demurred charmingly.

"All right. I keep a little flat nearby. We can go there."

"You have an apartment in town?" Mercedes asked with wonder, gathering together her papers and shrugging into an old but still handsome fur coat.

"I often stay overnight," he explained, taking her by the arm as they left the building.

"Then why didn't we go there last weekend? Why book an

expensive inn?"

"Well, there's only one bedroom and I didn't want you to feel as though we had to be intimate."

"I did want to be. I told you that."

"Yes, dear, I know you did, but twelve hours too late for it to matter."

"I'm sorry Hugo. About that and everything."

"I'm down on Marlborough Street about seven blocks from here. Want to take a cab?" he asked.

"Let's just walk," she replied, tentatively putting one boot in front of the other until they reached the portion of sidewalk that had been sprinkled with sawdust. "Did you get my letter?"

"Yes, I got your letter," he said, lighting a cigarette. "It made me want to wring your neck."

"I'm sorry."

"Well? Did you consult your one or more therapists?"

"Yes."

"And?"

"Well, first I went to a psychologist."

"Female?"

"Yes."

"And what did she tell you to do?"

"Actually, she suggested I join a B&D support group."

"No kidding!"

"Yes, her take on the situation was something like: if it feels good do it, as long as you're not harming yourself or others."

"I'm impressed."

"Then I saw a sex therapist."

"Another female?"

"Another female."

"And what did she suggest?"

"She offered to bring over a surrogate that afternoon to play with me."

"You didn't take her up on that offer, I hope!" Hugo replied indignantly.

"No," she smiled. "But I thought it awfully nice of her to offer."

"Nice nothing. The very idea of a girl like you having to pay a man to play is ludicrous. Hell, I could find a hundred men in Boston who'd pay you for the privilege! And well!"

"Are you offering to turn me out, Hugo?" she smiled.

"Maybe later," he promised without humor. "Well, did you see anyone else?"

"Yes, a psychiatrist."

"Female?"

"Male."

"And what did he say?"

"He traced it all back to my father."

"Really? How so?"

"Well, my father was cool and never showed me much affection."

"Oh? I'm sorry to hear that."

"Thank you. The doctor thought it significant that the only time I had close physical contact with my father was the few times he spanked me as a child. He said this could be one of the reasons I tend to eroticize discipline."

"What else did he say?"

"Well, he brought up an interesting point about me being born during the 60's, the exact decade during which the woman's movement fully took hold. He said that the media conditioning I received during my earliest years was a mass of contradictions, juxtaposing the images and mores of the early 20th century, against the sexual revolution and feminist movement of the late 60's -early 70's, thus accounting for my confusion as to proper and improper behavior between the sexes."

"That is interesting," said Hugo, reevaluating his opinion of counselors.

"He suggested that to allow politics to circumscribe my sexual behavior, was as potentially limiting to real personal expression as the women of a hundred years ago permitting religion to repress their most basic biological urges."

"I told you repression is bad," Hugo reminded her.

"He said that it would be different if I was depressed about my orientation; but since I was only intellectually conflicted about the socio-political aspects of being mildly masochistic, he didn't feel that a protracted analysis of my problem would be of benefit to anyone but himself."

"I didn't think psychiatrists came that honest," Hugo marveled.

"They're not charlatans, you know."

"You got lucky," Hugo replied.

Ten slippery minutes later they were entering the extremely old brownstone where Hugo kept a small, well-furnished flat on an upper floor. Hugo lit a fire in the sitting room hearth and heated water for tea while Mercedes took off her coat and looked around.

"I would have asked you about your relationship with your father if you'd given me the chance," he said reproachfully, when she joined him in the old fashioned, tiled kitchen. "But you insisted on pretending that your interest was merely academic, and fled my company the moment we got close to discussing anything real!"

"I explained I was confused," she protested mildly, flicking back her straight, silky hair in characteristic style before sipping the hot tea.

"So now that you've gotten permission from the entire Boston medical community, are you going to start behaving like a normal girl in the scene?" he demanded.

"How does a normal... woman in the scene behave?" she replied provokingly.

"She tells a man what she wants, what she's about, what makes her tick. Would it kill you to discuss your fantasies with me?"

"It wouldn't be easy."

"How about writing them out? Most of my female subscribers can't wait to pour their hearts and souls out to me. You're as reticent as the sphinx."

Mercedes smiled softly and said, "I don't think I could tell you anything about me you don't already know."

"Nicely put, but I'd still like to get some sort of feel for your tastes and leanings."

"How should I know what I like or dislike when I've never done anything with anyone apart from what I've done with you?"

"That's crazy talk. Everyone knows what they want and don't

want, it's just instinctive."

She shook her head, "But I'm completely inexperienced."

"Never the less, you've read enough to know that the scene is rife with rituals, some of which you may love, others of which you may loathe. For example do you wish to be stood in a corner with your skirt above your waist and your panties pulled down?"

"No!"

"Do you fancy being spanked by another woman in front of me?'

"Of course not!"

"Have any desire to don a school girl uniform and be traditionally caned?"

"No!"

"Would you like to be put in a leg spreader bar and whipped in every intimate place?"

"...What's a leg spreader bar?"

"Maybe I'll show you next time," he threatened gruffly.

"I am intrigued by bondage in connection with ...discipline," she answered, with difficulty. The bondage tumbled off her tongue, the discipline following but reluctantly.

"Finally some relevant data! Classic B&D does make sense for someone like you."

"What do you mean?"

"Well, you're so horribly repressed, so painfully embarrassed to ask for what you want, the best thing would probably be for someone else to simply take control. Once you're in bondage, the problem of choice is removed. All you need do is react to the stimuli applied. Right?"

She buried her face in her teacup again, answering his question without words.

"At last we're getting somewhere!" he declared with some satisfaction.

They walked into the sitting room where the fire was crackling cheerfully. Hugo seated himself on a loveseat opposite the hearth and motioned her to him.

"Come over here," he said authoritatively. She came to him and he pulled her down to sit beside him. "You're such a solemn little creature," he said, taking her chin in his hand and leaning down to kiss her on the mouth. "I'd like to make you laugh some day."

"Read to me aloud from Diderot or Voltaire," she suggested seriously.

Hugo smiled and kissed her again, a little more expressively. Then he pulled her across his lap to enfold her in his arms and crush her to his chest. When he stopped kissing her mouth, her head fell back and he fastened his lips to her throat. Her small, full bosom heaved with emotion as he fondled her firmly through her cranberry wool open collared sweater, lightly pinching each nipple through the protective fabrics, which still shielded them.

She seemed almost to swoon in his arms as he romantically ravished her, now allowing his hand to slip up under her black wool skirt until came to rest between her slim thighs, snugly encased in black, textured tights above her good leather walking boots.

Pushing his palm between her legs he pressed it against her Venus mound through her tights and panties, kneading her there first lightly, then more resolutely, while still kissing her mouth and throat, lightly biting her velvet ear lobes and inhaling the natural perfume which emanated from her hair and skin, until the crotch of her textured hose became damp, then wet.

Turning her over on his lap so that her bottom became upturned, he pushed her skirt up to her narrow waist and beheld her slim, oval cheeks, tautly pressing up against the semi-opaque tights with their quaint woven clock pattern. Arranging her legs so that her feet were together on the floor, arching her bottom up across his lap, Hugo deliberately rolled her pantyhose down to her upper thighs, revealing a pair of plain black cotton high cut briefs, covering her pearly, silken bottom with stylishly skimpy simplicity. These were also patiently rolled down to her thighs, to finally uncover her bare pale skin, pristine, smooth and innocent of even a blush.

Smack, smack, smack! His palm came down on either cheek resoundingly.

"Oh!" she cried, and jumped at the first swat. "Oh, oh!" the next two smacks elicited an even more lively response.

"It feels different on the bare, I expect," he remarked, stroking the sting away with his hand, then commencing the spanking again. First one cheek then the other, received this stinging benediction, again causing her to shift and wriggle on his lap, to plunge and buck, pant and squirm.

"Yes! Different!" she agreed breathlessly, putting one slim, graceful hand back to shield her tender skin.

"What did I tell you about doing that!" he asked her, catching her wrist and pinning it to her waist in a way that caused a ripple of pure submissive bliss to radiate through her. Smack, smack, smack! Smack, smack, smack! He spanked her again and again while holding her hand to her waist. She merely whimpered as small orgasms flashed through her.

"Oh," he paused, "thank you for your letter!" Smack, Smack, SMACK! "I thought you'd never write. And then you did." This declaration preceded a flurry of resounding slaps, which dusted her oval cheeks from hip to hip with a patina of magenta.

"I was only stating my feelings."

"Which made you seem backward and slow, which infuriated me, because other than that, I like you."

"I am backward and slow," she protested.

"All the more reason to allow me to guide you," he admonished her.

"So I will!"

"But only because you've been given permission to do so!" Smack, smack, smack! The spanking continued to communicate Hugo's indignation.

"No. I have a confession to make."

"A confession?" This stayed Hugo's hand.

"Yes."

"Well? What is it?" Hugo clasped his hands together and rested his forearms on her waist, still pinning her to his lap.

"I didn't visit any doctors this week."

"What's this you're saying now?"

"I didn't consult any experts about us."

"Are you saying you dissembled? Unfolded a tissue of lies?"

"Yes. I lied."

"Well!" he said before an awful pause. "May I ask why you decided not to follow your original plan?"

"Oh, they all wanted between fifty and seventy five dollars for a consultation and I just couldn't afford it. As it is I'm on macaroni and cheese until payday."

"So why pretend?"

"It seemed easier than admitting the truth."

"Which is?"

"That I'm too intrigued not to want to pursue this," she explained, turning to look at him.

"All right, get up," he ordered, standing her in front of him and pulling a clean white handkerchief from his breast pocket. "Put your wrists together in front of you," he told her.

"But, why?"

"Just obey me," he ordered sternly, putting her hands together and quickly binding them with the handkerchief. Then he got up, took her by her wrists and bent her over a sofa arm. "I'm going to teach you the first cardinal rule of B&D," he told her, unbuckling his belt and pulling it out of his trouser loops; "Never lie to your master." Wrapping the buckle portion around his fist, he turned the belt into a single lashed strap.

He pushed her skirt up over her bare bottom and holding one hand in the small of her back, applied the belt end stingingly, six or eight times, to the centermost portion of her pinkened cheeks. Every time the strap came down she gave a little cry and moved against the sofa arm in response.

"Anyway," he said, pausing with the belt against her backside, "at least you've come to your senses, all on your own." A few more sharp swats caused her to catch her breath.

"Telling lies is, of course, very naughty. But since being naughty doesn't come easily to you, I hesitate to punish you severely for that!" He tossed the belt away and pulled her up.

"Look," he said, directing her gaze over her shoulder at her reflection in a long mirror opposite them, which showed her black skirt still pulled up to her waist and her oval cheeks dark pink beneath it with fine, darker red lines from the brief strapping running across them. She stared in fascination, her face becoming as pink as her backside.

He pulled her to him and taking her by the wrists, lead her into the bedroom. "I'll bet this is the one thing you have done before," he smiled, placing her on the bed with her hands above her head and pulling off her sweater, then unhooking her dainty, front closing bra and removing it to reveal her firm, enticing bosom, gracefully rounded and girlish but in no way large.

"What?" she asked.

"Been tied up in bed." Now Hugo lightly pushed her down on her back and looped the handkerchief, which still snugly imprisoned her wrists, around a wooden knob on the elaborately carved headboard.

"No," she replied innocently, though again she lied. There had been inept boyfriends with silly scarves in more than one chilly dorm room. But none of those awkward starts counted. What mattered was the consummate beauty and balance of this present moment.

In a few moments he had removed every garment from her slim, curvaceous body which was as pretty as that of a pinup girl, especially with her hands pulled up above her head, lifting her bosom and pulling in her slender waist even more severely. Two pinches and her nipples went dark pink and stood to attention for the rest of the afternoon. Her eyes, riveted to his own, were glowing with fascination.

He caressed her, slid a pillow under her bottom, spread her legs, sat beside her, grazed her navel with his lips, pressed his palm against her lower abdomen and then let his fingertips begin to explore her painfully aroused sex organs.

"You, who love to hide so much, now have no choice but to let me see you. Completely," Hugo told her, deliberately spreading her thighs and labia, touching and examining her, while now and then looking back into her tawny eyes. "I'm sorry, is this embarrassing you?"

"Yes!"

"It's just that we rushed so the first time, I won't have you thinking that's typical."

Continuing to stroke and fondle her damp, pulsating Venus mound with one hand, Hugo moved the other up to lightly squeeze her breasts, firmly pinch her nipples, then her velvet ear lobes, all of which made her twist and writhe in a ticklishly tormented style, against the sage green velvet counterpane.

"Sex and Bondage Interlude #1," said Hugo, deciding to strip off his clothes and allow his own animal spirits to emerge.

"I always wanted to be a bondage pinup girl," she confessed, opening her eyes for a moment.

"Would you like to see what you look like in bondage?" Hugo asked, vastly encouraged at finally being made privy to one of her secrets and able to lay his hand on his camera in fifteen seconds.

"You mean you'd photograph me like this?" she asked, intrigued.

"Why not?" he said, setting the flash.

"But not for publication!" she insisted.

He smiled. "Why? Planning to run for Congress?"

"Maybe some day!" she returned impudently.

"When you see how pretty you look, you'll change your mind. You'll want to be in the magazine," said Hugo confidently, taking a few shots of Mercedes before putting the camera aside to join her in bed.

A few hours later they decided to dress.

"This time of day always makes me feel blue," said Mercedes, looking out the bedroom window at the darkening sky.

"Things can get scary when the sun goes down."

"And it always gets colder. So very much colder."

"Did you drive into town?"

"No, I took the train."

"Good. I'll take you back in my car."

Once they were snugly situated in his sedan he passed her the first joint she had seen since college.

"Smoke that half way down," Hugo told her, "and you'll never feel the same way about twilight time again."

"God, I haven't smoked in four years," she said, taking a hit and coughing violently. "Jesus, that's strong!" She stared at the cigarette in wonder. "Wow." She laughed. She began to relight the joint, then put the lighter down and stared out the window at the taillights of the cars ahead, all winding their way out of town. It had become warm enough to rain and the raindrops on the windshield made the lights run together like watercolors.

"Put it out for a minute and put the windows down. The toll booth is coming up," said Hugo, getting out change. Once they were past the obstacle he put the windows back up, took the joint from her, lit it and inserted Bitches Brew into the cassette player.

Mercedes didn't say another word until they were half way back to Random Point and turning into an inn for dinner.

"Blues go away?" he asked, after giving the waitress their wine order.

"Yes, thank you. Except for my canvassing this morning, it's been a beautiful day."

"How's that going?"

"Oh, just horribly," she sighed. "I've been at this wretched job for six months but I still earn the lowest commissions of anyone in my department. I know it's because I'm not aggressive enough, but I don't have it in me to hustle. Not only does going door to door drain me physically, but it's emotionally deadening as well."

"I can imagine," Hugo said sympathetically.

"Thank you for letting me complain. Lately you've been the one bright spot in my otherwise dreary life."

"Look, we've got to get you out of that job," Hugo said. "Have you tried applying for grants?"

"No."

"Let me ask around for you. I might be able to come up with something."

"Thanks!" she replied brightly, sipping the wine that had been brought to them.

"Maybe I could get one of my collectors to put up the money for a grant in return for you dedicating your book to him," Hugo mused.

"Since the subject of the book is patronage, that would be decidedly ironic," she replied with enjoyment. Then she remained peacefully quiet until the first course arrived, staring into the fire, remembering the afternoon in Back Bay and wondering if and when she'd have the opportunity to wear the lace combination for him.

Then Hugo said, "Would you like to hear my short term plan for dealing with your work related stress?"

"Of course!"

"Quit your job at the Chamber of Horrors and come work for me. I've needed someone to help me on the magazine for a while. I'm getting behind. And the subscribers are getting restless. They send awful letters."

"You'd pay me a salary to work on your magazine?"

"I'll match what you're getting now anyway and throw in lunches."

"You mean, I just work on your magazine? That's it and I get paid?"

"It's more demanding than it sounds, but I think you would enjoy it and so would the readers."

"And you would be my boss? My only boss?"

"I would be your editor."

"So what would I have to do?"

"Edit stories and letters, write columns and articles, picture edit and caption, storyboard photo shoots, shop for wardrobe and props, answer queries from writers, schedule models. There are a lot of things you can help me with."

"You really think you can trust me with all that?"

"I can teach you to spec type and crop photos. You're impeccably literate and you said you've been researching the subject all your life. I don't see any problem with you stepping into the job tomorrow."

"But are you really sure you can afford an assistant? I mean to say that if you could, why don't you have one already?"

"Maybe I've been waiting for the right person to present herself."

"But, would I really be an official employee with all the dignity that word implies or just a sort of in-house writing slave?"

"Now, what's that supposed to mean?"

"Would I have to teeter around on stiletto heels wearing nothing but a green visor and a printers' apron?"

"That's an intriguing image, but apart from coming in to use the equipment and go through the files, I imagine you could do most of your writing at home. I might ask you to look after the shop the few days a month I'm out of town, but never in only an apron and high heels."

"Well, it all seems too good to be true, so I can't help but be suspicious," she remarked plainly. "I might be dreaming this entire conversation as an aftermath of what you gave me to smoke."

"The offer is good," he insisted. "I need help."

"But what about the spanking? How will that fit in?"

"Perfectly, I should think."

"Does that mean you plan to spank me at work?" She went on guard.

"I hadn't thought about that," he admitted with a grin. "But I notice it's becoming easier for you to say the word. We're making progress."

"But would I be your lover or your employee?"

"The two aren't mutually exclusive."

"I've never engaged in an affair with an associate or co-worker. But I've been warned against doing so often enough."

"That's nonsense. Why shouldn't people who are fond of each other work together, especially on projects of mutual interest? I think we'll both have fun and the magazine will benefit from your fresh, feminine voice. There is no down side to this, honey."

Mercedes ate her dinner with a superb appetite. Then they proceeded to drive the rest of the way to her flat in Provincetown. He carried her bag upstairs for her and followed her into her apartment for a final embrace. But her mind had been revolving on the possibilities of his proposal and she not only stepped out of hugging range but suddenly came out with a statement that took him completely by surprise.

"Hugo, you seem so mercurial. You might be capricious as well. Suppose I come to work for you and then you quickly tire of me sexually. Would I still retain the job? Or would I be dismissed?"

At length he replied, "Do you want another paddling?"

"Why?"

"What do you take me for?"

"I'm just saying, I don't know you well enough to predict your behavior."

"Ditto, but I'm willing to take a chance. Why aren't you?"

Mercedes looked down. "I'm sorry."

"Never mind," he said gently, helping her off with her coat and hat. "For some reason you're insecure and I probably haven't helped that. I don't tend to flatter with words, so you may not even know how attracted I am to you. And now more than ever since you seem to have finally stepped out of the closet."

"I am insecure. Horribly so," she admitted. "But you have helped, oh so much! And I can't wait to wear the beautiful undie outfit for you."

"I'll look forward to that," he promised, hugging her good-bye. "Now do as I recommended and give your notice tomorrow. And come to me as soon as ever you can."

Chapter Seven

The History of Hugo Sands Part 4
Modern Spanking Romance

The cruelest phase of winter was holding Random Point in its grip. Consequently, Hugo Sands Antiques stood virtually empty from morning to night. However, in the back offices, Hugo and his new editorial assistant, Mercedes, were putting out an esoteric magazine so intriguing that many readers were subscribing to it years in advance.

In addition to being his latest lover, Hugo's pretty new employee was also a grindingly accurate historical scholar whose field of interest overlapped with his own. Clearly she would some day write very good books and he liked the idea of being her first patron.

But in spite of her probity and focused intelligence, Mercedes was still an inexperienced girl without a clue of how to manage a dominant male. This fact was driven home to Hugo on the one-month anniversary of their first meeting. He had spent the morning ice-skating on the duck pond across from his shop and only came in around noon. On entering his office he was disquieted to see the mail already open on his desk.

"Mercedes, why did you open the mail?" he demanded when she entered his office a moment later.

"I just wanted to get the letters to type for the next issue," she explained, pushing a tendril of straight, shiny ash blonde hair back behind one delicate ear.

"Please don't do that again, dear," he said, managing to control his annoyance along with his impulse to slap her bottom very hard.

"I'm sorry," she replied, going pale. "I didn't realize I wasn't supposed to."

"That's just basic business etiquette, honey," he said mildly.

Sitting down he began to leaf through the letters. The envelopes she'd opened contained subscription payments and orders for sample issues. The letters specifically addressed to Hugo she'd left sealed. Hugo took a deep breath and felt calmer. These still unopened envelopes contained various missives from female readers; some confiding their dreams and frustrations, others submitting personal ads and a few extremely motivated individuals petitioning to personally correspond with the editor of the New Rod Quarterly.

Hugo didn't like to tell Mercedes that he had an unofficial fan club, composed of ardently submissive women, who wrote regularly to proposition, challenge, tease, bait, woo and seduce him. Nor did he wish to admit that some of them he encouraged.

Mercedes returned a few minutes later with a coffee tray.

"I wouldn't have opened this one, but it wasn't marked personal or specifically addressed to you," she produced a heavy, gold edged card on which was scrawled a short note, paper clipped to a photo of a striking brunette. "I'm sorry. It never occurred to me that you actually have women pursuing you," she said, unable to conceal her distress at the discovery. "Excuse me," she said and vanished back into her small office.

Hugo studied the photo of the smart beauty, then read the accompanying note. "*Dear Hugo*," it began, "*Your magazine is flawless and your photo is hot. If you're ever in Manhattan on a Saturday night, come play with me at The Vault. I would love to go submissive to a man in a tailored suit. Sincerely, Nikki Leigh*."

Hugo joined Mercedes in her small office where she was seated at her desk attempting to compose herself.

"Mercedes, you can't get upset about women writing to me. It's inevitable when one publishes. You'll have your own following as soon as the first issue with your photo appears. Then you'll get more letters than I do. And some of them will be from men you might actually want to play with."

"You mean let other men handle me?"

"Sure, why not?"

"But, I thought we were seeing each other."

"Seeing each other? We're practically living together," he laughed, for they had spent every other night for the past several weeks locked in each other's arms. "But that doesn't mean we shouldn't adventure now and then."

"You think of that as a good relationship?"

"Certainly!"

"Is that how you conducted your last relationship?"

"Uh huh," said Hugo.

"So you do plan to meet this woman in New York?"

"Why not? She might be uninhibited enough to pose for the magazine. She might give me a terrific interview. She might know other girls who want to place ads with us. One live wire can lead to twelve different connections."

"If you didn't publish the magazine, would you still be going out of your way to meet other women now?"

"Let me think about that one."

"Were you never faithful to one woman?"

"Of course, but that was before I found myself in the center of the scene. Naturally I now feel a greater obligation to be social than ever before."

"Why? If the personal ads coming in are any barometer, there's no shortage of single men available to satisfy the needs of the women who write you. In fact, there is a disproportionate number of available males to females right now. Isn't it selfish of you to dazzle these women and in all probability ruin them for the deserving but largely ordinary men they might have looked upon more favorably had they not met you first?"

"I love the way you put that," he commented without disagreeing.

"And your last girlfriend, the mystic? What did she think about your conducting yourself in this fashion?"

"She wasn't the type to set limits," he smiled as he recalled Cassandra's wisdom.

"So, you're going to New York?"

"Eventually."

"She looks very sophisticated," said Mercedes wistfully. "And she writes with such confidence. I envy her ease."

"Why don't you come to New York with me and we'll both meet Nikki at the Vault? You'll appreciate that hellhole on a John Waters level."

"You think I'd enjoy meeting a beautiful woman who has designs on you?"

"It might relieve your anxiety."

"How so?"

"I'll let you tell me that after you've met her."

"I can't go to New York. I'm too busy," she said as he turned to leave.

"You'll go," he said closing the door softly behind him.

"Do you want to write an article about spanking in the movies?" Hugo asked Mercedes later that afternoon.

"I don't think I know enough about the subject to speak with any authority on it," she demurred.

"Watch these then," he said, leaving several videotapes on her desk.

"What are they?"

"Compilation tapes of spanking scenes from mainstream movies."

"Where did they come from?"

"Various collectors put them together. Here," he said, handing her a sheaf of typed manuscript. "You'll find the stars, years of issue, production companies and titles on these lists."

"Is there a VCR here?"

"I've got one. I'll hook it up in your office."

Hours later, Mercedes emerged from her office in a palpable state of heat. She was so warm and pink in the face from watching the vast multitude of spanking excerpts that Hugo felt her forehead to see if she was feverish.

"Take the tapes home and watch them again," he advised her. "I have a dinner engagement, but I can come by later to tuck you in."

Mercedes knew what he meant and put her arms around his waist, pressing her cheek to his chest. "I'm sorry I was jealous," she murmured. "You take good care of me. I should be more grateful."

He turned her face up and kissed her red mouth. "I like the way you presumed to scold me today," he said, "though doing so was not in the best of taste."

"When I said it was selfish of you to interpose yourself between your few and far between female advertisers and the multitudes of men who so desperately need to meet them?"

"Again, your turn of phrase is incisive, but rude, considering that you are my protégée."

"If we really are in a relationship," she mused when he let her go, "haven't I the right to question your motives in meeting other women?"

"Sure, as long as you understand that I'm always likely to default to professional interest and thus remain perpetually unassailable."

"I see."

"At any rate, it's nothing to worry about," he assured her, "I'm growing fonder of you every day."

Mercedes' week of revelations continued to unfold the next day, which she spent entirely on editing letters to the Editor. She was starting her own column and had a large stack of epistles to choose from, which she began to attack with some excitement. But by noon, her spirits flagged and she merely sighed and shook her head as she typed in letter after letter from male submissives who wanted a spanking from Aunt or Teacher, male switches who mainly wanted to read stories about and see photos of women spanking girls; crusty old male dominants who requested photoplays and fiction which focused on girls in correctional institutions or college dormitories being harshly punished by their severe female matrons or attendants and an assortment of BDSM "masters" whose tangential interests extended to nipple torture, retention enemas and suspension bondage.

Mercedes read through twenty letters before she came across one which she felt even remotely reflected her own orientation, written by one of the few female subscribers. It was a charming letter, though it touched on a subject of little interest to Mercedes, namely, nostalgic spankings from the correspondent's grandmother.

"Most of these are from men," Mercedes told Hugo that afternoon when she placed her hard copy on his desk.

"That doesn't surprise me," Hugo said, looking up briefly from his newspaper and coffee.

"There was one sweet one from a lady named Elaine, talking about her childhood spankings. Do you know her?"

Hugo gave a short laugh. "Oh sure, everyone knows Elaine. She's been around the scene for years writing letters about her grandmother."

"Oh really? Have you ever met her?"

"First of all, Elaine's a man."

"Really?" Mercedes looked at Hugo, stunned.

"Oh, sure!" Hugo smiled without concern.

"That's awful! Why do they do that?" she cried, feeling her face go hot with anger.

"They enjoy reading their fantasies in print, I guess."

"It's perfectly hateful," Mercedes insisted. "No wonder the women all write to you first. Where are the real men, anyway?"

"They're there. But you have to realize that many more people subscribe to the magazine than bother to write to us."

"But why all these lesbian fantasies among the ones who do trouble to write? Do they get some sort of vicarious thrill out of imagining they are one of the women?"

"I expect that's exactly what the fascination is about," Hugo said.

"You don't think that way, do you?"

"I should hope not. Though I do enjoy watching one lady spank another."

"God, I hate that!" she replied without scruple.

"No bisexual urges?'

"Never."

"Anyway, get used to it. It's the number one male switch fantasy."

"Why don't they fantasize about being men getting spanked by women? Why do they have to be women in their fantasies?'

"Because in our culture, men are supposed to be strong and

authoritative, not submissive and yielding."

"I suppose I can relate to that," she replied, remembering how conflicted and frustrated she herself had felt about her own submissive needs only a few weeks before.

"Try not to judge these guys. They can't help being what they are any more than you can."

The next day, Mercedes began typing up the longer letters and memoirs that had arrived that month. Mid morning Hugo walked into her office with a tape measure.

"Stand up, I need to measure you," he told her, pulling her out of her chair. "Put your arms above your head," he instructed, proceeding to take her upper body measurements.

"What for?"

"I'm ordering you some fetish clothes from Holland and I need your exact measurements."

"What sort of clothes?"

"The sort that figures like yours were made for."

"Oh Hugo, these letters," Mercedes sighed. "They're making me hate life."

"What's the matter now?"

"They're so sadistic, the dominants. They don't seem happy unless they've induced screaming hysterics and inflicted livid welts."

"They're just fantasizing."

"But why such violent fantasies?"

"They were probably mistreated as children."

"Suppose these malcontents actually start dating our women through the ads? Aren't you afraid of what they'll do in their ignorance?"

"It's a valid concern," Hugo admitted. "But did you know that you have a twenty four inch waist?"

"So how are you going to address that concern?" she asked, blushing as he measured her hips.

"Only 33" around the hips," he commented, squatting in front of her to take her leg inseam measurements.

"Hugo?"

"Well, part of our job is to promote proper scene etiquette. That's why it's so nice you're here to express the female point of view," he told her, springing up to notate the measurement he'd just taken.

"You mean I can respond to these horridly sadistic confessions the way I really feel about them?"

"Of course, so long as you remember to be diplomatically equivocal at all times. For example, you'll find the phrases: "in some cases", "a notable exception" and "the vast majority of" indispensable to putting over your most heartfelt generalizations. Now your shoe size is six, right?"

"Yes. Am I getting new shoes as well?"

"Boots, baby, boots, boots, boots," he promised with a smile.

"There's a letter from a Victor K. that's perfectly vile."

"Yes, he's a player. European, very rich. Spends half his time in B&D clubs beating the holy hell out of the girls. Don't tell him off, whatever you do. I've been angling for him to come out and visit the shop. He collects 18th century furniture and art."

"So he's the kind of person who actually does the kind of things he writes about his letter?'

"Yes. He's the notable exception," Hugo replied, putting away his small notebook of measurements.

"And how am I to respond to his letter diplomatically?"

"Oh, easily. You say things like, 'While nipple torture may not be appropriate for every submissive, the vast majority of B&D enthusiasts will eventually experiment with milder forms of breast discipline, such as pinching, spanking and in some cases, the application of light to firm clamps."

"In other words, you narrowly justify the fringe behavior while offering less severe modifications?"

"Precisely. And obviously, when writing in the editorial voice, you would characterize someone like Victor as a classic martinet rather than a dangerous whack job."

"So we as editors must practice sophistry?"

"I wouldn't call it that."

"I would."

"I think you have to remember that even what you yourself enjoy might be considered harmful and dangerous to someone not in the scene, while a girl like Slave Amy might find a player like Victor just right."

"Who's Slave Amy?"

"A new customer. You'll find her ad in the batch I just put on your desk to enter."

As a new female ad was still a novelty at the offices of the New Rod Quarterly, Mercedes hastened to explore the brown-corded folio that Hugo had left on her desk. She found Slave Amy's ad on top of a stack of a dozen or so others and rolling a fresh piece of paper into her typewriter, arranged the neatly printed piece of loose-leaf paper on her copying easel. She quickly began to transpose the childishly rounded letters into crisp typescript as follows:

"Humble female slave, 23, natural, long, straight, blonde hair, blue eyes, 5'3", 105 lbs., slender, seeks master in greater Boston area to punish and use me as he sees fit. I need to be spanked until I cry to make me a better girl. I have many flaws and often make mistakes. Correct my willfulness with stringent corseting and tight bondage. Purge me of my naughtiness with embarrassing retention enemas. Force me to yield to you in any position or degree of exposure you prefer. Fill my head with your desires and my body with your essence. I am not beautiful and have no special genius, therefore I will be to you a modest, non-demanding slave. Kind and caring lover preferred for long-term relationship, excellent dominant of any stamp will be granted favors in return for proper discipline. Contact Slave Amy through this magazine and command me to reply."

Now Mercedes noticed the accompanying snap shot in the envelope sent by Slave Amy. She studied it with a pounding heart, for this Boston based submissive was a good deal more attractive than her self-deprecating description implied. The photo was of a young, slim, corseted blonde, apparently dancing onstage at a club or bar. The three quarter shot showed her lithe body in sensuous motion as she virtually made love to a silver pole, with her head thrown recklessly back and her pale blonde hair flowing to her waist. The sheer built in bra of the corset revealed a small, firm, rounded bosom with dark pink nipples. Her graceful legs, black hosed, seamed and gartered, were punctuated by five inch high heeled fetish pumps that elegantly lifted her trim, curvaceously seat, clothed in only a black satin g-string under the hip length hem of her elaborately sewn beige and black, brocade satin corset. The only flaw in Slave Amy's photo was a prominent nose, which Mercedes felt gave the girl's face some character. On the back of the photo Amy had penned in permission to publish it with her ad.

Mercedes took the photo out to Hugo on the floor of the shop where he had just accepted an antique clock repair job from that day's lone customer.

"This Amy Albright sent a very pretty photo, didn't she?"

"Yes, she should get snapped up in short order," Hugo agreed.

"I wish she hadn't pressed so hard with the ball point pen on the back of the photo," Mercedes mused. "The imprint comes right through."

"Why don't you call and ask her to send you another one? It looks like a publicity still from the club where she works. I'm sure she has more."

"Don't you think she'd prefer to hear from you?" Mercedes asked.

"I thought it bothered you when I got in touch with the female advertisers."

"Doesn't this one interest you?"

"Sounds like she needs a lot of attention," said Hugo, taking the photo and looking at it again.

"Don't you think she'd make a good model for the magazine? She's in Boston. Should be easy to schedule her for a photo shoot, especially if she's already exotic dancing."

"Good point. Why don't you mention that to her when you call about getting the new photo?" he said, handing the photo back to Mercedes and getting his clock repair kit out of a wooden drawer under the back counter.

"I'm not bad with a camera," said Mercedes. "I could easily photograph you spanking her for the magazine."

"I'd rather photograph you spanking her," said Hugo.

"Oh no, I don't want to do that. I told you how I feel about girl-girl stuff."

"It was just a thought," shrugged Hugo, rolling up his sleeves before laying out his tiny tools.

"Would it ... please you if I consented to pose in a photo shoot with this girl?"

"Certainly it would, but I don't want you to feel pressured."

"I don't," said Mercedes, thoughtfully walking back to her office with the photo.

Several weeks later, Mercedes and Hugo were arranging a corner of Hugo's Boston shop for a photo shoot featuring Mercedes spanking Slave Amy, who was due to arrive momentarily.

It was about seven pm and a light snow was falling on the city. The manager of the shop had long since gone home and the rest of the shops on Mass. Ave. were closed and shuttered. They had just come from a wardrobe house adjunct of one of the Back Bay theatres with several Edwardian costumes. Presently a young female stylist arrived to dress the girls' hair.

Now Mercedes went into the back office to don the outfit which had been obtained for her role as an elegantly dressed young woman of the early 1900's. The gown was of mauve and cream with antique gold looped fringes and a frothy white lace edged sweetheart neckline. The corset that went underneath, which had been designed especially for an Ibsen play, had been formed for a slightly larger woman than Mercedes and had to be laced to its smallest circumference in order to gird Mercedes' trim waist to greater advantage.

"This is comfortable," she said with surprise as Hugo expertly laced her.

"Don't get used to it," he warned, slapping her bottom smartly, "the one on order from Amsterdam is going to lace a lot tighter than this!" Then he helped her with the gown and buttoned it up the back. When she was ready he instructed the attentive hair dresser to arrange Mercedes' hair in a chignon with bangs. Since her hair was only chin length and not especially thick, this required some art and

Hugo left them to it while he waited in front of the store for Slave Amy to arrive.

The small, slim blonde, wrapped in a PVC trench coat and shiny black knees boots tumbled out of a cab a few minutes later with a round PVC bandbox containing her own personal, custom made Victorian corset from BR Creations in California. Hugo paid the driver then turned to look the girl over.

"Mr. Sands?" she asked shyly, smiling up at him and looking very young. "I'm Amy."

"I said seven sharp, Amy," he scolded her over folded arms. "You're fifteen minutes late."

"Oh, I'm sorry!" she cried, her blue eyes immediately moistening at the severity in his tone.

"Is this the way you make a first impression?" he demanded, ushering her into the warm shop. "And what kind of a silly coat is that to wear out on a cold Boston night?" He took the bandbox away from her, unbuttoned her raincoat and helped her out of it. Underneath she had on a short, pleated black wool jumper over a thin, pearl grey polo sweater. "Did you bring your I.D.?" he snapped, tossing her offending coat on a counter.

"Yes, of course," she replied, digging in her black PVC purse for her black PVC wallet and producing a driver's license that proclaimed her to be above the age of consent.

"In future, don't show up in Back Bay dressed for the Combat Zone," he warned. "It looks like I'm ordering outcall."

"I'm sorry," she replied meekly, peeking at him from under her long lashes.

"How long has it been since you've had a good spanking?"

"I've never had a good spanking," she admitted, her eyes glittering with instantaneous excitement as they met his.

"What do you mean, never? I thought you're Slave Amy?"

"I am. I mean, I want to be. It just hasn't really happened yet. That's why I sent you the ad."

"Why are you dancing in a club? Have you no education?"

"I have a degree in psychology from B.U., but there's a glut of psych majors competing for the same jobs this year and I haven't been able to find a position so far."

"H'm, that's too bad."

"I like dancing," she replied.

"Oh, don't be ridiculous."

Amy bowed her head in submission to this judgment and waited for instructions.

"And you're asking for trouble with that ad," he advised, seating himself on a tall backed wooden chair and motioning her to his side.

She came to him with a blush. "I'm sure you were late on purpose," he declared, pulling her lightly down across his lap, for she seemed to weigh nothing. She was a small girl who fit across his lap like a child. "After this you won't be able to say that you've never had a spanking," he told her, folding back her pleated wool skirt to reveal her small bottom and slender legs, snugly encased in nubby black wool tights. He raised his hand slightly and brought it down firmly, first on one cheek, then the other, one then the other, six times, eight times, ten times. "Oh! Oh! Oh!" she cried out in tiny gasps every time his large palm came down on her shapely yet compact bottom. Her legs began to kick almost at once and she squirmed at every pause. "You see, I'm barely spanking you and look how you're reacting. While your ad made you seem like the world's most experienced submissive. Don't you see you're asking (Smack!) for (Smack!) trouble (Smack, smack, smack!) ???"

"I didn't realize," she gasped.

"Stop wriggling and hold still," he recommended sternly.

"I will!" she whimpered, shuddering with abandon to his will.

"That was a reckless and highly immodest ad, in spite of its undertones of abject humility. You have to learn to be more circumspect when petitioning strangers in our scene to notice you. Hold a little back. Reserve your submission until you encounter a worthy object upon whom to bestow it. Otherwise you'll find yourself in a world of trouble," he told her, setting her on her feet without lowering her tights. She rubbed her bottom vigorously while looking down at the shiny round toes of her boots. "Understand me, young lady?" he demanded, lifting her chin.

"I think so," she replied, pink faced and glowing.

"As inexperienced as you are, you should start by requesting a daddy instead of a master in your ad."

"Really? Why?"

"Because you're altogether too compliant to be presented to a hardcore dominant. Most masters I've met would consider it their sacred obligation attempt to control your every thought and motion, and from the way you phrased your ad, you seem quite silly enough to let them."

"I'm not really as lame as I sounded," she protested mildly. "I just thought that was the way one was supposed to approach dominant men."

"We'll discuss the intricacies of writing personals later. Meanwhile get dressed while I finish arranging the set," he pointed her to the inner recesses of the shop. "Introduce yourself to my girlfriend and tell the stylist to pull your hair back in a bow at the base of your neck."

Still rubbing her bottom, Amy left him and Hugo began to light the Edwardian drawing room set he'd assembled.

Mercedes was grateful that the hairdresser was putting the finishing touches on her coiffure when Amy entered, for she preferred to keep the slightly younger woman, whom she perceived to be a tangible rival for her lover's affections, at a comfortable distance. The circumspect graduate student was still not sure why she had agreed to participate in the photo shoot, wherein she would immediately be called upon to spank another female, an activity for which she felt not the smallest inclination. Her acquiescence, so she mused, undoubtedly sprang from the awkward and uncomfortable concept of pleasing her man, which unfamiliar yearning had lately manifested itself in response to her fear of losing Hugo to a more obliging submissive.

The notion of losing Hugo was not to be born. Yet she could not avoid feeling disquieted at agreeing to perform like a puppet in a girl spanks girl scene, merely in order to stroke what was apparently the universal male libido. Now, in addition to dealing with her new relationship anxiety, Mercedes had also to contend with a sudden rush of post-feminist guilt at compromising her heterosexual orientation just to satisfy her boyfriend's desire to photograph her going through the motions of punishing a younger, blonder and clearly much more submissive female than herself.

Amy was warm, friendly and confiding as Mercedes helped her to dress quickly.

"I can't believe I'm getting paid for this," said the girl, lifting her skirt and pulling her panties aside to regard the blush left behind by Hugo's hand. She grinned with delight and touched the smooth pink surface of her skin with wonder. "It doesn't feel warm," she said to Mercedes. "The stories always imply that it's going to feel warm,"

"What's it like getting spanked by a stranger within minutes of meeting him?" Mercedes couldn't help asking, feeling violently jealous of the uninhibited girl.

"I wouldn't call Hugo a stranger," Amy smiled, "I take his stories to bed with me every night."

Mercedes felt a flutter of repulsion mixed with a curious excitement at meeting one of Hugo's groupies.

"You're so lucky to be his girlfriend. I wish I could find an alpha male to rely on. I can't wait until my ad comes out. I'll get to play a lot then."

When the exotic dancer was installed in a chair for the makeup artist to prepare, Mercedes went out to Hugo to receive his final instructions.

"Lovely," said Hugo, on seeing her in her costume. "How do you like the set?"

Mercedes looked over the parlor corner Hugo had arranged with approval. "So, what do you want me to do?"

"Go and stand in the set while I adjust the lights," he instructed, rolling and taping paper hoods on his large lights, fussily angling the smaller ones, experimenting with them and shifting them around incessantly until Amy appeared, adorably arrayed in her sailor style frock, her hair curled and tied in back with a large velvet bow. "Now Mercedes, you stand near the high backed chair and Amy, stand by her side. Mercedes, you're Amy's older sister. You have been looking for Amy all afternoon. There was note from the day school that Amy has been playing hooky for the past three days. She's been seen with the neighborhood hoydens at the Ice Cream Parlor, the tea room, the Nickelodeon and in the park with boys. As your parents are touring Europe, you, Mercedes, will have to act in loco parentis and punish your naughty sister with a good spanking."

"Am I to scold her before I spank her?" asked Mercedes.

"Yes. Look serious and try to communicate the nuances of the fantasy through your body language. Once you've got her over your lap, hold her close to you, grasping her firmly by the waist. There should be no mistaking who is in control here."

"Okay, scold, spank, serious," Mercedes reviewed before calmly composing her face.

"Amy, stop smiling and look as though you were going to receive a painful and humiliating punishment. Mercedes, you're doubly furious at your sister because you needed her this afternoon to write out wedding invitations for your June nuptials. Ever mindful of your impending responsibilities as a young matron, you must steel yourself to be extremely severe with your recalcitrant sister, now treading an erroneous path. Pause after you deliver each line and allow the meaning to penetrate. This will give me the time I need to catch your expressions."

Mercedes was an intuitively excellent model while Amy tended to lose her focus, giggle, look at Hugo instead of Mercedes and turn her face away from the camera.

"Amy, concentrate," Hugo urged, "be aware of the camera without looking directly at it, but never turn your face entirely away from it."

"It hurts to keep my neck twisted that way for a long time," Amy complained.

"Then lean up on your elbows or the heels of your hands and twist from the waist instead of the neck," he advised. "And don't make me tell you again about looking at the camera, Amy. If I have to tell you again, you'll get a cane stroke."

Mercedes stared at Hugo in shock. While Amy merely murmured, "Yes, Sir."

The shoot progressed slowly, due to Amy's apparent inability to concentrate. Since Hugo knew she wasn't stupid, this sloppy inattentiveness provoked him into taking dramatic action sooner than later.

"Excuse me, Mercedes," said Hugo, lifting Amy off her lap and pulling the younger girl by the ear to a nearby drum table, which he bent her over. Taking up a short, straight rattan cane, he laid one juicy cut across the back of her skirt.

"OW!" Amy cried, bursting into tears an instant later as she was repositioned across Mercedes' lap.

"Now let's proceed with the posing," said Hugo, picking up the camera he'd loaded with color film. "Amy, turn your face towards the camera but don't look directly at the camera. And don't make me tell you again."

"But, she's in tears," Mercedes protested, tenderly brushing a few tendrils of blonde hair off Amy's brow.

"I'm all right," Amy whimpered.

"She's fine," said Hugo. "Let's continue."

Paradoxically thrilled and appalled by her lover's imperious manner and the harsh measures he felt necessary to engage Amy's attention, Mercedes addressed her duty gravely, reserving all remonstrances for a more private moment.

Seizing a moment when Amy excused herself to fix her lipstick Hugo gave Mercedes' waist a squeeze and said, "You're doing brilliantly, my love. Your attitude, expressions, everything is perfect."

"Is this so?" she replied, in amazement.

"Wait until you see how photogenic you are."

"Hugo, aren't you being too rough on Amy?" Mercedes ventured.

"Ha!" he snorted. "Don't worry about that."

"But how can you speak so severely to her, and cane her for something she can't help?"

"Of course she can help it. You saw how much improved she was after a caning."

Amy returned to them.

"Well, young lady?" he demanded.

"I'm ready," she replied, seeming to have forgotten all about the cane stroke and his unkind remarks.

Moving into the bare bottom portion of the photo set, Hugo

instructed Mercedes to raise her victim's skirt and ruffled petticoat and separate Amy's split bloomers to expose her backside in the shape of a cameo. The bare oval of bottom that peeked up at Mercedes from between the openwork drawers was already creamily pink.

"Now take that small oval hairbrush and touch her up with it," Hugo instructed, picking up his black and white loaded camera now. "Amy, you're looking at me again. What did I say about that?" Amy looked down in trepidation and shame, giving Hugo a perfect expression. But this did not save her from another cane stroke. "No, hold her in place for me," Hugo told Mercedes, applying one sharp stroke across the centermost portion of Amy's bottom.

"OW!" the girl cried again and once again started to sob.

"Perfect," Hugo commended, moving back and picking up the color camera. "Now look far, far away, Amy, into the distant future when you won't be subject to your sister's whims," Hugo encouraged. "Look rebellious through your tears!"

This instruction was something beyond what was available to Amy dramatically and she merely looked confused. This also worked and Hugo continued photographing her face.

"Spank her harder with the hairbrush, Mercedes. Don't hold back, we're almost done here and I want some reaction out of her."

"But there's a mark from the cane. And she's already crying," Mercedes protested weakly.

"It's okay," Amy looked back and smiled at Mercedes. "I want this to look good."

"Are you sure?" Mercedes asked Amy searchingly.

"Make it hurt," Amy replied. "I deserve it for not paying attention."

"You see?" Hugo said. "She's fine, I tell you. Let's go on. It's time for both you young ladies to strip to your corsets and drawers. We still have to get through the posed caning shots."

About an hour later, satisfied with the photos he had taken, Hugo and Mercedes dropped Amy off at her house in Allston Brighton. Hugo helped her up to her second story flat with her bandbox and Mercedes saw them conversing for a few moments in the upstairs hall before the girl entered her apartment.

"Are you going to use her again?" Mercedes asked as soon as he returned to her and hurriedly got behind the steering wheel, for it was a very cold night.

"Depends on how the photos come out. She was pretty awful. You saw what I had to do to make her pay attention. Nice girl, though."

"She was very compliant."

"You noticed that, huh?" Hugo grinned. "I hope you don't plan to take me to task for the way I treated her."

"I was wondering what you were thinking, acting that way."

"I was only doing what she expected. Believe me, that was the mild end of the spectrum she's about to be exposed to when her silly ad comes out."

"Are you...going to see her again?" Mercedes asked softly.

After rather a long pause he replied, "Well, I do kind of owe her a scene."

"You do?"

"Sure. After all, she did the best she could tonight. I think she's counting on playing with me at least once."

"You think she still wants to after tonight?"

"Oh, honey," Hugo smiled. "You've got so much to learn."

"And you want to play with her?" Mercedes asked. "I mean, even though she's... not very bright."

"Oh, she's bright enough. She just has a problem concentrating. She probably watched too much TV as a child."

"So you find her attractive?"

"She's cute. I have to admit, her submissiveness is attractive to me."

"She's exponentially more submissive than I am."

"Yes," he agreed. "And no."

"What's that supposed to mean?"

"Let's just say I found you very charming tonight."

"But you turned me into a dominant."

"Turned you nothing. It came naturally to you. Wait until you see the letters pouring in after they get a glimpse of you wielding a hair brush."

"So you plan to exploit me as a dominant rather than a submissive?"

"Did you enjoy posing?"

"I'll let you know after I've seen the photos."

"Could you stand the loss of dignity involved in posing for a submissive scenario?" he asked.

"If it was as artistically photographed as today's scenario, of course."

"Happens quickly doesn't it, this loss of inhibitions?"

"You've seen it all before?"

"Once or twice."

"What I need help with is coping with the jealousy I'm suddenly feeling about every other woman who is fixated on playing with you."

"Help coping, huh?" he looked at her. "You seemed to be coping just fine tonight.

"I was working hard to give that impression."

"Well, you needn't feel threatened by Amy or anyone else," he said, squeezing her thigh. "In addition to being an exceptional person in every way, you've been coming in unexpectedly handy lately. Why would I run after other women? I admit I enjoy an adventure now and then, but I'm not disloyal."

"I suppose I'll have to become more sophisticated for you."

"That's a must," he agreed.

"When you do see Amy, what are you going to do with her?"

They parked and entered the fine old apartment house in Back Bay where Hugo kept his elegant flat.

"What am I going to do with Amy?" Hugo mused, "Probably fulfill one of her more esoteric fantasies, just so she has something proper to compare her future nightmare sessions to."

"Why nightmare?"

"I just think she's a little too submissive."

"But you like that."

"Lots of people like that. People without my consideration for example."

"You weren't very considerate to Amy tonight, caning her for being stupid."

"Mercedes, I already explained, she was looking for some sort of discipline tonight. She'd worked herself up for her first meeting with me and would have been crushed if she didn't get a spanking."

"I heard you give her a spanking, but I saw the caning and frankly, I was shocked. I thought it was cruel to punish her for her limited mental capabilities."

"Oh, nonsense. If more children were forced to pay attention the old fashioned way you'd see an immediate return of good manners and literacy. Amy is a prime example of someone who is failing to realize her full potential simply because she refuses to take anything seriously."

"I think you're wrong. They've recently identified a syndrome called Attention Deficit Disorder that seems to explain Amy's problem with remembering instructions."

"I've heard all about it. They've got little kids on speed to help them concentrate. It's completely absurd. I still say a discipline is what it takes to focus a lazy child," he insisted, letting them into the apartment.

Mercedes went into the bedroom to exchange her street clothes for a dressing gown and slippers. Hugo began a pot of coffee and cut up some bread, fruit and cheese. She came out as he began a fire in the small parlor hearth.

"By the way, you looked extremely believable spanking Amy," Hugo told her, handing her a cup of coffee. "Your natural gravity translates into dominance beautifully."

"Thank you, I think."

"I told you my last girlfriend became a dominatrix, didn't I?"

"You seem rather proud of that," Mercedes noted, "but I can't quite figure out why."

"I shouldn't be," he replied, adding liqueur to his coffee. "I really can't take any credit for the transformation. She was strong when I met her and only got more powerful after I introduced her into B&D."

"I would think that a traditionalist like you would resent a woman become dominant."

"I'm not a traditionalist," he replied. "I'm a player."

Later, in bed, she told Hugo, "I don't think I could stand the humiliation of being punished for an actual character flaw..." she hesitated, "...but I do want to be punished. Seriously punished. As sternly as you did Amy."

He tightened his arms around her and murmured, "I'll make a note of that."

The next morning while they were drinking their coffee the mail arrived and with it Mercedes' new outfits from the European leather maker. Mercedes was too new to the milieu of fetish couture to realize that it was Christmas morning and simply sat and stared in surprise as Hugo pulled article after expensive black leather article out of the big cardboard box he had so carefully opened. He checked the various pieces against the packing slip, reading aloud, "One pair of ankle length Victorian boots, one pair of thigh high stiletto boots, one back lacing dress with long sleeves and a sweetheart neck, one long line leather corset, one leather hobble skirt and matching vest. Looks like it's all here."

"How much did all this cost?" Mercedes wondered, not knowing what to make of the receipt in guilders that had fallen out of the box.

"I won't know for sure until my statement comes with the conversion to dollars," he replied readily, "but roughly two grand. So be sure to treat your new wardrobe with the respect it deserves."

"Wow," she said, pressing the leather dress to her nose to inhale its heady scent. "Is it going to be worth it?"

"When you see how you look snugly corseted, you won't ask that question."

"I was laced for the photo shoot last night."

"But not tightly. It makes a difference."

"I don't see how I'm going to walk in heels this high," she observed, holding the Victorian ankle boot up to the cool morning light coming in through the Venetian blinds.

"You'll just have to practice," he told her with a grin. "Meanwhile, hurry and pack your bag, I've just decided that we're going to Manhattan today."

"But I was going to work on my thesis tonight. I thought we'd be driving back to Random Point this morning."

"No, we're driving to New York."

"But I don't have enough things with me for another night."

"Yes, you do. You left an extra change of clothes and under things here last time you were in town. And we'll bring all your new leather for tonight and tomorrow night at the Manhattan clubs."

"You mean like that place The Vault, where you have a standing date with that self assured young woman who sent you the photo?"

"Yes. And the spanking club Paddles and maybe a few of the dungeons. Now hurry and throw your things into a valise, but don't get dressed until I lace you into your new corset."

"Hugo, I have to work on my thesis this weekend. I've already taken too much time away from it this week," she demurred.

"Mercedes, attend to me!" he said seriously, "We're going to New York today. Understand?"

Feeling butterflies, Mercedes fled to the bedroom to pack her bag. In a moment he joined her, the black leather corset in one hand and its accompanying g-string in the other.

"Come over here," he said, sitting on the edge of the bed and pointing to the spot on the floor between his legs. "Stand here. Now."

"Why? What are you going to do?"

"Help you get this on."

"But why put it on me now?"

"All these questions, all this arguing. You obviously need more discipline. And I can't think of a better way than with stringent lacing." Hugo untied the belt of her dressing gown and pushed it off her shoulders. Her nude body was smooth and redolent of botanical soap from her recent shower. "Put this around you," he handed her the corset he had unhooked and she wrapped herself in it. "Now stand up very straight and let me hook these," he instructed, fastening the five hooks and eyes down the front of the garment. "Now turn around and let me lace you. If you haven't gained any weight since I measured you a few weeks ago, the two back halves should completely meet when you're fully laced. And they do! Turn around and let me see."

Experiencing light constriction, Mercedes turned and gasped at the dramatic image of herself, which she now saw, reflected in the wardrobe mirror. A flirtatious built in bra, formed of a stiff nylon frill, peeked out of the top of the corset while the same black nylon edging added a suggestion of lingerie to the hem. This was a corselet worthy of Bardot, circa 1958 and having never seen herself in this glamorous a light, Mercedes could only stare in amazement.

"I look like that?" she exclaimed.

"You are adorable," he agreed, fastening his hands around her willowy waist. "And your modesty makes you all the sweeter."

Mercedes kept staring at herself.

"Put this on," he said, handing her the g-string."

"These are supposed to serve as panties?" she asked.

"You can't wear regular panties with a corset like this. You'd have to dig in too deep to get them on and off. You need to wear a g-string."

"But they're icky. And uncomfortable."

"You'll just have to get used to it for the sake of beauty and style," he told her firmly. "Now hold onto my shoulder so you can step into them. You'll find it hard to bend in a corset. Your movements will necessarily slow down and become more graceful."

"I don't think my jeans will go over this very well," she said.

"You're not wearing jeans for our road trip. You're wearing your leather hobble skirt. And stockings and your new ankle boots."

"You mean to say you want to drive all the way to New York with me in a leather outfit and high heels?"

"Why not? You'll just have to totter to the car and get in. If it's the slightest bit icy, I'll carry you."

"But, it's a four hour drive, isn't it?"

"Not quite. Now get a pair of stockings and put them on."

Hugo watched while Mercedes perched with difficulty on the edge of a loveseat to pull on her seamed, nylon hose.

"Now come here to me and I'll do up the garters for you," he commanded her back to him. "Always turn and look in the mirror to make sure your stocking seams are straight," he told her, watching her obey him with some satisfaction. "Now sit back down and I'll bring you the boots," he continued, kneeling before her to help her into them. "What you must do is lean down and grasp the laces, making sure they're even, then lace them up one row of hooks at a time. Go on and try it." Mercedes quickly accomplished the task. "Now stand up," he said, helping her to her feet. She swayed against him, never having worn five-inch heels before. "What a beautiful pin up you are," he told her, leading her before the mirror and turning her around so that she could examine her elongated silhouette from all angles.

"I can't possibly walk in these," she protested.

"Don't say can't," Hugo recommended, slapping her exposed bottom sharply. "You can and will wear beautiful shoes for me."

Mercedes' chin came up with a pout and she folded her arms over her pert bosom in resentment. "But this isn't possible!" she cried, with a tiny stamp of her foot that threw her off balance and into his arms.

"Yes it is possible," he told her firmly, sitting down on the bed and sweeping her across his lap to spank her. "We are traveling to New York this morning, by car. You in a corset, heels and hobble skirt!" Smack, smack, smack! His hard hand came down repeatedly on either bare, peach toned cheek, classically framed by the fancy corset hem and sheer black stocking tops. "Now if you waste any more time arguing, I'll add wristlets and a butt plug as additional controls."

This dire threat left Mercedes limp and trembling.

"Nothing to say to that, I note," Hugo laughed, putting her back on her feet. "It's what I'd do to Amy. You ought to thank me for allowing you to hold onto most of your dignity even as I conduct you through your first real training session."

"Thank you," she murmured.

"You're welcome. Turn around, I think I'll cinch your waist a little tighter."

"Tighter?" she cried.

"That's right, to punish you for arguing about the g-string," he told her, untying her back laces and retying them a half inch tighter.

"That's so snug!" she breathed, stealing a glimpse of herself in the mirror again.

"Doesn't it give you an enchanting waist?" he asked, closing his hands on it again. "Now lean on me and step into this skirt," Hugo said, unzipping the hobble skirt and holding it for her. "Turn around," he ordered. "Now I need to tighten up the laces of the skirt!"

"But how am I supposed to sit down in the car?"

"Don't worry, I'll lift you in. Now remember, there's a side zipper to the skirt that comes up from the bottom or down from the top so you won't have any problem in the powder room. Now I think a white blouse under the leather vest would be the perfect way to complete your traveling outfit."

Hugo helped her to put these garments on and buttoned them up for her.

"Now lets see how that nice old fur coat of your looks with the outfit," he said, opening the hall closet and pulling out her vintage fur and matching hat. He draped the coat over her shoulders and angled the tam to one side of her head. "Put on some dark red lipstick and don't forget your gloves," he told her, carefully folding her new leather dress and thigh high boots into his second valise.

Hugo took their bags down to the car then came back for Mercedes, who found it necessary to lean on him every step of the way to the elevator and out into the street. As soon as they got outside Hugo swept her up into his arms and carried her to the bottle green Jaguar sedan, placing her gently in the front seat.

Soon they were on their way, in a light rain that followed them all the way to New York.

"I should have spanked you harder just now," Hugo mused as they cruised onto the turnpike. "I should always spank you harder when you argue with me."

Mercedes looked at him speechlessly, her greatly reduced tummy fluttering at these attentions.

"Turn over and kneel on the floor," he told her coolly.

"What?"

"Bend over the seat."

Her leather outfit creaking tightly, Mercedes slowly shrugged out of the fur and obeyed, getting down on her knees to lean over the seat and present her slim, leather skirted bottom to the driver.

"Put your wrists behind your back and walk them up your back as far as you can," he said, grabbing both her wrists she put them back and helping her into the position. "Don't move," he told her, slowing the car as they joined the end of a tollbooth line. With three or four cars ahead of them, Hugo now leaned over to administer four hard swats to the seat of Mercedes' skirt. Then he said, "Get back up, we're coming to a toll booth."

Mercedes attempted to scramble back into her seat but the tightness of her skirt and corset caught her by surprise and she was forced to squirm and inch rather than jump back into position. Righting herself in the seat just as they came level with the booth, she took as deep a breath as the corset permitted and attempted to look out the window as though nothing had happened.

Neither of them spoke for several minutes. Then Hugo said, "Did you feel those through that skirt?"

"Yes. I still do."

"Since I've kidnapped you for the weekend, you may take Monday off to work on your thesis," he told her, throwing coins in the change box and surging back up to freeway speed. "And we should probably hit the museum while we're in town. It may inspire you."

"I'd like that," she forced herself to reply, though she hardly felt like chatting after what he had just done.

"You're flushed," Hugo observed. "Are you getting too warm in that outfit? It might help to take off the vest."

"I'll just remove my gloves," she replied.

"Yes, do," he said, impulsively taking her hand and kissing it. "I'm delighted I can still make you blush."

After a few hours on the road, Hugo pulled off at an Inn. The path leading to it was smooth and Mercedes found her balance on the high-heeled boots well enough to step gracefully through the oaken entryway without assistance. Catching her reflection in the foyer mirror she was thrilled to realize that the glamorous young lady, straight out of a John Willy cartoon, was herself. How remarkably dainty her torso could be made to appear through cunning corsetry! As they were ushered to their table under the window on the woods, Mercedes noticed the heads of the several businessmen lunching in the dining room turn to follow her swaying, willowy form as she minced across the small, handsomely decorated room. She tried to remember whether men ever followed her with their gaze before. If so, there had never been more than one at a time.

"Mercedes!" Hugo called her to attention a moment after they were handed the stiff, gold tasseled menus, "that's enough looking in the mirror for now."

Mercedes reluctantly drew her gaze away from the mirror to her right but immediately found it drawn by the mirror directly behind Hugo and opposite her. She found herself again begin to admire her impossibly small waist until Hugo sternly caught her eye and said, "Do you want me to spank you right here?" Mercedes quickly opened the menu and began to study it. "I'll let you look in the mirror all you like later. While I'm caning you in our suite at the Doral Tuscany."

"Have I been that bad?" she cried.

"Jealousy has always been a caning offense."

"But caning is so severe!" she protested. "I'm afraid."

"You'll love it," he told her, squeezing her knee under the table. Then he slid in next to her on the banquette and allowed his hand to creep between her smooth, hosed thighs to where the skin became bare and finally to caress and enclose her public mound. "Don't you think I know what my girl likes by now?" He inserted one finger between her labia. "How naughty to get so wet," he admonished her, pulling his hand free. "It's funny that you thought Amy so much more submissive than you. She'd have been chattering all the way from Boston. But you feel things too deeply for that. Of course I won't cane you hard."

Mercedes melted from her heart to her soul, for she had never been courted before. She realized she was receiving all these rarified attentions because she had petitioned for them herself, but carrying it out so delicately was all Hugo's style. Even so, she was still curious about the type of ordeals he would have chosen to subject Amy to, were she his companion for the weekend.

"Just order soup and a salad. You don't want to eat too much while you're that tightly cinched," Hugo recommended.

"Oh, I'm not very hungry," she admitted.

"Is the corset starting to feel uncomfortable?"

"Just a little," she replied.

"We'd better loosen it a bit after lunch," he said.

"How? I've got all these complicated things on."

"I'll bribe the desk clerk to let us use a room for a few minutes."

"Jesus Christ, Mercedes, is that you?" a young man's voice brashly demanded from the dining room doorway. He and several other junior businessmen were being shepherded into a smaller, private dining room across the hall for a cocktail lunch when the square shouldered boy in the Brooks Brothers suit called out to the leather clad, wasp waisted girl.

"Oh my god, it's my ex-boyfriend Anders," Mercedes whispered to Hugo as the Princeton man she had dated throughout her senior year at Sarah Lawrence descended on their table.

"It's me, Anders," said Mercedes, rising as nimbly as she could to embrace her annoying ex. "Anders Mudgett, my employer, Hugo Sands."

The men shook hands, Anders barely looking at Hugo, Hugo looking closely at Anders.

"I can't believe it's you," the crisply groomed young businessman exclaimed. "What have you done to yourself?" Anders wouldn't release Mercedes hands and she had to pull them free.

"Nothing," she replied, thrown off balance by the sudden appearance of her least gallant lover. "What are you doing here?"

"Business lunch. How about you?"

"We're on our way to New York. On business too," she volunteered, wishing him away with every fiber of her being.

"Really? What is it you're doing now anyway? I never hear from you anymore. It really hurts my feelings."

"Mercedes has been helping me in my shop and finishing her masters thesis," said Hugo, handing Anders Mudgett his Hugo Sands Antiques card. "She'd been working for the Provincetown Chamber of Commerce, but her talents were wasted."

"I can't believe the way you look," said Anders, still gazing at Mercedes. Hugo smiled and slipped his hand under the table, under her skirt and between her legs again.

"Thanks, Anders," said Mercedes uncomfortably squirming on her seat.

"I have to go," said Anders, scarcely able to tear his eyes from

Mercedes' torso in the white shirt, fitted vest and skirt, and boots which lent an extraordinary arch to her insteps. "Call me. Let's have lunch next time I'm in Boston!"

"Sure," she replied with a faint smile, willing him back out the door with every cell in her brain. Besides, Hugo's fingers were creeping back towards her Venus mound and she felt her face growing correspondingly warm.

"Think I'm going to let you see that idiot in Boston?" Hugo snapped, giving her bare thigh a pinch.

"Ow!" she cried, "I thought you weren't jealous!"

"I have no objection to you playing with a man in the scene who will appreciate you now and then. But that joker is obviously not in the scene and never did appreciate you."

"That's true, but –"

"But nothing. And don't argue with me," said Hugo tersely.

"I only said I'd have lunch to be polite," she explained, "I didn't really want to. Anders is boring and he always made me give him lots of head."

"But being submissive, you pleased him, always hoping he would spank you. And he never did. Am I right?"

"It's true. I wasted an entire senior year's worth of ripe sexuality on him. But what did I know? For all I knew, all men were like Anders. Did you see he couldn't take his eyes off my waist?"

"A corseted waist draws the eye," Hugo agreed; "I expect you'll be hearing from him sooner than later."

"Hugo, are you peeved at me for some reason?" Mercedes ventured timidly.

Hugo's chin came up and his blue eyes narrowed. "Yes, I'm peeved!"

"But, why? What did I say?"

"It isn't what you said, it's what you didn't say. Why didn't you tell him I'm your sweetheart?"

"I didn't know I had permission to tell people that," she stammered.

"Mercedes, do you want me to slap you silly?"

"I didn't think you'd appreciate it if I lay claim to you like that," she insisted. “Honestly. It was out of respect to you that I introduced you in that manner.”

“Is that so?” Hugo didn’t sound impressed.

“If he calls, I’ll explain that you’re my... boyfriend?” she asked timidly, “Master? Mentor?”

“I like mentor,” Hugo cheered up. “It implies respect and awe, but does not preclude a sexual relationship. That would have kept him guessing. However, I don’t want him guessing. I want him crystal clear on the fact that I’m the new man in your life. Understand?”

“Yes,” she smiled, “Thank you.”

After giving their order to the waiter, Hugo bribed the concierge to gain access to a well-appointed parlor suite. He conducted Mercedes in and locked the door.

He unzipped her vest and removed it, pulled her over to a chair, sat down and holding her in front of him, unzipped her skirt completely and allowed it to drop to the floor. “Pull up your blouse,” he ordered, then began to deftly unlace, lightly loosen, then relace her waist cinch, giving her back the half inch he had taken from her just before they’d gotten on the road. She sighed with relief and laughed with pleasure at the release. “There, dear, does that help?”

“God, yes! It feels wonderful now,” she breathed, falling into his arms and burying her face in his lapels.

“You’re doing so well for a girl who’s never corseted before. As soon as we get to our hotel I’ll get you out of the cinch. I’m told there’s nothing to match the sensation of getting out of a cinch you’ve had on all day.” He hugged her affectionately, then, couldn’t resist turning her over his knee and administering a quick spanking to her corset framed bare bottom cheeks.

“Hugo, someone will hear!” she whispered in acute embarrassment.

“It’s the least you deserve for introducing me merely as your employer,” Hugo told her firmly, smacking her hard a half dozen more times before lifting her from his lap. “Now put your skirt and vest back on and we’ll go and have our lunch.”

“But I’m so hot, I’m burning. Can’t we make love now?” she said with uncharacteristic candor, longingly eyeing the bed.

"No, our soup will get cold," he decided. "Now finish getting dressed, young lady." Hugo left the room and returned to the table first. Mercedes finished getting dressed and teetered quickly after him, getting better on the heels every moment.

Emerging from the private dining room in time to run into Mercedes, Anders Mudgett and his aura of bad aftershave suddenly seemed to come at her from all sides.

"Baby! Again, I can't believe it's really you! So what are you doing now? Something in the antiques business?"

"And working on my masters. How about you, Anders?"

"Investments firm," he replied. "Say, why not save me the search and give me your phone number now?" he asked, whipping out his notepad.

"Anders, I'd rather not. I'm seeing someone now and I don't have much spare time."

"So I'm getting the brush off, am I?" he grinned.

"I'm sorry!"

"No, you aren't. I can see that you're thriving without me. But how come you look so damn hot all of a sudden? Look at what you're doing to me!" Anders motioned to the conspicuous bulge behind his trouser zipper.

Before she had a chance to answer, Hugo came out to find her, took her by the wrist and led her back to their table saying, "Come, Miss Vonderai, your soup is getting cold." He held her chair for her and then sat down himself, looking piqued as he shook his napkin out. "Well? Did you set boyfriend straight about us?" he demanded.

"I told him I was seeing someone now and not to call me," she replied, lifting a spoonful of wild mushroom soup to her lips.

"Someone? You only said someone? Not me specifically?" Hugo asked sharply.

"I'm sorry," she said in confusion, "It was awkward. I mean, I'd just introduced you as my boss. He would have asked a lot of questions that I wasn't in the mood to answer. Besides, my shoes were giving him a hard-on and I felt altogether nonplussed."

"Well, if you're going to dress like that you'll have to learn to deal with hard-ons popping up all around you. At the Vault you might have to carry a crop just to slap them away. But that's no excuse for forgetting you're my girlfriend for the second time in five minutes. I'm going to be very severe with you later for that!"

Mercedes stared at him speechlessly.

"Eat your lunch," he ordered.

"You're a very bad girl," he scolded her as soon as they were back on the road. "You let Anders' sudden admiration go to your head and forgot yourself. I must say, this is not what I'd expect of you!"

Lightheaded from the admiration, corseting and wine, exhilarated as never before at finally having her core fetish indulged to the hilt, Mercedes felt acutely aroused. Being close to him again in the car, breathing in the faint scent of his soap and heather tweeds, she tingled with anticipation of his next glance, word, caress or cuff. She wanted most of all to be slapped, which made her bite her gloved knuckle with shame.

"I shouldn't have turned you into an elegant lady so fast," he mused. "I started you in finishing school when it should have been nursery."

"What's that supposed to mean?" she sat up straighter, for her back was beginning to hurt from the tight cinching.

"That you need a lesson in humility. For example, your first public spanking, tonight at Club Paddles. And you won't be going in leather either, young lady!"

Hugo checked them into their smart, continental flavored hotel on East 39th Street and immediately unhooked her corset.

"Oh god, that feels so good!" she sighed, flinging herself onto the rich counterpane of the bed and rolling to and fro in nude, liberated ecstasy. He unlaced her boots and pulled them off as well but didn't join her.

"Hugo?" she stretched her slender arms towards him.

"I have to go out and get a few things for tonight," he told her, evading her embrace with a faint smile. She sat up and stared at him.

"Aren't we going to make love?" she asked, springing up to her knees and impulsively throwing her arms around his neck. "I want to so badly!"

"Later," he said, disengaging her arms. "Order up sandwiches while I'm out. And take a little nap. I want you fresh for tonight."

"This doesn't seem fair," she protested, following him to the door with uncharacteristic boldness. "I'm in a perfect state. What am I supposed to do while you're gone, feeling like this?"

"Behave yourself. And don't you dare masturbate," he warned her, pinching her earlobe sternly. "If I find out you have done, I'll humiliate you worse than you ever dreamed possible at Club Paddles tonight."

Mercedes thought, "Why am I not protesting this?" But aloud she replied, "If you leave now I will masturbate. I'll have no choice!"

"You most certainly will not!" he insisted, pausing to turn her over his knee and spank the entirely nude girl hard and fast, several dozen times before setting her back on her feet to rub her bottom in shock.

"Now will you behave?" he asked.

"Yes," she replied, deeply embarrassed, pulsating, stinging and thrilled.

"Now remember what I told you. Order supper, rest and be a good girl until I get back."

Hugo went downstairs and had a few drinks in the bar before embarking on his shopping. Running into Mercedes' ex-boyfriend had been lucky, providing Hugo with a fine excuse to take her to task. Knowing Mercedes as he did, Hugo predicted that legitimate excuses to spank her would come few and far between so he rejoiced in finding one ever so often.

So far, it had been a perfect day and Mercedes a perfect playmate. But giving in to his tendency to push things as far as they would go, Hugo augmented his trip to Bloomingdales with a side stop at Dream Dresser and returned to Mercedes laden with packages.

He found her soaking in the luxurious bathtub.

"Where are the sandwiches?" he demanded, displeased to see no dinner cart in the suite.

"Oh, I forgot to order any," she cried, stepping out of the tub and wrapping herself in the fluffy white hotel robe.

"Bad girl!" he said, picking up the phone and asking for room service. Mercedes came to sit on the arm of a loveseat to look at him. After giving his order he put down the phone, folded his arms and looked at her. "Did I not tell you to order up supper?"

"I'm sorry," she said, very much abashed as he turned her over his knee yet again, this time to pull up her robe and spank her bare bottom, still pink from her hot bath.

"I think I'll just continue spanking you until the sandwiches arrive," he decided, bringing his palm down briskly on either cheek until each was a dusky rose in color and Mercedes was squirming across his lap.

"I'm really sorry!" she declared, attempting to wriggle out of smacking reach in earnest now, for his hand suddenly felt very hard across her tender bottom. "Oh please, that does hurt!" She put one hand back to shield her bottom but he caught her wrist and pinned it to her waist.

"You're an inconsiderate girl," he told her, relentlessly slapping one cheek then the other with metronomic precision, allowing each hard spank to penetrate her satiny skin deeply before laying on the next. "I'm going to train you to obey my simple orders much better from now on," he promised.

"It's true, I'm not thoughtful," she agreed critically. "I become distracted and let people down."

This candid admission stayed his hand a moment and he paused to stroke away the sting of the five or so minutes of solid spanking he had administered. "I'll help you focus," Hugo replied and commenced spanking her again, releasing her hand. Just then there was a knock at the door.

Hugo pushed her off his lap and opened the door for the dinner cart. The young waiter who wheeled it in smiled faintly at nothing in particular as he opened the wine and waited for the check to be signed. Mercedes realized he had heard some of the spanking while approaching the door and went to look out the window in embarrassment.

"Get over here, young lady," said Hugo, after the waiter had gone. "You need a proper meal." He held the chair for her and she sat down, then bounced back up.

"Ow! That last spanking really hurt!" she cried, looking reproachfully at him. He sat opposite her and poured their wine with a satisfied expression.

"I'm glad. You've been taking entirely too much for granted around me. Now I don't ask for much, but food and drink promptly provided is essential to keep me going throughout the day and night!"

"The way you spoil me, I should be more attentive!" she readily joined in her own condemnation.

He watched her delicately nibble at her sandwich and slowly sip her wine. "Did the corseting take away your appetite?"

"No, the horniness," she replied with a rueful grin.

"You're being awfully forward today," he commented, "why is that?"

"Why do you think? I'm in heat. I have been all day. And you keep denying me."

"That was good," he said, pushing his plate away and finishing his wine. "I think I'll shower now," he said.

She waited until she heard the water running and leaving her robe behind, joined him in the large, state of the art marble shower with its opposing dual shower heads above them and at waist height. This was a compartment designed for couples to enjoy and they did so in luxuriant abandon. As marble benches lined either end of the glassed-in stall, Hugo was able to take her in a seated position, perching her on his lap facing away from him in order to expose her front to a vigorous stream of warm water gushing from the waist high spigot opposite them. Hugo held her fast to his lap, his palm pressed against her lower abdomen, on the spot that always seemed to serve her best, making sure her entire sex, while filled by himself from behind, was bathed in a continuous freshet of rushing water. Quickly brought to a climax by the hard sex and soft water treatment, Mercedes fell limp as a kitten into bed and slept for several hours.

When she awoke Hugo was already dressed in a black suit and grey shirt.

"Is that your club outfit?" she asked.

"Yes, and here's yours," he said, showing her an outfit he'd laid out on the vanity consisting of a short black pleated skirt, a gray blazer with some sort of school emblem on the pocket, a white shirt and black tie. "The shoes decided me," he said, dangling a pair of fetish height stack heeled oxfords from one hand.

"You want me as a schoolgirl?" her tone betrayed her disappointment.

"More like post modernist preppie/B&D wanton," he corrected, pointing to the four-inch heels. "To be paired with sheer pantyhose and no panties. Tie to be worn at half mast, with attitude."

"I wouldn't know about things like that. I went to public school."

"Well I went to prep school and I can tell you for a certainty, the girls knew what they were about."

"And what were they about?"

"Giving us hard-ons and fucking our brains out. Now get dressed," he told her.

Mercedes said, "But what about the leather dress and boots?"

"Those are for tomorrow at The Vault. This outfit is more suitable to Paddles."

"But I never wear my skirts this short."

"Then it's time you started."

"Why must I not wear panties?" she asked, looking dubiously at the package containing the seamless, sheer to waist tights.

"Because it will be more fun when your skirt gets flipped up for your first public spanking."

"Hugo, you aren't really going to spank me in public?"

"No, of course not," he assured her.

"Oh, thank heaven!" she sighed.

"But someone surely will," he told her cheerfully.

"What do you mean? You plan to hand me off to a stranger tonight?"

"Certainly not!"

"Then, I don't understand," she mumbled in confusion.

"You can pick the stranger out yourself."

"Are you kidding? You expect me to walk up to a strange man and ask him to spank me?" she asked, carefully pulling the sheer nylon tights up over her calves and thighs and then to her waist. Next she slipped the little skirt over her head. It fit her elegantly, covering her bottom and three inches of upper thigh to perfection.

"You see," he said, "you have the legs to wear short skirts."

"Hugo, answer my question," she said, slipping into a front closing bra.

"No bra," he said, taking it out of her hand.

"No? Why not?" she asked, blushing as he embraced her from behind, enclosing her firm, well rounded little bosom in his hands and squeezing each peach shaped globe lightly while softly biting her earlobe.

"So I can pinch your nipples through your blouse if you misbehave in public," he murmured in her ear, letting her go.

She pulled on the fitted white blouse and submitted to his buttoning it for her and tying the skinny tie. Then he sat her down and helped her step into the oxfords, which he then tied for her.

"I'm not going up to a stranger and asking him to spank me!" she declared.

"So wait until someone approaches you," Hugo genially suggested. "They will."

"But I really don't care to play with a stranger," she protested, standing up in the shoes and walking across the room to regard herself in a full-length wardrobe mirror. Hugo helped her on with the blazer, unbuttoned the top two buttons of her blouse, lowered the tie to the third button and stepped back to look at her.

"Nice," he said. "How do the shoes feel?"

"I like them!" she declared, strolling across the carpet with relative ease after wearing the inch higher heels earlier that day.

Hugo called down for a cab and filled a hip flask with rum. Then he helped her on with her college fur, slipped on a black topcoat and gloves and escorted her from the suite.

"Did you hear what I said, Hugo?" said Mercedes, as they debarked on West 26th Street in a cold, whipping wind, a few minutes later and entered Club Paddles by the side door. "I do not care to play with a stranger!"

Hugo checked their coats, retaining the hip flask in his jacket pocket.

"That doesn't matter," he replied. "At your own suggestion, you're being punished today. "And today isn't nearly over." He took her by the hand and led her into the cafe, where he bought two cokes, to which he then added a liberal amount of rum from his hip flask. "Here," he said, "you need to loosen up. I don't know what I was thinking of not getting you stoned before bringing you here."

They began to tour the rooms, sipping their cocktails. Mercedes clung to Hugo's arm and allowed herself to goggle at the various tableaux of bondage, flagellation and esoteric teasing taking place between consenting partners of many ages and body types, most dressed in black and many in leather, rubber or PVC. Around the walls, wistfully watching the couples in action, ranged a silent battalion of single males, most falling into the young middle-aged category and none dressed in anything approximating fetish. A few mistresses were languidly flogging their near nude male and female slaves on several raised platforms about the inner alcoves, as well as a master or two with a bound and gagged submissive at his feet or on his whipping post. The room with the most straight-backed chairs was already occupied with people giving spankings.

Mercedes looked about her, thinking, "I don't want to play with anyone here! They're all so middle aged!" She excused herself to visit the restroom and upon emerging walked by herself around the club. One thirty-something master, muscular, in black leather pants and a pectoral framing harness, drew her attention as he fastened a tow headed boy in jeans and a plaid shirt over a whipping block and began to belabor the youth's backside with a thick razor strop. "How unlucky that the only cute top in the room is a leather man!" thought Mercedes.

"Did you pick someone out?" Hugo asked, coming up beside her and following her gaze toward the traditional strapping unfolding on the platform.

"He is awfully cute," she whispered, becoming mesmerized by the corded arm rising and falling with the measured lashes of the strop. The good-looking boy bent over the black wooden block stoically grunted with each stroke, but Mercedes noticed his eyes moisten under the increasingly vigorous swats. "Too bad he's gay."

"Don't let that stand in your way," said Hugo.

"If he's gay, why would he want to play with a woman?"

"I don't know. Why not? He's obviously a show off. For one thing, it's excellent P.R. I'd approach him if I were you."

"No. I couldn't possibly. It's out of the question. Besides, he's too hard for me," she hastened to reply.

"Nonsense. That's exactly what you need. I'm too soft on you. You know I am."

"Hugo stop teasing me," she said, marching back into the spanking room, where they sat down to watch the players while sipping their drinks. Men began approaching Mercedes to ask if they might spank her.

"Don't say yes unless you want to," Hugo had time to whisper in her ear before the first approached.

Mercedes said, "No, thank you," to one inappropriate applicant after another until Hugo asked her her criteria for rejecting them.

"My criteria is would I go out with them."

"That's too stringent for a place like this," said Hugo, topping off their drinks with more rum.

Just then an arresting young man strode into the room. He was tall, ebony complected and extravagantly well tailored, with a handsome, chiseled face and close-cropped hair. As a number of women in the room picked up their heads to grin at his entrance, Mercedes realized that this vision off the cover of GQ must indeed be a regular and hence a true enthusiast, but for what?

Looking away just a moment too slowly, Mercedes made eye contact with the beautiful stranger and sealed her fate. It took him only a few moments to get across the fast filling room to tower over her and politely request the privilege of paddling her.

Mercedes looked up in confusion, then looked at Hugo as if for permission. He nodded vigorously, even going so far as to place her hand in the hand of the nattily dressed young man. "By the way," Hugo explained cordially, "this will be her first public spanking so please make it memorable."

"Then I'm even more honored," said the courtly dominant, taking

Mercedes across the room to a convenient spanking bench and after pausing to enthusiastically compliment her shoes, turning her over his muscular lap. Telling her how lovely she looked in his cultivated, velvety voice, the second male ever to properly spank Mercedes smoothed her skirt down over her pert bottom and lulled her into a sense of security with flattering words and mild expressions of gentlemanly admiration. But when the spanking began, all such civilities ceased and all Mercedes became aware of was her courtier's hard, heavy hand. It came down rapidly and stingingly, each time with a sharp report. It was painful! And not only because she had already been spanked several times that day. No. This was quite simply the hardest she had ever been spanked!

Of course, she wanted to take a good spanking from the devastatingly debonair young man, but should not one draw the line at agonizing pain? During a pause in spate of searing swats, she looked up to see if Hugo was watching with approval or horror and noticed that he had left his seat. She lifted her head to look around the room. Hugo was spanking a plump, bouncy girl. Mercedes wondered whether this was one of his readers and if he had arranged to rendezvous with her there. This notion caused her a pang of jealousy, which might have preoccupied her, had not the spanking resumed with vim.

"Oh, please! Mercy!" cried Mercedes, for this was what Hugo had told her to say if anyone here spanked her too hard.

"Are you all right?" asked the severe gentleman, helping her off his lap.

"Yes, thank you," she stammered.

"That was too hard, wasn't it?" he looked abashed.

"Whatever gave you that idea?" she laughed. As she turned to walk away she found herself face to face with the leather man she'd observed strapping a boy earlier.

"Hi," he said, "I'm Todd. Hugo said you're picking up a little local color for your article on Paddles. May I help with that?"

"What do you mean?" she smiled.

"Don't you want to try out my whipping block?" Todd asked,

taking her gently by the hand and leading her into the other room.

"But I've just been spanked really hard," she protested, none the less allowing the experienced young dominant dispose her across the wooden block.

"May I?" Todd asked, flipping up her short skirt to reveal her well-spanked bottom in the sheer beige tights. "I see you have been spanked hard," he observed, running his palm across her taut, oval cheeks through the sheer nylon pantyhose. "You might even bruise. Don't worry. I'll go light. I'll just give you a little taste of a light tawse."

"Ouch!" Mercedes squeaked as the sharp split strap came down across the centermost portion of her cheeks. "That really stings, Todd!"

"A little lighter then," he amended his stroke to barely kiss her upturned backside, which was already stained a dark rose from the handsome black man's hard hand. Smack, smack, smack! The little split strap stung her lightly while Todd held her fast to the block with his hand in the small of her back. "Slowly getting harder," he warned her, applying the tawse with a slightly heavier hand.

"All right," she assented, steeling herself for the promised increase in intensity. Now the sharp, biting kisses of the tawse spurred pre-orgasmic tremors of excitement to ripple through her sex center in waves. Could she possibly be climaxing from a strapping alone, administered to her in a public place, by a gay man?

Looking up, Mercedes noticed that people were watching! Strange faces grinned at her discomfort, some belonging to men she had refused to play with only minutes before. Suddenly she felt overwhelmed by a sensation of social embarrassment and the elusively ticklish orgasm evaporated like a bubble instead of bursting like a firecracker.

Mercedes begged to be let up. Todd helped her to her feet and they hugged.

"You're adorable," he told her, raising both her hands to his lips. "Thank you."

"Thank you," she replied. And whispered in his ear with uncharacteristic candor, "I almost came."

He beamed with pride and pinching her earlobe said, "Naughty girl!"

Hugo was waiting to receive her when she stumbled back onto the floor, dazed with the excitement of a near orgasmic experience from a spanking alone in public.

"How's my girl?" Hugo asked, drawing her out into the corridor between rooms.

"I'm fine, Hugo. Todd was a sweetheart."

"The other guy was going way too hard on you," Hugo said disapprovingly.

"I said mercy and he stopped."

"I'm glad you had the sense to finally stop him. I can't believe you let him go on so long."

"He's so handsome, I couldn't help wanting to please him," Mercedes said.

"He looked pleased," Hugo reassured her.

"All the people staring really threw me," she confided.

"You have to learn to tune them out."

"Todd was nice," she said dreamily.

"So when is the prettiest girl in the room going to do some community service?" Hugo asked.

"What do you mean?"

"Show a little compassion and spank a man or two."

"Me? Spank a man?"

"A boy then. Pick out a cute one and do your duty."

"Like you did yours?" she asked.

"That wasn't a duty," he replied. "I like cute, chubby women."

"Really? Have you ever dated one?"

"Several!"

"Well, you're very democratic, I'm sure," she said, resting her back against the wall to take the weight off her high heels.

"Come on, honey, be a good girl and make me proud of you," said Hugo, slipping his hand in under her blazer and enclosing one pert breast in his hand through the thin cotton shirt. He squeezed her firm globe and pinched her nipple, causing mini-orgasms to begin washing through her again. "Find one deserving young man, give him a good spanking and I'll reward you by taking you home and putting you to bed."

"But why, Hugo, why?"

"Because I want you to have something to write about for the magazine to justify the expenses of this trip. This is just the sort of experience you need."

"Oh, very well," she grumbled.

"That's not the proper attitude," he said, shifting to the other breast and pinching her nipple a little more sharply. "You're the best looking, best dressed woman in this club. Every man has been fantasizing about you since you walked in. Since you can't play with all of them, be magnanimous and leave them with a perfect image they can take home a treasure for the next seven to twenty one days. Pick out the cutest boy you can find and turn him over your knee."

"All right, I'll do it!" she agreed, clasping his hand in both of hers and bringing it quickly to her lips. "But only because I adore you to the point of madness at this moment!"

She turned to find a blond-haired, blue-eyed boy at her elbow. He was dressed in a mock prep school outfit of shorts, white shirt, blazer and tie. He looked twenty-seven or eight with the cleanest cut features, straightest hair and fairest complexion in the room. This exact inverse of the handsome, suave black man she had just allowed to spank her smiled appealingly as he dropped to one bare knee, presumed to kiss her hand and begged to be corrected for his sins. Mercedes turned and looked at Hugo. He was watching over folded arms and raised his eyebrows as much as to say, "See what I mean?"

Mercedes took the young man's hand, pulled him to his feet wordlessly and led him off to a vacant seat against a wall.

"To spank a strapping boy like you would hurt my little hand," she said standing him before her as she sat down. "What do you suggest, young man?"

"Please use this!" he produced a small wooden hairbrush from his blazer pocket and handed it respectfully to her.

"If I let you go over my lap, you mustn't kick or fuss," she warned, reaching up to undo his shorts and lower them. Underneath he had on snug white briefs. She pulled him down over her lap, secured him to her thighs with one hand on his trim waist and tested the hairbrush against his taut bottom with a juicy thwack. He didn't move except to respond with the smallest jerk of recognition. Another smack, another twitch. It was a solid wooden brush and his was a well-padded backside, rounded but muscular and firm. She brought the brush down harder, first on one hemisphere, then the other. Tiny grunts escaped his wide, handsome mouth. Now she spanked him faster, in volleys of vigorous swats, still alternating from cheek to cheek through the tight cotton briefs. Many minutes passed, but she was not aware of this.

"A bold boy like you must be hard to embarrass," she commented, laying the brush aside to lower his briefs, "but I will try none the less!" When she had revealed his creamy white buttocks she was surprised to note how pink the lower portion of each had become. Now she began striking slightly higher up, to spread the spanking across the entire canvas of his bottom. "What an ample backside for such a slim boy," she commented.

"Oh!" he laughed but also winced at the criticism as well as the impact of the brush coming down repeatedly on his bare cheeks.

"You get pink very fast!" she said, smacking him methodically and not neglecting any portion of his upturned backside as he began to wriggle ever so slightly across her thighs. "But I told you to hold still!" she warned sternly. "Do not make me tell you again." And then she continued to spank him. More minutes ticked away, but Mercedes didn't notice. He was a handsome boy and this was not hard work.

Mercedes began to spank her captive more severely and faster, administering quick flurries of dozens of swats at time and noting that such treatment caused him to pant and tense with agitation, then dissolve bonelessly across her thighs when it ceased.

"A boy as cute as you must be very spoiled," she remarked, allowing him a respite while she rubbed each reddened cheek in circles with the palm of her soft hand. "Are you a very spoiled boy?"

"Yes, Mistress," he replied, grinning back at her over one shoulder.

"Not Mistress," she frowned, smacking him resoundingly several times with the flat of the brush.

"Yes, Ma'am!" he corrected himself quickly.

"Definitely not Ma'am!" she rejoined, swatting him a half dozen times even harder. "That makes me feel like a sixty year old school marm on the prairie."

"Well, how should I address you?" he gulped, unconsciously putting one hand back to shield his belabored bottom. She caught his wrist and pinned it to his waist, causing him to catch his breath with increased excitement.

"You may address me as Dearest Mercedes," she said, smacking him for emphasis. "Now say it!"

"Dearest Mercedes!" he replied with extreme enthusiasm.

When next Mercedes chanced to look up Hugo caught her eye from where he stood leaning against the bar and tapped his watch. Mercedes understood this was the signal to conclude her latest spanking adventure.

"What is your name, young man?"

"Parker Nicholson," he replied.

"And your profession?"

"I'm a stockbroker."

"With what firm?"

"Goldman Sachs."

"And have you a secretary?'

"About a dozen of us share a receptionist."

"Well then, in appreciation of the attentions I've shown you tonight, I would like you to bring your very overworked receptionist a two pound box of Belgian chocolates first thing Monday morning."

"Dearest Mercedes, I will do so without fail!" promised Parker fervently.

"Mind you do for I will check!" Mercedes assured him, delicately nudging him to indicate the spanking was over. He scrambled to his feet and had his briefs and shorts up in a moment.

"God, you're so dominant!" Parker gushed with admiration. "Is there any chance I could see you again?"

"Nothing is impossible," Mercedes replied with a soft smile.

"I don't suppose I could have your phone number?"

Mercedes shook her head but clasped his hand affectionately, stood up and gave him a hug. He took her by the waist and squeezed her to him so closely that for the first time she felt the full extent of his arousal. Pushing him away firmly she lightly cuffed his cheek, admonishing him to behave like a gentleman. He looked down and blushed.

"I'm sorry, but you're the most exciting woman I've ever met!"

Mercedes left him with another soft smile and joined Hugo at the bar.

"Do you realize you've been spanking that boy for a half hour?" he said with a grin. "Your shoulder is going to be sore tomorrow."

On the way out of the club four different men accosted Mercedes to beg for a spanking. "Maybe next time," she told each one, neither displeased nor intrigued by their admiration, but satisfied that she had accomplished the task Hugo had set her to the best of her ability and perhaps a little better than she thought she might have done.

Chapter Eight

At The Dutch
(Present Era in Random Point)

"The answer is no. Emphatically no!" David Lawrence declared to his uncommonly pretty wife, while applying a hat and sun glasses to the head of the season's first snowman, which they had built outside Cobweb Cottage, their snug domain set atop Pigeon Cove in Random Point.

"But why, David? Why, why, why???" Hope cried, sticking a cigar in the snowman's mouth and a pennant from the prep school where David taught English literature in the crook of its elbow.

"Why don't I think it's a good idea for my wife to tend bar - nights - for the man who's been trying to annex her away from me for the last six months? Let me count the ways. 1. You're already in love with Michael Flagg. So all I need is for you to be around him and the heady aroma of alcohol every other day. 2. It is completely inappropriate for the wife of a Braemar instructor to moonlight as a bar maid. 3. You already have a perfectly respectable job at the bookshop where you are valued for the good you do quite apart from your ornamental qualities."

"I can make beaucoup tips," Hope speculated mildly, careful not to display too much enthusiasm for what she knew in her heart to be quite a potentially naughty part time job. "I'll bet I could double my income just working two nights a week at The Dutch."

"It isn't worth it. Consider the unwholesome atmosphere," David replied, "the danger of stick-ups and the like."

"David, be yourself. You go drinking there every Thursday night.

No one's going to rob a place that belongs to a former cop."

"I suppose that's the linchpin of his glamour, the detective thing," observed David, leaning a golf club insouciantly against the snowman's thigh.

"David, this is just the change of pace I need," Hope reflected.

"The hell it is," he snorted, pulling a hip flask of whiskey out of a capacious overcoat pocket and taking a pull on it.

"You know how gregarious I am. I've always wanted to tend bar."

"I thought you always wanted to work in a bookstore."

"I can do both."

"You get to be plenty gregarious at the bookstore coffee bar," David pointed out, putting away his bottle and packing more snow onto their creation.

"Do you forbid me to do it?" she asked tentatively.

"Positively, unequivocally and finally!"

"Really?" she cried, amazed.

"Hope, did you honestly think I'd allow you to tend bar for your boyfriend???" He dropped down on a small stone bench overlooking the choppy, wind tossed waters of the cove and dug in his pockets for a pipe and sweet cherry tobacco.

"Darling, you're not usually so implacable," she observed, coming around behind him to knead his shoulders through the heavy tweed overcoat. "Can't I persuade you to see my point of view?"

"No!" he shrugged off her hands but then grabbed her and pulled her around the bench to sit beside him. "And nothing will make me change my mind on that account. Do you understand me, young lady? If I catch you sneaking off to work there, even once, I promise you you'll get your first real beating from me!"

"David, don't you owe me a concession? In exchange for the Alison Albrecht incident?"

"That was cancelled out five to eight times over by your repeated assignations with Michael Flagg."

"Those were just sessions."

"Don't try to confuse the issue with semantics. He's had you. More than once. Look me in the eye and deny that!"

Hope couldn't comply with this request.

"But I really want to do this!" she suddenly insisted, her blue eyes sparkling in a way he had never observed before.

"And I really don't want you to do it," he replied firmly, sensing she was about to throw her first tantrum of their almost two year relationship and trying to remember exactly where he had left his favorite strap.

Hope stood up, walked some distance away from him, formed a small snowball and violently pitched it at his head. He ducked to one side and it merely grazed his shoulder.

"Next time perhaps I won't miss!" she threatened direly before marching into the house.

Michael Flagg came to buy the Dutch through the happy coincidence of the small pub being put up for sale and his simultaneously receiving a substantial inheritance from an ancient relation in Ireland. He had retired from his career in law enforcement the previous year and had been earning a steady, if boring living conducting check fraud investigations for local banks, occasionally supplementing his income with the sale of detective stories to pulp fiction magazines. So when the Irish bonanza arrived in the mail concurrent with the availability of The Dutch, there wasn't a doubt in his mind about what he should do.

The idea of staffing his bar with scene girlfriends was an agreeable whim, born of the notion that they might enjoy helping him create another (sub rosa) Random Point scene social center, like the one already operational at the bookstore. Besides, pretty women never hurt any business. And this was one, which, to his mind, required no special training other than that which he could provide on the spot. All the women he knew had been taught to mix drinks for their men and were meticulously attentive to those demanding entities.

And the women he knew knew him. He could be as bossy as he chose without offending any one of them. If he wanted them to move, he could swat them on the bottom. Far from minding this mild encouragement, they would enjoy it. In fact, the more he pondered, the more the felt that scene women were the only kind of employees he ever wanted.

After Hope informed him with frustration, that she could only promise him one night, for now, which might well be abbreviated by David dragging her out from behind the bar by the hair, Michael called Laura Random, the second young lady on his list.

Laura was neither loquacious nor flirtatious, but the artistic brunette was extremely attractive, at ease with all sorts of men and smart enough to handle any challenge that might arise within a tiny tavern, just off Shadow Lane. Like Hope, she thought the concept of tending bar for Michael fun, sexy and the height of New England sociability. Everyone loved The Dutch. And of course, she had always entertained the warmest feelings for Michael Flagg, though he had spanked her only twice and kissed her once in their five-year friendship. But there was her lover to consider.

While Hugo Sands was seldom predictable, he reacted to Laura's statement that she might go work in Michael's bar in pretty much the same way that David Lawrence had done. More than a decade had passed since the pleasant era of Mercedes Vonderai and while a number of other interesting women had passed in and out of Hugo's life, Laura Random was currently, and had been for the last several years, the focus of his attention. For a variety of reasons, she had long eluded his grasp. Now that he could finally call her his, he had no intention of letting her slip away.

"Let you go work for Michael Flagg?" Hugo asked while uncorking a bottle of wine that night. "Certainly not!"

Laura paused in tossing a salad. "But why not? I have the time."

"Honey?"

"Yes, Hugo?"

"You're not working for Michael Flagg."

Laura sighed but made no reply, setting the table thoughtfully, Hugo's obvious jealousy of Michael bringing a faint smile to her lips.

"Why don't you paint a few murals for him instead?" Hugo suggested a few moments later, pleased with her for not pressing the argument. Laura looked up from sipping wine with excitement.

"What an excellent idea!" she replied.

"It's a much more appropriate contribution for you to make, dear," Hugo said, thus ending the discussion to their mutual satisfaction. This way she would get to hang around the bar for a few weeks or months at its inception, soak in the atmosphere, support Michael, but still come home before dark!

After dinner, while Laura was clearing the table, Hugo slipped into his study to call Sloan Taylor. Sloan was alone in the small apartment above the bookstore where he lived. He'd been working on the accounts, for he was now a half partner in Marguerite's shop.

"Hey Sloan," said Hugo, "just want to give you a heads up about something."

"Really? What's up?"

"Forgive me for asking but, you're still giving Pamela the cold shoulder, right?"

"Right," Sloan replied at length, realizing that Hugo wouldn't have introduced this topic frivolously.

"Forgive me for asking this too, but you're definitely not gay, right?"

"Of course I'm not!" Sloan sputtered.

"That's too bad, because you're about to get fucked by Michael Flagg."

"Hugo, what the hell are you talking about?"

"Michael Flagg's just bought the Dutch and he's trying to get all our girls to go work for him. He's already asked Hope and Laura. Well, guess whose going to be next? Believe me, Sloan, you don't want Pamela exposed to Michael. He's catnip to submissive girls."

"I see," said Sloan, a cold sensation in his stomach. "Thanks for telling me this."

"I thought it was important enough to disturb you with. It's still only nine o'clock. He may not have gotten to Pamela yet. He may just be thinking about her. I'd go over to her place and fuck the living daylights out of the girl while you still have some claim on her loyalty. He gets her in that bar with him, you can forget about her for one to two years."

Hugo being so wise in the ways of the scene, Sloan thought it foolish to entirely ignore the warning, but equally idiotic to go rushing over to Pamela's to affect a quick patch up of the love affair that she herself had torn by indulging in a passion for Hugo several months before.

Sloan had not made love to Pamela once since her confession of the brief and ill advised affair with Hugo, which had quickly culminated in Hugo firing her and Pamela going to work in Damaris' smart little dress boutique instead. Damaris was Michael's ex-wife and the two were now on pleasant terms.

Hugo had never intended to make love to Pamela, but after the first time he spanked her, it was rather inevitable. Sloan did not fault Hugo, but Pamela, and in this instance, Sloan was right. Pamela had put Sloan entirely out of her head during the Hugo infatuation and the bookstore manager was still smarting from that semi-rejection. He wanted Pamela back, but not before she was ready to give him the unequivocal appreciation he felt he deserved.

Now a third male was about to enter her sphere, Michael Flagg, that fair-haired, 6'3", spanking Casanova, who had at one time or another, captured every female heart in their clique. Sloan had the not the slightest doubt that Pamela would accept Michael's job offer. She didn't make much at the boutique and didn't do much with her evenings these days. Pamela was a natural for the job.

But Hugo's advice of running over to Pamela's apartment and ravishing her was simply too undignified to follow. It wasn't Sloan's way to move impulsively. And yet, the more he paced and fretted, the less riveting the business of paying open invoices seemed. But what excuse could he use to visit so abruptly? Then he remembered the bolt of lilac tulle he had ordered from Italy for Pamela's birthday present. That wasn't until several days hence, but Sloan thought, "Close enough," and dialed her number.

Pamela was amazed and thrilled to hear from Sloan at that hour and gave him permission to visit without hesitation. He hadn't been to her place since the night she'd made her terrible confession and he had told her that they needed to take some time off from each other while she sorted out her feelings. This was sheer punishment and nothing else. Pamela had been suffering keenly throughout her time off, the interludes with Hugo having tapered off to practically nothing and her longing for Sloan now at it's greatest.

Of course she felt immensely guilty for having initiated the affair with Hugo and yearned for an opportunity to prove her love for Sloan.

She kept his photo by her bedside so she could see it every morning and night. And some of his clothes which were still at her house, she sometimes put by her pillow, to breathe in his scent. Pamela had been infatuated with the older, more urbane Hugo Sands, but she felt truly stricken about alienating her beautiful, intellectual, cultivated Sloan.

When he arrived at her apartment, on the second floor of a Main Street triple-decker, he found her in a charming, gold brocade dressing gown and matching slippers, with her long, dark hair down and full lips painted dark red. She had opened a bottle of burgundy and handed him a glass as soon as he walked in.

"What's that?" she asked, glimpsing the bolt of fabric under his arm.

"Your birthday present," he told her, taking it to the table and unrolling the stiff, shiny, almost iridescent lilac tulle. "There's twenty five yards of the stuff, enough to copy that 1947 Dior model you like so much."

Pamela fingered the fabric with educated admiration. "Very handsome," she pronounced, holding some of it against her as she gazed into a looking glass. "Now I can make a real ball gown for the next party!"

Now they silently sipped their wine, looking at each other across her sitting room. Snow was falling softly outside the bay windows and a fire licked and leapt in the small hearth.

"So, what have you been up to lately?" he asked.

"Just working at the shop with Damaris," she replied. "How about you?"

"Same as ever," he said, feeling terribly awkward and not quite honest about what he was doing there.

"Oh, Sloan, I've missed you so!" she suddenly cried, flinging herself into his arms.

"And what about Hugo?" he held her away from him. "Is that over?"

"Yes!"

"In that case, perhaps I'll stay the night."

"Oh darling, please do!"

It was, therefore, a freshly forgiven and well-caressed Pamela who greeted Michael Flagg when he came into his ex-wife's shop to offer her a job the following morning, exactly as Hugo had predicted he would. Whether Hugo's other predictions about Pamela's tenure under ex-detective Flagg would come to pass remained to be seen in the fullness of time.

Meanwhile, the following Wednesday night presented Hope's first opportunity to put in at least a few hours at Michael's bar. David taught an English literacy class at the Community Services Center in Woodbridge from six to seven thirty and an SAT preparatory class at Woodbridge High from eight to nine. This meant he would not be arriving home until ten p.m., which would allow Hope to lend a hand at the Dutch from five until around nine thirty, as this was her weekday off from work at the bookstore.

When she arrived she found Laura Random taking measurements of the walls where she intended to paint murals and Michael removing and remorselessly breaking all the singles in the juke box that Random Point revelers had been forced to listen to relentlessly for the last quarter century. In about an hour he'd replaced the Beach Boys, Four Seasons and Supremes with vintage singles from his own collection going back, in some cases, 35 years, of The Stones, The Doors, Hendrix and Lou Reed. The first time the dulcet tones of Back Door Man filled the cabin the fur on the black house cat stood on end, but he soon got used to the change, especially considering the baked salmon and chicken his new owner had been thoughtfully feeding him.

Hope had been assigned to inventory but as soon as the customers began to appear she had no opportunity to do anything but serve. The cash register was manual and not difficult to use. There were ample lists of drink recipes behind the bar, though it being New England, most of the patrons requested mugs and pitchers of beer on tap, which she quite enjoyed filling. Her friendliness and efficiency, already well known to most denizens of the small Cape Cod village from their visits to the bookstore coffee bar, was instrumental in insuring running tabs. Even Michael noticed that people seem to drink more rapidly and cheerfully while Hope was serving them.

She was dressed pretty much the same as for the bookshop, in dark blue jeans, a white shirt and a cherry red apron. Her eyes matched the jeans, her nails and lipstick the apron and her blonde hair was pulled back in a long, thick ponytail that brushed her waist. Little rakish ankle boots adorned her pretty feet and allowed her to comfortably run around behind the bar. With her unusual beauty there was no need to dress any more provocatively than this and well she knew it.

Michael regarded his barmaid with undisguised affection, for she was quite a good, in addition to being a useful girl and had given him nothing but satisfaction during the course of their recent friendship. As a semi-retired professional submissive, Hope now and then made herself available to a few local dominants. Hugo Sands was one, Ambrose Bartlett, the department store owner from Woodbridge another, Anthony Newton the composer, when in residence, a third. But by far Michael Flagg was her passionate favorite and their professional relationship had quickly metamorphosized into a spanking love affair. Why David tolerated this sometimes puzzled Michael, but he knew better than to ever question his good fortune in finding Hope accessible every now and then.

Hope could have told Michael why David was prepared to let her go so far and then no farther. These little slips of hers into adultery were like money in the bank for a husband with a similarly lively sexuality. Their marriage was nothing if not a balance sheet of infidelity, with continuous entries being made by either one or the other of them.

Of course Michael did not expect David to allow Hope to work at the bar, any more than he expected Hugo to let Laura do the same thing. But he also felt there was no harm in trying. And after a few hours had passed, with business being brisk, both Hope and Michael forgot all about David. Laura had long since gone home and the after work crowd had been supplanted by a raucous group of young dating singles and various local alcoholics hugely appreciative of the new old music now being piped into the rustic room.

The crowd began to thin at ten, it being a weeknight and Michael was just wondering whether it was worth it to throw another log on the fire when Hope's husband David walked in.

Hope looked up from behind the bar and froze, realizing she'd lost track of the time. A soft, thick snow had begun to fall without and

David's overcoat was sprinkled with snowflakes. The Cramps "Psychotic Reaction" had just dropped down on the turntable and reflected David's mood to perfection. Giving her one steely look, David inclined his head towards the door then walked back out into the anteroom.

Hope knew better than to make her husband wait. Tearing off her apron and grabbing up her tweed reefer coat from behind the bar she cried, "Bye Michael," and ran out to the foyer where David was waiting for her.

On her way out she nearly collided with the incoming Marnie Price and Jane Eliot, the coordinator and assistant coordinator of the Women's Center in Woodbridge, a heavily lesbian non profit organization that was liberally funded by Marnie's wealthy family and friends.

"What made Princess take off like that?" the tall, lean, negligently beautiful, blonde Marnie demanded of Michael as she slid her blue jeaned backside onto a barstool.

"Oh, her husband just came looking for her," the new pub owner replied philosophically. "Hi Jane!" he beamed fondly at his ex-fiancée, with whom he had sundered romantic relations some five years before but who had become a dear friend. The slim brunette social worker had come out on the bi side in recent years and was in fact currently her lesbian companion's better half. "How nice to see you both. What can I get you girls?"

"Anything with a floating widget for me," said Marnie, shrugging out of her woolen toggle coat and helping Jane off with her camel overcoat.

"I'll have a Sammy," said Jane, looking around the room to note that Michael had no other assistants. "Hey Michael, is it true you're looking for help?"

"Why? You know someone?"

"Yeah. We got this girl who needs a job," said Marnie bluntly. "You should hire her."

"Marnie let me tell him," admonished Jane, who was often embarrassed by her companion's indifferent manners and inelegant turns of phrase. "We do know a highly deserving young lady --" Jane was interrupted by Marnie's snort of derision.

"She'd sock you one if she heard you calling her that," Marnie chortled, popping the top of her Guinness herself, listening for the fizz of the floating widget and expertly filling a mug down the side so as not to create a foam top.

"I like the way you poured that. How about you coming to work for me, Marnie?" Michael kidded the youthful millionairess.

"Anyway, Michael," Jane continued, "our girl's name is Carmen Farrell. She's twenty-five and altogether sweet. But she's had a rather unusual upbringing --"

"Raised by dykes," Marnie summed it up, with her wide, attractive mouth full of pretzels. "And it shows."

"Dykes, huh?" Michael wiped down the wooden bar thoughtfully. "Is she a dyke as well?"

"No, no, of course not," Jane hurriedly assured him.

"We don't know," Marnie corrected her friend, cramming peanuts in the place where the pretzels had gone. "But she looks like one."

"Oh Marnie, you know that's not true!" Jane cried in frustration at her painfully frank companion, who grinned back at her through sips of ale. "Honestly, Michael, she's a dear little thing, but she hasn't had the easiest time. Her real parents were just no good. So her lesbian aunt and her butch girlfriend took Carmen in when she was about seven. They've been excellent to her, but it was rather a frill-free rearing. I don't think she's ever owned a dress. If we're not sure of her exact orientation that's probably because she doesn't know what it is herself yet. Suffice to say, she's had boyfriends and doesn't appear to dislike men. The reason we were thinking of her for the bar is that she hasn't shown a real aptitude for anything else so far and she's wise guy enough for it."

"You must really like this Carmen to plead her case so eloquently. What isn't she telling me, Marnie?" asked Michael, topping off Jane's glass of Sam Adams.

"Don't you like surprises?" replied the blonde before draining her glass.

"She has a piercing or two," explained Jane, "because she's flirting with the thought of B&D."

Michael's head snapped up. "What's this you're saying now? The girl's a player?"

"Not as yet," amended Jane, "but I think she's intrigued enough to go from poser to player in the next few years."

"Oh, Jane," Michael smiled, "with all due respect, how could you know?"

Jane colored slightly but did not think this a proper moment to take issue with his remark. She had come a long way from the sort of feminist she'd once been, but Michael had very little knowledge of her adventures with Hugo Sands and subsequently, others. He only recalled the fire breathing womyn who had once condemned all spanking as violence and himself as a cad for choosing to be part of the scene.

"I know because I told Carmen that you're a dominant and this seemed to intrigue her even more than you being an ex-cop, which already intrigued her quite a bit."

"Get it? New talent for you," said Marnie, wandering over to the jukebox and punching the numbers for the Patti Smith song.

"You're sending me a girl to play with?" Michael incredulously asked Jane.

"Not necessarily. I just thought you might like to know what kind of girl she might some day turn out to be."

"I must say, that last bit of data helps her case. Send her by tomorrow," Michael decided.

Meanwhile, David had pulled Hope out to the porch where they gazed at each other for some moments in silence. Hope's heart was pounding violently and her legs felt painfully weak.

"What did I tell you?" David finally said, cuffing her on the cheek. It wasn't much of a slap, but it was administered sternly enough to cause tears to spring into her eyes. "You didn't even have the decency to pretend to obey me! You couldn't even be bothered to get home just a few minutes before me, to save me the humiliation of having to look for my wife in a tavern, waiting bar for her lover!"

This passionate harangue was punctuated by David dragging Hope out to the car and throwing her in the front seat. Getting in the other side with a slam of the door he laboriously started the rebellious old engine. “You’re probably enjoying this tremendously, aren’t you, Hope? You need to be the center of attention and what better way than having your husband snatch you out of your boyfriend’s arms. The whole village will be talking about it tomorrow.”

“I wasn’t in anyone’s arms,” she protested. David threatened her with the back of his hand and she subsided against the car door. “And I did mean to get home by nine thirty. I just lost track of the time since it got so busy.”

“Shut up. I’m not interested in your lame excuses for the chronic disrespect you show me,” David declared, still looking iron daggers at her. Finally the engine started and they moved forward down Shadow Lane and on towards the coast road that would return them to their cottage.

“David, I’m sorry. I didn’t mean to be disrespectful. I just really wanted to work at the bar one night.”

David did not look impressed and said nothing more until pulling up in front of Cobweb Cottage some ten minutes later. Hope huddled in the front seat in her tweed coat until David pulled her out of the car and into the house.

“Get undressed for bed,” he told her curtly, going into the kitchen to brew them hot toddies. When he opened the refrigerator to get the lemons he noticed a pretty platter left for him by Hope with sandwiches and pasta salad for his late dinner. Biting into one of the dainty sandwiches, David felt somewhat soothed. This was an old trick of Hope’s, but he never could resent it.

“At least she’s thoughtful,” he said to himself, sitting down at the table with the platter. A shot of the Bushmills he was planning to use in the toddies sent a feeling of deep warmth through David and his irritation at his wife’s disobedience began to decrease rapidly.

When he joined her in their bedroom the fire was crackling and Hope had encased her slim, well rounded form in a sheer black nylon gown and matching negligee, beribboned in black satin and evocative of a Vargas gatefold, circa 1958. As he entered, she was slipping her feet into black marabou trimmed high-heeled slippers, her wavy blonde hair streaming down her back and over her shoulders in silken disarray.

"Here," he handed her a mug of steaming water, Irish whiskey, lemon and honey.

"Thank you," she accepted the offering without rising from the footstool that she perched on by the fire.

David hung up his jacket, removed his tie, unbuttoned his collar and rolled up his sleeves. Hope watched him wordlessly and wide-eyed, sipping the toddy, though she sensed from his expression that the worst of his pique had evaporated in the kitchen.

"Is there even one damn cigarette in this house?" David finally demanded.

"Sure!" Hope immediately retrieved a joint from a painted box at the bedside, stuck it between his lips and lit it with a taper from the fire.

"Trying to soften me up, huh?" David said, taking his first hit in about ten years. "Think if I get full enough and stoned enough and thoroughly drunk on your beauty I'll let you off the hook, don't you?"

Hope smiled and shrugged, content to let the gown set work its magic on her husband. Finally he took the drink away from her and set it aside. Then he pulled her to her feet so that he himself could take the seat on the stool and pull her down over his lap.

Hope's bottom gleamed pale beneath the two layers of sheer black nylon which veiled it. David took a small, ebony hairbrush from the bedside table and administered twelve resounding whacks to alternate cheeks while holding her in place around her small waist. She cried out as each smack fell, attempting to twist away. But David held her fast and continued with the spanking.

After twelve of the best with the hairbrush, without any sort of warm-up, Hope was trembling on the verge of tears when he lifted her from his lap.

"Face down on the bed," he told her, removing his belt. Hope pouted at him, her hands going back to her rosy bottom. "Don't look at me like that. You brought this on yourself."

But after a hit or so more off the joint, David was inclined to pause, come sit beside her on the bed, arrange her hair, gently remove her provocative slippers and lightly stroke her punished cheeks through the gown and robe. Seeing her shoulders untense, he dropped a few light kisses on the back of her neck, shoulders and arms. He hated to feed her vanity, which was already huge, and so refrained from telling her how adorable she looked, but he let his fingertips speak as he caressed the silken backs of her knees and delicately turned back the skirt of both her robe and nightgown.

Now that her firm, round cheeked bottom was fully revealed he saw how deeply pink the wooden brush had stained her flawless alabaster skin.

"Not that this will teach you anything, but it will make me feel better," David said, bringing the strap down across her upturned cheeks several dozen times, slowly and methodically, letting each individual swat sink in and leave a light red mark in its wake before raising the leather again. Hope caught her breath every time the belt kissed her cheeks but instead of crying out, bit her knuckle.

At length, David tossed the belt aside, sat beside her on the bed and rolled her over. With misty blue eyes and parted red lips, she reached up to put her arms around his neck. He took her hands and held them in front of her. "Not so fast. I may not have the heart to give you the thrashing you deserve, but that doesn't mean I've forgiven you!"

"Oh David, you know I'm your slave," she murmured, forcing him to embrace her.

"I don't want you to work for Michael anymore. If I catch you there once more I'll have to retaliate in an entirely different manner," he warned her, while enfolding her closely in his arms.

Hope pulled away from him. "In what manner?"

"You remember Gigi, that cute little student of mine who had the temerity to crash Hugo's Halloween party with her boyfriend? I don't think I have to tell you what kind of crush she has on me. She sends me mash notes that would make D.H. Lawrence blush. She's already 18, as you know. We determined that the night of the party, before everyone took a turn spanking her. And she's just received an early acceptance to Harvard. Are you listening, Hope?"

"Yes," Hope nodded, feeling painfully uneasy.

"Gigi. Even the name is adorable, isn't it?" David refined the torment.

"It's always been one of my personal favorites," Hope agreed.

"Yes, Gigi loves me. Her love burns pure and bright. In fact she wants nothing more than to give herself to me, in every conceivable way. She's even worked out the details. As a graduation present to herself she plans to rent a suite at the Ritz Carlton and invite her favorite English teacher for tea. I would drive into Boston and spend the afternoon. She hasn't presumed to ask me to spend the whole night. But who knows? If I drink a bottle of wine with her, I probably won't want to drive back out to The Cape that same evening."

"I won't work in the bar anymore," promised Hope with an uncomfortable blush.

"Good girl," said David, gathering her back into his arms with a smile, for in all probability, he would never have to produce any of the mythical letters from Gigi.

The next afternoon Hugo visited the Dutch and was not so much surprised as disappointed to see Pamela already behind the bar, polishing glasses with a soft cloth. She was gracefully clad, in a black dress with a square cut neck, nipped waist and three quarter sleeves, with her black hair in a shiny, perfect French roll and a gold locket on a slender chain around her neck. As Michael was nowhere to be seen, Hugo walked straight up to her and demanded, "Pamela, what are you doing here?"

"Oh, hi Hugo! I'm working for Michael part time now," she replied guilelessly.

"You are, huh? Does Sloan know about this?"

"Of course. I consulted with him this morning after Michael offered me the position. Sloan thinks it a very good idea."

"What's this you're saying now?"

"He thinks it could be the making of me."

"Oh, I'm sure it could," said Hugo with an alternate meaning.

"At least one man in town doesn't mind me working for him!" Pamela said pertly, to which Hugo merely raised an eyebrow.

"Yes, well, just see that you behave yourself, young lady," Hugo advised, "and don't go falling in love with your new boss."

"Really, Hugo, if Sloan isn't worried, why should you be?"

"Because I know you better than he does. But I'm glad to hear you're back together. When did this happen?"

"He came over last night, with a lovely birthday present for me. And stayed the night!" she reported with contentment.

"And how does your other boss feel about you working for her ex-husband?" Hugo asked, pointing to the Guinness on tap. "I'll have a glass of that."

"Well, she didn't tell me not to," said Pamela, filling a stein for her ex-boss.

As Hugo was taking the edge off his thirst, Michael appeared in the doorway behind the bar and greeted his friend with a grin.

"Hey, Hugo, like my hired help?" Michael asked, repressing the urge to pat his new bar maid's slim bottom as he passed behind her.

"You're consistent anyway," Hugo observed, bringing the mug to his lips again as a new girl entered the Dutch and walked straight up to the bar to address Michael.

She was of medium height but delicately boned, with regular features, a fair complexion and ultra short, feathery, pale blonde hair. Her eyes were tawny hazel and her mouth wide and beautiful, but she'd spoiled the effect of these assets, at least for Michael, Hugo and Pamela, by piercing her nostril with one gold ball and her eyebrow with another. She was dressed in a pair of faded jeans, a long sleeved tee shirt and small hiking boots. Her chipped manicure was of frosted mint green, otherwise her arms and hands were very pretty. Her bosom was small, high and unrestrained by any bra. Her waist was intriguingly tiny and her hips slender. She looked shy and arrogant all at once as she demanded to see the owner.

"I'm the owner. Are you the little girl Jane and Marnie were sending me?" Michael asked pleasantly. Hugo and Pamela now paused to watch the proceedings with extreme interest.

"Yes. I'm Carmen. But I'm not a little girl," she claimed, looking Michael up and down.

"Jane tells me you don't have any experience," Michael said.

"Is it that complicated?"

"Come behind the bar here and show me how you pour a glass of beer," he told her, opening the gate, letting her in and pointing her to a tap. Carmen took the glass mug he handed her and tilted it under the tap so that the beer would run down the side instead of cascade into the middle. The proportion of beer to foam was perfect when she set it on the bar. "Good! Very good!" said Michael. "Now tell me, Carmen, if a customer asked for a merlot, what color wine would you be looking for?"

"Red."

"How about a pinot grigio?"

"White."

"Good! Now, tell me, Carmen, how much alcohol does a jigger hold?"

"One ounce and a half?"

"Excellent! Now let me see you write out a sales ticket," Michael told her, pushing a pad towards her across the bar. "Now write: 2 martinis @ $5 each, 3 Heinekens @ $4 each and one Bloody Mary @ $5 and give me a total."

Carmen scribbled on the pad. "I get $27.00"

"Let me see that," Michael snatched the pad. "God you have horrible handwriting. But you got the total right. Sometimes you won't have time to take your checks back to the cash register. What do you think, Hugo? Will she do?" Michael asked. Carmen didn't enjoy being discussed and glared at no one in particular while sipping the beer she'd just poured.

"She seems to have the basics down," Hugo agreed, smiling at Carmen in such a way that she couldn't help but smile back.

"This job pays $7 an hour plus your tips. I'll need you every day except Sunday from five to midnight. Think you can handle that schedule?"

"Hell, yes!" Carmen cried, delighted.

"Now there's just one more thing, dear," said Michael, "the question of appearance."

"Appearance?"

"You look too radical for our crowd. If you want to work for me you'll have to remove the hardware."

Carmen looked confused.

"The nose and eyebrow rings will have to come out," he said bluntly.

"That's fucked!" Carmen cried vehemently, folding her arms across her chest.

Michael shrugged, "Sorry, but I know my clientele and you'll scare them looking how you do now. Or at the very least put them off their drink."

Pamela, who was roughly Carmen's age but of an entirely different stamp, agreed with Michael's assessment of Carmen's appearance, but also sympathized with the pretty blonde, whose current look was the height of subterranean chic.

"Well, I'm not getting all frou frou, like her," said Carmen, tossing a glance at Pamela's exquisitely tailored dress, dainty accessories, porcelain skin and gleaming manicure.

"No one expects you to make that sort of statement, dear," said Hugo kindly. "Pamela's a dressmaker, so she's bound to show off."

"The jeans are fine. I'm just saying get rid of the armor," Michael added. "And you might clean up your language while you're at it. Leave the swearing to the customers."

"I'm feeling persecuted," said Carmen, narrowing her eyes at her new boss, "but I need a job and Jane says you're okay, so I'll agree to take my piercings out for work."

"Yay!!!" Pamela clapped her hands together softly, at which Carmen threw her a look. "I'm Pamela," said the brunette, extending her hand over the bar to shake Carmen's.

"Hi," said Carmen.

"This is Hugo," said Pamela.

"Hi," said Carmen.

"How do you do?" Hugo shook her hand also.

"Come back tomorrow at five," said Michael cheerfully.

"Can I finish the beer?" Carmen asked.

After she had gone Hugo shook his head at Pamela and said, "I don't have high hopes for that one."

"Why not?"

"The dyke influence is too strong to be eradicated at this late date."

"Hugo, you're awful," Pamela smiled. "Give me a month and I'll have her in a prom dress for you."

"Are you saying you'll turn her into a girl?"

"Well, one of us will," Michael put in, refilling Hugo's glass. "Think I was too rough on her about the piercings?"

"You'll know that if she sues you for discrimination," said Hugo.

"She's a lovely little girl," said Pamela.

"Well, at least you've given up this mad idea of staffing your bar entirely with submissives," said Hugo.

"This one may well be in the scene," said Michael, "according to Jane."

"What could Jane possibly know about that?" Hugo wondered.

"I expect pretty much what you taught her. God knows, I never touched her in that way while we were together."

Pamela looked up with interest. She hadn't heard of this Jane before and couldn't help but wonder what Hugo had taught her and why.

The next afternoon Carmen found Michael rearranging stock in the back of the pub and Laura Random in the main room drawing a chalk outline of her mural on one of the walls. Carmen had removed her nose and eyebrow rings and was wearing a new pair of jeans and a brick red corduroy shirt with the same low hiking boots. Like all natural blondes, she caught the eye, and the patrons already seated at tables with bottles of beer followed her with theirs as she slipped into the back to greet her boss.

The beauty of Carmen's face was now fully apparent and Michael rewarded her with one of his most winning smiles. When he stationed her at the sink to start washing glasses, he also observed for the first time, her remarkably high, round and jutting bottom. This he considered a bonus.

Telling her he'd call her when it got busy he left her to continue washing out the sturdy mugs by hand and loading the dishwasher with the delicate stemware. At the end of a half hour, he came back into the small kitchen to find her proceeding nicely, with the assistance of Sam Adams.

"Did I tell you you could drink back here?" Michael asked,

summarily relieving her of the half empty bottle and giving her one small, admonitory smack on the bottom.

"Sorry," she murmured, more embarrassed at being caught with the beer than being swatted by her new boss.

"You can have a beer on your dinner break," he told her, taking the bottle away with him.

Laura's mural was to be based on the scene in the 1925 film version of Scarlet Letter, where Hester Prynne is visited in the stocks by the Reverend Arthur Dimsdale. Laura's sister, Susan Ross, also an illustrator, was coming to the village that weekend to help with the painting. Their idea was to complete several murals inside the pub, depicting key scenes from New England literature. Captain Ahab and Moby Dick were reserved for the wall that the dartboard was on and the disastrous sleigh accident from Ethan Frome was going opposite the coatroom.

Bringing Laura a glass of Riesling and a sandwich, per Michael's instructions, Carmen looked at the photo of Lillian Gish and Lars Hansen that Laura was working from and asked, "What did they do to you after they put you in the stocks?"

"I think in many cases the victims were beaten or fatally pelted with stones," the brunette replied, accepting the glass of wine with thanks.

"Wouldn't all the village jocks have surrounded a girl in the stocks and performed a circle jerk?" asked Carmen guilelessly.

"I don't think jocks or circle jerks were permitted in Puritan Boston," Laura replied.

Suddenly an afternoon rush began and Carmen was drafted immediately into service at the tap. She knew the beer prices by heart, being a denizen of the Dutch for several years herself, but had to refer to the menu for everything else. Michael expected this to stymie her, but Carmen seemed to glide on wheels that afternoon. She filled the orders efficiently, had a quick, impish smile for everyone but replied not at all to the flirtatious remarks thrown out as she ran around to the tables. The way she handled the men impressed Michael. While Hope would have bothered to conquer every heart in the room, Carmen seemed content to politely keep the beasts at bay.

Conversely, within a very few days, Carmen began to admire her boss. She could scarcely fail to notice the steady stream of women who came to the pub specifically to see and congratulate him on his new business. There was Connie Barton, owner of the Bone and Feather Inn, who was selling Michael extremely good sandwiches for the counter. There was Laura's younger sister Susan Ross and her friend Diana Stratton Currie, up from New York and shedding all the glamour that locality implied. There was the leggy and elegant redheaded Marguerite Alexander, in to flirt deeply and meaningfully with her ex-lover. Marguerite gave Carmen more than a once over, pausing to chat with her for an hour and converting her to a fan. Carmen also met the fabled Hope Spencer Lawrence, who had worked one whole night at The Dutch before her husband dragged her home. And the new owner of the Random Point gym and European Spa, Polyxena Guzman, stayed a whole evening drinking in the bar, becoming more and more pink in the face and hilarious in her off color remarks to Michael, who wound up driving her home.

Polyxena was still estranged from her lover Dieter Brant and living alone in the lighthouse. She had been flirting with Michael for several weeks and now it was time to harvest the fruit of it. Michael was doubly fascinated by Polyxena. Her pin-up form and face, the cultured European accent, the fine education and vast quantities of business acumen melded into a highly attractive package of unattached womanhood. But it was the fact that the girl was a mistress, exploring her submissive side for the first time that by far interested Michael Flagg the most. Michael considered the taking of a dominant woman to be one of the greatest things a man could do for the honor of his sex. There was a piquancy in turning a mistress over one's knee that was difficult to match.

Carmen couldn't understand why she resented it so much when Michael took Polyxena home, or laughed at Diana Stratton's impertinences or gazed dreamily into the eyes of Hope Spencer Lawrence, but she did. At the end of one short week, Carmen was arriving at work early and staying each night until the last possible moment. Then, at the beginning of her second week, she amazed Michael by arriving for work in a dress!

Carmen had bought the outfit at the shop belonging to Michael's ex-wife, Damaris, for whom Pamela also worked most days. Carmen had never bought a dress in her life, no less any garment costing over a hundred dollars, but she had been studying Pamela's style and saw how much she could learn about presentation from the design school graduate.

The dress Carmen finally chose was of smoky blue wool with a surplice top and full skirt. She also wore chestnut riding boots, which represented the remainder of her week's pay. Never in her life had she spent $350 on apparel in one day. Her reward was Michael staring at her agog as she entered.

Pamela made a great fuss over Carmen's new look, demanding that Michael pay her a compliment.

"Couple more inches of hair and she'll look like a real girl," he agreed.

"He's only teasing you," said Pamela to Carmen when Michael stepped into the back. A crimson blush had spread from Carmen's throat to her brow at Michael's off hand remark, showing Pamela exactly how the new girl felt about her boss. And after she had tried so hard too. Pamela thought it was really too bad of Michael to speak so to the new girl. Carmen gazed into the mirror over the bar, pulling at the ends of her hair.

"I wonder why he even hired me," said Carmen with a sigh. "I'm clearly not his type."

"You're everyone's type," Pamela reassured her.

Carmen discovered that her tips went up with a dress on. And the men spoke more respectfully to her. But when her aunt, her aunt's girl friend and a group of their lesbian buds came in to raise hell mid-evening, the teasing was merciless. None of these good natured forty something dykes had ever seen their little Carmen in a dress and some of them wolf whistled as they thumped their table for ale. Michael came to serve the women himself and was duly needled by the large, raucous group. They loved finding out he was a former cop and wanted any lesbian cop stories he could provide. He wound up sitting down and drinking with the women, learning Carmen's entire history and making seven new friends. Carmen blushed continuously all night.

As the two of them cleaned up around midnight Michael thanked her for bringing in the new customers.

"You think I'm a dyke too, don't you?" she suddenly accused.

"Oh, no," he smiled, dimming a few of the kitchen lights. Carmen began to snap crumbs off the wooden table with a towel, leaning over to flick the edges. Michael's eyes were once again drawn to her round, jutting bottom, almost the buttocks of a black girl, so fully molded were they.

"Why do you even mention such things, Carmen?" he asked, sweeping up the crumbs she brushed onto the floor as he circled around the table in her wake.

"Because I want you to notice that I'm a female, damn it!" she cried, folding her arms across her pert bosom.

"Think I haven't?" he grinned.

"So, how long does my hair have to get before we can have sex?"

"Direct, aren't you?" he replied with another smile.

"Well, you're not getting any younger," she returned.

"Don't you have a boyfriend?" he asked, not bothering to rise to the bait. It had been so long since he'd made love to a woman who wasn't in the scene that he didn't he know whether he was even capable of getting it up for one anymore.

"No."

"How come?"

"Maybe I've been waiting for a man friend instead."

"Well, you're more than sweet to think of me like that, in spite of my advanced age, but I don't think we'd be compatible."

"Oh," she said, surprised, distressed and embarrassed. "Forget it then."

"Don't get me wrong," he added hurriedly; "It's more to do with me than you."

"You already have too many women in your life?"

"No, it's to do with personal preferences."

"Like for longer hair and no piercings?"

"No."

"What then?"

"Well, basically I only date submissives. That's why I broke up with Jane. We'd been planning on getting married. But on the eve of the wedding, I discovered the scene."

"The scene?"

"The spanking scene, here in Random Point. There are lots of people into it around here."

"You mean like, over the knee spanking?"

"Exactly. I've always been fascinated by it. But it wasn't until about five years ago that I started to meet others who were also. Ever since then, I've turned to the scene for my social life, my love life and my sex life. And it's worked out so well that it doesn't seem to make sense to go outside it anymore."

"Spanking, huh?"

"I don't expect you to understand."

"I'm not completely unsophisticated, you know!"

"No?"

"So, you won't ever fuck me unless you can spank me first?"

"Well, ideally," he replied, looking at her.

"And what do you get out of it?"

"It's a special kind of bliss, but unless you have a fetish of your own, I don't expect you to understand it."

"So, I would think you're really into bottoms, huh? Because I happen to have a really good one!"

"Yes, I've been noticing that," he agreed.

"I can't imagine what it feels like to get a spanking. Couldn't you give me a little demonstration before we decide it isn't for me?"

"Are you serious? You want to try it?"

Carmen looked at him as much as to say, "If it gets me any closer to that marvelous hunk of masculinity known as Michael Flagg, yes please!"

"I'm not afraid to, anyway," she replied defiantly.

"Leaving that to one side for a second, why do you want to start something with your boss?" he said, squatting to sweep the crumbs into a dustpan.

"You have more good looking women hanging around you than a gentleman of leisure. There must be a reason."

"Well, I do appreciate the interest, but I don't think we should rush into anything."

"Is that a polite brush off?"

"No."

"You're not attracted to me. That's the problem," she declared, removing her apron and hanging it up.

"I just hadn't thought of you that way," he replied truthfully. "Being as you're not in the scene, as I said."

"So, is spanking pretty much all you can do?" she suddenly challenged him. "I mean without Viagra?"

Michael sighed and looked at Carmen. Holding her gaze, he reached into his pocket, pulled out a foil wrapped condom and placed it on the table in acceptance of her challenge. Reaching out with one hand he grabbed her by the wrist, spun her around and bent her over the edge of the table. She looked at him over her shoulder but registered no protest.

Pushing her skirt up to her waist Michael revealed her round, muscular buttocks, clad in a pair of smoky blue lace briefs, also acquired at the boutique of his ex-wife. Carmen's pink and white skin gleamed through the lace. Careful not to snag them, Michael rather quickly tugged her panties down and made her step out of them. Her legs were bare to her knees, where her boots began. He separated them and stood behind her, regarding her remarkably shapely backside with extreme admiration and running his hands over its curves.

"Are you going to spank me now?" she asked.

"I'll save that for when you need it," he replied, unzipping his trousers and allowing his stiffening cock to escape. The sight of the young woman so compliantly bent over the edge of the table was sufficiently stimulating to inspire a splendid erection. This now was snugly wrapped in a condom and poised at the proper portal for insertion. Michael spread her with his hands and explored her blonde fuzzed Venus mound with gentle fingers until her slit became moist and her clitoris stiffened. She opened to him. Her whole body yielded as he began to penetrate her, first with one finger, then with two.

"Sure you want this, honey?" he asked, stroking her waist and reaching up to briefly cup each firm, small breast in one hand for a squeeze.

"Oh my god!" she cried, turning to see how large her boss was in readiness. "Hell yes, I want it!"

Soon thereafter, she got it. For in spite of not being in the scene, she had petitioned for sex with such determination and bent over so nicely for it that Michael would have felt himself a lunatic to protest any further. Besides, it was interesting to think about turning her into a player.

Their initial encounter was over in fifteen minutes. But afterwards they wanted more of each other. Michael took her back to his house in the woods and put her in his bed. There they made love more completely. She shyly confided that she found it almost impossible to climax unless given some anal stimulation. ("Jackpot," thought Michael.) She showed him how she had accomplished this goal in the past, mounting him as he lay on his back and placing each of his hands on a bottom cheek. They experimented with her riding him and him digitally penetrating her bottom. She came fast and her flutters triggered his second climax of the night.

The next morning, when she crawled across Michael to get her cigarettes, Carmen got her first spanking, consisting of five or six swats. Then she was turned the right way around and even more soundly kissed.

Carmen, who had woken up with bikers, but never with a man of taste, marveled at the architecturally ingenious house in the light of day. Michael told her that it had been redone for him and his then bride, Damaris Perez, by his friend William Random some years ago and agreed that it was probably far too nice for a bachelor. Carmen, who lived in a shabby Provincetown single disagreed. She liked it fine at Michael's house.

As he gave her coffee and a bagel Michael wondered whether they should discuss what had happened the previous night. But she looked so content at his kitchen table, turning the pages of the lurid detective magazines to which he contributed fiction, that he decided not to disturb her with hypothetical discussions as to why this was probably not going to work out.

Besides, he couldn't think of any way to tell her that he was not the faithful type without insulting the evening they'd spent in each other's arms. She would just have to figure that out for herself, he decided. For after all, she had been the one to come on to him, not the other way around. As he saw it, more than half of the responsibility for what had happened belonged to the girl. If she did not see fit to ask any questions or exact any promises before their tryst, she could not expect him to alter his behavior in any way as a result of their night together.

Carmen left Michael's house on a cloud. But she didn't stay up in the ether very long. For when she arrived at the pub that evening, a new woman was seated at the bar, leaning on her elbows and looking dreamily up into Flagg's blue eyes. This blonde was sleek and finished, slim to a fault and dressed in a chalk gray flannel suit, with elegant four-inch pumps to match.

Carmen was informed by Pamela, whose shift was just ending, that the girl was called Patricia Fairservis and that she was Michael's most recent ex-girlfriend, visiting from New York for the night. The words pierced Carmen's heart. It seemed that however many of them showed up, Michael's supply of exes would never be exhausted.

Patricia looked Carmen over and dismissed her with a half smile, for Carmen was back to her pegged jeans, plaid shirt and hiking boots that day and apart from being pretty and fresh faced, appeared entirely unremarkable to the Prada clad blonde.

The former editor of Cape Cod Style was now working in the accounts department at the ad agency Chipper-Knight and enjoying a whole new life in the milieu she most admired. Of course she missed her monumental Celtic warrior sex god, but a tiny coastal village was never the berg to contain her ambitious energy and she had faith in the NY scene to eventually provide her with a replacement for Flagg. Meanwhile, she wasn't about to waste a visit to her precious ex-lover. This night would belong to Patricia and Michael alone. They would flirt and drink and with a final twist of the knife, they would dance, for all to see.

While Patricia was in the bar, Carmen didn't exist for Michael, or so it seemed to that young lady. It was the worst night of Carmen's life. For over the past few days, she'd fallen harder and harder in love.

The previous night, with its glorious culmination had catapulted her through heaven's happy portals. But the observation of Michael with the very beautiful Patricia plunged her straight into the depths of hell.

At last the evening ended. Michael dismissed Carmen at twelve sharp with a pleasant, absent smile, and had Patricia stay to help him lock up. Carmen went home feeling dead. She hadn't eaten any dinner, for loss of appetite. Now she felt completely hollow. She lay on her bed without even undressing, looking through the window at a tiny patch of inky sky and stars until her tears blurred the stars into the ink.

The next day Patricia returned to New York. Pamela came in at five to help with the evening shift. Carmen arrived moments later to leave Pamela speechless with shock. Carmen had been to the barber and had obtained a radical buzz cut. Now there was naught by a fine fuzz of blonde between Carmen's skull and the sky.

At first Michael didn't even recognize her. He thought a young boy had walked in. Then he realized what she'd done and turned that particular shade of red that belongs uniquely to those of Celtic origin when angry or embarrassed.

"What the hell did you do to yourself?" he demanded. Carmen's chin came up defiantly but before she could frame any sort of reply he grabbed her by her wrist and dragged her into the back. "Get over here!"

"You're doing this here?" she cried as he dropped down on a wooden bench and yanked her across his lap as though she were a serviette.

"Think you're cute?" He brought his hand down hard, spanking her with all the indignation which he deemed her defiance deserved. "How dare you come in here looking like this?" Smack, smack, smack! His palm descended vigorously on alternate cheeks, warming her well-worn jeans thoroughly with dozens and then scores of swats. "You did this because of Patricia, didn't you? Answer me!"

"Yes!" she replied on a sob.

"What an idiotically childish thing to do!" he accused, continuing to spank her resoundingly. "You think you have a right to be jealous? Of me?"

"No," she squirmed, trying to shield her bottom with her hands.

For her trouble she had them slapped and pinned to the small of her back. "But I was hurt."

"That's nothing to how hurt you're going to be," he promised, smacking her repeatedly. "Do I have to remind you that you propositioned me?" Smack, smack, smack! "That you practically dared me to take you?" Michael brought his hand down even harder now, causing her to kick her little booted feet up so high that he nearly caught one in the head. "Hold still and take what you have coming," he ordered, finishing with another vigorous volley and pushing her off his lap.

"If I had any sense I'd fire you!" he declared, shoving the bench back into place. "Looking like that you'll scare the customers away," he added with unnecessary cruelty. "Now pull yourself together and get back on the floor. Since you've entirely ceased to be ornamental, you might as well make yourself useful!" Michael's exiting remark, much more painful to bear than the spanking, called fourth a torrent of tears, which Pamela found Carmen bathed in when she entered a moment later.

"Oh, honey," cried Pamela, delicately dabbing at Carmen's face with a fresh handkerchief, "why in the world did you have your head shaved?" Pamela couldn't resist running her hand over the freshly shorn nap of her new co-worker. "Oh, it feels like velvet though," the brunette exclaimed. "Lovely to the touch." Carmen swallowed her tears and managed a smile. She allowed Pamela to keep stroking her head in wonder. "It really feels nice!"

"It will grow back quickly," Carmen said on a sob.

"Did he...spank you?" Pamela asked with hesitation. Carmen nodded.

"I think that means he likes you," Pamela smiled.

"Not any more he doesn't," said Carmen sadly.

"Come on, let's get back to work," Pamela encouraged, pushing a hand mirror in front of Carmen's face and handing her a lipstick.

"I don't wear lipstick," Carmen resisted.

"Oh yes you do," said Pamela, neatly applying the cherry shade to Carmen's luscious lips.

Michael didn't look up when the girls emerged. In fact, he had decided not to look at Carmen at all until her hair grew back. But he was far too managing to ignore his girl as she went about her work, and he couldn't help but notice with a slight pang of guilt, that he'd effectively wiped the impish smile off her face for the rest of the day.

In fact, she seemed sadly subdued, though not inattentive throughout the entire evening as well. People who knew her reacted with surprise rather than horror to the buzz cut. Strangers didn't even seem to notice, for she had a finely shaped head and set off by small golden earrings and with the cherry color on her mouth, Carmen was still decidedly feminine in appearance.

A tangible warmth from the spanking stayed with her for over an hour. Far from resenting this, Carmen hoped the sensation would linger, for she knew it would be the last physical contact she could expect with Michael Flagg for some time.

As the evening progressed, the big parade of Michael's comrades of both sexes arrived in ones and pairs, each noting Carmen's haircut with amazement. Little Susan Ross and Diana Stratton Currie made the largest fuss over it. Thoroughly bi herself and always attracted to the edgy, Diana kissed Carmen's hand for her boldness. Michael scowled at them and sent Carmen to wait on a table at the other side of the room. "Don't distract the girl," he growled at Susan and Diana, "she has work to do."

Pamela's tender heart went out to Carmen and she could not help remonstrating with Michael the moment they were alone in the back at the same time. "How can you be so unkind to Carmen?" Pamela softly protested. "Can't you see she's on the verge of tears?"

"There's more going on here than meets the eye," he told Pamela, who was still in ignorance of the fact that Michael and Carmen were already lovers. "But suffice to say, it's none of your concern!"

Pamela stiffened haughtily and grabbed a bottle of white wine out of the cooler. "And don't baby that brat either," her boss warned her. "She's in the corner with me and she's staying there!"

Chapter Nine

Love Isn't Born

Carmen Farrell's G.I. Jane look didn't last long. By the week before Christmas her fair hair had grown out to the pixie cut she'd originally walked in with when she'd been hired to tend bar the month before. But Michael Flagg continued to nurse a grudge against Carmen for her jealous act of defiance in having her pretty head buzzed.

"Don't you think it's time to unbend a bit, Michael?" Marguerite Alexander asked the new owner of The Dutch as he set a steaming Irish coffee in front of her that drizzly afternoon. "She's languishing for love of you and I know you can't be indifferent to the girl, so why the lack of gallantry? This isn't the Michael I know," the sable swathed redhead observed, her green eyes tracking Carmen's wistful figure as the slim blonde went about the tables refilling salt and pepper shakers and wiping the wooden tables down.

"Gallantry?" replied Michael. "For that uncouth brat?"

Carmen paused by the one jock stuffed table at the back of the pub, set opposite the TV monitor, where a boxing match was in progress. As Carmen's voyeuristic excitement grew, she could be heard to exclaim, "Fuck, those Puerto Rican bantams can move!"

"See what I mean?" said Michael to Marguerite. "No manners, no education, no vocabulary, just as common as can be."

"Surely you're being very severe upon the young lady," Marguerite murmured.

"She's not a young lady," he insisted. "She's not any kind of lady."

"I had no idea you'd become so fastidious," said Marguerite.

"That ref is fucked!" they heard Carmen declare, in response to a decision on the bout. All the jocks agreed and ordered another round.

"See? That's the only word in her lexicon," said Michael, glaring across the room at Carmen while snapping crumbs off the bar with a towel.

"So, was that an idle rumor I heard about you taking her home one night last month?" Marguerite expressed only mild interest.

"It happened," he admitted reluctantly. "Once."

"Don't tell me once was enough with that little darling!"

"Maybe not," he said, "but it won't happen again until that one is properly trained!"

"Michael, what in the world do you mean?" Marguerite laughed.

"She needs civilizing worse than any girl I know."

Marguerite blushed at the implication but saw exactly what he meant. Between herself, Damaris, Patricia, Susan and most recently the dazzling Polyxena Guzman, Michael had in recent years consorted with a highly refined breed of woman. Even his original girlfriend Jane Eliot, albeit too politically correct to prove his perfect match, had developed into a little diplomat of tact and courtesy.

Whereas Carmen was a college drop out who had been casually raised by unpretentious dykes, a tomboy who dated bikers and drank beer straight out of the can. She rode a motorcycle, smoked whatever came to hand and had never heard of Jane Austen. She had tattoos in silly places and piercings in her nostrils and eyebrows, (which she was forbidden to wear for work). There were vast reserves of purity and beauty within her, especially deep in her heart and soul, but a surface element of crudeness had taken hold early and would only be eradicated through a sustained and conscious effort.

"You could always play Pygmalion," mused Marguerite after a wondering, "Can't they fucking see that eye is already closed???" issued from the rosebud mouth of Carmen as she continued to monitor the match.

"That would be more in Hugo's line." Michael replied.

"But dear," said Marguerite, "isn't there something to be said for a humble helpmeet? Think of how grateful she'll be. Ponder her adoring compliance."

"Ha!" Michael laughed without mirth. "Remember how adoringly compliant Damaris was when I first rescued her? That part doesn't last."

"Well what about the fact that of all the girls you know, Carmen is the one who needs you most."

"If that was true it would be pathetic," he snapped back.

"God, you're hard. And at Christmas too!" Marguerite sighed, then couldn't help but wince when a resounding, "Unfuckingbelievable!" left Carmen's lips in response to the next decision.

"Can you see why she's getting a birch in her stocking?" Michael asked.

After Marguerite departed Pamela came on her shift with a stack of wrapped packages to put under the Christmas tree. The bar filled up fast with villagers who'd left work early for Christmas parties. It had been like this for several weeks and the cash register sat stuffed at the end of each night.

Anthony Newton contributed to the general merriment surrounding the reopening of The Dutch by sending over a stand up piano and coming to play it himself that evening, accompanied by Susan Ross and her best friend, the newly wed Diana Stratton Currie.

Carmen was introduced to the Broadway luminary and was once again made much of by Susan and Diana, who admired the new length of her hair and presented her with sweaters for Christmas. Michael scowled from across the room and presently came over to bark at Carmen to get behind the bar and tend to her customers there. Carmen flashed him one rebellious glare behind his back before gathering up her presents and taking them with her. "And after you take those orders meet me in the back, I want to talk to you, young lady," Michael added curtly, causing the tiny hairs to stand up on the back of Carmen's neck.

But presently it became too busy for either of them to leave the floor. Anthony Newton's playing kept people from leaving and the pub soon became filled to capacity. Also with the New York entourage was Phoebe Casper, the petite chanteuse who was to have an important role in Newton's next musical.

Phoebe's husband, photographer Pascal Robbins, sat at the bar chatting with his ex-model Pamela but casting uneasy looks toward the piano where his wife was singing "Love Isn't Born" in her rich contralto, to Newton's accompaniment.

Pascal and Phoebe spent a good deal of time apart due to the traveling requirements of their respective professions and this had kept their two-year marriage rather fresh. But Pascal was not a little jealous of Phoebe's important admirer and possibly with good reason.

Pascal knew all about the casual morality which pervaded Newton's clique, whose members justified their bed hopping by claiming membership in an all pervasive entity known only as The Scene. He'd discovered the previous year, when he and Phoebe lived a season in Random Point, that she herself was part of this secret society of spanking enthusiasts and had been all her life. But it took Random Point to give her the courage to admit it to her husband.

Once Pascal learned that his wife craved domestic discipline, it wasn't hard to make her innocent little fantasies come true. Phoebe possessed certain traits that cried out for correction by the lights of her exacting mate. And Pascal knew how to play his role. Apart from possessing a naturally forceful, bossy and dominant personality, he'd seen enough spankings in old movies to facsimilate the proper attitude, pronounce the appropriate words, achieve the optimal positioning and deliver the goods with verve.

Phoebe went for it all, falling in love with her good-looking husband in a whole new way. Nor did she give him the slightest reason to doubt her constancy, even when faced with the temptation of an entire scene to play in. She had chosen the man she desired and now he even spanked her. As far as Phoebe was concerned, Pascal could rest easy in her loyalty and love.

But Pascal had a jealous nature and in spite of his faith in Phoebe, he mistrusted every man who looked at her, especially the ones in Random Point and particularly the brilliant and powerful Anthony Newton, who besides offering his wife the most enormous chance of her career, was good looking, personable, and decidedly "in" this increasingly ubiquitous scene.

Compared to these life long enthusiasts, Pascal felt himself to be an outsider. He resented their universal comradery and merry, indiscriminate, incestuous lovemaking. He really couldn't understand how Anthony Newton could tolerate his girlfriend Susan Ross flirting with every dominant man she met and sleeping with most of them as well. He was sure he could have Susan himself, any time he chose. She liked him, found him attractive, had sat on his lap and posed for him. The taking of Susan Ross would be as easily accomplished as turning her over his knee. He had learned that much about these bad children! But of course he hadn't acted on this dangerous and scandalous knowledge. He considered himself sophisticated, up to a point, but in many ways he was as old fashioned as the fedoras he enjoyed wearing.

Pamela was the only one whom he believed to be true hearted, since he had traveled with her for almost a year and their relationship had remained strictly professional. But he recently learned, through the Susan and Diana grapevine, that even Pamela had succumbed to the siren song of infidelity and cheated vigorously on her lover Sloan Taylor with Hugo Sands in recent months. This was disillusioning and Pascal felt somewhat piqued at Pamela for having behaved so badly. He meant to scold her for it too, as soon as he had downed an unspecified number of vodka tonics.

Michael Flagg's new bar Pascal could not help but regard as just one more hotbed of illicit scene activity, designed to undermine his influence over his vivacious, curvaceous, bisque-complected songbird.

"God, that girl has a fucking gorgeous figure," murmured Carmen with honest admiration as she brought Pascal a fresh drink.

"Well, she's corseted," Pascal revealed, smiling across the bar at Pamela, who had been the first to lace his slim but voluptuous wife into a waist cinch. "She's reduced her waist two inches corseting."

"No fucking way!" Carmen marveled.

"Carmen!" Michael snapped from behind her, "I need you in back!"

Carmen followed him into the kitchen, pulling nervously at the ends of her hair. That day she was dressed in a handsome (allegedly) cast-off outfit of Pamela's, a nubby brown tweed skirt and a close fitting pumpkin colored merino wool polo sweater, along with the new chestnut riding boots. Michael couldn't help but notice how well she looked, but this only made him more impatient with her.

"What did I tell you about swearing, young lady?" he demanded.

"I wasn't swearing," she protested, trying to remember to whom she'd just spoken and what she'd said.

"No? I've heard some variation of the word 'fuck' pass your lips at least seven times today, and it's still early."

"Sorry," she said meekly.

"Don't you realize how vulgar and ignorant it makes you sound to talk that way?"

Carmen looked at the floor. He continued in a milder tone, "Carmen, you're a very nice girl, but you manage to make the worst impression. I really want you to concentrate on choosing better words."

"Okay," she mumbled, turning to return to the floor.

"If I hear one more swear word out of you tonight, I won't call you back here just to talk!" he threatened sternly. "Now get back to your customers."

Carmen fled with a warm, pink face, her heart throbbing with a mixture of shame and pleasure. He had scolded her, but not without saying that he thought her a very nice girl. He had threatened her (with another spanking?) but not with firing. And just for a moment, she saw him look at her waist and the upward curve of her bosom with something like approval. Perhaps she had a chance with him after all.

"Is this what it's like, being in love with a grown up?" Carmen asked Diana, gazing across the room at her boss as he delivered a pitcher to a table. She'd just set a Brandy Alexander down in front of the small, sleek brunette, who now sat at a corner table with Susan.

"Why? What do you mean?" Diana asked, grabbing Carmen's hand and placing it against her cheek.

"Isn't my boss the handsomest man?" Carmen sighed.

"Oh, you love Michael, do you?" Diana pulled Carmen down to sit on her lap, locking her arms around the delicate blonde's slim waist and nuzzling her throat. "Well, I'm sure he loves you back!" Diana cooed.

"He's sure not acting like he loves her back," Susan commented, noticing the scowl on Michael's face every time he tossed Carmen a glance.

"I know," Carmen agreed, jumping off Diana's lap and quickly clearing the table.

"Carmen, tell Michael we want a bottle of really good champagne," said Diana. "I've got a brand new charge card and PC has ordered me to run it up so he can have an excuse to beat me when he gets back from Europe."

"I'm so proud of you, I could burst," said Susan, spontaneously embracing her college friend, who had plunged so dramatically into the scene as to end up the wife of a wealthy and indulgent spanking and bondage daddy, who had not only been to Yale with Anthony but also owned the firm of Chipper Knight where Susan worked as an illustrator. "As they say, those who can't do, teach," Susan sighed, looking at Anthony and Phoebe across the room.

"Anthony may not be fond of marriage," Diana soothed, "but he adores my best friend."

"He thinks it would ruin everything to add his initial to my monogram," Susan mused for the thousandth time, as if she still didn't really understand her (five times divorced) lover's attitude. "But I don't think it would!"

The warmth and interest the girls from New York were showering on his bar maid displeased Michael. The last thing he wanted was for Carmen to be taken up, spoiled and possibly even ruined by Susan and Diana before he had even had a chance to train her.

Michael delivered and opened the hundred dollar bottle of champagne himself, pouring the amber liquid into flutes. The girls pressed him to join them in a glass and he sat down. "I don't know what I did to deserve all this, but I'm enjoying the hell out of it," said Michael, still marveling at Anthony and the piano.

"Then why don't you show it by being nicer to young Carmen?" Susan demanded. Michael threw her a look.

"Has she been complaining?" he asked.

"Heaven forbid," replied Diana, slipping her tiny hand under Michael's huge one. "But we have eyes."

Realizing that Carmen had everyone from Marguerite to Pamela to Susan on her side only annoyed Michael more and he became shorter with her as the night progressed.

By half past eleven, only a few topers remained. Pamela had gone home. Carmen wiped the tables down and delivered final tabs to the drunks. Michael stood behind the cash register, merrily counting its contents twice. Carmen came to him with the rest of her receipts and cash.

"Bet you did well off Anthony Newton and those brats," Michael commented sagely. The next moment Carmen began unfolding her special tips from Susan and Diana, which she'd simply crammed into her apron pocket.

"My god!" she exclaimed, "These are hundred dollar bills! They must have made a mistake. I'd better call them tomorrow."

"Nonsense. Do you have any idea how wealthy Mr. Newton is? Didn't you notice him leave us a piano? And Diana just married one of the fattest cats in New York. They meant for you to have the cash."

"It doesn't make sense. I just brought them some drinks," she shrugged to herself, going back to clearing tables and putting up chairs as the last few patrons shuffled out into the wind and rain.

"Carmen, go grab those tweak heads and make them come back for some coffee before they get on the road," Michael ordered, looking up from the happy occupation of rubber banding twenties.

"Okay!" she replied, dashing out after the experienced drunks, who were long gone by the time she got outside. She returned shaking her head, reporting, "It's really raining hard too!"

Carmen disappeared into the bathroom to change into her jeans, sweater and jacket for the ride home.

"Carmen!" Michael shouted for her before she was done, in a tone that indicated he had found the wad of checks at the bottom of her stack upon which she had playfully scrawled either "Fuck you," "Fuck you, asshole," "Fuck off and die," "Get fucked," or her personal favorite, "Merry Fucking Christmas to you and your entire Freak Show." She had written these little essays on the receipts of departed patrons entirely for her own amusement, but her boss wasn't enjoying Carmen's sense of humor.

Carmen emerged from the bathroom in jeans, a black leather jacket and her black motorcycle boots. But Michael grabbed her by the wrist and jerked her into the kitchen as paternalistically as if she was still wearing the Pamela skirt and sweater set.

"What's this tomfoolery?" he brandished the sales checks in her face. "Do you want another spanking?"

"I was just teasing you," she admitted, blushing carnation pink.

"What happened to the skirt?"

"I'm going home on my bike."

"In this rain?"

"I've done it before."

"I'll drive you home."

"Okay."

When they were in his car Michael said, "Did you bring the skirt and sweater?"

"They're in my pack," she said, indicating a leather satchel.

"You live in Provincetown, huh?" he asked, throwing the car into gear. The rain had become thunderous but beat on the windowpanes no more loudly than the pounding of Carmen's heart at being so close to her idol.

"Yes," she replied out loud, but inwardly prayed to the Goddess, "Don't let him take me there. Make Michael take me home with him instead."

"Maybe we should just go to my house. It's so close," he said mildly.

"Your house?"

"Terrible driving in this weather on the coast road," he explained.

"Oh, yes!"

"And you are starting to look like a girl again," he added.

"Oh! You give me hope!" she cried.

"Hope for what?"

"Hope for yum yum. You do it better than anyone," she replied unselfconsciously.

"Yum yum?"

"Sex, I mean."

"Oh, that."

"I just loved it with you."

"Knowing what I now know about you, I could make you come in about ten different ways before we ever got to yum yum," he mused.

"Really? How?"

"Oh, various forms of corporal punishment mixed with penetration. There's an infinite number of possibilities just within that category alone."

Carmen admitted candidly, "That sounds sexy, but I'd die of shame."

"Really?" Michael couldn't help but be charmed.

"You're the first man I ever met who knows anything about sex," said Carmen.

"Not very experienced, are you?" he asked. She shook her head.

"But I'm interested in becoming more so," she insisted.

"Copy that," he replied.

They didn't exchange another word until they arrived at Michael's house.

"You never told me how you felt about that spanking I gave you," Michael said, handing Carmen a hot cocoa a few minutes later in his sitting room.

The mention of the spanking, given to her as a punishment for willfully having her head shaved, caused the color to once again flood her face, but she smiled too. "It was more embarrassing than painful," she finally replied, causing Michael's brows to arch. He then realized with a start that what the girls were saying was right. Carmen was in love with him. How else to account for a girl not in the scene scarcely feeling the sting of a patented Michael Flagg paddling?

"I've failed in my duty unless I punish in a way that is equally painful and embarrassing. You must have a very hard bottom, young lady. I wonder if it comes from the motorcycle?"

"Whenever I think about that spanking, I get a sort of spasm right here," she placed her hand atop her flat stomach. "I just wish you hadn't gotten so angry at me along with it."

Michael looked down. "I'm sorry," he said. "But you did cut your hair to make me furious and you got what you wanted."

"I guess I wanted attention, because I was jealous of Patricia. I know I had no right to be. We'd just had the one night together, after me throwing myself at you. So who the fuck was I to protest?"

"Carmen, what did I tell you?"

"I'm sorry! Damn it!" she clapped her hand over her mouth.

"I warned you what would happen the next time you swore!" Now Michael captured Carmen around the waist, sat on the arm of a broad leather chair and turned her over his knee. Then Michael spanked Carmen.

"Why is it that you're unable to remember the simplest directive? No swearing is what I told you I wanted to hear out of you and no swearing is what you will do around me from now on!" Smack, smack, smack! The palm of his hand came resoundingly down again and again on the seat of her pants, causing a layer of heat to be trapped between her flesh and the denim.

Michael realized that once again dungarees were lending an inappropriate amount of protection to Carmen's tough little bottom. "Get up!" He lifted the lithe blonde from his lap. "Go and change back into the skirt and sweater." Carmen disappeared without question, which pleased him no end.

Was she in the scene or wasn't she? She was certainly behaving like a woman who was. When Carmen came out again he said, "Carmen, Carmen, Carmen, what am I going to do with you?"

She looked up at him with the gold-flecked hazel eyes of a cat. Or was that a trick of the firelight?

"You don't really care about being politically correct do you?" he asked, running his hand lightly through her inch of baby soft blonde hair.

"No, I couldn't give a fuck about that stuff," murmured Carmen before she could think to stop herself. Michael grimly seized her by her cream velvet earlobe and this time taking a seat on a hassock, flung her face down across his lap.

"You're unbelievable. Can't you concentrate for a minute on what you're saying?"

His hand came down on her thick woolen skirt for three or four smacks before he realized that she'd never feel a thing through it. Up came the skirt presently, revealing a pair of white lace cotton briefs through which her pinkened skin could already be glimpsed.

"I'm going to teach you to think before you speak."

Now he paddled her soundly for several minutes. She panted but made no outcry. She knew she should be feeling severe pain, but instead she only felt tremendous stimulation and excitement. His hand made a loud report. It caused heat to emanate from her flesh, but she still could not define what she was feeling as hurtful.

Carmen had no wish to break free. She knew that she could wriggle off his lap, out of his grasp, if she chose to do so. He was holding her firmly, but not in an iron grasp. She was certain that if she begged to be released, that Michael would let her go. She had no fear and she had no pain. But something kept making her stomach clench with the most intense pleasure she had ever known, something about control.

"I'll try harder," she promised as she felt him tug her panties down and begin afresh on her bare skin.

Thirty smacks later, he let her up, pulled up her panties and sat her back down in a chair. "As I had begun to say, a sort of relationship might be possible between us, but only if you accept the fact that I am not now nor will I ever again be politically correct," Michael said.

She replied, "I've dated bikers. How bad could you be?"

"I'll tell you how bad. I want you to start behaving like a lady."

Carmen stuck her finger in her mouth as though she were gagging herself.

"Do you want another spanking?" he demanded. She looked contrite.

"Well, what does being a lady mean? Gloves and girdles? Spitting instead of swallowing?"

"It means you don't say the first vulgar thing that comes into your head, even if it does seem clever."

"Okay, I stand corrected. But I associate the word 'lady' with the embalmed."

"I mean 'lady' in the sense of a girl who doesn't comport herself like a jock."

"I can't help being a wise guy. It's an integral part of my personality," she protested.

"Fine. Part of my personality is to smack your bottom when you irritate me. Which seems to happen every two minutes."

"I'll try my best not to swear," she promised. "And I accept that you'll keep administering Pavlovian beatings to me until I learn," she replied deadpan.

"Then you're smarter than I thought."

"What else do ladies not do?" she asked.

"They don't get any more tattoos if they know what's good for them," he told her sternly.

"They do," she said timidly.

"I can't be your exclusive boyfriend," Michael frankly explained. "I have too many on-going connections."

"Boyfriend?" she murmured. "I just thought you'd kind of use me for sex whenever you felt like it."

"Are you being funny again?"

"I don't expect you to be my boyfriend," she assured him, with downcast eyes.

"Maybe not tonight. But you will," he sighed.

She shrugged. "I'm really not a ball buster," she promised, adding, "And as you said, I came on to you."

"Yes, you shouldn't do that sort of thing. That's an example of unladylike behavior."

"Why?"

"You should always make the man press for sex. It's more exciting for us that way."

"You're the first man I've ever come on to," she explained. "I didn't think you'd ever get around to noticing me otherwise."

"Well, that's where you were wrong."

"I guess I don't know much about men. I always thought they wanted women to be casual and easy, like them."

"I prefer them well dressed and perfumed. This was one of the areas in which Jane and I differed."

"What was the other one?"

"Oh, the spanking thing. Wouldn't you know it though, the year after we break up, she stops equating feminism with austerity, starts wearing smart little dresses and bizarrely enough, lets Hugo Sands spank her."

"Why didn't you try to get her back then?" asked Carmen, for Jane Eliot was one of her favorite people.

"Oh, all sorts of reasons. I was married to Damaris by that time, for one. Then Jane got the job at the Women's Center and suddenly came out as bi if not lesbian. She's been with the irresistible Marnie ever since."

"And why did you break up with your Damaris?"

"Marguerite."

"Marguerite Alexander?"

"I was running after her too at the time."

"Even though you were married?"

Michael shrugged, "I could never resist her."

"She is very feminine," Carmen reflected.

"However, she's married now."

"And faithful to her husband?"

"Almost continuously, I believe."

"Why didn't you ask her to marry you after your divorce?"

"Marguerite? I didn't think she'd consider it. Then she goes and marries someone with half my imagination, just because he owns a bookstore chain. And is in the scene."

"Is everyone in this village in the Scene?" Carmen wondered aloud behind the bar the following afternoon as she poured a Sam Adams on tap for Pascal Robbins.

He said, "Have you noticed it too?"

"Hell, yes!" she replied. "I hadn't worked here a week before I got spanked by my boss." She had to smile when she said it.

"Phoebe and I lived in Random Point last fall and we got invited to a few parties. In fact that's how she met the maestro."

"Oh, Mr. Newton, you mean?"

"Who could be more irresistible to an actress than a celebrated Broadway composer, with parts to cast and apparently, spankings to administer!"

"Are you saying that your wife might get a spanking from him some day?"

"I expect she already has. But she'd never let on. She knows how I feel about things like that."

"How do you feel?"

"I'm adamantly opposed to it!"

"Mr. Newton is a lovely man," Carmen observed.

"Thanks, you're helping a lot," Pascal replied morosely.

"But doesn't he have his hands full with that cute Susan Ross?"

"She is cute, isn't she? Can't believe he doesn't keep a tighter rein on her."

"Want another one?"

"Sure."

"She and her friend Diana were really nice to me last night."

"They can afford it."

"Do you think they're going to try and seduce me?" Carmen asked casually.

"I doubt it," Pascal laughed. "Though you're cute enough for anyone to want to try and seduce."

"You think so? My boss hates my short hair."

"Really? I think it's charming. Reminds me of Jean Seberg in Breathless."

"I'll have to look for that one at the video store."

"You let your boss spank you? Just like that?"

"I didn't let him. He just grabbed me, dragged me back there and did it."

"You could have filed a complaint with the labor board, I think," Pascal pointed out.

"There were special circumstances. I had shaved my head for spite after he spent the night with an old girlfriend."

"Oh, I see," said Pascal. "Petulant, are you?" Carmen dropped her gaze. "If I'd have seen you that day I probably would have spanked you myself!"

"Really? Are you in the Scene then too?"

"No, I just happen to think that women who act like children ought to be spanked."

"I suppose it was childish. He's only just begun to forgive me," Carmen admitted, going to wait on a table. Pascal followed her in the mirror, continuing to admire her. Pamela had told him she was working on this rough diamond and already his ex-model's handiwork was evident. She had given Carmen a few key wardrobe items, such as the taupe woolen skirt, vest and khaki shirt she had on that date. With the top boots the outfit rather suggested a smart little uniform and Michael noticed this with approval when he walked in a few minutes later.

Now that they had spent their second night together Michael began to feel differently about Carmen. He couldn't help but be impressed by the way she had taken her spankings. She hadn't argued with any of his criticisms. And she was as responsive as could be wished. She was cozy to sleep with, adorable first thing in the morning and didn't talk too much. All of this compliance, mixed with the smart new outfits and lengthening hair added up to a quantity of girlishness that Michael found very appealing.

The first time they crossed paths in the kitchen he seized her by the waist, lifted her to the table and sat her there.

"I was thinking," he told her, "that Saturday night should be our night."

"Our night?"

"There could be other nights, but Saturday can be our permanent date night."

"Really? You're giving me a permanent night?"

"It's a good idea to have one," he said, ruffling her hair and kissing her again.

All that day she felt him looking at her anew. She was careful about her language that afternoon but in the midst of what she felt to be an entirely irreproachable conversation with some local jocks, Michael pulled her into the back.

"Are you flirting with those boys?" he demanded, seizing her by the earlobe.

"No, of course not!" she sputtered. Then she saw the look in his eyes and realized he was teasing her. She blushed all over as he let her return to the floor with a smart smack on the bottom and an injunction not to flirt with the customers.

That day Michael seemed to finally notice how perfectly lovely Carmen was.

Pascal was to photograph the girls for some ads for the pub. Carmen was reluctant to pose but Michael insisted on placing her behind the bar with a tray of ale mugs balanced on one hand and a saucy smile on her lips. It was extremely difficult to get her to smile for the camera, though she had no problem doing it naturally and unconsciously all day long. Since there was only so long Michael was willing to have lights and reflectors set up in the bar, he finally threatened to slap her silly if she didn't start obeying Pascal's orders and she became amused enough to smile.

After Pascal shut up his kit, he sat down to relax behind a series of martinis, and Carmen went back to serving customers. It was Friday and the bar was filling up fast with numerous familiar faces as well as some new ones. Around six, when Pamela came on to help with the evening shift Michael called Carmen into the back with a serious expression.

"What's up?" she asked.

"Carmen, do you know anything about that blond kid in the booth, the one who owns the trick Harley outside?"

"I actually do. That's Joe Stringer. I went out with him a couple of years ago. Why?" Carmen replied, pleased, in all innocence, to be able to answer her boss' question.

"Really? Why'd you break up?"

Carmen shrugged and sighed, "He just started going out with someone else."

"You meant that joker had the nerve to dump you? Now I'm really ticked."

"Why?" Carmen laughed.

"Was he dealing while you were dating?"

"He used to sell weed to friends now and then, when he came across something choice."

"That all?"

"Maybe some crystal."

"Carmen, did you know he's set up shop here today?"

"No! Honestly, I didn't," she cried, becoming pale.

"Calm down. I believe you. Now listen, ordinarily I'd throw him into the parking lot head first, but I couldn't help but notice that most of his customers are dear friends of mine, so I'm going to let you deal with him."

"Who even talked to him?" Carmen wondered, trying to remember. But Pascal's lights had been shining in her eyes and between the beer steins and the smiling to concentrate on, she hadn't paid the slightest attention to her handsome ex-boyfriend. She'd said hello, brought him a Heineken and forgot all about him.

"Well, his first visitor was Marnie Price. Which sort of explains how Jane and Marnie found you, doesn't it?"

"That's true. I met Marnie through Jeff," Carmen recalled.

"Then Hope Lawrence breezed in, sat with him for five minutes and scampered out again. Fifteen minutes later, he entertained Mrs. Ambrose Bartlett briefly. She didn't even stay for a drink. And I just saw him slip something in an envelope to Pamela!"

"Wow. He is bold!" Carmen observed. "You're not going to do something horrible like have him arrested, are you?"

"No, but I want you to scare the hell out of him when you tell him to leave, as I greatly resent him doing business in my establishment. But before you do, find out exactly what he sold Mrs. Bartlett, Hope and Pamela."

"What about Marnie?"

"Don't bother, I can't have any fun with her, but the other three can be made to answer for their actions!" Michael replied with a great deal of satisfaction.

"What do you mean?"

"I'll tell you later. Maybe. Meanwhile get the information I need and throw that joker out." Michael pushed her back out onto the floor.

A few minutes later, the Harley roared off in the rain and Carmen rushed over to her boss with the exciting news that both Mrs. Bartlett and Pamela had been the recipients of crystal meth and Hope a quarter ounce of hydroponically grown grass.

Carmen didn't feel comfortable informing on Pamela but Michael convinced her to do the right thing by taking her in the storage room, bending her over a stack of crates and smacking her a few dozen times. It wasn't that the smacking hurt that badly, especially through her skirt, but the possible embarrassment of Pamela coming in and finding them in this position, or of the customers actually hearing and figuring out what was going on, caused her to finally produce the information Michael sought. Carmen resolved to make it up to Pamela somehow.

With the valuable information in his possession, Michael planned his collection route.

He stopped at the bookstore the following afternoon and confronted Hope with her insolence, of conducting an illegal transaction in his pub. Michael pointed out to her, over her own coffee bar, how wrong it had been for her to use his establishment in this way. Hope acknowledged the faux pas with an apology and blush.

"I'll expect you at my house on Sunday afternoon for your punishment," Michael told her firmly. "I happen to know that David will be at the book fair in Boston, so don't try to wriggle out of it!"

Hope smiled and served him coffee, saying, "When have I ever and what should I wear?"

Michael confronted Pamela as soon as he got back to the bar.

"I want a word with you, young lady," he began sternly over folded arms. Pamela looked up from folding red napkins, startled.

"Did I do something wrong?"

"I should say you did. Where do you get off buying crystal in here?"

Pamela turned white. She felt sick and dizzy.

"Pamela! Did you hear what I said?"

"Yes."

"No wonder you're so thin, doing that stuff. Don't you know that stuff is bad for you? You have to stop it at once. Do you hear me?"

"Yes. I understand." Pamela murmured, unable to meet his eyes.

"What do you think Sloan is going to think of this?"

"You're not going to tell him, are you?"

"Of course I am. Someone has to take you in hand."

"Please don't tell Sloan. We just got back together, and things are going so well."

"No wonder you're so thin!"

"You already said that."

"Well, I'm sorry, but someone is going to have to spank you for this."

"Oh!" Pamela understood. She got her color back and shyly

polished the tabletop.

"So, you're adamant I not tell Sloan, are you?"

"Please, Michael! He's only just forgiven me for the Hugo thing."

"There was a Hugo thing?"

"I just can't have him disillusioned about me again so quickly. I've barely had time to recapture his heart yet."

"But you do need to be punished," Michael insisted.

"All right," she looked at him. "When?"

"My house, Sunday afternoon. I believe Sloan is going into Boston with David Lawrence to the book fair."

Michael Flagg wasn't normally wicked, but the concept of having Hope and Pamela together in his own private disciplinarium and under his personal paddle was too entrancing to forego. He was the first to admit that his tactics were the opposite of ethical, but from Michael's point of view, the girls had brought this on themselves by flaunting his authority as the owner of a reputable establishment.

His Sunday afternoon settled, Michael turned his attention to the delicious Mrs. Ambrose Bartlett, nee Paula Rohan, the formerly voluptuous, now svelte blonde guidance counselor of Braemar Prep and a woman with a higher profile than most. Michael knew her husband Ambrose Bartlett, owner of the most exclusive department store on the Cape. Bartlett was a sophisticated player, who thought he had found his ideal counterpart in the compliant and beautiful Paula. But it was the clever David Lawrence, an instructor at Braemar, who had been the first to uncover Paula's latent spanking affinities and introduce her to the Random Point scene.

Michael had met Paula on a number of occasions, including Hugo Sand's Halloween party and knew her to be a sincere submissive. Otherwise he wouldn't have thought of approaching her the way he did when they crossed paths at the gym on Sunday morning.

Michael had been idling by the front desk while the gym owner, Polyxena Guzman, in a pale blue cotton wrap dress and clogs, meticulously arranged a rack of bathing suits. Michael had only just begun paying court to the Dutch millionairess, whose white blonde hair was braided into the same coronet that he had undone in the lighthouse where she lived, several nights before. The intensely curvaceous, thirty year old immigrant was alluring for all the obvious reasons but perhaps the most fascinating aspect of this well educated, razor sharp young businesswoman was that until quite recently, her sexual orientation had been purely dominant.

Polyxena had arrived in Random Point with her submissive Dieter Brandt, a personal trainer, masseur and for years her hard working partner in the spa business. Good looking, affable Dieter was pleasant, thoughtful, reliable, and as respectful towards his mistress as a woman like Polyxena could wish. But beside the fresh, new crop of strictly dominant men she was beginning to meet in Random Point, with their intriguing ways and unabrasive style of taking control, Dieter had begun to seem just a little dull. Then the curious Polyxena decided to perform an experiment or two with the hitherto unexplored submissive side of her nature. She accepted her first spanking from Freddie Johanson and would have welcomed others from the same quarter, if Freddie's girlfriend Allison hadn't intervened and put a stop to these adventures.

Michael Flagg was the next logical choice. He was tall, muscular, just old enough to display some character in his face, but still bristle with virility. He'd attempted to appropriate Polyxena for his own from the first day of her arrival. The ever-present Dieter, a thoroughly nice young man and not deserving of a backstabbing, had clamped a certain amount of restraint on Michael's flirting. But like a shark scenting blood, the moment Michael ascertained that Dieter's exclusive option on Polyxena had been breeched by Freddie, he had moved in on the gym owner himself.

At Hugo's Halloween party, either slightly before or slightly after Diana and Currie's wedding ceremony, Michael had convinced Polyxena to allow him to bind her to a whipping post and flog her nude shoulders and bottom. Dieter had walked in and glimpsed the mistress he'd revered for years being soundly whipped by a strange man! The effect upon the young German athlete was not pleasant. Polyxena turned her half lidded blue eyes towards the door to see a Dieter neither meek nor mild, but a blazingly angry lover, who took the liberty of untying her without asking anyone's permission, thrust her black ball gown at her and ordered her to stop making a fool of herself.

Stunned, and also angry at being thus interrupted, Polyxena had shrugged back into her gown, turning to have Michael hook up the back. Dieter had ruined the mood anyway, so why allow him to see her naked, she reasoned, adjusting her dress in a mirror opposite, her face rosy with indignation. But there was much worse to come. The more Dieter looked at her in Michael's grasp, the more furious her lover became. Finally he seized Polyxena by the wrist, dragged her out into the hall and sitting on a lounge, took her across his knee and spanked her! This was not only humiliating but painful to the little mistress.

Naturally they had to separate for a time after that. This was entirely Dieter's choice. Polyxena wouldn't have dreamt of throwing out her unofficial husband. He was so useful, for one thing. He did everything one needed done, cheerfully and efficiently. She also enjoyed his expert attentions. She planned to punish him for what he'd done of course, by denying herself to him for a time. But he didn't allow her that pleasure. Instead he moved into the Bone and Feather Inn, trading massages for a room from Inn Keeper Connie.

Michael was the first to know when Dieter moved out. Not that it was entirely finished between Polyxena and Dieter. There was that incident a week or so before, when she had taunted and pushed him beyond bearing and he had finally responded by once again spanking her and taking her, in a whole different way than ever before.

Michael didn't like the fact that Dieter had learned about spanking women so fast, but supposed it was the flip side of his mistress learning to take spankings from men. Michael realized he had to work fast if he wanted to play with Polyxena, for moving at his current speed, Dieter might be back in the lighthouse shortly. And Michael enjoyed spending time at the lighthouse. His ex-lover Patricia had been a tenant for a time and it was a very sexy place to hold a discipline session.

The fact that Polyxena was an avowed dominant made mastering her that much more piquant for Michael. Nor did he feel he had to skimp on the esoteric side trips of which he was so fond. He took her sophistication for granted. Even on their first night together, nothing was out of the question, including bondage, toys and sodomy. By comparison his first night with Carmen had been a still life. Naturally it was hard to decide how far one should take a tourist, whereas with a seasoned player, options were limitless.

Michael had just brought Polyxena a hot chocolate and was chatting with her when Paula Bartlett exited the spa, glowing from a massage.

"Hi, Michael," the immaculately groomed young matron greeting him in passing. He caught up with her and accompanied her outside where she put up her umbrella against a fresh, chill downpour.

"Hi Paula. Do you have a minute?"

"Sure," she closed her umbrella again and stayed with him on the porch as the rain soaked the woods around them. "I came by the bar yesterday. It's already a jumping place I see."

"That's what I want to talk to you about," he began, leaning against a post. "And rather seriously too."

"Excuse me?"

"Paula, I saw you with that dealer Joe Stringer. I saw you score, right there in my place. It didn't make me happy."

Left momentarily speechless by Michael's accusation, Paula gazed at him in wide-eyed alarm. Then she murmured, "It really wasn't much of anything."

"I know exactly what it was."

"How? How do you know?" She was genuinely puzzled.

"Never mind how, I just know. And what's more I think it's awful you're doing crystal. An intelligent woman like you should know better. It's quite dangerous."

Paula made no comment.

"I have a good mind to tell David."

"David?" Paula looked up at him, startled. "Why David? Why not my husband?"

"Because David and I have discussed your figure and both of us agree that you shouldn't get skinny. It will ruin your beauty."

"Well, Ambrose doesn't agree. He prefers the social x-ray type," she replied, folding her arms and frowning.

"Then come to the gym more."

"I will, but I also need drugs to control my appetite," she insisted.

"Then get a legal scrip from a doctor."

"They're not as effective."

"Even so, you need to stop doing crystal."

"You're probably right," Paula sighed.

"I'd like a more emphatic agreement than that."

"Why are you taking such a personal interest?"

"I wouldn't have if you hadn't been indiscreet enough to make your connection at The Dutch."

"I apologize for that."

"That's not good enough."

"What do you mean?"

"I want you to give me what you bought yesterday."

"What?"

"It's the only way I can be sure you'll stop doing it. And I don't advise you to call Joe again. He'll be under surveillance from now on and I don't think you want to be there when he gets busted."

"Is this true?" she demanded. It wasn't but Michael nodded anyway.

"Do you have it on you?"

"Even if I did I don't know if I want to give it up."

"Even after everything I've just said?"

Paula shrugged.

"Have you no guilt? No shame?"

"Why should I feel guilty? I'm not the one who ordained that no woman of fashion shall wear a dress size in excess of one digit. Do you want me to disgrace my husband? Because I've been assured that I do so every time I wallow in a size ten!"

Michael was taken aback by her vehemence and set aflame by her sparkling eyes. "I'm sorry," he said, "I didn't realize it was like that. You're husband is an idiot."

Paula smiled.

"But you still committed a crime in my place of business," he insisted. "How do you think Ambrose would feel if people made connections at Bartlett's? And look at what you're buying, the worst form of speed there is! I'm really disillusioned by you, Paula."

"I said was sorry."

"That's not good enough."

"You said that before."

"You're being pretty fresh for a girl who's entirely in the wrong," Michael observed, an edge creeping into his voice for the first time.

"I blame society and I'd advise you to do the same," said Paula, putting up her umbrella and stepping off the porch.

"Just a minute, young lady," he pursued her to her car, "I have more to say to you!"

Paula paused with the key to her new Mercedes in her hand. "Yes, Michael?"

"You make me almost wish I was still a cop."

"Oh? And why is that?"

"Then I could throw the scare into you that you deserve for fooling around with stuff like meth."

"Oh, so you miss the power to intimidate at a glance, do you?"

"Sure!"

"And suppose I were intimidated, what would you do then?"

"Turn you over my knee!"

"Oh!" Paula started and blushed.

"I see you do have some shame," Michael said, briefly caressing the soft skin of her pinkening face. Now she went a deeper red, looking up at him with full comprehension. The next moment a peal of laughter burst from her highly kissable red mouth.

"What's funny, Mrs. Bartlett?" Michael demanded with increasing irritation. This was not going as he had planned.

"Are we about to enact one of those improbable scenes out of bad spanking literature, where the man blackmails the woman into letting him spank her by threatening to expose her to the authorities?"

"Hope and Pamela went for it right away," Michael replied casually, refusing to be thrown by her penetration.

"It's tremendously tempting of course," Paula looked at Michael with appreciation, "but my husband would consider it far worse of me to play with another man than to discover I'd been sneaking speed."

"Who said anything about playing," Michael snorted, refusing to be defeated so quickly. "I happen to think you should be punished!"

"Ambrose would kill me."

"What if I told you something about your husband?"

"What?"

"He's engaged Hope Lawrence for several sessions, including once after your marriage."

"How shocking!"

"Yes, isn't it?"

"Not shocking that Ambrose would do such a thing but that you'd betray him to me like that! I thought men never gossiped. Isn't there some austere male code of honor you're supposed to adhere to?"

"Normally, I would, but there's something about you that's making me want you more every second we talk."

"I can see why the girls all say you're dangerous," Paula lightly flirted, getting into her car.

"I can't believe you're getting away from me like this. Don't you care about what I just told you?"

"About Ambrose and Hope? Well, I have slept with her husband, so I suppose it was only fair. But let's let the seed germinate. Perhaps I'll feel differently the next time we talk."

"Very well, but I'm not satisfied," he told her, pressing her gloved hand.

"I can see that," Paula looked pointedly at the iron bar his jeans.

"I hate Ambrose for making you so self conscious," Michael said candidly.

"It's fun being pampered," she admitted, waving her hand about the new car, "but I don't know how long I can live under this sort of pressure." Then, on impulse, she placed the paper containing the half-gram of meth she'd bought from the dealer in Michael's hand. "You're so right about this stuff. Take it."

Michael had to smile as she drove away, even though she had gotten the better of him. Anyway, two out of three wasn't bad. And, Mrs. Bartlett would be single again some day, perhaps soon. Time was on his side.

Christmas Eve was still several days away, but Michael decided to celebrate his with Carmen on their Saturday night. They didn't get back to his house after closing the bar until one. Carmen was very sleepy after many hours on her feet and several gulped mugs of eggnog. But she came back to life when Michael lit a fire and turned on the lights of his Christmas tree, under which a dozen richly wrapped presents had been piled. Carmen was amazed to learn that all the presents were for her.

"Then, you really like me?" she asked, looking up from opening boxes of dainty things. There were pearl earrings, a golden locket on a velvet cord, a black velvet dress, black velvet pumps, a dressy black cashmere winter coat, suede gloves, a velvet cloche, French perfume, a black satin corselette, silk stockings with square heels and seams and a smoky blue silk satin gown set.

When she got to the box with the coat she sat stunned. He had spent several thousand dollars on her Christmas, a thing which no one had ever done for her before. "This is so unexpected," she cried, feeling an embarrassing lump in her throat. "I didn't think I'd even get a turkey," she murmured, adding, "I'm awfully sorry but I didn't get you anything."

"I know what I want from you though," he told her.

"What?"

"I know a doctor in Woodbridge who removes tattoos. I want to arrange for you to see him."

Now Carmen really wanted to cry, but not from sentimental joy. She turned from him feeling deeply wounded. "Oh!"

"Carmen, don't take it like that. You have no idea how much more beautiful you would look without the Harley tramp stamp on the small of your back."

"I hate you," she pouted.

"Carmen, you're wearing a company logo. Think about it."

"You don't like me the way I am. You want to change me. It's just like I thought. You're making me frou frou."

"Girls are supposed to be different from men."

"It hurts to have a tattoo taken off."

"You deserve that for being stupid enough to get it in the first place."

"Do you think I should be spanked for getting the tattoos?" she asked tentatively, as though she'd been thinking about spanking and wondering how to reintroduce it.

"Of course I do!"

Carmen blinked sleepily at him. He told her to put on the satin gown and robe. Once she had donned the sumptuous garments she stood in front of the mirror for a long time, admiring herself. He sat in the window seat with a scotch, looking at her.

"Now pull up the skirt and see how ludicrous the Harley logo looks in contrast to your flawless skin in satin."

"You know, you've been nicer to me than anyone so far, but you can also be very mean," Carmen protested simply.

"I'm sorry."

"So you really, really hate my tattoos, huh?"

"Especially the one just above your bottom."

"I suppose Polyxena Guzman doesn't have any tattoos."

"Perish the thought," said Michael.

"She looks at you like you were a torte."

"She's a nice girl. We play once in a while. It's nothing serious."

"You mean she doesn't have a regular night?"

"Not so far."

"That woman gives me a pain in my stomach," Carmen declared.

"Come over here," he said and took her in his arms. "Give me a kiss and we'll save your spanking for New Year's Eve."

"New Year's Eve?"

"Yes, I'm about to create the next Random Point institution, New Year's Eve at The Dutch, a private party, with playing."

"Playing?"

"You and I will break the ice. I'll give you a spanking in your new black corselet."

"You mean in front of everyone?"

"That's right. So they'll know you're one of us," said Michael.

"One of us or one of yours?"

"One of the players instead of the posers," he qualified his statement, pushing up the sleeve of her robe to sadly regard yet another tattoo, this one on her upper arm. "This to me is poser stuff," he said, tracing her devil bat tattoo with his hand. "Paint on defiance.

It's childish."

"Whereas getting spanked in public is mature?" she laughed.

"Call it a rite of passage."

Late Sunday afternoon, Hope was pouring tea when Pamela arrived. When Michael showed her into the sitting room, Hope jumped to her feet and the girls stared at each other.

"What's she doing here?" Pamela spoke first and sharply. Michael folded his arms and looked at her.

"The same thing you are."

"What do you mean?" Pamela cried.

"She's here to answer for drug shopping in my bar."

"You do crystal?" Pamela looked at Hope in surprise.

"No, she was buying weed," Michael explained, taking her coat and going out of the room with it.

"What's he up to?" Pamela demanded of Hope, who shrugged, not a little hurt that Pamela should still hold herself so aloof.

Michael returned.

"You know, it's really time you two became better friends," Michael observed. Pamela folded her arms across her small, pert bosom and lifted her chin. "Don't you think that sharing a punishment will bring you closer?"

"You can go to hell with that little idea!" Pamela snapped, her slim elegant foot tapping on the hard wood floor as she glared at her host.

"Why?" Michael asked.

"Because I for one don't consent to participate in a stupid, awkward, male jack-off fantasy of you domming both of us at once!" Pamela asserted indignantly.

This was unanticipated! Michael hadn't reckoned with such antipathy from Pamela and wanted to seriously thrash her for her insulting attitude towards Hope, but instead forced himself to reply in a tone completely devoid of heat, "In that case, let's forget the whole thing."

"Forget it?" Pamela looked at him suspiciously.

"Sure. You're dismissed."

"What do you mean?"

"I mean since you don't consent to participate, you might as well go."

"But what about our agreement?"

"I said forget it."

Pamela hesitated, started for the door, turned and murmured, "I'm sorry, but I just can't do this," before marching out. Hope and Michael looked at each other. He held up his hand to silence her, whispering, "Wait, she'll be back."

They heard the closet door open, then shut again. A moment later, Pamela returned.

"What's up?" Michael asked.

"All right, I'm back. Let's get this over with," Pamela said angrily.

"I thought you didn't consent," said Michael.

"I can't have this hanging over me," Pamela protested coolly. "I'll submit."

"Incredibly magnanimous of you," Michael commented.

Hope handed Pamela a cup of tea, asking,

"Or would you rather have a whiskey?"

"Neither, thank you," said Pamela, putting down the cup and saucer without tasting it. "I'd simply like to discharge my obligation and leave." Again Michael wanted to shake Pamela for being so unkind to Hope, who had never done her one iota of harm and whose only crime was working under Pamela's lover Sloan as his assistant at the bookshop.

"You see how crystal can change someone's personality, Hope?" Michael said. "I recall that Pamela used to be, well, not exactly warm, but almost amiable. Now she's about as rude a young woman as I've ever met."

But Hope did not feel comfortable being dragged into the fray. Her female loyalty quotient was high and she was particularly wary of injuring the sensitive and highly strung Pamela, with whom her boss Sloan Taylor was in love. Hope knew full and well that the reason for Pamela's coolness was jealousy alone, which wrung Hope's tender heart. Sloan had refused to fire Hope and replace her with Pamela as his assistant, and Pamela had not gotten over it yet. Even working part time for Michael at the bar had not really changed her point of view.

That fact that Sloan continued to bask in Hope's fair radiance daily tortured the willowy brunette.

"You seem to know where every thing is," Pamela observed as Hope poured herself a tot of whiskey. The implication was clear and Hope felt Pamela's reproach. Like most girls, Pamela adored Hope's husband David Lawrence. Now Hope realized that someone must have told Pamela about her on-going affair with Michael Flagg.

"Just what the hell is that supposed to mean?" Michael snapped, becoming deeply irritated by Pamela's arrogance.

"I can't believe your husband lets you make a fool of him the way you do," said Pamela. Hope almost choked on the strong Irish whiskey.

"Don't dignify that with a response, Hope," Michael advised, now quite angry with Pamela. "And you, young lady, I can't believe your insolence! In fact, I've had about enough of it. Come over here," he demanded, seizing her by the wrist and yanking her over to a chair. "God, you've made me angry!" he declared, dragging her down across his lap, locking his arm around her waist and bringing his other hand down on her slim, oval bottom through her thin fawn wool riding pants.

Pamela had on a rather smart replica of Myrna Loy's riding outfit from The Rains of Ranchipur, complete with boots and blazer. Her straight black hair was pulled back in a pony tail and she wore gloves, which Michael noted, thinking he must get his little Carmen more gloves. He had been shocked to see her get on her bike that morning without any at all.

Michael spanked Pamela vigorously for ten or twelve minutes, while Hope watched, timidly perched on the arm of a chair, sipping whiskey. Pamela responded with whimpers and kicks, as opposed to shrieks and wails, so as not to give him the satisfaction of knowing how badly his big hand stung her slender bottom. Hope admired her stoicism and noticed, with her practiced eye, that even though Pamela winced, a ripple of something went through her, every time Michael finished an enthusiastic volley of smacks.

Hope had been in Pamela's current position often enough to recall every uniquely masculine aspect of Michael's lap, from marble thighs to iron truncheon pressing in between them. He had a way of holding one around the waist with his large hand that possessed and protected at once. He was a man to take one's breath away and Hope felt Pamela's ill-concealed excitement vicariously as she voyeured the scene from the sofa arm. But this innocent enjoyment was not to endure and the next words out of the lips of her beloved dominant chilled her to the bone.

"Who do you think you are," Michael asked Pamela, "to put on such airs? When by your own admission, you yourself were Hugo Sands' plaything, in spite of your engagement to Sloan!" Smack, smack, smack! "You have a lot of nerve to reproach Hope for doing a session with me now and then." Michael's hand descended tirelessly throughout the scolding, prolonging the warm-up into fifteen or eighteen minutes and creating such a deal of heat in the seat of Pamela's pants that Michael could actually feel it with his hand. "I'm very disappointed in your lack of friendliness towards Hope!" Michael added furiously, smacking her all the harder. "You ought to have better manners. And if you wish to continue working for me, you will!" Smack, smack, smack!

Now the pants came down, but the spanking continued, over her white, figured silk panties, which covered but a small portion of her darkly pinkened bottom.

"I ought to make you beg Hope's pardon on your knees," Michael mused, spanking her olive hued thighs now. Pamela jerked on his lap in real pain, vainly attempting to escape his hand. She put back one of hers to cover her thigh but only had it pinned to her side and slapped for her trouble. "But I have a better idea."

"No," Hope silently prayed, "don't say it! I can't. I won't. Anything but that!"

"What idea?" Pamela turned, glad to divert him from spanking her for a moment.

"Male jack off fantasy #2," said Michael, lifting her off his lap, putting her to one side and crooking his finger at Hope.

"What? Why? What do I have to do?" Hope stammered, jumping off the sofa arm and hiding behind it.

"Come over here," said Michael.

Hope crossed the room as to an execution, for she knew what was coming. Michael pointed at the chair he'd just vacated.

"No, Michael, I can't. I won't," Hope resisted. "She'll hate me for the rest of our lives." But Michael made her sit on the chair anyway.

"Male jack off fantasy #2. Remember, drug offender????" Michael frowned at Hope. Pamela now realized that Michael meant for Hope to continue with the spanking and recoiled. This time he didn't give her the opportunity to argue or protest, but simply lay her back down across Hope's dark blue jeaned thighs. Pamela, who was taller than Hope, though around the same size 5, felt awkward, but the chair was substantial enough to allow her to extend and plant her legs and arms.

She didn't bother struggling to get away, as that would have been revoltingly undignified, considering Michael's determination to humiliate her, but her cheeks burned fore and aft at the position he had placed her in.

It didn't get worse than this in Pamela's girlish universe. She was Veronica over Betty's lap and it burned into her soul like carbolic acid. She fancied that she hated Michael at this moment more than she had ever hated any other man. Even Hope had ceased to matter or exist, for a split second anyway, as Pamela felt herself transported to a place filled with guilt, shame and yet, a curious excitement.

"Go on. You know what you have to do. My hand is tired," Michael encouraged Hope, handing her a small wooden paddle. "Oh, wait, let me do this first," he offered, kneeling beside the chair to firmly lower Pamela's panties to mid thigh. "And, wait," he stopped Hope's hand in midair to sharply separate Pamela's thighs as much as the binding riding pants would allow, lowered to her knees.

"Tsk, tsk," Michael sighed, "look how thin she's become. She can't take very much more."

Michael stroked Pamela's dark pink cheeks, slightly spreading them. Then he placed one of Hope's hands on each of Pamela's buttocks and motioned for her to affect a full exposure of Pamela's charms.

"You're going to stop taking that drug, Pamela, if I have to whip you every day, you're going to," he advised, flicking a miniature flogger between her cheeks.

Michael looked at Hope, as much as to say, "Don't be coy, really spread her!" Hope winced but obeyed the silent command, pressing Pamela's bottom open to give Michael complete access to her tiny anus. "I suppose you're familiar with the fact that bad girls get whipped here?" he demanded, flicking the spot between her cheeks sharply and repeatedly.

"Yes!" Pamela cried, in such a way as to cause Michael and Hope stare at each other. That had been the first sincere remark out of Pamela's lips all afternoon.

Michael tilted Pamela's bottom up slightly, jerked her pants down as far as they would go, made her arch up from Hope's lap a few inches and began to apply the smooth little paddle lightly to Pamela's sable muff. "You can tell she's had her pussy spanked before," Michael commented to Hope, who still held Pamela firmly open for him and was herself beginning to relax a little as she saw Pamela responding to the strict humiliation. Pamela was panting along with whimpering now instead of sobbing.

"You see how you're no better than anyone else, Pamela?" Michael asked, insinuating the slim handle of the paddle between her slick labia, just to get it wet enough to flourish in front of her eyes. "Now that we've proved you're a slut, we can continue with the discipline portion of the program," said Michael, pressing her back down on Hope's lap firmly and putting the paddle back into Hope's hand. "Spank her," he said. "Just until your arm gets tired." Then he went to pour himself a Bushmills.

Hope hesitated with the paddle in her hand and her arm about Pamela's waist. "I'd rather not," said Hope meekly.

"It's your penalty for buying weed in my bar. Do your penance and make the best of it. Pamela won't hold it against you. Will you, dear?"

"No," Pamela said, through gritted teeth.

Hope hadn't been called upon to spank other women very often in her career as a professional submissive, but she had a technique for delivering a spanking to a woman that she herself had developed. In this case, she pretended she was Sloan giving the spanking to Pamela and spanked Pamela as she imagined Sloan would, briskly and deeply. Hope plunged into her role, her intensity increasing with every passing second. Sometimes she thought she should write stories, her spanking fantasies were so rich. In this case, Pamela's equestrian raiment was the trigger to Hope's romantic involvement. Pamela's bottom, pre-pinkened by Michael's stern hand, was ravishing.

Hope decided when the spanking was over and helped Pamela to her feet. Michael wasn't satisfied that Pamela had been punished sufficiently, but Hope had felt Pamela reach a climax over her lap during the pussy spanking and she had enjoyed several successive ones at various other stages of the spanking. Pamela was spent and ought to be released. She would never hate Hope again.

"I should make you stand in the corner for how bad you've been," Michael said coldly to Pamela. "And I haven't even heard one sincere apology out of you." Pamela set herself promptly to rights then looked down at her boots, in rather a pleasant daze, though still angry and upset about being put in such a position by him that afternoon.

"I'm sorry," Pamela murmured. Then she spontaneously threw her arms around Hope and hugged her. Hope smiled at Michael around Pamela's shoulder.

"Very well then, you can go," he said. "But remember, I'd better not catch you doing any more speed. I won't have to institute drug testing to tell if you are. I was married to a speed freak and I know all the signs."

"Do you still want me to come into work?" Pamela asked nonchalantly.

"Why shouldn't I?"

"You seem as though you're still upset with me."

"Of course I am. You're a very bad girl. I only hope I can help you reform."

Pamela looked as though she would burst into tears if she were sent off without a hug. Hope looked at Michael urgently. Michael shook his head and let Pamela leave without another word.

"How could you be so cruel to the poor girl after all that?" Hope asked, when she was sure that Pamela had driven away.

"That girl needs schooling," Michael replied. "I wanted to smack her much harder for the way she talked to you, but you saw how thin she's let herself get."

"I wonder why Sloan doesn't smack her harder," Hope mused.

"Maybe someone should let him know how impossibly conceited Pamela has become."

"He thinks she'll grow out of it."

"Hard whippings are what she needs, and lots of them."

"Me too!" Hope said, jumping into his arms.

Chapter Ten

Two Weeks

Anthony Newton and Susan Ross had agreed to witness the quiet civil ceremony that would unite William Random and Damaris Perez in Boston on the first day of winter. But when Anthony remembered that he had pledged to perform at a benefit concert in Las Vegas on December 21st, the wedding party was rerouted to Nevada.

It is probable that had Marguerite and Malcolm not joined the Vegas excursion, that Anthony and Susan would also have returned to Random Point as one, but fate put Marguerite in the room while the travel plans were being made, and the invitation which she immediately received to join the party unfortunately included her increasingly incompatible spouse.

William was delighted to have a rock-climbing partner with him for the weekend, but Malcolm's chemistry was at terrible odds with that of the group. In the first place, Malcolm resented being signed on by Marguerite without being consulted, even though William was his friend and business partner and he was fond of Damaris.

Secondly, ever since reading his wife's diaries, Malcolm had never been comfortable around the immensely wealthy Anthony Newton, who had been intimate with Marguerite in the recent past and was insisting on underwriting the whole trip.

Finally, Newton's flippant brat of a young paramour Susan Ross, had seldom charmed Malcolm. To Malcolm, Susan was just one more decadent influence on his wife, someone to make Marguerite dissatisfied with her own circumstances. The recently failed entrepreneur, being currently reduced to a humble half ownership in a climbing gym, experienced a heightened sense of disgust at the profligacy he was witnessing that day every where he looked, from the superb Bellagio penthouse suites in which Anthony's party had been installed to the insidious casinos below.

A better businessman would have seen the value of cultivating more friends like Anthony Newton, but Malcolm Branwell was proud and austere. He'd no more think of calling in a favor or begging a referral than he'd contemplate shooting heroin or buying a Ferrari.

"A pain in the butt, is what my dear husband is," Marguerite complained as she brushed out Susan's long, wheat gold hair in Anthony's suite.

"Why is he being no fun?" Susan wondered. "Doesn't he realize this is Damaris and William's wedding day?"

Just then Anthony entered with Dennis, wheeling a wardrobe cart loaded with zippered black bags.

"Hi Girls. Well, I managed to bribe the Chapel to let us in for twenty minutes at eleven o'clock tonight."

"Did you bring me presents?" Susan jumped up and clapped her hands. "Marguerite, look, Christian Dior and Yves St. Laurent!"

For once Anthony did not go straight to the piano but folded his arms and leaned against the mantel to watch them open the bags. "Open the big puffy one first," he advised, nodding to Dennis, who knew that he was now supposed to open champagne.

"Oh, this one must be for Damaris," said Susan, beholding a YSL wedding fantasy gown, size 2."

"Of course it's not for Damaris. She's already got her own outfit," said Anthony impatiently. Susan stared at him.

Susan took the gown out to inspect and hold up to her body.

"I am in the mood to get married today," said Anthony.

"Susan!" Marguerite hugged her small friend to her magnificent bosom. "Do try on the heavenly gown and I'll call Damaris and William!"

Susan looked at Anthony with acute suspicion. "I'm serious!" he told her.

She came to him and felt his head. He wasn't feverish and hadn't been drinking. Dennis brought in the champagne and Damaris emerged in the suite. The petite brunette knew how fervently Susan had been longing for a proposal from Anthony and almost wept with joy for her small friend. This was too delightful!

William came in next. He'd been climbing at Redrocks with Malcolm all morning but was now properly dressed in a crisp, grey pin striped suit for his second wedding ceremony photos.

"Look!" Susan showed him her dress. "We're going to take wedding photos with you, just for fun."

"Susan, I told you, I'm serious," Anthony insisted, pinching her pink earlobe, and kissing her red mouth.

Marguerite found her husband sprawled on the bed, watching the current war on television.

"Darling, hurry and get dressed! We're going to take the wedding photos outside in that divine garden and guess what? Anthony and Susan are getting married too!"

"You're kidding me!" Malcolm sat up. "What for?"

"No other reason but love, I should think," said Marguerite gaily, choosing a sage green satin suit to compliment her light red hair.

"They should leave things as they are," Malcolm growled, pulling a suit out of the wardrobe.

"Really, Malcolm, if you're going to display that sort of attitude you'd better not come," cried Marguerite, "I wouldn't have Susan upset for the world today!"

"Fine!"

Marguerite was so angry she almost stamped her foot, but instead retired to the dressing room, thinking, "If I had only left him home!" It was horrid to discover one had married a churl, but she mainly blamed herself for insisting he participate in a gala jaunt for which he was not in the mood. Now she was learning a lesson about forcing her husband to conform to her wishes, even in so innocent a diversion as a wedding party of close friends.

"He's been in an abysmal funk ever since his Book Bag Chain got acquired," Marguerite confided to Susan as they strolled arm in arm through the casino after taking the wedding photos, bundling Anthony off to his rehearsal and changing their clothes. "He feels like a gloomy failure and all displays of frivolity offend him accordingly," the statuesque bookshop owner continued, steering Susan towards the $1 slots to teach her about the machines.

Marguerite had changed into a smart wool jersey dress and thigh boots. Susan had gotten back into her favorite pegged jeans and out tucked shirt for maximum casino comfort. Marguerite had scolded her, reminding her they might want to sit at a table and bet like ladies. Susan protested that she would put on an evening gown later for Anthony and sit at his side at a table while he lost enormous piles of money, just like in a movie.

Susan had been looking forward to being treated like a grown up in public by Anthony for years, but because of his celebrity, he had been cautious of exposing her in this manner. However, this weekend anything went. He'd be keyed up after his performance and a few hours of gambling would relax him. Then there was that eleven p.m. appointment at the chapel to think about. Susan shivered with anticipation. Was it really going to happen this suddenly?

Then Susan looked at Marguerite. Marguerite was married. But she wasn't happy, at least not at that particular moment, with a sulky husband in an endless funk. It didn't seem fair to Marguerite, who was such an outstanding woman in every way, to have to settle for this. Yes, Malcolm was good-looking and apparently immensely virile, but so were many other men of their acquaintance.

"So long as you're still fond of him," Susan sighed, squeezing Marguerite's arm.

Malcolm surfaced after they had migrated to the $5 slots, from which he attempted to drag them the instant he discovered just how much they had both lost.

"Anthony gave us money," Susan protested. "He told us to have fun."

"So because someone else earned the money it's okay to waste it?" Malcolm demanded. Marguerite sighed.

"Look -" Susan began to retort, but Malcolm cut her off.

"How can you waste so much money when people are starving and freezing to death in Afghanistan even as we speak?"

Susan looked at Marguerite who excused herself to flag down a waitress.

"Don't be silly," Susan replied calmly, though her heart was pounding with indignation. "Anthony's only reason for being here is to perform in a relief benefit."

"I wish you wouldn't corrupt Marguerite. She has little enough to spare even if you have endless amounts!"

"Look Malcolm, this weekend is on Anthony. It's his present to William and Damaris. Can't you just relax?" Susan tried again to placate him, while still pressing the buttons of the five-dollar slots. "Oh, look! I got my first fishing trip. And it was on a maximum bet! Woo hoo!"

Malcolm walked away in disgust as Susan won a three thousand dollar jackpot.

After posing for the photos, William and Damaris had gone back to their suite to make love. They were lying amid their wedding finery and rumpled bedclothes when Susan called to report her win and Malcolm's unacceptable behavior.

"I knew we shouldn't have dragged Malcolm along," William reported to Damaris as he went off to shower. "I told Marguerite so." Damaris wondered why, but was anxious to experience the spa and quickly tossed on some jeans and threw her keys into a bag. She met Marguerite some ten minutes later in the steam room where the tall, russet haired beauty had gone to lose some tension.

"I just heard homegirl hit a jackpot," said Damaris tentatively.

"I'll bet you also heard about my husband's tantrum in the casino? I tell you, Damaris, I'm nearly fed up."

"I understand," Damaris sympathized. "He seems edgy, like a speed freak."

"He's been just impossible lately. And he's half way to ruining Susan's wedding day!" Marguerite cried.

They encountered Susan a few minutes later in the Jacuzzi. She was modestly clad in a two-piece swimsuit with her hair twisted up. Damaris and Marguerite got in nude.

"So, what do you girls think? Should I take advantage of Anthony's Vegas madness and marry him? Or should I do the decent thing? We all know it's a whim," said Susan.

"Don't be mad," cried Marguerite indignantly. "This is the proposal you've been waiting for for five years. Of course you're going to take advantage of Anthony!"

"So you see it that way too?" Susan replied thoughtfully.

"You put that badly," Damaris chided Marguerite.

"I just don't think I can do it to him," the pretty blonde decided. "He's never wanted to get married. It's always been me nagging him to. Why should I go against his will after he's been so good to me? Shouldn't I take the word of someone who's been through five divorces that marriage doesn't work?"

"Susan, you know that your reign has exceeded that of all the ex-wives by far. You're his chosen one. Now you must take your rightful place!" Marguerite begged, her heart sinking at the thought of her own husband giving Susan Ross such a disgust of the married state that she could dream of calling off the much desired union with her beloved provider.

"Don't force her," warned Damaris. "She knows her man better than we do. The married state isn't right for some."

"You can say that again," Marguerite sighed, subsiding in the water as she realized that the sensible younger lady in the pool had already decided the outcome of the evening. But it made her angry and resentful against Malcolm. Everything had been so happy, so perfect, and now the double wedding was reduced to a single one.

"Tomorrow he'll thank me," Susan chuckled and emerged from the Jacuzzi to shower off.

"Oh God, Damaris, Malcolm's ruined everything!" Marguerite cried.

"Don't worry," Damaris soothed, still immersed in the vision of herself in her own wedding dress, reflected in the mirrors of their suite earlier that afternoon while William took her.

"If only he were submissive, or even a switch, how I'd thrash him!" Marguerite fumed, emerging from the bubbling waters of the whirlpool Aphrodite-like.

Marguerite held this thought all the way back to the suite, where she found Malcolm fast asleep in just a pair of trunks on their bed. He awoke at her return and tried to pull her into his arms.

"Don't! I'm furious at you," she snapped over folded arms.

"Why?" he seemed surprised.

"The way you scolded Susan. As if you had the right to! It upset her terribly!"

"Really? She didn't seem terribly upset," Malcolm replied, trying to nibble her ear. She pushed him forcefully away and jumped to her feet.

"I said don't," she said seriously.

"All right, I won't!"

"The mood I'm in, I'd sooner flog the living daylights out of you than let you touch me tonight!" she declared, astonishing Malcolm into sitting up.

"That'll happen when hell freezes over," said Malcolm.

"Fine!"

"Marguerite, where are you going?" he asked, watching her change into a knit dress and matching cardigan.

"Anthony should be through with the benefit by now. I'm going to see if he's back."

Marguerite fled the suite before Malcolm could grab her, deciding, "One way or another, he will be disciplined!"

Immediately after watching Anthony's performance, Susan and Damaris walked out together on a casino tour of the immediate strip, allotting themselves two hours of gambling before returning to the Bellagio to dress for the ceremony at eleven.

Anthony was enjoying tea and a light supper in his suite when Marguerite joined him.

"Have you spoken to Susan since earlier today?" the redhead asked anxiously.

"She waved to me from the wings. I hear from Dennis she won a jackpot earlier and now she has gambling fever," Anthony smiled.

"Anthony, I don't think she's up for getting married anymore," Marguerite reported.

"Don't be silly. She's been pestering me to marry her since she graduated Vassar."

"I know but something changed her mind."

"What could have possibly changed her mind?"

"She says it's out of consideration for your true wishes, but Malcolm upset her today. He scolded her for gambling and blamed her for corrupting me. He was behaving boorishly and she could see that I had no control over him. I think it gave her a sudden horror of husbands."

"Where does Malcolm get off scolding Susan?" Anthony demanded. "And upsetting her on the one day I'm in the mood to get married! What the hell is his problem?"

"I don't know," she lied.

"Marguerite, when are you going to admit that you made a terrible mistake when you married that dolt?"

Marguerite hung her head in despair.

"You really should have known better than to bring him to Vegas if he feels that way about gambling."

"I'm so sorry!" she cried.

"It was quite thoughtless of you," Anthony declared, getting up from the table and calling Dennis to remove it. When the English boy arrived Anthony told him that he didn't wish to be disturbed for the next hour and then locked the door.

"Now Marguerite, you and I must have a serious talk," said Anthony meaningfully. "I won't bother to point out that your error in judgment has cost Susan Ross that extra initial on her monogram she's been longing for these several years. As I've already told you both, I'll never be in such a mood again."

Marguerite could hardly feel worse and miserably nodded, "I know!"

"But it isn't Susan I'm worried about. It's you, Marguerite. You haven't been yourself since you married Malcolm. Why did you marry him, anyway?"

"He was good looking, rich, in the scene and gave brilliant head," she replied reflectively. "And he did me the honor of reading four and half of my favorite novels during our courtship."

"That impressed you enough to marry him?"

"They averaged 800 pages each."

"Marguerite, Marguerite, what am I going to do with you?"

"What are you going to do with me?" Marguerite remembered the locking of the door.

"I think someone has to punish you for marrying Malcolm and it might as well be me."

"What did you have in mind?" Marguerite asked with some anxiety, thinking of how she would explain the marks of a fresh chastisement to Malcolm that night.

"I'll give you a hint," said Anthony, removing his suit jacket and unbuckling his thin leather belt.

"But I can't be marked!" she cried, jumping up and moving away from him.

"Why not?"

"Because Malcolm would be furious."

"Who cares?"

"Anthony, please don't!"

"Come over here, Marguerite. Don't make me chase you because that wouldn't be dignified. We'll get this over quickly and then we can practice our song for later," he said, patting the back of an armchair and motioning her to him.

"Song?"

"I thought it would be nice to play Dearly Beloved by Jerome Kern for William and Damaris in the chapel tonight. You know the words to it, I'm sure."

"Oh, yes, of course," Marguerite smiled. "With all that's going on I forgot that the wedding ceremony was primarily to be for William and Damaris."

"Marguerite, do you remember the first night we met, five years ago?" Anthony took her gently by the hand and led her to the chair. He removed her glasses and placed them on a table. "It was at Hugo's Halloween party at the Cliff House, just before I bought it. You were terribly unhappy that night because you'd just found out that Michael Flagg had married Damaris. Remember?"

"Of course! But why do you bring that up?"

"Because Michael's been free for years now. Don't you think it's time you claimed him?"

"He has a girl friend now," she softly replied, allowing him to bend her over the back of the chair.

"Yes, I know. And he has a crush on Hope Spencer Lawrence and visits the Dutch gym owner once a week, but none of them will offer much obstruction if you return to being the Marguerite we know and love instead of continuing to submit to that cranky and colorless Puritan you've been pleased to call a husband."

The strap came down firmly and resoundingly across the centermost portion of her ample bottom, now so attractively clad in a fawn wool straight skirt.

"Ow! That's very hard to start out with!" she protested. "I'm certain I'll be marked!"

"Yes. It will be good for you," said Anthony, bringing down the strap again, a little lower across her bottom this time. She jumped and squirmed. He placed his hand in the small of her back. "If you jerk around like that I might miss my mark and wrap your hip," he warned unnecessarily, for his aim was quite exact.

"Please, darling Anthony, can't you just use your hand instead?" She turned her green eyes to him appealingly.

"Perhaps just for a little," he conceded, flipping up her skirt and summarily lowering her beige mesh nylon briefs to her knees. Marguerite kept her legs straight and together and arched her back, adding a provocative bottom wiggle to soften him. It only made him harder.

Now he smacked both her bare cheeks with his open palm dozens of times, rapidly and hard, until the creamy bisque hue of her flawless skin was tinted a deep shade of pink. He paused only to blow on his hand.

Presently, Marguerite attempted to distract him by rolling her bottom in small circles as she shifted her weight from one foot to the other. Her years as a submissive, both professional and private had taught her the power of an undulating backside to stimulate a male to action more erotic than disciplinary.

It wasn't that Marguerite objected to a good, sound spanking, especially from one of her favorite men, but the potential marking factor made her anxious to the point of barely feeling the pain or pleasure of the spanking.

While Anthony's palm unremittingly struck first one exposed cheek, then the other, Marguerite's mind raced to calculate how many hours might elapse until her husband saw her bottom again. From an average spanking, she would retain no marks and even the pinkness would fade in minutes or an hour. Not so with the measured, broad strokes of a methodical strapping.

"Step out of your panties and spread your legs," Anthony ordered, giving Marguerite hope of a discontinuance of the discipline and a commencement of the penetration. "And your bottom," he added, spanking her between her cheeks smartly. Then he reached below and spanked her pussy rather lightly. As though a secret switch had been thrown, Marguerite began to lubricate. Her undulations became more rhythmic and seductive. "Instead of worrying about marks, you should be thinking of how you might explain your labia being so swollen to this husband of yours who gives such brilliant head."

"Why should they be swollen?" she cried.

"I can't give you the scientific reason," he said, continuing to spank her Venus mound and creamy slit, somewhat more firmly now, "but pussy spanking does that," he informed her, inserting first one and then two fingers into her slick, hot glove. He fingered, then spanked her, fingered then strapped her, fingered, then pussy spanked her, over and over until she could no longer refrain from grinding on the chair back in a frenzy of excitement.

"That's my Marguerite," he told her, "Come for me, baby." And she did.

When Susan returned to the suite a few hours later she found Anthony dressed for the ceremony.

"Oh, hello!" he greeted her enthusiastically. "Been having fun?"

"Damaris and I had the best time," she replied, coming over to the piano to sit next to him while he practiced playing Dearly Beloved.

"Marguerite says you no longer want to get married," said Anthony conversationally.

"I know it seems schizophrenic of me, but I suddenly don't think we should change a thing about our relationship," she sighed, wrapping her arms around his trim waist and laying her head against his chest. "Besides," she added, "we forgot to get the license."

"Susan, you're getting smarter all the time," he told her, then handed her a large, flat, black velvet jewelry case. "Since you have your wedding gown and your wedding photos, you might as well have your wedding jewelry."

Susan looked at her new pearl and diamond pendant necklace, matching earrings and ring. Anthony took out the ring and put it on the appropriate finger. "There. Now you have your wedding ring. You can wear it when you want to feel married and take it off when you don't."

"You know, that Malcolm Branwell could learn a lot about being a husband from you!" murmured Susan, looking at her outstretched hand with its glittering adornment.

The last thing Marguerite and Malcolm did that strangely happy yet unpleasant day was to quarrel in the casino over Marguerite's shooting craps in a low-cut gown surrounded by a dozen hooting males. Since Malcolm didn't know how to play he could only watch Marguerite lose money while the men all but ate her up. He honestly couldn't understand how she could put herself in the midst of that drunken, drooling, shouting, tobacco marinated rabble and appear to enjoy herself and told her so at the first opportunity.

Following her across the casino as she went to put on lipstick, Malcolm told her exactly what he thought of her undignified and profligate behavior. Rather than arguing, Marguerite simply smiled and disappeared into ladies lounge. When she returned, he had gone, which suited her extremely well as his glowering at her had been ruining her luck.

She spent the next three hours in the casino, eventually joining Anthony and Susan in the high stakes card salon. They drank several bottles of champagne and then Marguerite won three hundred dollars on a Cleopatra slot machine. She was eager to tell Malcolm that she had recouped all her loses when she entered their suite around three, where she found a brief note that read, "Dear Marguerite, I'm sorry but I just can't take this anymore, any of it. We're obviously not suited to each other and should separate. I'm going to Boston to make the arrangements. Your future ex-husband, Malcolm."

One Week Later, In Random Point

"Isn't that a Braemar boy helping Hope behind the counter?" Freddie Johanson asked Allison Albrecht as they drank espressos at one of the hearthside tables in the coffee bar of Marguerite Alexander's bookshop that mid-Christmas week in Random Point. "Why isn't he home for the holidays? And why is he working at all?"

"That's Dru Baxter," Allison replied, "he's a townie on full scholarship. Don't you remember him and Gigi Frank crashing Hugo's Halloween party?"

"You know all the kids by name?" Freddie marveled. As the Network Manager for the Braemar Academy he knew all the hard discs by name.

"I am the Assistant Comptroller," Allison reminded him.

"They did crash the party, didn't they? But why ever did Hugo let them stay?"

Allison shrugged, "They're eighteen."

"Only just, I should think!"

"Makes it legal."

"I for one was amazed," Freddie admitted, watching the young man follow Hope Spencer Lawrence around the cafe with a bus cart as she cleared the tiny tables of soiled china. "Look at the way he's following Hope around!"

"I think she's training him."

"She's training him all right," Freddie chortled.

"What's that supposed to mean?"

"Can't you see that he's already in love?"

"That's nothing new," Allison said philosophically. "Everyone is in love with Hope."

"Except for the people who are in love with Hope's husband," Freddie said, uncomfortably reminding Allison of her momentary defection to David Lawrence several months before.

"That would include every girl at Braemar," Allison nimbly replied.

"They do maintain a balance, Hope and David," Freddie observed, starting as he noticed Hope playfully swat Dru Baxter's blue jeaned backside when he bent to load some dishes into the cart. Dru blushed as only a fair-haired boy can but also grinned mischievously at his new boss, who was just about eight years his senior and arguably, the principal beauty of Random Point.

The first year of the millennium was not a bad one during which to resemble Prince Harry of England, who was getting so much press lately and about whom American girls had just begun to fantasize. Dru took full advantage of being thus adorable and pressed his luck with every magnificent girl or woman he met. In Hope Spencer Lawrence, his English teacher's flirtatious young wife, Dru clearly recognized a goddess and was prepared from the first instant of his employment to serve her impeccably.

Hope was tempted to bestow a second smack on the seat of her cute new assistant's snug dungarees, but ruffled his flaxen hair instead and told him, "I'm so thrilled to have you here!"

After being kept waiting one too many nights in a row for his wife to finish cleaning up the coffee bar and come home to dinner, David Lawrence had registered a formal protest with Marguerite and Sloan to the effect that the cafe had become too successful to be maintained solely by Hope. She needed a busboy at once! David suggested Dru because he remembered how fond Marguerite had been of the brazen boy at the Halloween party. This would be the perfect type of kid for Hope to mentor, which she desperately needed!

Hope felt madly exhilarated at finally achieving a position of superiority in Random Point, even if it was only over a good looking prep school boy. She had lived in the village for almost two years and had always answered to everyone! David, who was her husband, ten years her senior and subtly manipulative, obviously (though ever so lightly) dominated her, but she also had her two bosses, Sloan and Marguerite, to obey, as well as an array of established and generous Random Point males to whom she sometimes went submissive.

Hope hadn't always been so thoroughly controlled. When David had first discovered her, she was top girl at a popular Hollywood B&D club, second to none in earning ability. With this proud mantle came respect, experience, and vast quantities of scene related wisdom, which Hope was prepared to impart to anyone in need of it.

Hope had helped many girls to glamorize themselves, teaching them to corset, to balance on heels, and properly draw on their gloves. She loved telling people how to do things, discussing the origin of customs, and sometimes initiating the novice into the secrets of life as she understood them. Dru seemed an ideal receptacle for much of Hope's instructional largess.

This clever boy had already proven his affinity with their group by agreeing to take a spanking from Marguerite on Halloween. In fact, the alacrity with which both Gigi and Dru had agreed to take spankings that night as a penalty for crashing the party, had astonished everyone except Gigi and Dru, who could not help but look at each other and burst out laughing; as much as to say, "You idiotic adults, we're into it! Can't you see we went to a lot of trouble to penetrate this legendary party????" But Gigi and Dru said none of this. They preferred to play giggling children as Marguerite took Dru away to one room and Hugo kept Gigi right where they were, so that not only he, but all the men present could vigorously spank the Braemar senior.

David Lawrence had long suspected that his two best students were players. They had been in his classes for two years and their reports on great works of literature always explored dominant, submissive or sexually perverse themes. David had also observed that Gigi was capricious and always retained the upper hand over her boyfriend, though it was obvious that Dru had been spanking her regularly. How else could such an elfin minx boast the immense tolerance for spanking, which she had displayed on Halloween?

Gigi remembered exactly how many men spanked her that night and detailed the event in her diary. But the party had left her dissatisfied with Dru and disposed to torment him. Their body language in class testified to the fact that Gigi had put Dru on notice.

David thought gleefully what a good lesson it would teach the arrogant little Gigi to have Dru suddenly under the doting tutelage of both Marguerite, whom Dru worshipped, and Hope, whom he adored.

Dru only hoped he had the fortitude necessary to concentrate on academia to the slightest degree during his final semester at Braemar. With Hope constantly before him and Marguerite periodically clicking by on her impossibly high heels, he could spend every spare minute fantasizing and not count a second lost.

Gigi suddenly strode into the bookshop, only to scowl at Dru as he beamed under Hope's approval. When Hope went to wait on a customer, Gigi snapped, "What was wrong with your job at The Pearl?"

"This job pays much better," Dru replied so innocently that Gigi wanted to slap his face.

"You're going after Mrs. Lawrence, aren't you? You think you may get her to play with you, don't you? Tell me!" Gigi demanded above folded arms and a small tapping foot.

"I have to work now," said Dru apologetically. "So nice to see you." Then he disappeared into the back with the cart of dishes. Gigi turned on her heel and marched outside, running into David as he entered the shop.

"Oh, hi Gigi, you still hanging around town?"

"Oh, I'm not going home for the holiday, Mr. Lawrence," said the pony-tailed brunette, kicking at some snow with the tip of her black oxford. She was dressed in a short, grey, pleated skirt, charcoal cardigan, white blouse and black wool tights. "I'm going to start my second semester reading list instead."

"I love that you're such a grind. Listen Gigi, we're having a little open house at Cobweb Cottage on New Year's Eve if you and Dru would like to stop by. It's from seven to ten."

"Then what happens? The grown-ups all go to the real party?" Gigi jumped up and down, momentarily forgetting her anger at seeing Dru fawning on David Lawrence's enchanting wife.

"As far as I know, there's a party at The Dutch. But it's by invitation only and I'm not sure whether Michael is allowing youngsters."

"Oh please, Mr. Lawrence, can't you get us an invitation? You know we don't care anything about drinking."

"I'll see what I can do. If you do something for me in return."

"What, Mr. Lawrence? You know I'd do anything for you!" Gigi swore.

"Gigi, did you just come from telling Dru off?"

"What if I did? He deserves a telling off. The way he drools over older women! That Marguerite Alexander must be old enough to be his mommy and he practically pants when she walks by!"

"Gigi, be nice. You know, Dru's not a child of privilege, like you. He has to work."

"Cry me a river, Mr. Lawrence. I can see how horribly he's suffering in there." Gigi gazed daggers back into the shop then strode to the smallest sized Mercedes parked at the curb and opened the door.

"Anyway, you two come to New Year's," said David, continuing into the bookstore. He soon saw why Gigi had come away upset. Marguerite had annexed Dru to help her carry boxes of books from the stock room to the stacks, undulating before him in a wool cashmere dress, with her flame colored hair down on her shoulders.

"Hey, Dru," said David, sliding onto a stool at the coffee bar, "I just ran into Gigi and invited you both to our open house on New Year's Eve."

"Thanks!" Dru exclaimed before following Marguerite out of earshot.

"You think Michael would mind Gigi and Dru showing up at The Dutch on New Year's?" David asked his wife as she placed a cup of coffee before him.

"Hardly," Hope grinned, remembering that Michael Flagg had been one of the gentlemen privileged to spank Gigi on Halloween.

Meanwhile, Marguerite was back in the stock room with Dru, supervising the loading of another trolley for the stacks.

"Dru, have you given much thought to what happened on Halloween?" Marguerite asked, climbing up a wooden ladder to hand him down a box, which he stacked on the cart, his eyes irresistibly drawn to the curves, which the snug cashmere dress with its fuzzy nap outlined so splendidly.

"Much thought!" he replied with a grin as his color came up fast.

"You do realize that I only spanked you to teach you a lesson, about how wrong it is to crash a party," she teased mildly, coming down the ladder again.

Dru replied gallantly, "I only hope I didn't hurt your beautiful hand."

"And did you learn a lesson?"

"Did I!" he sagely replied, his eyes penetrating into hers with a sophistication beyond his years.

"And what lesson did you learn, dear?" she asked, stroking his smooth cheek.

"That I love you!" Dru replied enthusiastically, planting a very small kiss on the smooth white hand that had caressed him.

"You silly boy," cried Marguerite, delighted, allowing her lips to lightly brush his before continuing on with the restocking.

Not content to leave the party invitation in David's hands, Gigi drove straight to The Dutch, located a mile out of town at the edge of the woods on Shadow Lane.

At that hour there were only a handful of regulars scattered around the pub watching the sports network over frothy pitchers. Michael was polishing glasses behind the bar and trying to persuade Pamela to stay on part time in spite of her exalted new position to come at Bartlett's Department store in Woodbridge after the first of the new year.

Pamela was to run the new Damaris boutique at Bartlett's to expose the line. This would not leave her any spare time to help Michael and his full time girl Carmen tend bar at The Dutch. However, Pamela was finishing out the year in high style, dressing exquisitely for her afternoon shifts and agreeing to help serve at Michael's private party on New Year's Eve.

Gigi slid onto a stool and politely requested a coke. Michael grinned with recognition at the youthful gatecrasher he (and a dozen other men) had spanked at Hugo's party. "Hi Gigi," he said, getting her the coke himself and putting a cherry in it. "Nice of you to visit. I thought you'd completely forgotten me."

"I know you've forgotten me!" Gigi pouted.

"Honey, how can you say that?" Michael demanded.

"I didn't get invited to your New Year's party."

"Oh! I'm sorry! I suppose I never thought you'd be in town. Of course you should come to the party. And bring your boyfriend too."

"Thanks!" Gigi cried, bouncing on the stool. Pamela smiled and Michael beamed. But when he went back to the kitchen he noticed Carmen stomping about it sullenly. She had just finished preparing a double order of French fries and was stealing fries off the two plates she was about to hand through the sliding window to Pamela when Michael walked in.

"Carmen, what did I tell you about eating off the customer's plates?" Michael demanded, swatting her firmly on the seat of her jeans.

"Sorry," she sighed, carrying a tray of sandwiches through the swinging door and out to the floor. When she came back he caught her and made her look at him.

"What's wrong?"

"You're making me go to the tattoo removing doctor this afternoon."

"Oh, don't be such a baby about it. I've told you he can give you a local. You won't feel a thing," Michael promised, ruffling her short, pale blonde hair affectionately. "However, if you continue making a racket back here, you will feel something, from me," he promised, turning her under his arm and smacking her five or six times.

"Ow!" she protested half heartedly, though the little spanking made her smile more than frown.

"Get on the road early so you're not late for your appointment," he warned. "And take the car, not the bike. It looks like rain."

It was in fact raining hard when Gigi returned to the bookstore to triumphantly inform Dru of their New Year's Eve plans. This time she found him alone, in the back, doing dishes. She negligently perched on a counter top and dangled her small feet while she watched her sometimes boyfriend up to his elbows in suds.

"Well, I got us the invite to the big scene party at The Dutch on New Year's Eve," she reported with satisfaction. "Direct from the host, I might add!"

"I'm not surprised he wants the cutest girl in Random Point to come to his party," said Dru gallantly, though the only woman on his mind at that instant was the fabulous Marguerite Alexander, recently abandoned by her husband and disposed to caress Dru's cheek at a moment's notice.

"Don't try to kiss up to me after what I saw you doing before," Gigi cried indignantly.

"But I like kissing up to you," Dru said, infuriating her by stealing a quick, dry kiss from her wide, beautiful, cherry mouth. "If only you hadn't stopped loving me," he added wistfully.

"Who says that I have?"

"Oh you may still love me, but only as a puppy," he pointed out insightfully.

"Idiot!" cried Gigi, irritated by his composure.

"See how you talk to me?" he observed.

"Sorry, unlike Mrs. Branwell, I haven't yet mastered the art of cooing!" Gigi rejoined before departing in a swirl of provocative pleats.

Marguerite did find Dru very charming and even mildly exciting. For even though the eighteen year old had not yet experienced his final growth spurt and was still rather slight and only of medium height, his physical beauty was not to be denied. And his adoring mien was balm to her insulted pride. The flush that rose to his alabaster cheeks, the rod that rose up and tented his jeans, whenever she flirted with him, were also gratifying. After the emotional going over she'd been given by her husband, the crankiness, the criticisms, the surliness that had marred her contentment ever since Malcolm had lost his Book Bag chain, the unconditional worship from the well groomed, well behaved, well read prep school senior restored her faith in herself as sex goddess and she loved the boy for that.

Therefore it was natural that Marguerite invite her new employee to afternoon tea at her house on the tip of Random Point just a few day's before the year's end. She brought her guest directly to her attic playroom and left him to examine everything at length while she prepared a tea tray below. She returned to find Dru with his head buried in her toy chest, intoxicated by the scents of leather and wood which emanated from it.

As she served him tea and English muffins they agreed that rain on skylights was the most perfect thing about winter on the Cape, that mirrors were remarkably exciting to play before and that age was no obstacle to compatibility in an esoteric relationship. Then Marguerite did many wonderful things to him, just as though she were the man and he was the girl. Dru didn't question anything she suggested or resist any gentle command. He wanted to learn how to serve a real woman, but at first she wouldn't let him.

She was very serious as she set her straight-backed chair before a mirror, motioned Dru to her side and pulled him across her lap. He noticed there was a mirror in front of him as well which caught the reflection of another placed behind and above Marguerite's chair. Dru realized with a hot flash of embarrassment that he would be able to see her spank him in the mirror as he felt it!

The perfect spanking was only the beginning. Marguerite knew so many ways to punish a boy. Dru had never been bent over a spanking horse before but was electrified from the first swish of her cane. She gave him such a long warm up over his jeans that he feared for her arm and protested. Meanwhile, he'd never felt so aroused in his young life and that was saying a good deal. The jeans kept in the heat of the caning while preserving his tender flesh for continued discipline. When she finally pulled his pants down he was pink, but not yet striped. That was soon remedied.

The cane felt so much more stringent on the bare bottom! But Dru loved the sensation with an aching pleasure. He had always read that canings were fearful things. In Marguerite's hand the rod seemed like nothing so much as a magical wand of endless stimulation. Gradually the strokes grew more serious. The sound of the cane swishing through the air and then the rapid series of strokes which followed close upon it sent flutters from Dru's loins to his heart.

She had a way of pausing, rubbing, then giving six sharp strokes in a row, rather quickly. After he was trained to take six, she increased the rapid strokes to one dozen, then two dozen at a time, faster and faster. Dru had once felt uncomfortably warm while watching the 1938

Tom Sawyer, when Tom takes Becky's birching from the master of the class. A fast one it was and even at age eleven, when Dru first saw the film, the birching scene stirred him intensely.

"Do you have a birch?" Dru turned to ask Marguerite.

"Of course I have a birch. I have three or four birches!" she replied, gaily throwing open her crop and flogger closet to retrieve the variety of birch rods she'd collected in recent months. Dru soon felt them all, turning his bottom dark pink as Marguerite repeated the same rapid volleys she'd given with the cane.

The strap was reserved for last, while Dru lay face down on a leather upholstered bench she was pleased to call a "bondage bed" though of course there was no need to restrain her guest for what he so fondly craved.

At first Marguerite wasn't precisely sure of how much pain was pleasurable to Dru and went rather lightly, but as she observed the motions of his muscular flanks, undulating with excitement to the rhythm of her strokes, she knew she could safely accelerate to medium high and redden him deeply for several hours before letting him go. Dru considered these the most perfect two hours of his life and begged her to let him express his gratitude. She did.

Several hours later Marguerite kissed her beautiful boy good-bye at her door and tried to ignore the fact that her new lover was going home to sleep in his parent's house.

Over Christmas week in Boston Malcolm became so depressed that he could barely go to the gym. (He did go, but had terrible workouts.) This not being like himself, he scheduled an appointment with a therapist to discuss what was going on in his life. They talked about him losing his large business and being reduced to a smaller one and his subsequent alienation from his wife, whom he felt he had disappointed.

The therapist, who'd heard much worse problems recently, advised the confused young man to stop taking himself so seriously and go back to his wife. No meds were prescribed and no further appointments scheduled. Because the advice came from a doctor and not a close friend who knew him well, Malcolm listened and saw the sense of it.

Walking around his rooftop condo in Back Bay he remembered for the first time in weeks that he still owned that property free and clear. His entire investment in the climbing gym with William had come from the sale of the faltering Branwell's Book Bag chain and the new enterprise promised to become viable in six months. He owed nothing, was only thirty-two and in splendid physical condition. There were no limits to what he could yet achieve. For example, he could still prove worthy of Marguerite.

Driving out to Random Point that New Year's Eve Malcolm rehearsed his speech to Marguerite. First he would apologize for his behavior in Vegas. Then he would explain that he'd been so distraught since losing his business that it had completely robbed him of his sense of proportion. He would say he had been wrong to try to tell her how to have fun in Vegas, especially with her own money and hypocritically prudish to take issue with her cleavage gown. Finally, he had been inexcusably rude to Anthony and Susan, for which he also intended to apologize.

He would ask Marguerite to forgive him. He didn't deserve a second chance, but she was kind and had once cared for him. Malcolm's old optimism returned on that sleety drive out to the Cape under a darkening sky.

He remembered how difficult winning her had been. All those damned books she'd made him read! The fact that he had won the peerless Marguerite could be counted one of his most spectacular achievements. But how poorly he had treated her! His behavior made no sense in retrospect, even to himself. But temporary insanity was surely a condition Marguerite could understand, capricious creature that she was. He felt reassured by the presence of a thin, narrow box in his inner jacket pocket. He knew his wife. Without a substantial bribe she might not even take his apology seriously! Malcolm smiled at Marguerite's absurdity, suddenly finding it much more endearing than annoying.

Susan and Dennis were sharing duty at the door of the Dutch that party night and she beamed at Malcolm's appearance.

"Susan! I'm so sorry I scolded you," Malcolm said, clasping her tiny leather gloved hand to his lips. "I was completely out of line. The truth is, I've been depressed. I have a doctor's note to prove it. Please forgive me?"

"Of course I do!" Susan said, hugging him. "We should never have forced you to come to Vegas."

"Susan, was it really my fault you decided not to marry Anthony?"

"Don't be silly," laughed Susan.

After Malcolm continued on through the anteroom Dennis said to Susan, "Shouldn't you have warned him?"

"Perhaps what's going on won't be perfectly obvious to Malcolm," Susan replied.

At first it wasn't perfectly obvious. Malcolm certainly expected to have to peel the men away from Marguerite by layers on New Year's Eve, but he never guessed the favorite one would be too young to drink in the bar.

Malcolm saw Marguerite, sleek in a leather halter dress and glove tight thigh boots, her red hair brushing her white shoulders, salsa dancing with the Braemar boy Malcolm remembered from Hugo's last party. The boy was dressed in a black sharkskin suit and white shirt with no tie and looked exponentially more confident than any 18 year old had a right to look, though Malcolm saw nothing peculiar in that. He recalled that Marguerite had taken the boy to her bosom at the previous party, spanking him as a penalty for gatecrashing. Now she was obviously amusing herself with the most unselfconscious dancer in the room. Malcolm looked around for Michael Flagg, always his most serious rival, and saw the proprietor behind the bar dispensing overflowing steins of ale on tap to his friends.

Assisting Michael behind the bar was Pamela, performing her last active duty as an employee of The Dutch. Beginning the following Monday she would work exclusively at Bartlett's department store in Woodbridge, managing the Damaris boutique, of which she was part owner. This opportunity had been created for her by Ambrose Bartlett, now seated at the bar with his wife Paula, who had not as yet begun to guess that there might be something more than business between her new husband and his newest department manager. Pamela was in a cranberry velvet Victorian corset gown, gathered and trimmed with cream lace and pink satin rosettes. On her long, elegant feet were high lacing evening boots of cream leather. Her black hair was twisted up into a loose topknot, and around her throat she wore a pearl on a black velvet choker.

Michael's other assistant, his permanent barmaid Carmen Farrell, was bound to a post in the middle of the pub, dressed in a black satin waist cinch corselet and bare bottomed, receiving her first flogging, (from Hugo Sands), during which Malcolm observed Michael keeping a watchful eye on the proceedings from across the room. Malcolm had heard that Michael was having an affair with his new barmaid but hadn't seen the proof until this moment. This was a relief. It meant Michael was less likely to be running after Marguerite.

Anthony Newton was in his usual position, behind the piano, playing the mambo music Marguerite and the boy were dancing to. William and Damaris were just getting up from their table to dance, but they motioned Malcolm over first and sat him down beside little Gigi Frank, who was dressed in a short navy blue velvet suit with cream lace at the collar and cuffs, her straight brown hair touching her shoulders and a rather dark shade of red on her beautiful, wide mouth.

Gigi had been glaring at Marguerite and Dru for being so obviously drunk on each other's charms. Not that she even wanted Dru for herself anymore, but to see him cleave to a woman in her middle thirties in public felt deeply embarrassing. But before Gigi could express any of her angst to Malcolm she was swooped down upon by Monty and Portia, an attractive, fairly dominant couple from Manhattan, who made a hobby of charming the pants off submissive girls.

"What an adorable little girl," said Portia.

"Do you like bondage?" asked Monty.

"I've never tried it," rejoined Gigi with interest, for Monty was tall and tawny.

"Where shall we take her?" Portia asked.

"As I understand it, there's an attic, a stock room, a kitchen and a cellar," Monty replied.

"I'll go check them out and see which would be best," Portia said, leaving Gigi to Monty.

"Do you like to play with women?" Monty asked her candidly.

"I don't think so," Gigi replied.

"Would you like to try it?"

"Not really," she said.

"Would you like to play with me?" asked Monty.

"Oh, yes!" cried the eighteen year old enthusiastically.

"In that case, let's get out of here before Portia comes back. We'll go back to my room at the inn."

"Your girlfriend won't get mad?" Gigi asked with excitement.

"She won't even notice we're gone," Monty assured her, shepherding her to the door.

Laura was helping to serve drinks to the guests and came to Malcolm's table with a sort of pink martini. "It's a vodka and cranberry sort of thing. Try it!" Laura urged.

"Oh, what the hell," said Malcolm, downing the drink quickly and wincing with every gulp. Then he smiled. "I may have another one," he suggested to Laura, who was delighted to see her best friend's husband finally relax and rushed behind the bar to make him a second drink.

"Everyone, Malcolm's drinking tonight," said Laura to Pamela and the recently released and freshly whipped Carmen.

"Malcolm's drinking tonight?" Michael echoed in astonishment. "What could this mean?"

"Haven't you ever heard of Dutch courage?" Laura laughed. "He'll need plenty of it to approach Marguerite!"

Michael sighed as soon as Carmen was out of earshot. Of course it had been too good to be true, Marguerite free at last. He'd managed to see her twice in the last week! But if Malcolm was back, that was the end of that.

The next revelers to sit down with Malcolm were Hope and David Lawrence.

"Malcolm, you're drinking?" Hope exclaimed, pressing his arm in congratulations. Hope had playfully seduced Malcolm the previous year, to take the pressure off her beloved boss, Marguerite, who had recently slipped with Michael, marriage being perhaps too tight a fit for the voluptuous redhead.

Ever since that day in the bookstore gallery, when Hope had permitted him to spank her, among other exquisite liberties, Malcolm had felt warm in the embrace of Random Point. Which was why, in spite of his lunacy in leaving Marguerite, his chronic crankiness at the decadence of the group as a whole, and the fact that the bar in which he sat drinking belonged to his wife's favorite lover, this was where he felt he should be on New Year's Eve.

"Hope, what's going with Marguerite and that kid?" Malcolm asked the village enchantress, suddenly noticing the way Marguerite was holding the boy and gazing into his eyes and that they hadn't broken their hold on each other through three songs as he'd sat there.

"Oh, you mean Dru?"

"He's one of my students," David volunteered. "He's been working part time at the bookstore helping Hope bus the tables."

"Yes, he's an angel," Hope murmured, grabbing champagne glasses off a tray being carried by Pamela and passing them around the table.

"But why is he all over Marguerite?" Malcolm demanded.

"She's just as much all over him, sport," David advised.

"Yes, Malcolm, brace yourself," said Hope.

Malcolm drank a glass of champagne instead of waiting for another martini.

"Of course we all know that she can be very silly, but I refuse to believe Marguerite would be interested in a teenager!" Malcolm asserted.

"I refused to believe they were discontinuing the rotary phone, but just try and find one today!" David remarked, on his fourth martini and not mixing them with champagne.

"Hi, Mr. Lawrence," said Lupe Freeman, appearing at the table with Carl-Adam Johanson.

"Lupe?" David was unprepared for the sight of his favorite former-pupil in a PVC jumpsuit that clung to her curvaceous little size 5 body like shiny black paint. Her black hair brushed her small but jutting bottom and her smile was more irreverent than ever.

"We drove all the way from Poughkeepsie in a snow storm to get here," Lupe confided. "And we got a flat on the way." Lupe's strapping companion looked no worse for being out in the sleet and gazed about the room in a trance, drinking in all the beautiful female forms as they flashed by him in velvet, leather or silk. "Well? Aren't you going to hug me or even pat my perfect bottom in this awesome cat suit?" Lupe demanded of her former-teacher.

"I'll hug you anyway," David grumbled, "not drunk enough to pat you yet."

Malcolm got up to make room for the new arrivals and drifted irresistibly over to Marguerite, who stopped dancing at his appearance.

"Malcolm! How nice to see you," she smiled, then turned to Dru and asked him to bring her a glass of champagne. The boy, who knew exactly who Malcolm was, hastened to obey his new mistress, though with a sinking heart.

"Do you mean that?" Malcolm asked, taking her hand and kissing it. Marguerite stared at him and smiled again.

"Why? Have you missed me?" she asked, withdrawing her hand from his and leading him to the table that had just been vacated by Freddie Johanson and his girlfriend Allison after Freddie spotted his younger brother Carl-Adam enter with Lupe. Though born 19 years apart, Freddie and Carl-Adam shared an uncannily similar interest in dominance and submission and had discovered the interactive portion of the scene at pretty much the same time, Freddie in Random Point and Carl-Adam at college.

Now leading Carl-Adam a frustrating chase was Lupe Freeman, a confident freshman who allowed him to possess her often, but not always, and was as likely to treat him as a servant as her lover, according to her whim. Lupe's callous indifference to the genuinely nice young man's needs, was largely due to her knowing that he'd had begun his odyssey in the scene as an abject, instep-nuzzling submissive rather than a self determined dominant male, which was the type she preferred. While Lupe wished submissive men well, she did not find them sexually interesting and was deeply shocked to find herself dating one. In Lupe's view, Carl-Adam had only become a spanking man through attrition and was therefore only about fifty percent as exciting to her as a natural player.

Carl-Adam had adored Lupe's Vassar mentor, Diana Stratton, to the extent that he had begged to be Diana's slave, her dog, her bear, her anything. Moderately charmed by the dollops of devotion pouring out of her Ivy League Viking boy, Diana had wallowed in his worship for a less than a semester before becoming bored by his tame genuflections and deciding to tutor him in the refined art of spanking a girl to orgasm instead. This dangerous training plus love had rather turned Carl-Adam's sexuality around.

Since he wanted Diana so painfully much, Carl-Adam had forced himself to adapt to the role of spanking stud. She still told him off regularly, abused him, and behaved with a general tone of insolence no truly dominant male would tolerate for a day. But she gave herself to him without restraint and in every way and a big boy of 20 needs that. Ideally, several times a day.

When Diana graduated, Lupe inherited the chairmanship of their on-campus B&D support group and Carl-Adam. In an effort to help that group to continue to thrive, Lupe momentarily abandoned her passionate persecution of David Lawrence to track down Dru Baxter, with whom she'd been close friends while at Braemar, and elicit his promise that he'd apply to Vassar and if accepted, join her there in the Fall.

Dru was happy enough to hand off the champagne delivery errand to Pamela as the proximity of Marguerite's husband was giving him butterflies of the most unpleasant variety. Pamela arrived at the table in time to see Marguerite open the flat jeweler's box that held a sapphire necklace.

"You are serious!" Marguerite commended Malcolm, admiring her gift with glowing eyes. "Thank you!"

"Oh, Marguerite!"

"Oh, Malcolm," she laughed.

"Marguerite, will you forgive me and let me come back?" Malcolm covered her hand with his. She pulled it free with a gentle tug. "You see, for months I've been depressed."

"Yes, darling, I know," she sighed.

"But I'm better now!"

"Really? Are you on meds?"

"No. The doctor told me the only cure was getting you back."

"Silly!" Marguerite laughed again.

"Seriously!"

"Unusual doctor."

"Really, Marguerite, I'm a changed man. I don't feel terrible about losing the bookstore chain anymore for one thing. It's not my fault the market changed. And I can make another business work just as well."

"I'm delighted you've finally come to your senses about that, darling," said Marguerite.

"Have you missed me at all?" he wondered.

"Of course I have. Quite a bit at first. Less lately though," she reflected, smiling up at Laura, who refilled their champagne glasses again. Malcolm drank thirstily. "You see, I've also come to my senses, Malcolm. Marriage was never the right choice for us."

"If you'll try again I'll make it right," he vowed.

"No!" she declared gently but firmly. "The freedom I've enjoyed this week has reminded me that I'm not a one man woman and I don't intend to suppress my natural urges any longer."

"When did you ever?" he demanded.

"Lots of times!" she replied indignantly, downing her glass in a couple of gulps. "But that isn't even the main issue. The truth is, you were a very cranky husband!"

"I know," he agreed guiltily.

"You never seemed to appreciate me."

"Never?"

"Okay, you did one thing right," she smiled again. Now Pamela passed by with a champagne bottle and refilled their glasses. Marguerite drank deeply then made a move to leave the table.

"Wait, where are you going?"

"I promised Susan I'd spell her at the door."

"When may we continue our discussion?" he asked, as she stumbled up on her 5" high heels.

"I think we've covered everything," she airily replied over her shoulder as she began to totter away. He sprang up and slipping an arm around her tiny waist walked with her.

"What do you mean? You've barely given me a chance to plead my case!" Malcolm was now inebriated enough to nibble Marguerite's ear. She turned to look at him in some amusement.

"You know, you left me," she reminded him. "Rather brusquely, I might add."

"Hi Marguerite, Malcolm," Diana Currie cried, having just entered the warm, crowded bar dragging her new husband by the hand. "Look who I got to take time off finally!"

Diana was 22 and her husband 40 but it was a love match built on spanking and bondage that defied criticism. They had met by chance in an exclusive B&D club and the attraction had been instantaneous. Currie was big and tall, confident and powerful while Diana was doll-like and meticulously pampered. She had always dreamt of a daddy and he had always longed for a baby. They idolized each other at first sight.

"Now there is a marriage that is working!" Marguerite pointed out to Malcolm as they continued to make their way across the crowded room. "Because P.C. adores Diana."

Right outside the cloakroom, Polyxena Guzman stood arguing with her ex-submissive boyfriend and still current business partner Dieter Brant in German. "And there's a relationship that's just failed," Marguerite informed Malcolm; "Because Dieter no longer adores Polyxena! Now instead of being selflessly devoted to his mistress, he's critical and cranky from morning to night. Women like us deserve better!"

Malcolm was left to digest these words as Marguerite went to join Susan.

Five minutes later, Michael Flagg found Marguerite, Susan and Laura in the attic smoking resinous skunkweed with abandon.

"Well, if it isn't the three original trouble makers," exclaimed Flagg with satisfaction. "What did I tell you girls about smoking dope on the premises?"

"Come on, Michael, it's New Year's Eve," Susan protested as her host turned her over his knee and administered a dozen sharp spanks to the seat of the black mesh panties which her summarily raised skirt revealed.

"Stay right where you are, you two!" he ordered Laura and Marguerite who had begun to move towards the door. "You all broke the rules so you're all getting spanked," he declared.

Marguerite said to Laura, "Five years ago he was just another guy with a girlfriend who wouldn't let him spank her. Now look at him, throwing his own spanking party in his own establishment. And all because we took an interest in the big brute!"

Michael grinned at Marguerite, put Susan off his lap and motioned to Laura. Susan rubbed her bottom but would have willingly remained an hour across that monumental lap, of which she had so many fond memories.

Laura came to Michael and allowed him to turn her over his knee. Like Marguerite, Laura was clad in a glove tight leather dress, but hers had a convenient zipper running from the hem of her skirt to the middle of her back. Michael unzipped it to her waist and revealed her black garter belt, panty and hose ensemble. Like her little sister, Laura's panties were so sheer that as soon as he began to spank her oval cheeks, the pink came up under the nylon mesh.

Marguerite was content to finish the joint while Michael spanked her best friend. After a dozen swats had been administered to Laura, she was also released.

"You!" Michael nodded at Marguerite. She pouted but went to him. Their eyes met before he pulled her down. "I ran into your husband downstairs. Are we returning to the old regime? If so, I'll make the most out of this."

"Make the most out of it anyway," Marguerite said, abandoning herself to her favorite lover's lap.

"Do you want us to leave, Marguerite?" Susan asked respectfully.

"No," said Marguerite.

"Yes," said Michael. "Run along girls. And behave yourselves!" A moment later the sisters had clattered down the rickety wooden ladder and Michael had Marguerite all to himself.

After three resounding smacks he rolled her over on his lap, took her in his arms and told her, "The hell with the spanking. I'm taking you while I can!"

Meanwhile, Susan and Laura thoughtfully stood guard at the foot of the ladder to prevent anyone else from ascending while their two friends were blending above.

"Hey, Malcolm, how's it going?" Hugo Sands shook hands with Malcolm.

"Not so well," Malcolm admitted, too besotted to be standoffish with his wife's original patron in the scene.

"I heard you were getting a divorce."

"I wasn't in my right mind when I suggested that. I'm sane again but Marguerite won't listen."

"You mean you want to go back to her?"

"Hell, yes!"

"Well, good luck!" Hugo said hastily, moving away, before he could be drawn into the morass of Malcolm's marital relations. Hugo was understandably loath to dispense advice to Malcolm about getting Marguerite back. Like Michael Flagg, Hugo was delighted to find Marguerite suddenly single again. She was such an intensely squeezable girl. "Excuse me, Malcolm, I need to talk to Ambrose Bartlett," said Hugo, finally shaking off the semi drunk husband in favor of his urbane contemporary.

"Malcolm's trying to get Marguerite back," Hugo told Ambrose, sliding onto a stool beside him at the bar, "and he's getting nowhere fast. Should I give him the benefit of my advice?"

"Has anyone felt Marguerite out?" Ambrose chortled.

"Oh, don't you know what she's been up to?" Hugo laughed, then lowered his voice to whisper something in the department store owner's ear. Ambrose glanced over at the table where the younger set were drinking cokes and raised his eyebrows at Dru, who was now being teased by Lupe and Diana.

Paula Bartlett, seated on the other side of her husband, heard Hugo's comment and it didn't surprise her. As the guidance counselor at Braemar, Paula wondered if it wasn't her duty to offer Dru Baxter counseling over having an obvious affair with an older woman.

"No!" grinned Ambrose. "I'm shocked! What a bad girl that Marguerite is. I hope she gets a public spanking tonight."

"What are you doing later?" Malcolm pounced on Marguerite as soon as she came back into the pub.

Marguerite looked at her husband with bemusement. "I haven't really decided yet," she replied honestly.

"Let me come home with you."

"No, I want to be free."

"Free to seduce little boys?" Malcolm demanded.

"Why not?" she gaily replied.

"So it's true, you're really sleeping with that kid?"

"Who told you that?" she laughed.

"Well? Are you or aren't you?"

"What do you think?"

"I don't know what to think!"

"That's true. You hardly know me."

They arrived at the bar and Carmen placed two fresh glasses of champagne before them. Marguerite leaned back against the bar and drank her flute while examining the room.

"I hope you don't let him -- let him --" Malcolm couldn't even say it.

"Oh, no! It's quite the opposite with us. I spank him!"

"I thought you only did that for allowance," Malcolm remarked.

"That's not strictly true. If a young man has a beautiful body and is extremely compliant, then I find it a pleasure."

"Humph!" Malcolm grunted, folding his arms across his chest.

"Have another?" Carmen asked, filling his empty glass.

"Thanks!" Malcolm gulped the next glass, his eyes fixed on Marguerite. "So you're going to make me beg, are you?"

"No."

"Then what will it take?"

"What will what take?"

"To get you back. What do I have to do?"

"Oh Malcolm, you don't really want me back badly enough to do something, do you?"

"Don't laugh. I'll do whatever I have to."

"No, you won't. You don't have the imagination!"

"The hell I don't."

"You don't want me back badly enough."

"I want you back so badly it hurts."

"You don't know the meaning of that phrase."

"Just tell me what you want me to do."

"Look Malcolm, since I've been playing in our scene, I've had my dignity assailed in a dozen different ways. I've been submitted to every sort of corporal punishment, put in bondage, made to stand in the corner, trained to masturbate on command, strictly corseted, butt plugged, double dildoed, ordered to give head, sodomized, given enemas, and once someone actually compelled me to wear a red union suit - but darling, I've never felt quite so keenly humiliated as when my husband walked out on me in the midst of a pleasure jaunt with my closest friends two weeks ago. Therefore, if I decreed a penalty for you, it would necessarily be extremely severe and not at all to your liking."

"I have to go submissive to you, right?" he replied at once, for he remembered her remark in their suite. "Okay, I will."

"Not to me. Nothing would ever be the same between us again. But perhaps to one of my girl friends," said Marguerite.

"With you there?"

"No," Marguerite surprised him by saying.

"No?"

"If you're coming home tonight I have to tie up some loose ends before you get there," she said casually.

"Well, when can I get there?" Malcolm's heart leapt at the invitation to return to her, blocking out the ordeal to come.

"After you've been to see my friend. Certainly no earlier than three a.m."

"Well? Who am I to see? When and where?"

"I have to work out those details but stick around and I'll get back to you within the hour," she murmured before slipping away from him again.

Chapter Eleven

New Year's Eve

Following Marguerite's instructions, Malcolm Branwell arrived at the grey painted lady with the pink and cream trim on the graveyard side of Shadow Lane, overlooking the thin strip of rocky coast that rimmed Random Point. The house belonged to Susan Ross and Malcolm found her awaiting his arrival in the downstairs sitting room. A fire was blazing in the hearth and the lithe, 23 year old blonde had changed from her party clothes into riding boots, wool leggings, a light merino wool shirt and a dark corduroy hacking jacket. Her waves of honey blonde hair rippled provocatively to her waist and played about her body as she moved with an interesting life of their own. The negligent, equestrian outfit encased Susan's pert form to perfection but did not really help her achieve the authority she'd been hoping for.

"God, you look good in those riding pants," Malcolm said, accepting a glass of wine and small sandwich from Susan as she showed him to a chair by the fire. "I don't suppose you'd let me spank you instead?"

"I would, if I were in a different mood," said Susan over folded arms, "but tonight I'm disposed to follow Marguerite's orders. Oh, and we're not alone either!"

"No? Who else is here?" Malcolm asked with a flutter, for he realized that if he were indeed really going through with this insanity, he certainly did not want it witnessed!

"Gigi, come in here, please," said Susan, going out to the hall and calling her newest young friend to join them.

Gigi Frank, a pony tailed brunette of 18, dressed a blue velvet, short skirted suit, emerged into the room. Malcolm recognized her from the party at The Dutch. He'd also spanked her briefly, at Hugo Sands' Halloween party.

He held his out his wine glass for a prompt refill. With his upcoming ordeal in view he saw no reason to halt his march towards complete inebriation.

"What is she doing here?" he asked.

"She's my assistant," Susan replied, taking the younger girl's hand and petting it.

"Why do you need an assistant?"

"In case you become insolent she's my witness. Otherwise you might find it too easy to turn things around."

"I wouldn't have agreed to come here if I planned to do that."

"Anyway, she's going to help me with the bondage."

"Why bondage? I'll hold still."

"Light bondage. A minor handicap. After all, you're a such big strapping male ..."

"I see," Malcolm replied. "Okay, bring it on."

"Come help me find what we need," Susan said, dragging Gigi from the room by the hand. In the hall on the way upstairs they held a rapid conversation.

"What are we going to do with him?" asked Gigi. "He seems too big to fit across our laps."

"He's just tall, he's not big. And I have a pretty sturdy little lap," said Susan. "I will spank him over my knee!"

"You? That just seems silly."

"That's the point. We can't let him wriggle out of a proper over the knee spanking from a girl. It's part of the humiliation."

"Why must we humiliate him at all? He's so handsome! Why can't we just use him for fun instead?" Gigi suggested.

"This will be a form of fun," said Susan. "It's something we have to learn how to do and even enjoy sooner or later. At least that's what everyone tells me. Why not practice on a beautiful man? Think of it like that! Plus, he's been a total jerk to Marguerite and even so, she's about to take him back. He just can't get off Scott free."

They entered the upstairs playroom, still a work in progress, and Susan threw open a few cedar chests. From one she extracted leather handcuffs, from the next she took a series of implements ranging from brushes to birches to straps. These she piled onto Gigi's waiting arms.

"How am I supposed to comport myself during this?" Gigi asked.

"Funny, I would have thought you already spanked that adorable boy you go out with, Dru," commented Susan on the return trip down stairs.

"Honestly, I never realized Dru had such a strong submissive side until this gentleman's wife took him for her pet."

"I can see that doesn't go down very well with you," Susan smiled. "But you shouldn't blame Marguerite. She was treated rather badly by this Malcolm we're about to discipline. He may look cute, but he can be horribly cranky."

"And we're going to try and cure that?"

"No. I'm sure that's a chronic condition. We're just a penalty that Malcolm has to pay before receiving permission to return home to Marguerite."

"Do you think she'll continue to see Dru after Malcolm returns?" Gigi asked with a quickening pulse.

"Oh, I shouldn't think very often," said Susan sagely.

They found Malcolm as they had left him. Gigi flung her pile of implements down on the hearthrug. He stared at them.

"You don't plan to use all those, do you? We'll be here all night!" he protested.

"We'll be here as long as it takes," said Susan sternly. "And you Sir, for the next half hour to forty five minutes, will speak only when you are spoken to."

"Fine!" Malcolm replied casually, "I just can't help but wonder if you've ever done this before."

"Ordinarily a little detail like that would matter, but after the way I saw you act towards Marguerite and all of us in Vegas, do you think I really care if I make a few mistakes?"

"Do you even know where to aim?"

"Gee, Malcolm, how afraid are you?" Susan laughed.

Malcolm shrugged and said, "Carry on."

"Good! I didn't think you were a wimp. All right, come over here to me and put your wrists in front of you," Susan commanded. When

Malcolm complied she attached the leather cuffs to his wrists and linked them with a boat hook as Gigi watched.

"I want some of those," said Gigi, stretching out her small hand to caress the leather cuffs and also Malcolm's hands.

"Get Dru to buy you a pair for Valentine's Day," Susan suggested.

"We're not going out together anymore," said Gigi. "I could never date a submissive."

"H'm, yes, I do know what you mean," said Susan, leading Malcolm to a slipper chair by the hearth. "No offense, Malcolm," she continued, sitting down, then looking up at him, "we know you're only submitting because you want Marguerite back. You're not really submissive."

"And if you happen to be after tonight it won't be our fault," Gigi laughed, struck by the hilarity of two inept, inexperienced submissives trying to control an athletic adult male at least ten years their senior. She remembered what an excellent spanker Malcolm had been on Halloween. It had been her first scene party ever. She and Dru had snuck in and got to stay by agreeing to take a spanking. Dru had been taken away to a private room and spanked by Marguerite. He had emerged from that room in love, both with Marguerite and being spanked, while Gigi had been spanked by every man in the room at the time of their discovery. About a dozen took turns. Even thinking about that half hour when a dozen different men had spanked her in a row, Gigi felt a rush.

"Come on, over my lap," said Susan, pulling Malcolm down into position. He still had on his wool gabardine suit trousers and a textured dress shirt. The trim, muscular, 6' tall, 170 lb. male disposed himself awkwardly until Susan pulled him up close to her waist. She was only 5'3" and 106 lbs. herself, so proper positioning was vital. "You can support yourself with your hands on the floor in front of you," she informed him, without unhooking the cuffs. "Gigi, bring me every small wooden object in the pile, would you?" Susan asked. "Comfortable, Malcolm?"

"No."

"Okay, we'll proceed then," said Susan, taking up a shiny maple paddle and smacking him resoundingly once on each cheek. He barely moved. Susan looked at Gigi. Gigi shook her head. They understood each other perfectly. “Malcolm, get up.”

“Are you done?” he asked.

“Just stand up,” said Susan without humor. Malcolm got to his feet with some difficulty, as his hands were still cuffed. Susan unbuckled his belt and unzipped his trousers then yanked them down to his ankles. His plain blue cotton boxers followed and both girls nearly gasped to behold Malcolm’s robust and fully erect penis stick out at right angles from his silken furred groin like a thick pink flag.

“Jesus, Malcolm, are you getting off on this?” Susan demanded, nonplussed by the new development.

Malcolm was just drunk enough to not care what either of them thought of him but demurred, “It must be the riding pants.”

“Damn it, you’re here to be humiliated,” cried Susan, bestowing a light smack on the hot dog special that suddenly seemed to be the focus of all eyes in the overheated room. “Just get back across my lap. And you’d better react this time or I’ll go right to the cane!” she threatened. “And damn it, put that thing somewhere. It’s sticking into my thigh.”

Malcolm asked, “What am I supposed to do with it?”

“Tuck it between your legs,” she recommended, picking up the paddle again.

“Can’t I tuck it between your legs?” he asked, suddenly grasping the full erotic potential of being over a woman’s lap.

“Certainly not!” cried Susan, commencing the spanking a second time, now with his firm, jutting, lightly fuzzed buttocks bare. Smack! Smack! She brought the paddle down hard on one cheek, then the other. Pink marks immediately appeared against his creamy hued buttocks. She smacked him hard and fast several dozen times. He grunted every time the paddle struck his muscular backside but barely flinched each time it connected. Redoubling her efforts to make an impression on Malcolm, Susan smacked him several dozen times more, and a good deal more severely, raising her arm as high as she could and bring it down with a thunderous crack each time the paddle kissed his flesh. Gigi stared in wonder, transfixed by the deepening pinkness staining the skin of their captive. If anyone had stuck her that hard, she feared she might die of the pain. Truly males were a different breed.

"Stop!" he suddenly cried. "This isn't working."

"What do you mean it isn't working? Aren't you feeling it?" Susan paused with the paddle against his radiant bottom.

"I am, sort of, but if you keep on the way you're going, I'll come."

"Are you being a joker?" Susan grabbed a handful of Malcolm's soft brown hair and forced him to look at her.

"Honestly!" he couldn't help but laugh. She pushed him off his lap and onto the hearthrug. The girls saw he wasn't lying. A tiny bead of crystal fluid lay atop the smooth pink mushroom cap of his fully erect and rather magnificent penis, which was wagging at them unselfconsciously as he scrambled to his feet. "I'm sorry, Susan, I couldn't help it," he said in the manner of a man who had drunk more than he could remember in one evening. "It has to be the riding pants."

Gigi stared at him in fascination. Susan stood up and paced, scowling at Malcolm, who had begun to make himself decent.

"I thought you were a dominant," Susan said. "Now all of a sudden getting spanked gives you a hard on? What gives here?"

"I don't know," he shrugged. "I never had that done to me before and I didn't know how I would react. Maybe it's because I'm so drunk. Maybe it's because I'm thinking about being with Marguerite again. But if you'd gone on, I'd have come."

"You should have shown more control. You've defeated the whole purpose of you being here. Oh never mind, just go! We can all honorably tell Marguerite that you took a spanking!"

"Don't be mad, Susan," said Malcolm, trying to hug her before departing. She shrugged him off. "I'd let you punish me some more, but I'm sure the same thing would happen. I just can't seem to think of anything but sex right now."

"Get the hell out of here you horrible man!" Susan said, stamping her foot.

Returning to The Dutch at 3 a.m., the girls found Dru Baxter pacing the windswept porch in an irritable state.

"Gigi! How come you didn't tell me where you were going?" the fair haired high school senior demanded in a tone that his ex-girlfriend had never heard before and which produced a queer sensation in the pit of her stomach.

Susan scurried inside leaving Gigi to reply, “I didn’t think I had to check in with you throughout the evening minute by minute!”

“Minute by minute! You disappeared for six hours! I’ve called Braemar five times to see if you got back there.”

“Well that was idiotic. After all it’s New Year’s Eve. Although I’m not surprised you didn’t notice me leave, you were so immersed in Mrs. Branwell’s cleavage!”

“God, you’re a brat!”

Gigi shrugged, walked to her compact Mercedes and opened the door. “Are you coming?”

Dru got in the front seat beside her. Before starting the car she paused to light a cigarette.

“Since when did you start smoking?” he demanded, shocked.

She threw the car in gear and they clattered over the gravel and out onto Shadow Lane, now dangerously ice glazed. “You want to just drop me off home?” he asked, carefully scrutinizing her for signs of fatigue or inebriation. Noticing neither, he untensed and stared out the window at the rime-frosted firs that lined the road. It had been a long and rather heart breaking night for Dru, what with losing Marguerite back to her husband and he wasn’t in the mood for Gigi’s sharp edges.

“I don’t feel like going back to school tonight,” she said, suddenly. “Aren’t your parents out of town? Can’t I come home with you?”

“If you like,” he managed a smile.

“Fine!” she bounced on the seat, suddenly reenergized. “But we’ll stop by Mr. Newton’s house first. Susan says they’re throwing together a late supper.”

“I am hungry,” Dru said, in his eighteen-year-old way.

A few minutes later, after several heart stopping skids on the way up the cliff road, Gigi and Dru arrived.

“So where have you been all this time, anyway?” Dru asked Gigi as they made their way towards the enormous kitchen, where Dennis and Laura had spread out sandwich platters, casseroles, cheeses, dessert plates and dozens of bottles of wine. David Lawrence, their

English teacher at Braemar and his wife Hope were already seated at the long refectory table restoring themselves with food and drink. Places were found for Dru and Gigi at once. Hope beamed at Dru, who was her part-time assistant at the bookstore coffee bar. He smiled back somewhat wanly as Gigi resumed tormenting him.

"I've been helping Susan Ross give Malcolm Branwell a big, fat hard-on to take home to Marguerite," Gigi serenely replied.

"What did you say?" Dru paused with his sandwich in midair, then put it down without tasting it. Being reminded of his broken heart took away his appetite and instead of eating he poured himself a glass of wine and drank deeply.

"Marguerite sent Malcolm to Susan to be punished for offending her and Susan brought me along to help. But instead of embarrassing him, being across Susan's lap only inflamed him so we sent him home to Marguerite."

"I see," Dru finished his glass of wine and poured another.

"What's the matter?"

"Nothing."

"Surely you didn't think that you really had her?" Gigi demanded.

"Let's not talk about it anymore," he asked.

"After all, she is married to a big, tall, strapping, pony hung man," Gigi taunted, topping off their glasses.

"Gigi, I said change the subject," Dru replied.

"What if I find the subject terrifically amusing?"

"Excuse me," Dru said, rising and leaving the table. Gigi followed him out of the kitchen and down the hall to the small, jewel toned green and gold gilt sitting room where he'd flung himself into a chair beside a pretty, little, pink veined marble hearth. Looking at him with his blond head in his hands gave her a pang of remorse.

He started when she entered the room, then sprang angrily to his feet. "What?"

"Nothing. I was just wondering whether you were ready to go."

"You can drive yourself back to school. I'll get a ride home with someone else," he told her curtly.

"I don't want to go back to school now. I want to go over to your house."

"Oh really! After the things you just said to me you expect me to entertain you as though everything was perfect between us?"

"Isn't it?"

"Ever since Hugo's Halloween party -- when you found out that I have a submissive side -- you've held me in contempt. Don't try to deny it!"

Gigi gave a tiny shrug.

"But even though you no longer want me for yourself," he continued, "you hate the idea that any other woman might enjoy herself with me, as evidenced by the brutal things you've been saying tonight!"

"Dru, quit over reacting. I was only teasing you. I'm sure you'll wriggle your way into Marguerite's pants again, as cute as you are. By the way, do you actually wear girly panties when you play the girl with Marguerite, or is it all a mental thing?"

"You know, Gigi, I used to find your cynicism amusing, but now that I can see how cruel you really are I don't seem to find it so funny."

"You make me sound like a character in a Noel Coward play," said Gigi, not displeased.

"He did say that some women should be struck regularly, like gongs." Dru swiftly returned.

"Look, I apologize for the crack about the girly panties," she declared, "but you simply can't send me back to school alone on New Year's Eve."

"Can't you go back to Monty at the Inn?" Dru demanded coldly.

"He'll be with his girlfriend by now."

"I'm sure Susan could find room for you here."

"I barely know her," Gigi protested.

"You said she asked you to join her tonight. She must like you. You can probably even get their good looking English manservant to tuck you in."

"No, I want you to tuck me in."

"If I take you home it won't be to tuck you in, it'll be to beat the living daylights out of you," he promised.

"Let's go!"

"Gee, it's cold in here!" Gigi said as they entered Dru's parents' house, which was another of the colorfully painted Victorians opposite the cemetery at the edge of Random Point. Dru turned up the thermostat and began lighting lamps.

"Come on," he said, drawing her up three flights of narrow wooden stairs to his loft, which featured an oak sleigh bed and porthole windows overlooking the grassy knoll, thin rim of shoreline and foam capped, inky sea beyond.

"I need to get out of these clothes," said Gigi, going behind a screen. She had brought a satchel with the intention of sleeping over and now extracted from it the sage green satin gown set that had been Dru's Christmas present to her. She had added a pair of pale green morocco slippers, which looked indescribably dainty on her tiny feet. Before emerging from behind the screen she took her hair out of the ponytail and allowed it to cascade down her back and over her shoulders. It was shiny walnut brown to match her eyes and perfectly straight. In contrast her skin was as fair as could be and tinged carnation pink.

"Well! I didn't think I'd ever see that on you!" he remarked over folded arms. She bowed her head in repentance but Dru wasn't impressed. "Come over here," he ordered. She came and he caressed her satin covered limbs. "It feels as good as it looks," he commented, but abruptly stopped stroking her in order to seize her by the earlobe. "Too bad you're not as good as you look!" Dru declared, pulling Gigi over to the bed and dropping down upon it, then drawing her straight across his lap.

Gigi tensed and waited for the first smack to fall. Even so, it took her breath away! His palm descended on her upturned, satin swathed backside with a resounding crack, first on one cheek, then the other. Smack, smack, smack, smack! Four more hard swats imparted heat and pain to her bottom.

"Ow, Dru! Ow! That's so hard!" She put back one small hand to shield the target area, which was not very large but jutted like the bottom of a miniature goddess. "Ow Dru! Don't be mean!" Gigi cried, as he caught her wrist and held it fast to her waist, punishing her for attempting to cover her bottom by slapping her on the back of the offending hand. “Ow! That hurt too!” she snatched her hand back and nursed it to her cheek.

“Hold still!” he ordered, spanking her soundly on alternate cheeks at as brisk a pace as he’d ever achieved. After a night of frustration and disappointment, insult and indignity, this was the ideal restorative! Dru looked up and glimpsed them in the wardrobe mirror opposite the bed. Gigi, turning back to look at him with her almond shaped eyes so appealing, her full, red lips parted and her teeth so white suddenly reminded him of all that was feminine about her.

Since she was being quiet and passive now he softened and leaned down to nibble on her ear and bite her neck. Before they’d played any spanking games she had gotten him to play vampire games with her, revealing that her throat, ears and shoulders were key erogenous zones. The moment he began to bite, she went limp across his lap, holding onto the counterpane with both hands.

But it was too soon to make love to her. After the many dreadful things she had said to him, Dru wondered if he even should make love to her again. He resumed the spanking, looking at her sternly. “The things you’ve been saying to me!” he scolded, pulling up the satin robe and nightgown to bare Gigi’s already pinkened oval cheeks. “The way you’ve been treating me!” Again and again, he brought his hand down, covering every inch of exposed flesh with firm, sharp smacks. Presently Gigi began to squirm and kick. But she stopped protesting, except for issuing small whimpers each and every time he struck her. “I never met a girl who needed this more,” he swore, increasing the intensity and velocity of the spanking to the point where she could no longer bear it stoically and resumed her original chant of protest.

“I’m sorry! I’ve just been jealous of you and Marguerite. Couldn’t you see that?”

“It’s crazy. I play with one woman at Hugo’s party and you get jealous. Whereas you played with twelve!”

“But I didn’t have an affair with any of them!”

“Well, I would never have thought of it if you hadn’t completely abandoned me after the Halloween party!” He pushed her off his lap and she stood before him, unconsciously rubbing her bottom.

Dru got to his feet and paced. “As I see it Gigi, you became jaded after playing with all those older men at the party and I suddenly didn't seem interesting to you anymore." Gigi couldn't meet his eyes. "Right?" he pressed. When she didn't answer at once he pulled her back into arms reach and slapped her bottom smartly. "Right, Gigi?"

"I suppose so," she replied, stepping out of his reach again.

"But then when you saw me with Marguerite, I suddenly became interesting again. Didn't I?"

"Yes!" she replied at once, to avert another smack.

"That's amazingly childish and at the same time perverse."

"The same can be said for what you're doing right now," she pointed out.

He looked at her cynically. Her sudden shyness was intriguing, if it was to be believed.

"How do I know you won't be bored with me again tomorrow and resume treating me like a pet cocker spaniel?"

Gigi's lower lip began to tremble and she turned her back on him. As she started to sob his erection threatened to burst through his trousers.

"Get to bed!" he ordered, putting out the lights and lighting one candle. Gigi scrambled under the bedclothes, dashing the tears from her eyes. Dru stripped and tossed his suit on a chair. "I'm taking your bottom tonight," he told her firmly, getting into bed beside her and drawing her into his arms.

"No Dru, no!" she hid her face against his chest. "It will hurt too much!"

"No, it won't," he insisted, biting her earlobe. She shivered and turned her back towards him, grinding back against him. Dru pulled off the robe but left the satin gown on Gigi, pulling it up to her waist and then locking his arms around her. He wasn't about to admit that Marguerite had taught him the secrets of sodomy and had pronounced him adept in the art. "You deserve it - for withholding yourself from me for weeks on end!" Dru smacked her thigh.

She looked back at him and pouted, "You're not being very gallant."

"Where did being gallant ever get me with you? Meet the new D.B.," he told her, pulling her up close against him and briskly penetrating her from behind. It happened so quickly that it took her breath away. And yet she was so wet!

Dru's palm pressed against her lower abdomen triggered a riot of subtle sensations. When he reached up to squeeze her small, peach shaped bosom and tweak her erect nipples she was stunned to experience her first breast related mini-orgasm. She felt wildly surprised as it happened again, the spasm of pleasure in response to the pinching of her nipples in conjunction with Dru's sturdy engine of young manhood now deeply pistoning into her clinging and copiously lubricated sex.

The same thing happened when he pinched her earlobe or bit her neck and shoulders. Shudders rippled through Gigi from one dainty erogenous zone to the next as Dru inflicted these sharp little attentions on her warm, slim, slightly rounded and silken smooth young body, now limp with surrender.

It had never been like this between them before, but Gigi realized with a painful pang of jealousy, that he had been studying with a local love goddess who had given him a doctorate in B&D foreplay over the past few weeks.

"Dru, please don't take my bottom now," she pleaded.

"Why?"

"Because I came."

"But I didn't."

"Let me go."

"Forget it."

"Don't be cruel!"

"Get used to it."

"No, don't!" she weakly protested as she felt him fully withdraw from her still faintly contracting vagina, only to thrust his throbbing mushroom cap between her pinkened cheeks. Lubricating her with her own creamy effusions Dru spread and penetrated her bottom. "Please, it hurts!" she whimpered.

"Don't fuss and it will stop hurting in a second," he insisted, enclosing her damp Venus mound in his hand and manipulating her deftly. Pulling her open he nudged further into her small bottomhole.

"Ow," she protested, half heartedly, for now he was fully inside her and it no longer hurt. But it felt thick and uncomfortable, deeply humiliating and intensely awkward to be anally filled. Then he began drumming his long fingertips against her clit and spanking her pussy ever so lightly while ramming his cock into her glove tight bottom ever so firmly from behind. "O God, o god, o god!" she cried, a clear signal to Dru that she was about to climax again. Which also made him burst with manly pride.

On recovering their senses they disentangled and got under the covers. In the semi darkness they lay in each other's arms.

"Can I stay and play house with you until your parents get back?" she asked.

"You can stay and play my submissive," he told her, tightening his arms around her waist.

"Why so bossy all of a sudden?"

"I'm just letting you know that if you choose to be around me, it's going to be on my terms this time."

"What do you mean?" she leaned up and looked at him. He laced his hands under his fair head and stared back at her.

"Gigi, as a girlfriend you chumped it. As a submissive, you seem just right. So if you decide to spend the night, realize that first thing in the morning, I'll very likely want you again. These weeks on end without sex at your whim is completely unacceptable. I'm a healthy, growing boy. I need sex at least twice a day. Nor do I intend to tolerate any more of your condescending remarks, sarcastic cracks and out and out insults as regards my relationship with Marguerite Branwell. You might as well know that I consider her my muse."

Gigi felt angry and hurt that he should talk to her so harshly after sharing such intimacy and bliss. It was true that she had behaved hatefully to him for weeks but hadn't her compliance over the last hour, the multiple orgasms and first submission to sodomy put paid to that bill?

She slowly got out of bed and began to look for her clothes, her eyes clouding with tears. How dare he even mention the name of her rival in that very bed where he had just taken her so thoroughly? So he'd have her whenever he wanted, would he? Gigi shot him one look of white-hot contempt before going behind the screen to dress. Of course he could no longer be her boyfriend. He had to be perfectly free in case Marguerite should summon him!

"Gigi, what are you doing?"

"I'm going back to school," she replied, pulling on the jeans and sweater she had brought in her bag. "I just remembered I have to start working on a paper first thing tomorrow morning," she continued, trying to sound natural. Why should Dru have the satisfaction of knowing how brutally he had just hurt her?

But more importantly, wasn't it best to exit on a high note, leaving the door open to additional supernaturally good sex? There were no other boys at school she trusted enough to initiate into her secret fetish world and she seemed to crave more of it every day. Since Dru had just gotten to the point where he was beginning to really know something about sex, it seemed foolish to completely cut herself off from this precious and infinitely practical knowledge. For the first time in her young life, cool self-interest asserted itself, causing her to emerge from behind the screen with the blandest of smiles and a tiny wave, scoop up her bag and flee the room before he could utter another word.

Dru listened to her clatter down the stairs and out of the house with a pounding heart. He stuck his head out the window and called down to her, "Gigi, are you okay?" She looked up at him and waved again, got directly into her car, started it and drove away.

Dru closed the window against the damp, cold air and tried to analyze what had made her go. Probably mentioning Marguerite in that reverential way, he thought, getting back into bed. But he couldn't help feeling the way he did and it was only fair that Gigi know that.

There was only one short Spring and Summer left before he went away to college, during which time his beloved, bespectacled, spectacularly beautiful mentor might once more make use of him. He wanted to feel free to accept this honor without compromising his integrity.

It was painful to think that he'd hurt Gigi's feelings, because he simply wasn't like that, but perhaps it was all for the best. The old Gigi would have told him off sensationally before such an immediate departure. The new, circumspect Gigi was showing control. He was no longer her cuddly toy, but at least he was getting some respect. And even though she had run off rather strangely, Dru felt that a new natural order had been established out of the chaos of their previous relationship wherein she now belonged to him.

Dru smiled at the irony of his relationship with the dominant Marguerite teaching him to be dominant with Gigi. But he'd never seen Gigi so transported. The magic had worked.

Chapter Twelve

January

As dawn broke over Random Point, the late night supper party at the Cliff House at last began to wane. Sloan Taylor was still searching for Pamela Crane along the upstairs corridors when he collided with Paula Bartlett, wrapped in a fur, carrying her pumps and looking fresher than any thirty year old woman had a right to look, after having been up all night.

"Going home so soon?" she joked.

"If I can ever find Pamela," Sloan replied.

"I'm tired of waiting for Ambrose too," Paula sighed, adding conspiratorially, "They are together, you know."

"Pamela is with Ambrose? No, I didn't know. But surely everyone's played out by now, aren't they?"

"You and I never got to play," Paula flirted lightly.

"I wish I'd known you wanted to," he smiled, taking her hand and kissing it.

"Sloan, why don't you drive me home and I'll tell you something," she said mysteriously.

"Certainly!" he said, intrigued.

Charging Dennis to inform Ambrose and Pamela of their departure, should the missing husband and sometimes fiancée ever choose to emerge, Sloan ushered Paula out into the frosty morning.

"That coat almost makes sense here," he commented as they carefully began their descent down the winding, ice-glazed road in his Jeep.

"It was one of my Christmas presents from Ambrose. I feel horribly guilty wearing it, but isn't it wonderful?"

"What were you about to tell me, Paula?"

"Let's wait until we clear the cliff road," she said mildly. Sloan didn't argue and they drove half way down the hazardous hill in silence. "This little road here leads up to our house," Paula said as Sloan negotiated the turn off and began to ascend an even narrower, winding road.

"We'll have coffee," Paula suggested, leading him inside her husband's elegant house. "And maybe they'll be by to salt the roads meanwhile."

Leaving the capably domestic Sloan to brew the coffee, Paula slipped upstairs to change from her party dress into a pair of wool trousers and a sweater set. By the time she clattered down the stairs he had already set cups and saucers out in the dining room. The coffee followed quickly and at last Paula took a deep breath and disclosed, "Ambrose and Pamela are having an affair!"

After a moment's reflection, Sloan replied, "Knowing Pamela, I'm not surprised, but what makes you so sure?"

"Did you notice that diamond pendant Pamela was wearing this evening? I saw it in Ambrose's desk drawer Christmas week. It retails at the store for three thousand dollars. The note that went with it said, 'Merry Christmas, Darling. Ambrose.'"

"And you received no such necklace or note?"

"I got other jewelry. And he never calls me darling. He calls me sweetheart. There are other indications as well. For example: what perfume does Pamela wear?"

"Channel No. 5."

"So do I. But just recently I switched to a different scent and had all my suits cleaned. But I still can smell No. 5 all over Ambrose when he gets home at night."

"Honey, that means nothing. In a department store scents hang heavy in the air."

"Dreamer. I know from whence I speak! Hasn't Pamela seemed distant or distracted lately?"

"That's her normal state."

"Well, there's a reason for it now," said Paula.

"If it is true, what are you going to do?" Sloan asked.

"What are you going to do?" she replied.

"I wonder," he mused.

"You don't seem very upset, Sloan."

"Oh, Pamela's disappointed me before. If what you say is true, I expect a lot of the attraction has to do with them both being selfish, shallow, glamour driven individuals, who can look into each other's eyes and bask in their own reflection. They actually belong together."

"So you're not going to do anything about it?" she asked.

"What do you suggest I do?"

"Well, she's your submissive, isn't she? Give her a good spanking and force her to stop stealing my husband."

"Do you really want me to? I'd do it for you if you wanted me to."

"Not for you?"

Sloan shrugged, "People don't own each other body and soul."

"You sound as though you've slipped yourself!"

Sloan smiled.

Just then Ambrose entered the room and started at Sloan's appearance.

"I had Sloan take me home," Paula explained pleasantly.

"Sorry," the department store owner said briefly, annoyed at the presence of a guest so early on New Year's Day.

"I'd better go," said Sloan, rising.

"Thank you for the ride," she said, seeing him to the door.

"Happy New Year," he said, squeezing her hand and kissing her lightly on the cheek.

"That Sloan Taylor is a very attractive young man," Paula commented, sitting down at the table with Ambrose to finish her coffee. "What a shame his girlfriend treats him so badly!"

"You might offer me some coffee," her husband commented, looking up from his newspaper. Paula brought him coffee.

"What do you mean, she treats him badly?" Ambrose asked from behind the business section.

"Oh, well every one knows that she's terribly unfaithful," Paula revealed. "My theory is that she has some wealthy older man on the side, who give her expensive presents and the like. Did you see that necklace she was wearing tonight? It wasn't cheap."

Ambrose lowered the paper and looked at Paula. "What's this you're saying now about Pamela?"

"I think she's got a decadent, affluent male in his forties who spoils her shamelessly. Poor Sloan hasn't got a chance against that sort of charm."

"H'm, I had no idea," he commented and went back behind the paper.

"Neither did he, until I clued him into all the telltale signs," Paula admitted. The paper came down once more.

"What do you mean?"

"He was in ignorance until I opened his eyes to the truth just now."

"You did? But why?"

"Well, because he's too nice a fellow to be made a fool of."

"What makes you think he even cares?" Ambrose demanded in frustration.

"What man wouldn't care to know if his lover was sleeping with another man? Wouldn't you want to know?"

"Why? Are you sleeping with someone else?" Ambrose demanded.

"Would you care?"

"What do you think? I hope you aren't contemplating any such thing!"

"Why?"

"Because you belong to me."

"No I don't. I'm just married to you. At the moment," said Paula, rising from the table. "Well, I'm sleepy now. I'm going to bed."

Ambrose followed her upstairs and also stripped off his clothes and got into bed, fatigued to the bone from staying up all night. When Paula got into bed beside him she curled up against him as usual with no further comment on the subject of extramarital affairs. But he was troubled by her remarks and inflamed by her cool insolence. "If I wasn't so exhausted I'd give you the beating you deserve for saying such things to me," he murmured in her ear before dropping off to sleep.

Late that afternoon, while Ambrose slept on undisturbed, Paula went looking for Sloan and found him skating on the frozen village duck pond. The sky was silver grey with yellow edges as the sun began to set. Paula remembered that her skates were in the car and presently joined him on the ice. She was dressed in grey wool leggings, a matching turtleneck and black wool pea jacket cropped at the waist. A grey wool peaked hat hugged her flaxen head and grey mittens covered her small hands.

Correspondingly all in black, tall and reedy, Sloan glided in stark relief against the wintry white pondscape of icicle-draped trees and quant village shop fronts in the background. Established as a township in 1700, Random Point was paved with original 18th century cobblestones and retained a certain eldritch quality, especially on a winter's afternoon. The few black birds that had not flown south yet were cawing on the bare tree limbs above them as Paula waved to Sloan and skated out to meet him.

"Well met!" she laughed, allowing him to catch her hands in his. "You were just the boy I was looking for."

"Paula, how nice!" he cried, wrapping one arm around her attractive waist as they proceed to skate around the perimeter together. "Why were you looking for me?"

"I was thinking over what you said earlier, about how Ambrose and Pamela are actually better suited to each other than they are to us."

"Did I say that?"

"Yes, and I think you were right," she confided, looking up at him with her candid blue eyes and hanging onto his waist just a degree or two more securely than the moment before. Sloan felt a thrill as he realized her intent.

"Whereas you and I are extremely well suited to each other," Sloan filled in the blank exactly as she expected.

"Doesn't it seem that way?" Paula asked, beginning a second circuit around the pond with him.

"I already admire, approve of and appreciate you exponentially more than your idiot of a husband could ever dream of doing, you know," Sloan declared, squeezing her waist. "And I'm certain I can make you like me."

"Why do you think I'm here? You're a gentleman, a scholar, and the polar opposite of that pompous, custom suited, walking double standard I married!"

"Of course, I can't offer you anything material," Sloan sighed. "I'm only half owner in the bookshop."

She smiled at him and Sloan had to kiss her. Once their lips connected it was hard to break apart.

"Have you noticed lately that Pamela isn't available for dinner just about every other night?" Paula asked.

"She says she's been working late at the store getting the boutique organized," Sloan replied.

"Ambrose has been working late every other night as well," Paula revealed.

"So you're saying they've been together each time?"

"Want to have some fun, Sloan? Let's us start getting together whenever they tell us they're working late. That way it could be weeks before either of them are the wiser."

"How naughty you are," Sloan said, squeezing her waist again.

"I'll bet you a dinner at The Owl that Pamela and Ambrose will work late tomorrow night," said Paula with a grin.

Pamela did work late the following evening, assisting Ambrose Bartlett at the Private After New Year's Sale, that invitation only event calculated to flatter the vanity of the local carriage trade. Champagne, watercress sandwiches and petit fours were served as the wealthiest women on the Cape browsed delicately though the freshly pressed and steamed racks of Versace and Valentino for fifteen hundred dollar bargains.

Pamela never expected to see Hope Spencer Lawrence among the matrons and professional dynamos shopping that night, but her young rival strode in boldly, dressed in a grey tweed top coat over a black turtle neck and black pants, her black zip boots adding three inches to her medium stature. She was hatless and her silky, light blonde hair fell to her waist in natural waves. Pamela envied that hair and attributed to it all of Hope's good luck.

"Hi!" Pamela met Hope at the rack of Dutch made leather cat suits, of which there was only one size small remaining, and which Pamela expected to be given as a present from Ambrose Bartlett, provided it was not purchased during the sale.

"Hi!" Hope was holding her gold tasseled invitation in her gloved hand, and Pamela noted with a flush of indignation that it had been hand signed by Ambrose.

"Hope, are you seeing Ambrose Bartlett on the side?" the slender brunette demanded urgently.

Hope started at Pamela's vehemence and protested, "No, of course not!"

"Oh! Then why did you get an invitation to the sale? It's not as though you can afford anything here."

"A brutal but fair assessment," Hope smiled. "The truth is, I do a session with him every now and then and he gives me some store credit in exchange."

"A session?"

"Just a little spanking session," Hope informed Pamela, unerringly picking out the size small jumpsuit and holding it up to her slim, shapely body.

"I have dibs on that one," Pamela said, adding scrupulously, "if no one buys it tonight."

"Oh," said Hope, obligingly putting the cat suit back on the rack.

"Oh God," thought Pamela, "That was wrong to say!" Then she murmured aloud, "I'm sorry! Go and try it on. If it looks amazing on you, I'll yield."

"Are you sure?"

"Sloan tells me we can overcome our baser impulses if we try," Pamela smiled, pressing the cat suit into Hope's arms and dragging her off to one of the elegant, private fitting rooms. To complete her penance, Pamela helped Hope into the cat suit, deemed it perfect on Hope and insisted that Hope ask Ambrose Bartlett for it, even putting it aside with Hope's name on it. Hope could only raise her eyebrows and wonder at the change.

"David will spank me just for putting this on," Hope admitted with delight as she viewed her girlish form in three gilt mirrors, hugged from throat line to ankle in the world's most supple, fragrant leather cat suit.

"That was close!" thought Pamela as Hope departed ten minutes later to visit Ambrose in his private office suite. She shuddered to imagine how her executive associate might react if he knew she had proprietarily deprived Hope of the cat suit. Ambrose expected Pamela to behave impeccably at all times. Displaying grasping behavior before another sublunary mistress would be a punishable act.

Ambrose could be remote, critical and difficult to please. Therefore Pamela adored him. Ambrose was a powerful, sophisticated older man, with numerous seductive charms. His marriage to Paula and her engagement to Sloan seemed to disappear into the ether whenever he summoned her to his office, took her to a late supper or visited her at home. She could still count the number of times they had been together on less than two hands, but to Pamela it felt like a love affair. The necklace at Christmas had proven that. She felt guilty about all of this and didn't know how much longer she could go on deceiving Sloan, but as she felt she stood on shaky ground with Ambrose, due to his married state, she hesitated to even inform Sloan of the change in her emotions.

At the end of the night, long after Hope's departure, Pamela straightened up the floor as Ambrose merrily totaled the receipts. All the customers and saleswomen were gone and they were alone in Couture. The vast amount of revenue, which the sale had generated, rendered Ambrose more jovial and confiding than Pamela had ever seen him.

"Look Pamela, Mrs. Constance Blandings brought us cash!" he fanned a quantity of hundred dollar bills out on the countertop. Rapidly counting out ten, he pushed the little wad towards Pamela. "This is for you," he told her, sweeping the rest of the bills into a leather billfold that then disappeared into an inner breast pocket of his suit jacket. She blushed and put the money away, murmuring her thanks.

"That's just your cash bonus for selling big on the floor tonight. I still want you to pick out some outfits," he told her, bestowing a modest kiss on her smooth cheek. "Why don't you do that while I finish up here?" he said, turning to the computer to gleefully scan the credit card sales.

"Am I ever allowed to be naughty?" she asked, thumbing through suits.

"What do you mean?" he glanced up briefly and vaguely then returned to gloating at the figures. "Oh, you've done very well tonight, Pamela. You wrote up some great sales."

"Oh!" said Pamela.

"Oh, what?"

"I wanted that cat suit that Hope took."

"So why didn't you just put it in the back?"

"Am I allowed to do that?"

"On a fifteen hundred dollar item marked down to seven-fifty, after writing a book like you did tonight? I should say so! Silly girl."

"I thought you'd be angry at me for revealing to Hope that I had so much interest with you."

"Well, you are my favorite," Ambrose smiled. "Sooner or later, people are going to figure it out."

"You know this and don't mind?"

"You know how fast news travels in a small New England town," he quoted Peyton Place.

"Shall I go home?" she asked.

"Let me take you to a cute little inn in P-Town for a late supper first," he suggested brightly.

"I'll call Sloan and tell him not to wait for me," Pamela agreed eagerly.

About a half hour later, Paula tapped on the window of the bookstore, where Sloan was working late, reorganizing stock.

"I just got the call," she reported, bringing a gust of cold air into the shop before he shut the door against it. "Did you just get the call?" The blonde's cheeks were rosy and her perfume sweet.

Sloan admitted that Pamela had just called to report that she would be working too late to have dinner with him and not to wait for her that night.

"They're going to have a late supper, perhaps at some charming inn, and then they are going to make love, probably repeatedly." Paula informed him trenchantly.

"You're wonderful to take it so calmly," said Sloan with admiration, getting back on his knees amid the 18th century novels he was reshelving.

"Look at you!"

"I must admit, ever since our conversation at the pond, the thought of losing Pamela is bothering me less and less."

"Why? What do you mean?" Paula tossed her sable on a counter top.

"I've been thinking about you," said Sloan. Paula knelt beside him and put her red mouth within kissing range. He kissed her. She let him take her in his arms and kiss her again. "Did you wear this beautiful cashmere sweater for me?" he asked, pinching her velvet earlobe between two fingers, then nuzzling her throat.

"I knew you'd notice it," she murmured.

"I feel I should take weeks to court you, but I want you this instant," Sloan confessed, kissing her deeply again and lightly squeezing her full, perfect bosom through the soft sweater.

"Do you think I came here at this hour to help you shelve books?" Paula asked, kicking over a pile he had just carefully arranged.

"So that's the kind of girl you are!" Sloan said, rolling her over on his knee and smacking her round bottom smartly through her woolen skirt. "That was very naughty!" He pushed the skirt up to her waist. "What kind of undies did you wear for me?" Slate blue lace tap pants attractively encased her ample, shapely, peaches and cream hued buttocks and all the recent personal training had given her a leg advantage as well. "Oh, you are beautiful," Sloan said, caressing her bare thighs with something approaching adoration. Then he remembered the books and recommenced the spanking he had begun on her skirt. "But you're going to put every one of those books back in their proper order before you leave here tonight, young lady!"

"Then I won't leave until morning," she rejoined.

"You're in a wicked mood," Sloan observed, nonchalantly rolling the blue lace panties down to entirely expose her voluptuous, pink-tinged hemispheres. "Coming in here looking for trouble, knocking over my books, talking about staying out all night! What next?" Sloan demanded, rapidly spanking her three times on each cheek, then another three and another, over and over, until each creamy half moon grew rosy under his palm. "I can't tell you how long I've wanted to get you in this exact position, Paula," Sloan confided unselfconsciously, as she compliantly but whimperingly received each successive smack.

"You and several others," she reminded him saucily, in spite of the hardness of his hand.

"So you know about your fan club, do you?" Sloan stayed his hand to rub away the sting from each glowing cheek.

"I know men into spanking like to ogle big bottoms!" Paula replied with an air of superiority.

"Now I'm really going to spank you," Sloan threatened, and administered a swift volley of hard swats to alternate upturned cheeks. She put back one small hand to shield herself, which he promptly caught, smacked and sternly pinned to her side. "You do not have a big bottom. It is merely full, round and jutting. It's ideal."

"Oh, that's right, you like me the way I am. I guess that's why I'm here," Paula confided, sensual and dreamy, in spite of the sharpness of his smacks, which made her catch her breath, pant and sometimes cry out.

"I love you the way you are," he stopped to bestow kisses on her glowing bottom, stroking her up and down her legs and between her thighs. "Paula, you're excited!" Sloan brought his fingers, wet with her essence, to his own lips. "You taste so good, I might just eat you up," he murmured, pulling her panties entirely off and reaching again between her legs to entirely enclose her dewy public mound in his hand, resting the heel of it directly against her swollen clitoris.

"Oh, I never let men go down on me," she conscientiously informed him, turning her head.

"Why not?"

"It's just silly, that's all."

"We'll see about that."

"No!" Paula stubbornly insisted.

"No? How about I don't stop spanking you until you plead with me to go down on you instead?" he threatened, though still tenderly kneading her with his whole hand.

"You'd be spanking me for hours," she predicted.

"That's the whole idea," he replied, lifting her off his lap and to her feet. "Let's go upstairs."

Sloan took Paula up to his apartment in the second floor back of the bookshop. Paula poked around in the sitting room while Sloan went into the other room and turned down the four-poster bed. The flat was small, but wood paneled and charming. The narrow kitchen, equipped for a gourmet cook, had windows looking out on the brook. Everything was immaculate and stowed with nautical neatness. Paula reflected sagely that an extremely tidy partner was almost as convenient as a wealthy one. Either way, one never had to do much straightening up oneself.

It was true that she had grown comfortably attached to her full-time cleaning staff and unlimited spending money, but on balance, Sloan was young, handsome, gallant, caring, and as she was discovering this evening, he also had a lovely style of playing. Where her husband was jaded and detached, Sloan was idealistic and brimming over with animal spirits. Where her husband would "work late" four nights out of seven, Sloan would cook for her and read her novels by the fireside. Where she was a mere ornament to her husband, she would be Sloan's soul mate. She knew all of this to be true, just from the touch of Sloan's hand and the honest affection in his eyes.

She walked into his bedroom stretching as though she belonged there. "I'm having such a good time," she murmured. "Was it forward of me to suggest my staying the night?"

"You mean you were serious about that?" he asked, patting the seat beside him on a little sofa adjacent to the hearth, which was already crackling. She came to cuddle against him, laying her blonde head against his chest.

"Yes, please!" she said, looking at him with ingratiatingly innocent blue eyes.

"You mean blow the whole thing wide open, as soon as tomorrow?"

"Why not?" she shrugged with careless simplicity.

"Fine. If you don't care, I don't care," Sloan willingly agreed.

"I'll get a little flat in the village. Like before," said Paula, stretching her boots towards the fire.

Sloan pulled her across his lap and flipped up her skirt, saying, "To continue!" He renewed the pinkness in her cheeks with the palm of his hand while she squirmed and bounced at the sudden severity of the strokes.

"Ow!"

"Ready to submit completely, Paula?"

"No!"

Sloan sighed, and apologized insincerely, "Then I'm very sorry!" and continued spanking her hard. Now he brought his palm down crisply, pausing a beat in between each spank to add anticipation to her pleasures. Because of the way she moved across his lap and the adorable sounds she was making, Sloan was positive that Paula continued receptive, but just to make sure, he insinuated a hand back between her legs and darted a long middle finger into her slick vagina. "Now you're even wetter," Sloan told her. "Aren't you ashamed? You must be a very naughty girl to get so wet just because I'm spanking you."

"I am very naughty," Paula gladly revealed. "I'm a bad girl!"

"And proud of it, I see!" Sloan chided her, smacking her hard.

"I could never be naughty around Ambrose. I always have to be serious and on my best behavior," Paula turned to confide. Sloan bent to kiss her lips then made her turn her head back. "I'll do just as I like around you," she added impertinently. Sloan smacked her vigorously until she yipped in reply.

"You were naughty to come to me tonight," Sloan observed, stroking and caressing her punished cheeks with tender hands. "Your husband won't be amused."

"You mean my future ex-husband?"

"He'll probably beat you."

"He will," Paula smiled, excited at the idea of enraging her sophisticated husband. "But not badly. Just for good measure."

"That's true. He's got Pamela on his side of the ledger," Sloan remarked, remembering his fiancée for the first time in hours. Paula sat up and asked him. "What will you say to Pamela now?"

"This morning you wanted me to force her to give Ambrose up," Sloan reminded her. "You wanted your husband back."

"Now I'd like to bribe her to keep him," said Paula, hugging Sloan.

"I'm going to break up with her," said Sloan in such a serious tone that Paula felt a flutter of conscience.

"Do you think it proper to abandon Pamela before Ambrose has announced his intentions toward her?" said Paula scrupled. "He could turn into a Mr. Rochester or a Mr. Heathcliff in his fury at my defection."

"Well, isn't that exactly what Pamela deserves?" Sloan demanded.

As much as she wanted to spend the night with Sloan, Paula had to be up early for school the next day and decided to head home at around two a.m. Returning at the same hour from his sojourn at the Provincetown inn with Pamela, Ambrose, in his BMW, followed Paula, in her Mercedes, up the winding road to his estate, more slowly than he thought it possible for any human to drive.

Bristling with annoyance at finding her out at that hour, Ambrose ripped off his topcoat and demanded to know where she had been.

"Oh, Marguerite was having an at home for the girls," Paula tossed off without a particle of concern.

"And you've been there all this time?"

"Why?" she grinned; "Where have you been all this time?"

"What do you mean, where have I been? Dining with business associates, as I told you I would."

"Brandy?" she asked brightly, shaking a decanter in the air.

"Sure," he replied, suspicious of her perkiness. They sipped from small snifters, staring wordlessly at each other. "What have you really been up to?" he suddenly snapped.

"Why? What have you been up to?"

"We're not going to start this again, are we?"

"Sure. Why not?" Paula couldn't control a burst of inappropriate laughter from escaping her lips at the absurdity of their conversation.

"Paula, you have an uncanny sense of when I'm too tired to beat you," Ambrose declared, going upstairs.

"Oh Ambrose, I have about the juiciest piece of gossip you're likely to hear all winter," cried Paula, running upstairs after her soon to be ex-husband. "Marguerite told all us girls tonight. What do you think?"

"She's divorcing that pill of a husband, I hope," Ambrose remarked dryly.

"That too, but even more importantly, she's expecting. And she's not sure which of her lovers is the father."

"No kidding! Who are the primary suspects?" Ambrose asked.

"Michael Flagg, Dru Baxter, Hugo Sands and Anthony Newton, all of whom consoled her after Malcolm walked out on her in Vegas a few weeks ago. But it really doesn't matter, because she already considers it Michael's."

"So you're saying she's going to have it?"

"Oh, most certainly!"

Chapter Thirteen

Marguerite and Michael Play House

One wet, October night, Anthony Newton's Bentley glided to a stop in front of Marguerite Alexander's house on the tip of Random Point, Cape Cod.

Newton's driver, Dennis Cowper, the young Englishman who had been the affable composer's Man Friday for the past six years, got out first. Opening the back door with reverential care, he assisted Marguerite Alexander out. Next came his younger sister Belinda, cradling a small, fuzzy bundle.

Sheltering the three rosy-cheeked females under an enormous umbrella, Dennis escorted them to the front door of the white wooden house and taking Marguerite's proffered key, opened the screen door and was about to unlock the front door when it swung open.

Michael Flagg stood looking at them. "So you're here!" he grunted, revealing a rich, well nurtured resentment at being abandoned for ten and a half months by Marguerite. Never the less, he held out his arms for the baby, unwrapped the cashmere blanket that held her, pronounced her cute, cuddled her briefly, then handed her back to Belinda in order to continue scowling at his future wife.

"Dearest Michael, don't be cross," murmured Marguerite, emerging out of her furs to lock her arms around the tavern keeper's trim waist and lay her tawny head against his impressive chest. He returned the embrace but coolly and the kiss he gave her barely grazed her cheek.

"You're giving Belinda the worst possible impression!" added the tall redhead, who had very nearly gotten her figure back in the six weeks that had passed since the delivery in Europe of their child.

"Belinda, this is Michael."

The tweed coated twenty four year old London import smiled demurely and then politely asked to be shown to the nursery. Dennis said he would bring in the trunks and Michael went to help him.

Marguerite followed Belinda, bearing little Felina, into the suite of rooms which had recently been remodeled to accommodate both baby and nursery maid.

"He seems cranky," Belinda observed to the beautiful new mother who had become her best friend during the previous summer. In her capacity as a domestic employment agency administrator, Belinda had at first merely attempted to help Marguerite find a suitable nanny to bring back with her to the states. But the more time they spent sifting through applications, enjoying luncheons, touring museums and visiting the theatre, the more the forceful Belinda began to perceive that no one but herself would do to tend Marguerite's only child.

Besides, she had been missing her brother and was madly envious of the luxurious life he had long enjoyed with Mr. Newton. Of course Belinda was well aware that minding an infant was infinitely more demanding than acting as personal assistant to an immensely wealthy and extraordinarily agreeable creative genius, but the notion of hard work did not alarm her. In return, she would be amply compensated, courtesy of Mr. Newton, for the next four years, in respect of his being the infant's unofficial godfather.

Marguerite had frankly admitted, as soon as she knew she was pregnant, that the child might belong to any one of four men. However, since Michael Flagg had long been her choice of life partner, she decided that baby would be his.

This was not what Michael was indignant about. He was in fact, perfectly willing to acknowledge that Felina was his, whether she was or not, for his passionate love of Marguerite had been the one constant in his emotional life since first meeting her and he was more than ready to start a family. What angered him was being deprived of his lover's company for the better part of a year. In Michael's view he'd been cheated out of the last unencumbered period of Marguerite's life, the time he'd most wanted to be there to spoil and enjoy her.

"What's your sister like?" Michael shouted to Dennis over the shiny black vastness of Marguerite's largest steamer trunk as the hard, spiky sheets of rain loudly bounced off it and into their faces.

"Bossy," Dennis grinned.

"Great. That'll make three of us," Michael replied candidly.

"But she's a darling," Dennis added, lest his sister's new employer misinterpret his remark as a criticism. On the contrary, Dennis adored determined women and was bored by the other kind.

"I like the girl Damaris brought out from the city to look after her little one," said Michael, who'd been most favorably impressed by Bianca Perez, the newly hired nanny of his ex-wife and her husband, William Random.

"She does seems well bred," Dennis agreed blandly, as he felt only mildly attracted to the quiet girl the Randoms had chosen as nursemaid for their first child and whom he had met several times at Newton's Cape Cod home.

Bianca had just graduated from City College with honors when her cousin Damaris offered her a three year position in her house, with the promise of a bonus, upon that term's completion, which would greatly help finance the graduate school degree which she craved.

In addition, Bianca would be given a computer, a studio and all the leisure time she needed to begin her Masters thesis in Spanish literature. All these concepts thrilled Bianca, who was sick of subways and longed for ivy covered walls, eventually to find within them, a sexy, tweedy someone to rip her bodice open and release her inner vixen.

Dennis had briefly entertained the notion of courting the Randoms' nursery maid. But the sober demeanor of this focused female scholar could not but cool the ardor of a young man who fantasized almost exclusively about stiletto booted, severely corseted and fantastically capricious love goddesses.

"Give Damaris a month or so and she'll have Bianca turning heads all over town, " Michael predicted, visualizing the magnolia skinned Bianca with hair set free from her scalp pulling braid, her fine, full lips stained dark red and her slender form clad in one of his ex-wife's smartly tailored suits.

Leaving Dennis to help Belinda unpack, Marguerite and Michael repaired to Michael's house in the woods off Shadow Lane, located about a mile and a half from her own.

"Did you prepare a room for baby here as well?" Marguerite asked, bounding into the house with something more than her usual enthusiasm.

"I thought we'd just pitch her in a drawer," Michael replied, unable to remove his gaze from the finely proportioned, long legged Marguerite, who appeared especially fresh and attractive striding around his house in a grey tweed dress with an insouciant zip front and shiny black boots.

Reading his thoughts, she demanded, "Well, how do I look?" placing her hands on her womanly hips below an astonishingly nipped waist for a woman who had delivered so recently.

"Spankable!" he replied, pouring himself an Irish whiskey and offering her one.

"I'm only drinking good red wine," she demurred. "For the baby's sake, you know."

"Let me open a bottle for you," he offered.

"That's right, you own a bar now," she smiled. "You must have a glorious cellar."

She followed him into the kitchen, sighing with pleasure. "It so strange," she murmured, "I was sick with envy when William designed this cottage for you and Damaris. The whole world went black for a couple of years."

"And now William's married to Damaris and they have a baby of their own," he agreed, delighted to follow her into the nursery he'd created for Felina.

"Ah, yes," Marguerite approved, examining the wooden cradle, the shutters carved with stars and moons, and all the charming nuances of a rustic nursery.

"Are you sure you don't want to get the DNA tests done?" he asked yet again. It was a theme they'd touched on many times in their daily emails over the last ten months.

"Darling, wouldn't you rather let time tell?"

"Well, what color eyes does she have?"

"Dark eyes," Marguerite replied.

"Like Anthony," Michael said.

"And my mother," Marguerite reminded him.

"What color hair?"

"Looks to be a rather light, coppery brown. Very much like my natural color," Marguerite replied candidly.

"God, I've missed you!" Michael said, catching her by the waist and swinging her around in his arms. "How did you get your figure back so fast?"

"I didn't yet. I've been corseting."

He picked her up in his arms and carried her into the bedroom.

"It's chilly in here!"

"Girls always say that," he replied, depositing her on the sofa in front of the hearth. "I'll make a fire."

"Speaking of girls," Marguerite began, accepting a glass of wine from him, "How is yours?"

"You might say, how are yours," he corrected her, sitting down beside her after the fire began to crackle. "When you left I only had one girlfriend. Now I have two."

"Two?"

"This is why I begged you not to leave me, Marguerite," Michael accused her. "And why you deserve to be spanked so hard."

"Look, when I left you were having a modest, once a week affair with your adoring bar maid Carmen."

"Carmen is still the good girl she always was. She's heart broken we're going to be married of course, but she's pretending she doesn't mind."

"What about this other one? Is Patricia back?"

"No, but she is a blonde and her name begins with P."

"Paula?" Marguerite asked with a sinking sensation.

"No, silly. She's just married Sloan. They're deliriously happy."

Marguerite thought a moment then said shakily, "Not Der Lorelei?" referring to the young Dutch woman who'd bought and remodeled the gym the previous year.

"Yes, Polyxena Guzman. She's likes me to distraction."

"You never mentioned it in your emails."

"I didn't want to irritate you with it."

"I thought she was dominant."

"So did she until she got to Random Point. Then things began to happen. Freddie Johanson turned her onto spanking. But she'd had her eye on me from the start. Now she can't get enough of me. She's been trying to tempt me over to the lighthouse with promises of homemade Dutch apple pie all week. I haven't had the nerve to tell her I'm getting married tomorrow."

Marguerite raised her arched eyebrows and said. "Let me guess, it's been whipping, whipping and more whipping."

"Wish I could say that was all, but you know me."

"Sounds like you've been on a blonde holiday all year."

"And to make it worse, you bring in another one. And speaking of the English nanny, I hope you told her we like our martinis shaken, not our babies."

"Don't be dreadful," Marguerite grinned.

"Dennis says she's terrifically bossy."

"I know, but baby will need at least one firm and forceful presence in her life. Otherwise we'd simply spoil her to death."

"I suppose you're right. But why was Belinda ready to leave a managerial position to change diapers?"

"Oh, it wasn't a very wonderful job. She'll have many more opportunities here, especially since Anthony has taken a personal interest in her advancement."

"How long before you have to go back and nurse the baby?"

"Oh, at least three hours."

"How long before we can play?"

"At least three minutes."

"Are you serious?"

"I wouldn't go all the way, just yet. I'd give that a week or two more. But all other attentions would be most welcome. For unlike you, I haven't been the slightest bit adventurous for oh, say the last six months!" Marguerite disclosed, stretching with deep relaxation.

"It's been so long I can hardly remember what to do with you," he mused.

"Afraid?" she asked.

"Terrified. After all, you've performed a heroic feat since I've seen you last. And all by yourself."

"Frankly, I only would have found it annoying to have a man hovering around at that time," she smiled.

"Oh, Marguerite, why did you steal this last year from me? I still can't forgive you for that!"

"I'm sorry, darling, but I just couldn't follow my belly around Random Point for nine months."

"So it was nothing but your vanity that kept us apart?"

"I'll make it up to you," she vowed, taking his hand and rubbing it against her cheek.

"Oh, you deserve to be thrashed!"

"Very well," she grinned, standing up, unzipping her dress with one gesture and stepping out of it to reveal her newest black satin corselette, lightly boned, nipped at the waist and full to the hip, with satin eyelet trim. Her white thighs were bare between the hem of the exquisite foundation garment and the tops of her lacing thigh high boots and sheer black panties girded her full bottom. Her bosom was more ample than ever, with round, cherry nipples straining against the built-in, black net, push up bra, which barely contained her swollen breasts. "How do you like it?" She turned slowed so Michael could admire the effect from front, back and side.

"You look divine," he remarked, locking his hands around her waist and pressing his lips to her throat. Now his hands slipped down to squeeze her bottom cheeks. Then he pulled back and gently cupped her bosom in his hands. "And your new proportions are nothing short of spectacular. Comes from nursing baby, no doubt."

"Better touch me here instead," Marguerite put his hands back on her bottom.

"Are your breasts too sensitive to touch?"

"Not precisely, but you know how aroused I become when you touch them. Let's save that for last," she recommended, postponing the rarified pleasure she had dreamt of for the last few weeks, namely that of lying in her lover's arms, having him take each whole nipple between his lips and gently kiss and bite her to orgasm. She had no idea if Michael had ever tasted mother's milk. Such child rearing practices were not in vogue during their infancies. But she was certain that he would taste it before many more days had elapsed.

"Tell me what you want," Michael said, sweeping her up in his arms and carrying her to the large sleigh bed, which dominated the bedroom.

"A long, slow, meaningful spanking, possibly until I cry tears of sheer release," admitted thoughtfully, disposing herself across his lap like a well-trained house submissive.

"You want me to spank you hard enough to make you cry?" he was shocked.

"It doesn't have to be hard, just long and slow," she pointed out. "Here and here," she said, pointing more to the upper rather than the lower central portion of her cheeks. "That's where I want it, right where the bottoms of my jeans pockets would be," she instructed.

"Not here?" he asked, caressing her bottom where her thighs began.

"No, it hurts too much there. I like it a little higher. But not too high, of course."

"I never knew that!"

"It's a new discovery I recently made. Try it!"

Michael locked one hand around her waist and slowly began to smack first one and then the other cheek with a firm, heavy, deliberate stroke. She relaxed across his lap, letting the weight of her torso sink into the large, solid base formed by his muscle-corded thighs.

"Oh!" she cried, gnawing on one knuckle, "Yes! That's exactly right!" As his hand rose and fell she whimpered and wriggled ever so slightly across his lap, now and then kicking up her high-heeled boots.

"You honestly deserve this for leaving me so long," he murmured, still spanking her slowly and methodically but just a little harder now. Then he paused to tug her panties down and off, exposing her voluptuous, bottom, snowy at the edges but with the center of each hemisphere already glowing hot pink.

Beginning to feel the sting acutely, Marguerite put one beautifully manicured hand back to momentarily shield her bottom from his punishing palm. "Don't you dare," he warned, catching her wrist and locking it to her waist in such a way that made her feel as helpless as a child. The next three or four smacks on her bare flesh sent perfect ripples of ecstasy through her.

She took back her hand and the spanking continued, as slowly and deliberately as before, but perhaps a shade more severe. However, he now began to pause between volleys to separate her thighs and inspect her copiously lubricating inner pinkness. A few more smacks and another pause, this time to spread her cheeks and examine her even more intimately. When the spanking resumed she tingled.

Again and again he spanked her upturned cheeks, staining her fair flesh dark rose with his big, relentless hand. Once more she put her hand back to momentarily stay his blows and once more he caught her by the wrist, this time slapping her sharply on the back of the hand before pinning it to her waist. Michael was nothing if not surprised when this simple gesture of control triggered a tremendous, body-rippling climax in the play-starved sensualist across his lap.

"I can't believe how hard you let me spank you," he admitted, turning her around and gathering her into his arms.

"Were you spanking me hard?" she wondered, giving him her lips, pressing his hand to her bosom and straining her body against his in complete abandon. She pressed his palm to her lips. "I love your hands," she sighed, adding naughtily, "but I've missed your cock."

She could feel it under her, as rigid as a truncheon as she bounced her bare, pink bottom on his lap.

"Didn't you say we should wait a week or two?" he reminded her, pushing her hand away from his zipper. "I don't want to hurt you."

"You already hurt me!" she rubbed her bottom.

"You just said you could barely feel it!"

"While it was happening. But I feel it now!" she replied roundly.

"Come here," he told her, pulling her into his arms and gently pulling down the sheer cups of the corselette bra to expose her rosy, swollen nipples. Turning her on one side and getting in bed behind her, he pulled her back against him and began to fondle her breasts and pinch her nipples ever so slightly. She reached back to pull his zipper down and Michael released his cock to rest between her bottom cheeks.

"I could sodomize you," he suggested, nibbling on her earlobe while continuing to manipulate her nipples in the manner she desired.

"Would it be too perverse if I asked you to never stop playing with my nipples the whole time?" she asked, looking back at him over her shoulder. Michael smiled and lightly bit that fair shoulder, in a style that made her swoon in his arms.

"You're not exactly hard to please," he told her, happily reaching for the lubricant.

"Thank you for waiting so patiently for me to come back," she said, closing her eyes and preparing herself to be taken in the deepest possible way. "I've loved you from the start, but it had to be perfect for us."

"I've loved you from the start as well," he replied, "but we've lost so many years. Can you forgive me for all the mistakes I've made?"

"Michael, a man will go where his penis leads. The fault was mine for not making my true feelings for you clearer, sooner. But perhaps we had to experience all these different lovers to fully appreciate each other."

"H'm, one of these days you'll have to tell me about your experiences with the toddler," Michael said, suddenly remembering Marguerite's last notorious love affair of the previous winter.

"He was fully eighteen before I lay a glove on him," she protested, pulling away.

"You stay right where you are, young lady," Michael recommended, pulled her back against him by her waist. "Though I'm sure it's embarrassing to admit to seducing a prep school boy. Oh Marguerite! Marguerite, Marguerite."

"Shut up, let me go!" she cried, furious at the teasing.

"I will not," he replied, slapping her upper front thigh lightly. "Hold still."

"There was nothing wrong with my darling Dru," she declared. "He was perfectly adorable."

"Well endowed too, I expect," he put in, slowly working his palm across her abdomen, and down to her soft-fleeced Venus mound.

"Well, of course!" she replied. "Otherwise, he really would have been a child, wouldn't he?"

"Did he spank you, Marguerite? I've got to know!" Michael interviewed her in the manner of a talk show host.

"Certainly not!"

"How could he resist?" Michael slid his hand around back to her still pink bottom cheek.

"Very easily, he's submissive!" Marguerite rejoined. "Or at the very least, a switch. And you know how seldom they get the opportunity to receive spankings. Why would he squander his attempting to top me?"

"Oh, honey, with you it's not a matter of topping or bottoming, it's a matter of irresistibility. Your bottom swishing around in those tight skirts, atop those high heels, simply draws the male eye and hand."

"Oh Michael, don't you realize that at least half if not more of all men in our scene are submissive?"

"Really? I'd much rather be the one controlling you than vice versa," he said, inserting one long middle finger into her creamy vagina from the front, while nudging his penis deeper between into her bottom crease from behind.

"At least you only try to control me in bed!" she complimented him frankly.

"No one can control a force of nature."

"Your enlightened attitude is why I chose you to be the father of my child. You may proceed with the act of sodomizing me!"

The next afternoon Marguerite and Michael were married in a private ceremony at Anthony Newton's house. The small party consisted of: William, Damaris, their baby Ricarda, tended by Bianca, Hugo Sands and Laura Random, Dennis and Belinda, David and Hope Lawrence, Sloan and Paula Taylor, Susan Ross, Anthony Newton and Michael and Marguerite's new baby, Felina.

The two young nannies, Bianca and Belinda, naturally gravitated toward each other and began to discuss their respective origins and goals. Dennis hovered around his sister and the Flagg baby, bringing her and her new friend refreshments while stealing secret looks at Bianca, who ignored him.

The Puerto Rican girl was slight and lithe, with lustrous, straight, black hair to her waist. She wore a short, black velvet dress with an empire waist, three-quarter sleeves and an edge of stiff white lace at the sweetheart neckline. Her arresting, oval face, large, dark eyes and extremely pale skin were all so suggestive of a Dostoveyskian heroine that Dennis expected she was asthmatic, anemic or epileptic. However, he not seen her dressed so beautifully before and was particularly riveted by the round toed, high heeled, black patent leather t-strap party shoes adorning her elegant feet.

After the ceremony, while Dennis was busy opening bottles of champagne and handing around finger sandwiches, Belinda left Felina in Bianca's charge and took her brother aside to whisper, "What do you think of young Bianca? Isn't she adorable? Why don't you offer to show her some local sights on her day off?"

"I might do," Dennis replied lightly, handing her one of the flutes of champagne.

"Perhaps I shouldn't while on duty," she said, while taking the glass and sipping.

"You should. You don't realize how long this day has been in coming," he returned before leaving her to bring Bianca a glass.

"No thank you, I don't drink," the dark eyed girl replied graciously.

"Never?" Dennis marveled.

"I don't have the head for it," she confessed.

"One small glass?" he tempted.

Bianca was seduced and sipped. She liked his clean, bright, English boy good looks, his immaculate grooming, his politely attentive demeanor. Of course this boy could never be her type, she decided at once. She had set her romantic goals high and would settle for none but a college professor. Who else would understand or value her? And if her man to be were not a well-read intellectual, what would they have to discuss? If she only knew he'd been thinking of Dostoyevsky the moment before, how her attitude might have differed!

Just then Susan Ross came over to invite Bianca and Belinda on a tour of the mansion. Restoring the babies to their mothers, the younger women followed Susan out of the room. Dennis went behind the bar to mix martinis for Laura and Hugo while Marguerite and Damaris experimented with putting the babies in the same cradle together for the first time.

"Any regrets, honey?" Hugo asked his lover as she observed this stupefying cute spectacle with a faint smile.

"Huh?" Laura turned to accept the Cosmopolitan Dennis had just prepared for her.

"You were married to William once. That could have been your baby."

"Hugo, be yourself," Laura grinned.

"Just checking," he replied, relieved.

Susan led the girls up to the distant North tower attic playroom where she then delighted Bianca by producing the largest possible joint and igniting it with a flourish.

Belinda refused to partake of the proffered hand rolled cigarette and reverted to English type by lighting up a filter tipped Marlboro as she walked about the room, so strangely furnished with leather upholstered beds, spanking benches and X-frames.

"Is this a gymnastic studio?" Belinda asked innocently.

"Looks more like a B&D salon," commented Bianca with her New Yorker's innate sophistication.

"It's our playroom," Susan replied.

"So you're the sister of my employer's ex-wife?" Bianca asked, taking her first hit with appreciation then coughing long and loudly.

"Eye watering, isn't it?" replied Susan gleefully. "Yes, my sister Laura was married to William for several years."

"She's downstairs too, right?" Bianca said. "The girl with the chestnut hair? Doesn't she mind that the new Mrs. Random has her house and husband and well, everything that once was hers?"

"My sister Laura?" Susan laughed. "Not at all. After all, she has Hugo Sands and he's completely magnetic. As for what my sister gave up, Anthony Newton, the owner of this house, has pretty much been providing for both Laura and me ever since Hugo Sands introduced us."

"What's it like having a celebrity for a lover?"

"Entertaining!" Susan replied without exaggeration.

"He's been awfully good to my mistress as well," Belinda commented, to Bianca, "and my brother Dennis is his personal assistant."

"The boy downstairs passing around drinks is your brother?" Bianca marveled. "He seemed so poised. I didn't even realize he was an employee."

Belinda said candidly, "Oh he's a proper employee all right. In fact, I'm fairly certain that I'm only here on the strength of Dennis' reputation as an exemplary family retainer."

"Oh, I'm sure that isn't true, Belinda," said Susan. "Anyone could tell talking to you for a minute how exceptional you are."

"Thank you, but the truth is that I have as little experience with infants as Marguerite. We took classes together in London while we were waiting for the baby to arrive."

"Strange, both families choosing completely inexperienced nannies!" mused Bianca. "I took a class before I arrived as well."

"Let me explain," said Susan. "Marguerite, being all sensibility, chose you for your personal charm. You also turned Dennis into a splendid submissive and she admires that."

"Dennis is submissive?" asked Bianca.

"Actually, he's a foot and boot slave," said Susan, "note the way he looks at your perfectly shod feet."

"And what's your theory on why I was hired?" asked Bianca, looking down at the shiny t-straps Damaris had given her that morning to go with the new dress.

"You were hired for your well bred demeanor and intellectuality. Damaris wants her baby read to in two languages and tended by a soft presence to counterbalance her husband's strictness."

"Oh, is he going to be strict?" Bianca asked.

"Just don't ever let him catch you smoking weed in or around his house," Susan warned, "or you'll find out."

Just then Dennis arrived to call the girls back for photos to be taken. As they wandered back down to the second floor sitting room, from which Anthony's piano could already be heard, Bianca watched carefully until she saw Dennis steal a glimpse at her shoes, then returned the gesture with an impudent wink. Dennis was startled and confused. He pulled his sister back and let the others proceed before asking her to explain Bianca's behavior.

Belinda pulled Dennis into a smaller parlor and closed the door then disclosed with a rising color the various facets of his personality, which had been revealed to the new young lady by his mistress, Susan Ross. The roses in Belinda's cheeks were pale in comparison to the crimson flush that immediately sprang into Dennis' face on hearing that Susan had betrayed his humiliating secret to a lovely girl he'd just been considering approaching for a date.

"How could she do this to me?" he groaned, reluctantly following Belinda into the larger salon and allowing himself to be placed in the family picture beside Susan.

When Susan smiled up at Dennis and tried to take his hand he locked his behind his back and looked straight ahead.

"Dennis?" she whispered.

"Everyone hold your positions," said William Random, adjusting the camera, setting the timer and quickly stepping into the group shot just as it went off. After the group pose, William busied himself with smaller set-ups and Susan was able to again confront the young man who had served her patron and herself so flawlessly for the past six years. Their relationship had been typical given their personalities in that he had worshiped her and she had taken him for granted, but there had been real affection on both sides almost from the outset, and on sensing his displeasure, a chill went through the small, spoiled, minx who had long made Dennis' life such a joy and torment.

"What is it?" she demanded, pulling him forcibly from the room by the hand.

"You really want to know?" he asked.

"Of course, if something's wrong!"

"I'll tell you, but not here," he said firmly, suddenly coming to an incredible resolve.

"Fine, we'll go downstairs. It's time to get the desert trays anyway," said Susan, still mystified and alarmed. Dennis ran downstairs with Susan behind him, leading her into the second kitchen pantry and closing the door behind them.

"Why, Susan, why?" he demanded.

"Why, what?"

"Why did you feel it necessary to tell Bianca I'm submissive? Yes, you may well stare! I've just heard all about it from my sister. I was about to ask the girl out. Now she's laughing at me, and all because of your outrageous indiscretion! Let me tell you something, Susan, I'm not feeling very submissive at the moment. In fact, just the opposite!" Dennis cried, grabbing an antique butter pat off a hook on the wall and catching Susan by the wrist with the other.

"Dennis, what the hell do you think you're doing?" Susan cried indignantly as the chauffeur turned her over his knee and applied the square wooden paddle to the back of her thin, fine, charcoal wool gabardine skirt.

"Spanking you!" he replied, smacking her firmly with the butter pat on either cheek ten or a dozen times. "Maybe this will teach you not to gossip and ruin people's chances at happiness!" he cried with more emotion than she had ever heard in his voice.

"Ow! Let me go! Someone will hear!" she protested, trying to wriggle off his lap. But Dennis held her petite hundred and five pound form with an arm of iron and began a second volley of juicy thwacks across Susan's skirted bottom with the wooden paddle.

"I don't care if they do. Why should I? You humiliated me today, now it's your turn!"

"Dennis, you're hurting me!" she cried, attempting to kick him in the head. Diabolically, he locked her legs under his thigh and continued with a third set of one dozen swats, each smack landing exactly in the center of each pert, round cheek. "Let me go!" she pleaded one more time before bursting into loud sobs across his lap.

Suddenly coming to his senses, Dennis threw aside the butter pat and pushed Susan off his lap, jumping up as though he'd touched fire. She sprang away from him, her hands pressed to her bottom and tears running down her face. Then she turned her face to the wall and sobbed. Regaining his own composure he brushed his hands off and exited the pantry with some dignity.

The sounds of Susan crying, though momentarily exhilarating, began to make Dennis feel quite ill as he calmly loaded the dessert trays into the dumb waiter and sent them upstairs. He followed by the stairs, leaving Susan to her conscience in the pantry. When he reemerged in the large sitting room to hand around desserts, his face was still a deep shade of pink from his unaccustomed exertions and this was noticed by both Bianca and Belinda.

Having avenged his own honor so thoroughly, Dennis felt emotionally fortified and actually smiled easily at Bianca as he handed her a dish of petit fours.

"You mustn't credit anything Susan Ross may have said about me," he felt compelled to urge the slim brunette. "She's just trying to make mischief because she knows I like you."

"Why would she do that?" Bianca replied, in surprise.

"Because she thinks she knows it all and doesn't mind what she says as long as she achieves an effect. For years she's been accustomed to discussing me with her friends as though I were her pet squirrel. As her servant, my feelings don't rate. She's not really a bad sort, just unbelievably arrogant. It comes from being so dreadfully spoiled by Mr. Newton. Still, she means no harm. I expect that by now she actually believes I enjoy the way she treats me!"

"Does she use you for sex?" Bianca asked with academic interest, as the human passions were her overwhelming preoccupation. The question took Dennis' breath away for its boldness and penetration. He had never confided to anyone about the several glowing interludes he'd enjoyed in intimacy with his employer's love and had planned to go to his grave with this precious secret, but the notion of impressing the suddenly bewitching young woman before him was extremely tempting.

At last he shook his head, for in spite of Susan's recent treachery, he was honor bound to keep their charming secret. "But she has used me to amuse her friends, time and again," he revealed enigmatically.

"I hope they were nice friends," Bianca murmured.

"They were very nice," he granted with a grin. "And you're too clever by half."

"Your sister and I plan to become great friends," Bianca changed the subject quickly, feeling her face grow warm beneath his gaze. "We plan to meet tomorrow and spend the entire day together."

"Let me meet you for lunch?"

"Of course!"

After this Bianca returned to the baby who was her charge and Dennis retreated behind the wet bar to mix the next round of drinks for

Hope and David Lawrence. Susan never reappeared that afternoon. Leaving a hurried note for Anthony, she escaped in her Jeep to her playhouse, the refurbished "painted lady" on the graveyard end of Random Point, which Anthony had presented her with the previous New Year's Eve.

As Susan wound slowly down the cliff road in a cold, driving rain she realized that this was the first time she had ever deliberately fled Anthony's house to retreat to her own. And all because of Dennis! Susan didn't think she could ever look him in the face again. Far from being angry at the spanking, she felt painfully guilt stricken at having unfairly prejudiced Bianca against him before realizing that the pretty Puerto Rican scholar might be an object of his desire.

It struck Susan forcibly that Dennis had changed! The way he had behaved that evening was certainly not the act of a submissive male. It was more the act of someone who had been subliminally studying for years under the most devastating dominant Susan had ever known, her own master, Anthony Newton.

Was it possible that Dennis, between the ages of 25 and 27, (those years during which he had first tasted intimacy with his young mistress), should have subtly begun to change from a submissive into a non-submissive or even a dominant male?

Or could it be that Dennis was never really as submissive as she thought? Susan remembered the time he (almost) refused to follow Anthony when she suspected her lover of keeping a Mistress on the side. She had pressured Dennis using finely honed dominant techniques, absorbed mostly from fetish novels, until he had yielded, (though not without some resentment), and acting against his better conscience, shadowed his beloved employer, and reported back to Susan.

She thought back to the previous summer, when again, Dennis had betrayed his employer's trust on a whim of her own curiosity. This time his indiscretion had been discovered by Anthony, who was far too attached to Dennis to fire him, but much too peeved to let the incident pass. He had sent Dennis to an uptown mistress for a caning, with a note, as from the principal, admonishing the elegant but strict Isabel Bruno not to spare her arm, and Dennis had submitted to the painful (and exciting) ordeal without a murmur. Was this the act of a dominant male?

And yet, the way he had behaved that afternoon was beyond shocking in an ordinary male friend, no less an employee, no less the former foot slave, Dennis Cowper.

In their entire 6-year relationship, he had only spanked her once, on her madly unexpected request, sensually, while they were snowed in one night and Anthony was in Europe. On one other occasion, while traveling together, she'd allowed him to sleep with her and make love to her repeatedly, again on a whim. That had been nearly a year before. It was true that Dennis' attitude toward Susan had altered slightly lately. Perhaps it could be said to now contain more affection than respect, until tonight, when so much accumulated rancor had been aired!

The worst part was having possibly been the cause of wrecking a romance for Dennis before it had a chance to begin. That notion tormented Susan, as Dennis had never shown much interest in dating before.

A few hours later she called Anthony and asked him to come to her. The genial host hated to leave his piano and guests but came without question at once, for he could count on one hand the times Susan had specifically asked him to do anything for her. In the course of their surprisingly smooth relationship, he had generously provided and she gratefully accepted, but her demands had been practically nil.

Generally she was at hand when he wanted her, and busy enough not to bother him when he didn't. She went to work, didn't do many drugs, chose her lovers discreetly, spent his money modestly, always introduced him to her most charming friends and improved her mind daily with good books. For a very young lady, Susan Ross had a very calm spirit. So to go to her now was no hardship. Once arrived he was happy to be away from the bustle of so many guests and stretched out in front of her fire in perfect relaxation.

"Wasn't this place a good idea?" he asked, "What a perfect end to a beautiful day. I want credit for part of it too. When we were all in Vegas last Christmas I urged Marguerite to dump the baggage and claim Michael Flagg once and for all, and she actually took my advice.

I mean, wasn't it making you sick, them being madly in love with each other all these years and doing everything but being together? Why do people so seldom know what's good for them?"

"Because most of us aren't that smart," said Susan.

"Susan, tell me what happened at the house that made you leave like that."

Susan took a deep breath then said, "I unthinkingly insulted Dennis and he's furious at me."

"You insulted Dennis?"

"I blurted out to Bianca Perez that Dennis is submissive. Dennis heard about it from Belinda and confronted me. He said I destroyed any chance he might have had with Bianca, on purpose, just for my own amusement. But I had no idea he was interested in her! Or I never would have said word one about him being a foot slave, which apparently he isn't anymore. What a difference a day makes!"

"And that's why you left? Because Dennis told you off?"

"Hell, yes! I feel guiltier than Emma Wodehouse after she insulted Miss Bates at the strawberry picnic and Mr. Knightly so forcibly expressed his disapproval."

"Susan, I appreciate the magnitude of your faux pas, but things aren't as bad as you think. When I left the house Dennis and Bianca were making plans to meet for lunch tomorrow."

"Seriously?" Susan's heart bounced in her chest. "He made that much progress just after -- telling me off?"

"You may have actually done him a favor, igniting him like that."

"Anthony, do you think it's possible for a man to go from submissive to dominant?" she asked.

"Oh, undoubtedly. Especially with someone like Dennis whose been exposed to our particular facet of the scene for years. He was bound to get curious about the other side sooner or later."

Susan returned to the Cliff House with Anthony the following morning and managed to avoid Dennis most of the remainder of the weekend. Normally she would have plied him with questions upon his return from his outing with Bianca, Belinda and their charges, but she felt excruciatingly embarrassed at the thought of their last encounter and hid from her lover's manservant pretty much until they all returned to New York by charter plane on Monday morning.

Since Susan was already late for work at the Chipper-Knight ad agency, where she was an in-house graphic designer, Anthony instructed Dennis to drop him off at home in the Village first, then deliver Susan to the Madison Ave. office building where she worked.

Susan was grateful for the first time that a glass divided Dennis from herself and exchanged not a single word with him until he opened the door for her departure. She turned to look at him before going up into the building and was taken aback by the coolness of the stare he returned. "Well?" he said, over folded arms.

Susan stared back at him for a moment, her embarrassment giving way to indignation. "Well, I was going to apologize for my inappropriate behavior the other day, but how dare you strike that attitude with me? And for that matter, how dare you lay hands on me?"

"I'd do it again if you gave me a reason," he replied steadily.

"And I'd have you fired!" she cried.

"Doesn't matter. I'd still do it. And I'd enjoy doing it!"

"Oh shut up! You're insufferable. Just go away. I'm heartily glad you're going to Europe day after tomorrow. Not seeing you for three weeks is exactly what I need!"

"I'm not accompanying Mr. Newton to London this time."

"Why not?"

"He wants me to stay at the house in Random Point and make myself available to Marguerite and my sister if they need me."

"Is that so?" Susan asked with wonder. "Anthony can get along without you for three weeks?"

"I'll pack well for him."

"You realize he's doing this out of the goodness of his heart, so you can be near Bianca for a while," Susan said unthinkingly.

"Oh, so he knows the whole story as well?" Dennis returned angrily.

"He observed you two going out to lunch together and drew his own conclusions," Susan wriggled out of admitting she had spoken to Anthony about her grievous error.

"You told him," Dennis accused coldly. "God, I only wish I'd spanked you harder!"

As there was no possible reply to this statement, which caused Susan to experience a curious stabbing sensation in the pit of her stomach, she turned on her heel and entered the building, only turning once to see with a shock, that he still stood there looking at her, with a terrible scowl on a clean, chiseled face, that seemed to grow more attractive every day.

About the Author

In Random Point, everything is linked to spanking and this is true for the author of the Shadow Lane novels as well. Eve Howard has been writing and producing spanking erotica since the 1980's, when she began freelancing for one of California's largest fetish magazine publishers. While editing *Spank Hard* magazine (as Lizzie Bennett) in 1985, she was discovered by the video producer Nu-West and offered a chance to perform in spanking videos. In 1986 she published the first Shadow Lane story and the following year formed the video production company Shadow Lane with her partner Tony Elka. The Shadow Lane novel series, originally published by Eve in serial form in her magazine *Stand Corrected*, was brought out in paperback volumes by Blue Moon books beginning in 1992. There are nine titles in the Shadow Lane series and Eve is currently working on Volume 10.

Since 1988, Eve has written, directed and produced over 150 spanking videos, the vast majority featuring the same male-spanks-female dynamic portrayed in her novels. Female-friendly and designed to make people feel good, rather than guilty, about being into spanking, Eve suggests an irreverent alternative to the all or nothing B&D subculture portrayed in such beloved classics as *The Story of O*. Many spanking fans have discovered the real life spanking scene by following the same patterns of social networking as described in the Shadow Lane novels. And for almost twenty years, Eve's company Shadow Lane has been one of the primary social organs of the real life spanking scene. She lives with her husband Tony and three cats in Las Vegas.

Reader Reviews about the Shadow Lane Series

"I've become addicted to the "Random Point" series so much that I can't wait until the next chapter. I've ordered the first two Shadow Lane volumes and have re-read them over and over. I never tire of them. Eve is the only person I know who can make an enema sexy."

"I discovered Shadow Lane about a month ago via AOL. Prior to that time I thought I could write excellent spanking erotica. Then I ordered, "The Problem with Laura." This is just a note to commend Eve Howard's spectacular talent and to say thanks for an incredible erotic experience."

"I have just completed "Return to Random Point" and decided that I had to write about how much I enjoyed it. I have not been so aroused since reading my first discipline novel many years ago, about a girl raised in England and "coming of age" as I believe they put it. More recently I have enjoyed reading Grant Andrews' My Darling Dominatrix and Ann Rice's "Beauty" series. It seems that women, though, have the right touch when it comes to writing about this subject. Eve, especially, knows how to touch that erotic nerve and bring it to a pure, raw sensuality until one feels that he/she is near bursting with lust."

"I, for one, have always loved (and by loved I mean devoured... breathlessly) Eve Howard's novelettes. To read them… especially when I was just 'coming out'... was to feel completely validated. I truly identified with each and every heroine; the feisty, sassy ones, the shy, demure ultra 'subby' ones... the young ones, and the more mature. I loved the gentle yet firm "taken in hand" nature of the romantic variety of spanking D's that Eve always incorporated into the stories. I loved that the plots were not complicated… but, feasible nonetheless. I loved the depictions of sexual escapades after many of the spanking interludes. I appreciated that the girls were cherished and adored by the affably rogue-ish gents… that the submitting was willing and desired… that it wasn't like 'rape.'

I like the settings... having grown up in New England and living here almost my whole life. I LOVED the idea of the bookstore (which I always find sexy). Then and now. I could cite many passages too, but I fear I've rambled enough. Eve was/is always my favorite spanking author."

www.ingramcontent.com/pod-product-compliance
Lightning Source LLC
Chambersburg PA
CBHW020504020726
47493CB00001B/180
9781926585574